AN
IMMORTAL
SPY
NOVEL

THE
PLAGUED SPY

K. A. KRANTZ

The Plagued Spy; The Immortal Spy: Book 2
Copyright © 2018 by Kristine A. Krantz All rights reserved.
First Print Edition: April 2018

Cover and Formatting: Gene Mollica Studios, LLC

Published 2018 by K.A. Krantz

www.KAKrantz.com

Print ISBN-13: 978-0-9862537-5-1
eBook ISBN-13: 978-0-9862537-4-4

Printed in the United States of America

To the Snotapods
Moist, mobile, petri dishes. Thanks for the plagues.

CHAPTER 1

"**S**neak, sneak, sneak, creepy guy. I see you," Bix sang to herself. Perched on the steep roof of an old church turned leather bar, she clacked her garish purple-on-pink pumps against the roof rake. Below, a barfly in a peacoat and ball cap exited the club and trailed after a teenage boy ambling along an urban street in Washington, DC, Primary Mid World.

Late autumn's bitter wind tugged withered leaves from the smattering of trees in their designated concrete plots and wrought iron cages. The leaves danced through the industrial city streetlights being swapped out for historical replicas with cleverly integrated cameras. Large dumpsters blocked street parking in front of brick row houses in the throes of million-dollar renovations incorporating residential security systems that covered every inch of a property inside and out.

Gentrification and the modern surveillance state, inordinately useful.

Bix tilted her arm, allowing the projection from her smartwatch to play over her fitted dress's dark sleeve. Camera feeds from across the District flickered in high-def color, night-camera green, or antique gray scale as peacoat and his prey moved through their range of coverage.

Too bad for peacoat that his chosen prey was the newest member of Bix's intelligence team. Cian was a teenage Sage, one who'd pwned all the human public and private networks within a five-mile radius of the bar. The team was in the throes of a retrieval mission. Peacoat had picked the wrong club kid to follow home tonight.

Cian headed through a neighborhood one mile from the US Capitol. The occasional passing car illuminated his olive beanie and frayed flannel jacket. His shaggy hair was long enough to keep his face obscured from the cameras, but the subtle hitch in his gait identified him better than anything else.

Peacoat kept pace behind Cian, maintaining his distance.

"Okay, Cian, you've picked up one street tail, thirty yards behind," Bix spoke softly, still adjusting to the mic and earpiece she wore as one spectacularly sci-fi ear cuff. When it came to multifunctional jewelry, the Sage hadn't quite grokked discreet.

"That's Lonny," the Sage mumbled. "He's a rando from the bar who doesn't understand 'no,' but he tips really well. Don't beat him up."

"I don't do beatings," Bix objected.

"I'm talking to the Berserkers listening in." Cian turned down another quiet street. "I'm going to shake him, then loop back for the package."

"Cian, no," Bix cautioned. "Do not deviate from the plan. You're part of a team now. Let the team handle him."

Three Berserkers emerged from the shadows and set off after peacoat, splitting up to box the guy in. Two dozen more Berserkers and their commander lay in wait between Cian and the small national park where the Sage had hidden a very important package. As long-lived soldiers in the Mid World Army, Berserkers were not always on deployment, but they were always on active duty. This battalion's latest mission was the protection of the Sage and the evidence he was on his way to retrieve.

Not a lot of people knew the package of evidence against some very powerful players existed, but those who did could smite city blocks at will. Bix had offered up a half-dozen ways of fetching the evidence without risking the Sage, but she'd been overruled by soldiers who did this sort of thing all the time. Letting the Sage participate was supposed to be good for the kid, build confidence, encourage collaboration, and teach trust. Chest thumping and bro hugs all around. That sort of thing.

Whatever. As long as the unopened package landed in her grubby mitts without additional pit stops, she'd play her assigned part of overwatch without complaint.

Team player. She are one. Ayup.

Until the kid moved off camera.

"What did I just say about deviating from the plan?" she carped. "Now you're in a dead spot. Talk to me so we know you're okay."

"Give me a sec," came the annoyed answer. "I want to mark it on the map. I can put a camera up here tomorrow."

"Do not stop moving," she insisted over the static in her ear. A clatter and a curse said the Sage had dropped his phone.

Peacoat moved into the last frame, then vanished.

"Cian, move, now." She listened for his voice. "Cian, Cian?"

Scuffling. Grunting.

"Damn it, kid." Bix stared at the picture on her sleeve, at the last place Cian had been on camera. As a gatekeeper, all she needed was an accurate mental image of the origin and the destination to create a pathway—small as a snail or large as a stadium. Tonight, she needed one a bit wider than her hips. She opened a gate in the air above the bar's double oak doors and another at the site of Cian's disappearance.

She pushed off the edge of the church roof and slid through the gates.

Half a heartbeat later, her heels struck cracked asphalt as she landed on a side street that had yet to know the influx of financiers and developers. The stale scent of tobacco, outdoor grills, and malt liquor gave the area a personality. Nonsensical arguments shouted down alleys and across blocks added to the character.

Humanity and all their pent-up aggression. They really weren't that different from the many magical races of Chwedlonol. Humanity just couldn't cope with the minor variances within their own race, so they weren't emotionally or intellectually ready to know about the thousands of other races milling around them. Humans were, on the whole, immature. Chweds who didn't look like a human either had to use glamours or stay out of the human-centric Primary Mid World. None of the magical races wanted to provoke a war with the humans, because humans served to ground native and disparate magics. Humans, for all their ignorance, were extremely necessary to ensure this World and many others didn't implode.

Plus, their ability to entertain was exceptional.

Bix picked her way along the broken sidewalks, earning a few catcalls from darkened porches and entryways. She found Cian's phone first, a few steps from a thick tree root breaking through the concrete sidewalk. The kid had probably been staring at his tech and tripped. Fortunately, the phone's dull green rubber case had protected it from the fall.

Muffled sounds of a fight came from a nearby trash-bin alley.

Following the noise, she came face to flannel with the Sage staring aghast as ball cap and peacoat got his ass served to him by seven feet of brawny blond Berserker. A black skull cap with wards stitched into the fabric covered the wealth of the Berserker's long hair. His oxblood leather jacket hid the seam of his prosthetic arm but not the bulging of his dinner-plate biceps. The beads securing the war braids in his thick beard clacked as the commander of the Berserkers casually schooled the stalker in the fundamentals of hand-to-hand combat.

Bix almost pitied Lonny the Stalker. Almost.

"You okay?" she murmured to Cian.

"A syringe," the boy whispered, rubbing his neck. "Lonny had a syringe."

Bix slid her arm through Cian's and tucked his phone in his jacket pocket. "Did he stick you with it?"

"Yeah." Cian held out his hand, and across his palm balanced a short needle attached to a thin tube with the dregs of black liquid that left rust-colored legs on the barrel. "I'm no doctor, but I'm pretty sure anything that looks like used motor oil isn't meant to go inside people."

Bix turned the kid to face her. "Do you want me to take you to a hospital? Pick your favorite, any Mid World. We'll be there in a breath."

"Doctors will want to know what he shot me up with." Cian gawked at the skirmish. "No point going anywhere until I have that answer."

"Tobek will get those details, don't you worry," she said, tipping her head at the Berserker commander. "Let's take you to a human doc to monitor vitals at the very least."

"I've done enough party drugs to know when I'm headed on a trip. Right now, it's just shock jacking me up." He shrugged off her hold and pulled the collar of his jacket tightly around his neck. "The last thing we need is the ER calling in the cops or social services, especially while my mom's in a coma. They're not going to care that I'm in grad school with a part-time job, only that I'm barely seventeen and employed at a leather bar."

A host of logical arguments came to Bix's mind, but so did decades of experience gathering intelligence from folks of assorted ages, races, magics, and demographics. Sure, she could exploit Cian's current state to coerce him into doing what she wanted. However, he was a teenage boy. One who'd survived multiple homes within the foster system before he'd landed with his forever mom—whom he adored. On his best days, he was a big bundle of fluctuating testosterone slapping around a hyperactive genius brain. In this shitty moment, his racing pulse betrayed his fear. Being surrounded by big Berserkers probably made the kid feel better.

As long as he didn't drop dead before retrieving the package from wherever he'd hidden it in the park, the choice was his to make. If he died first, then she'd have to strike a deal with a god to get the info from his soul. Any deal with a god was not going to be a good deal for her. It was the nature of the divine to be malicious assholes.

"Fine," she conceded. "Tell me if you change your mind. Meanwhile, does Tobek know you've been injected?"

"I do now," shouted the Berserker commander as he snapped the club stalker's wrist, then dislocated his shoulder, forcing the man to his knees.

Lonny surrendered with a low scream through clenched teeth.

"Don't kill him, Chief, please," Cian pleaded. "He's just a perv."

Tobek smiled his slow easy grin and winked at Bix. "What do you think, sweetheart?"

To many, the Berserker commander was known simply as Chief. To Bix, he was Tobek—immortal slave to an undisclosed House of Fate, powerful high warlock, generous roommate, and occasional pillow.

He also patently refused to call her by her name. Weirdo.

"Oh, I suppose we could let the guy live. I have a soft spot for humans, even when they're being stupid." She patted Cian's arm.

"Hey," Cian objected.

"Cian's stalker is a Chwedlonol, not a human. He's let his glamour slip." Tobek whipped Lonny's hat off and tossed it in a heap of rat-shredded trash bags.

Pointed ears, curled lobes, skin the hue of rich fertilizer, straight hair two shades darker than his skin, and the eyes of the deepest axinite branded Lonny as a dark elf. Thick webs of amber scars in the palm held aloft by Tobek continued under the elf's sleeve.

Bix knew exactly how this particular elf had gotten those scars; it had involved a dwarven high council meeting, a grid of magic-infused laser beams, and the elf's inability to follow directions. Despite her damning report on his performance, he'd still made it into the ranks of special agent with the Cross-World Intelligence Guild. To add insult to injury, he'd been assigned a few times to support her Dark Ops team because of his regional knowledge. A region that was not the Primary Mid World. He had too little respect for humans to exist among them.

All that to say he shouldn't have been anywhere near Cian.

The dark elf looked her in the eyes and smirked.

Her lips couldn't form the warning fast enough.

The elf punched his free hand into the pavement. Elven magic surged underground, shoving against Bix's Other World magic. Roots alive and dead roiled and writhed, breaking through pavement. Fences toppled. Cars tipped. Alarms blared. Old clapboard houses groaned.

A fat snarl of splinters and thorns knocked Tobek to the far end of the alley. With a roar that cut through the chaos, the Berserker commander regained his feet. Brilliant green and silver magic built around his natural hand, then blasted the dark elf, throwing the idiot into the air.

Lights in windows of the surrounding row houses went dark. Slatted shades split and curtains gaped. The glow of phones betrayed surreptitious recordings in progress.

Bix opened gates to obscure the fight and to shield humanity as warlock battled elf in the ever-watchful urban streets. Elves' deep connection to Mid World magic put them in the upper-upper caste of Chwedlonol, one step removed from the superpowers. Still, the elf was no match for the commander of the Mid World Army.

Tobek advanced on the elf, dominating him in magic, strategy, and mass. The elf trembled and redoubled his efforts. To no avail. His skin leached color, and the earthen hues of his magic paled. Tobek seized the opportunity, pressing his physical advantage until his rubber-coated mechanical fingers closed around the elf's throat.

"Yield or die," the Berserker demanded.

"Her. First." The elf flung out his hand, launching something small at Bix.

Bix glanced down at the vee of her dress. A full syringe

teetered on the swells of her breasts, snared by the wires of her bustier. Fragments of a shattered needle glittered on the unbroken surface of her skin.

"Big mistake, Lonny." Blue light dawned in Tobek's eyes, the telltale sign of a Berserker's rage. A rage that made his kind stronger, faster, and unable to tire.

"Lonny isn't his name, and 'stalker' is a bit of a misnomer too, isn't it, Loncalaz?" Bix plucked the syringe from its precarious position and waggled it at the elf. "Did you just screw up another official op, or are you off the range?"

"Op? He's an agent?" Tobek glanced at Bix, then glowered at the elf. "Did the CWIG put a hit on her or the boy?"

"Never. Safe. Again." Loncalaz the dark elf sucked his cheeks into hollows and clawed at Tobek's wrist. No, no, the hollows weren't intentional. His clothes hung loosely on him now, where minutes ago his pants had been skinny-fit snug. The buttons of his peacoat had come off during the skirmish with Tobek, allowing the coat to gape. The more he struggled in Tobek's hold, the more frequent the glimpses of his emaciating body.

"Loncalaz, did you infect the kid with the same cooties you have?" Bix asked as fear skittered up her spine.

The elf sputtered and gasped. If any of those things made it to actual words, she couldn't tell. His shoes fell off his feet. His toes curled into the arches, and the arches rolled back to the ankle to disappear under his pant legs. Boneless.

"Guys?" Cian called with a tremor in his voice, rubbing his neck. "There's something growing on his skin."

Crystals. Everything visible around the loose waistband was covered in crystals. And they were spreading.

"Let him go, Tobek, now," Bix urged.

Tobek dropped the elf and retreated. "What did you do, elf?"

Loncalaz rolled into a fetal position. The sleeves of his coat no longer held the withering stumps of his arms. The harsh, haughty planes of his face softened, not from expression but structurally, as if his skull was collapsing. Malformed eyes filled with agony fixed on her.

"One thirty-two," Loncalaz garbled as his jaw disintegrated.

"What is that? What does that mean? Is that the number of people affected?" Tobek demanded.

Bix shuddered as crystals completely covered the elf's face. Within heartbeats, all that remained was a geode the size of her fist. From its hollowed center, lights pulsed in the colors of the rainbow.

"Wh-what just happened?" Cian whispered. "Is that elf magic?"

"No." Tobek yanked an emptied syringe and needle from his thigh. "Sweetheart, any idea why the CWIG sent an assassin after the boy?"

"They didn't." Bix crouched beside the elf's remains and inspected the immediate area. Everything was dry. Clothes and concrete. No bodily fluids dampened anything despite the obvious desiccation of the body. She examined Loncalaz's clothes. The peacoat's inner pocket was stitched shut. A silica bag was in the front pocket of his pants. Scuffs marred the tops of the shoes, clearly from the set-to with Tobek, but the heels showed no wear at all. All of it was new, as though acquired purely for tonight. She looked over her shoulder at Cian and frowned. If Loncalaz had never worn this outfit before, how did Cian know who was following him? The bar had a coat check, and the kid had left before the elf.

"How can you be so sure he's not after me?" Cian shuffled closer. "Is one thirty-two your secret agent code name or something?"

"One thirty-two is a CWIG protocol number." Bix stood with the geode in her hand and met Tobek's glowing gaze. "Loncalaz injected you to force your organization to help. It's what CWIG agents are trained to do when they're infected by whatever biologic is at the heart of a clandestine mission gone pear-shaped."

"He was undercover?" Tobek blinked rapidly as his rage ebbed and dimmed the brightness of his eyes. "Why prick the Sage and not one of the other Berserkers at the bar if he wanted the MWA's help?"

"Easier target, maybe," she mused, studying Cian. "He couldn't *ask* for help since the op would take too long to explain and it would allow you a chance to refuse."

"What? I'm not the weak link," Cian cried. "He tried to inject you too."

Maybe not the weak link, but the kid *was* linked to Loncalaz. The elf had gone through the CWIG academy with Cian's mom, an Oracle. He'd been the agent to her analyst. The elf and the Oracle had gotten a reputation as the Wonder Twins. Every academy graduate and washout kept tabs on their classmates because everyone had had their deepest, darkest, dirtiest secrets exposed during training. For agents, monitoring the folks who knew your weaknesses was a matter of survival.

No question Loncalaz had known exactly whom he'd infected. He'd known the kid wasn't part of the Mid World Army, just a temporary ward of Tobek's battalion. He had no obvious reason to draw Cian into a blown op; however, he'd had to infect Tobek to ensure the MWA was onboard.

The question was whether the kid had known the elf before tonight.

"Loncalaz wasn't aware my skin is practically impenetrable," Bix dismissed, handing over the loaded syringe to Tobek. "But I'm not surprised he'd try to take me down with his dying breath. To everyone in the intel community, I am a pariah who betrayed her team for personal gain. I may have been paroled and the bounty taken off my head, but the backlash from my peers is bound to happen anyway."

"Aren't you immortal, though?" Cian scoffed. "He can't have been a good spy if he didn't know that."

"Keep in mind, due to me missing ninety-five percent of my memories, *I* didn't know I was immortal until recently." Bix slid her nail along the edge of her teal bangs, straightening them. "You two well enough to complete the retrieval mission tonight?"

Tobek shook his head. "Not with both of us injected with an unknown bioagent. Everything we touch, everyone we encounter, hell, our very breath could spread whatever this is. I'm sorry, sweetheart, the mission is aborted. For now."

Bix's guts sank, and clamminess settled on her nape. The longer that evidence was unsecured, the more time more bad guys had to learn about its existence. She didn't like this delay. Not at all. Not one bit.

She turned on the kid. "Tell me where exactly you hid the thing and I'll get it, sans drama and botched war games."

Tobek had the decency to grunt his chagrin.

"I put a biolock on it," Cian said with too much pride. "I have to be the one to get it. Anyone tries to bust into its hiding spot sets off one of those troll bombs Mom lifted from the CWIG armory."

"Troll bomb," Bix groaned. "Are you... That could destroy the package and create a mile-wide crater. The park's a half mile from your Capitol. Do you have any idea the shit storm—"

"That shit storm is intended to maximize political damage," Cian interjected with a shrug. "I didn't know who would go after it, but Mom stole it from the CWIG to keep it out of more dangerous hands. Now she's in a coma because of it."

"So you opted for blowing it up with a troll bomb." Bix looked to Tobek with both brows raised. The Berserker didn't cover his grin fast enough. She muttered nothing kind under her breath. "Fine. We'll focus on this mess and getting you cured, so I can retrieve the package your mother should never have removed."

Cian opened his mouth, but Tobek coughed loudly and pointedly, shutting the kid up.

"Elves are arrogant, but even they wouldn't tote around loaded syringes without some sort of case. If we find that..." Her words trailed off as Tobek pulled a white ceramic case from his jeans' pocket.

"Lifted it from him during the hand-to-hand portion of the evening." Tobek slapped the case against his palm. "Sad to say it is empty, however. My guys will run it for prints and latent magics to see who else had their hands on this thing."

"Okay. CWIG HQ isn't far from here. Loncalaz should have gone in instead of invoking a one thirty-two. That he didn't is cause for concern. I'll own that ball." Bix tightened the gates around their little threesome as a police car stopped at the edge of the destruction made by elven magic. Red and blue lights flared.

Cian retreated, stepping dangerously close to an open gate. "Why does the CWIG train their agents to resort to terrorism?"

Tobek caught Cian before he toppled into the gap creating the distortions.

"Small acts of bioterrorism in the field are the flags CWIG agents raise for the express purpose of alerting HQ to the distress call while maintaining cover." Bix reexamined their surrounds. Of all the security cameras in the area, this was the one dead zone. This was where Cian had chosen to go off plan. "The agents enacting a one thirty-two protocol do so with the expectation of being arrested by the CWIG and shuttled off to HQ's clinic while their reluctant coconspirators are interrogated and the research coopted. It's how HQ effects a rescue and gets a jump start on a cure without burning the legend of the covert agent."

"Since we don't report through the same chain of command as the CWIG, I don't have to contend with a political pissing contest over who gets to run lead on this." Tobek tapped his earpiece twice. "Deploying off-World quarantine protocols. Three definite infected and one possible. We need this area cleaned and local LEOs managed."

"Aye, Chief," came a voice over the comm Bix had forgotten she was wearing.

"Wait, off-World?" Cian squawked. "I can't go off World. I-I have to read to Mom tonight. I have exams and a double shift tomorrow, and—"

"You're a potential plague carrier, Cian. Until we know what we're dealing with, you and I are in lockdown." Tobek pulled his phone from his pocket, tapped the screen a dozen times, then showed Bix the picture on the screen. "If you would be so kind as to deliver the three of us here, along with Loncalaz and everything he touched, sweetheart?"

She studied the details of the Spartan field house with a matte-gray floor, stainless-steel walls, and the coat of arms for the MWA frosted on wide glass doors. In the center of the huge room, four cells of clear walls abutted each other. They offered all the hominess of a prison cell's cot, toilet, and sink.

She wrinkled her nose. "Where, exactly, is that?"

"MWA Quarantine Facility, Grimtebel." Tobek put his phone back in his coat pocket.

Grimtebel was a Mid World covered in rocky desert. Those rocks happened to be alive and carnivorous. Not a place Bix ever wanted to visit again, mission or no mission. The Mid World Army was welcome to it.

"What about my mom?" Cian insisted. "She's going to wake up any day now. Any day, and I have to be there. I have to be there to explain to her why she doesn't have legs anymore and that the people who—"

Tobek gripped Cian's jaw and tilted Cian's head toward the streetlight, stopping the kid's babbling. "You're high right now. That's why you were fumbling with the phone. That's why you didn't want to go to the hospital when all this started."

"Humans legalized weed here. It's not that big a deal anymore." Bix stared at the glow of the geode. The colors and rhythm in which they changed niggled at her memory. She'd seen it somewhere, recently.

"It's not weed. It's designer." Tobek snatched the beanie off Cian's head and unrolled the cuff. Three small plastic baggies held different colored pills of assorted sizes.

"I just needed…" Cian let the excuse drift off, and he looked everywhere but at Tobek or Bix.

"Tell the doctors at Grimtebel exactly what you took and

when." Tobek handed the kid his cap and pills. "By the way, that place is wired. If you're a cooperative patient, the staff might let you near a computer. They may even work with the men guarding your mother to arrange a virtual bedside reading with her, okay?"

Cian bit his lip as his jaw quivered. He managed a nod. Tobek gave Bix the good-to-go glance. A thought delivered the boy and Loncalaz's clothes to the MWA Quarantine Facility.

Tobek arched an expectant brow.

"You know I'm not going with you, right?" Bix frowned and poked at the inner crystals of the geode still pulsing with light. Where *had* she seen the pattern before? "I've got a dinner date I can't miss. I'll shoot out to the ether and let it kill whatever Mid World–created gunk Loncalaz may have gotten on me for safety's sake. That'll have to do."

"I understand any kind of confinement is out of the question." Tobek scratched his beard. "However, it would be helpful if you'd let the MWA doctors check your clothes and skin for transfer or contamination. In my thousands of years, I've never seen a man die quite like that."

"He's not dead." Bix held up the geode. "Look around. It's been five minutes, and not a single psychopomp has shown up to deliver his soul to whichever god owns it. Someone from the soul-delivery service should have been here thirty seconds before he kicked it."

"Maybe the psychopomps can't get past your shadowbox here." He jerked a thumb at the pocket of distortion shielding them. "Thank you for doing that, by the way."

"Even a burned spy knows there are rules about wielding magic in the Primary Mid World. Didn't want you to get your butt chewed for defending the kid." Bix closed the gates shielding them from lookie-loos. Around them, a dozen Berserkers helped to right cars while they chatted up the cops and the neighbors.

No sign of a psychopomp.

"You sure I can't convince you to come with me for a spot check?" Tobek cajoled.

"Based on the last time I was poked and prodded, I'm pretty certain I'll have an unintentional yet highly destructive reaction to your doctors' best intentions. Rather spare your guys my weird." She eyed the hand Tobek held out to her. "I'm going to hang on to Loncalaz for a little bit and get a second opinion on his status. I'll deliver him to your docs when I'm done, if you'll send me a pic of where I should put him."

"If you insist on carrying him into inhabited areas, at least use a secure transport." Tobek spun his natural hand around his prosthetic over and over. Green magic built in brilliance until a glass ball manifested in his palm. He unscrewed the top half and waited for her to put the geode inside before closing it.

She hugged the secured geode to her chest. "Do me a favor? Don't turn into a rock."

"I'll do my best." He flashed his easy grin, then sobered. "Be careful, sweetheart. I don't like the CWIG's involvement in this. That the elf waited until you arrived on scene to truly fight back makes me very suspicious."

"I'll do my best," she echoed, opening gates that delivered her roommate to his new and hopefully temporary home.

She, on the other hand, had a dinner date with a god to get to; one who might know something about the geode glowing in her hand.

CHAPTER 2

The Woolly Barrel existed on a Mid World where trees grew larger than skyscrapers. The nightclub catering to slumming superpowers and social-climbing Chwedlonol one-percenters had been built into the hollowed trunk of one of those trees. Tonight, the amphitheater, recessed on the main floor, had been filled with water to host a merfolk symphony. The music enthralled but, with this particular crowd, lacked enough magical oomph to ensnare. Under warm ambient lights, demigods canoodled with dilettantes on tufted loungers, sipping concoctions outlawed on most Worlds. Games of chance and skill happened at stations recessed along the perimeter. The second floor of the Woolly Barrel overlooked the first, hosting a long bar and small tables with optional screens for intimate conversations. The third floor, sparsely decorated with a black leather bench that wrapped around the entire balcony, was reserved for Very Important Gods.

A dozen VIGs glowed with the primordial essence that made them so damn delicious.

Bix licked her lips and made her way along the plush carpet to her impeccably dressed dinner date. His three-piece suit of navy windowpane never went out of style. A deep burgundy shirt brought out the crimson of his pupils while complementing the amber of his irises. The paisley pocket square pulled everything together.

"Phobos," she greeted.

The Greek god of fear shook his dark mane as he glanced up at her. His cold smile showed his pointed canines. "Chimera."

Bix winced at the use of the moniker she'd recently discovered belonged to her. As far as her impaired memories spanned—a whole thirty years, which was a nanosecond for an immortal—all the references she'd encountered of the Chimera described former-her as a ruthless judge and punisher of the superpowers. Emphasis on ruthless. Double emphasis on former. These days, she barely held her own against moderately friendly superpowers. The ones who didn't like her—which were most of them—relished any opportunity to make her life miserable.

Phobos's cruel chuckle skittered over her skin as he refolded his pocket square. "Still getting used to being the bogeyman?"

"That's really more your sandbox."

"Flattery isn't necessary. Neither is that gift you're hiding behind your back." He stuffed the nattily folded scrap of silk into his chest pocket. "It holds the piquant aroma of elven fear with an earthy undertone that tells me dark elf. Transmuting mortals now, are we?"

"I didn't change him." Bix held out the glowing geode in its glass case, then pulled it close. "Wait, could I have if I'd wanted to?"

"Let's focus on one aspect that you no longer remember how to control at a time, shall we?" He sighed. "To that point, I have located someone willing to make introductions to those who can instruct you in the art of Shadow Casting."

The darkness within Bix rippled beneath her skin at the mention of being a Shadow Caster. There were so many things about herself she didn't know, including her possession of incredibly destructive magics. She really should get schooled on those, but right now her priority was to recover the evidence pouch before it fell into wrong hands, or, worse, got blown to smithereens. There was also the problem of Cian and Tobek morphing into rocks. She needed to understand what, exactly, Loncalaz had been turned into and how long her friends had before they turned into it too. From there, she could make a plan.

"The costs of the referral and training are yours to negotiate. I imagine they'll be steep." Phobos took Loncalaz's remains from her and opened the orb.

"I'll take that referral, thanks," Bix said, not wanting to reject the god's generosity because miffed gods did not let a girl feed off them.

Phobos flipped his wrist and handed her a business card of a bear holding a spear. "Devana of the Slavs. She's expecting you."

Bix slid the card into her bustier and waited while Phobos set the halves of the orb aside to inspect the geode. That he hadn't casually dismissed it as gods were wont to do made her worry. That worry doubled as he wafted his hand over the geode, inhaling deeply.

"Since you can smell the elf's fear, I'm going to take that as confirmation he's alive and passably sentient."

"Sentience is overstating it grossly." He undid the first four buttons on his shirt, then patted his lap, all with distraction. His focus remained on the geode. "How did you happen upon this?"

She straddled the god's legs and grabbed hold of the lapels of his jacket, holding his shirt wide with her thumbs. The energy he exuded tickled her skin. She nuzzled the crook of his neck, savoring the anticipation of a heady meal. "Literally fell at my feet."

He tangled his fist in her hair and pulled her head back. "A straight answer, Chimera. This soul is trapped, still tethered to a body I cannot discern by threads of Fate that have solidified."

That explained the glow.

Bix sat up and looked again at the geode. "Of course. I thought I recognized the pattern of the glow. The blood of a Fate looks like that."

"That it does, but their blood is not solid." He stared at her with eyes full of threats. "I wish to know more about this."

"Me too," she answered frankly. "If you'd let me have my dinner, I could get on with figuring out what the hell caused a man's body to desiccate, leaving behind only the skin to which the crystalized threads bonded."

"Ah, the skin. That is why there is a dark outer casing and a distinct smell," he murmured, gentling his hold on her hair and pushing her face into his bare chest. "Feed. We both have work to do."

Bix didn't have to puncture his flesh to get at the nutrients she needed. Divinity wept from his pores and built in his aura. A touch of her lips upon his skin and a flick of her tongue over the goose bumps rising along his sternum began the glorious feast. Intimate without being vulgar. Vulnerable without being a victim, she drank the primordial essence he exuded. A soft moan escaped her as the power of a god filled her Other World body and reinforced her magics. She reveled in the frisson of her cells surging with renewed vitality, heightening her senses and fine-tuning her spatial awareness.

Sated, she loosened her grip and looked up into the hooded gaze of the god of fear.

"I begin to understand why your last provider had difficulties separating sustenance from sex." His voice was thicker, husky.

Bix shoved herself off his lap as caution twisted with anxiety. The darkness within her pressed against her skin, eager for release. "That hasn't been a problem for you in the past."

"I did not say it was a problem." He extended the geode to her. "Find another provider for your next meal."

She snatched the geode and returned it to its glass case. "Odd request if it's not a problem."

"I wish to know if I will suffer the jealousy that plagued your last provider." He spread his arms along the couch. "Jealousy will complicate things for both of us."

Couldn't argue with that. Cooling her erratic temper, she gave him a brittle smile. "Thanks for dinner."

He inclined his head. "Do keep me apprised of your progress with that bauble."

Bix checked her watch for the image from Tobek. Sure enough, a picture of a cot against the wall of a clear cube filled the screen...along with a shot of a hairy blond toe in the corner of the pic. She dispatched the orb and geode into the waiting hands of the MWA's doctors. The text she sent to Tobek read simply:

Definitely alive.

CHAPTER 3

Bix closed gates inside a frigid cave high up in a crag of ice located in Jotunheim, a Mid World populated by giants. Bitter wind lashed at the long icicles covering the opening, thickening them with the spray from the choppy glacial sea raging below. Nobody in their right mind visited Jotunheim's northern reaches. It was home to cantankerous frost giants. The constant thunderous booming of the giants going about their lives caused the landscape to tremble and drowned out smaller sounds, which made this a great place to hide. The lack of a preprogrammed gateway anywhere in the region made this patch of frosty hell a perfect place for a bolt-hole.

Any spy worthy of their craft had multiple bolt-holes, off-grid havens that only the operative knew about. Each bolt-hole had a stash of whatever the agent needed to vanish. For some, it was a change of clothes, cash, new identity papers, and travel tickets. Really good agents kept at least three pieces of evidence for blackmailing authority figures. Really, really good agents kept access keys to proprietary systems in case of regime changes. Dark Ops agents kept all those things plus an arsenal that would allow them to complete a mission should one or more of their teammates fall. Since each team member had a specialty, the items in the arsenal had to come as close as technology and magic could provide to fill the gap.

It'd been ten years since Bix had been in the spy game. A year or two longer than that since she'd visited this bolt-hole. Bolt-*pit*, technically. Beyond the reach of the ice's glow, there was a cavity six miles deep. At the bottom was a heavily warded prison cell that had once harbored a beloved pet belonging to Ogun, the Yoruba god of war and metalwork. Possibly the only thing Bix liked more than her extensive shoe collection were the loyal beasts of the Other Worlds. She'd freed the creature and returned it to its master. As a token of his thanks, Ogun had forged a small gargoyle pendant that she wore on a leatherlike cord alongside another pendant of special meaning.

The vacated prison made for an excellent bedroom; its many wards shielded her from prying magics. The walls of the pit leading to her bedroom provided plenty of space for cubbies to hide her emergency stashes.

A girl could never be too safe.

The density of the icicles at the front of the cave suggested that no one had found her bolt-hole during her absence. So, with security verified, she popped down to the prison-turned-bedroom. Everything was exactly as she had left it. The stack of mattresses, the pile of comforters, and one boomerang-shaped pillow looked like they belonged in a dollhouse box due to the scale of the humongous prison. It was way too cold for spiders and such, so there were no cobwebs or insect carcasses. The enchantments that had provided water for Ogun's pet were still active, still refreshing the Olympic-pool-sized water bowl with enough frequency to prevent ice or algae from forming. The gate she'd left open to recycle the food still worked too. On another Mid World, there was a tribe of gentle giants who probably believed their chosen deity really did give two shits about them due to a reliably refilled pantry.

As much as she wanted to crawl into bed for a long nap, she had a blown CWIG operation to investigate, friends to cure, and a package of evidence to claim. The best time to infiltrate the CWIG HQ was when the graveyard shift took their lunch break. Getting in was easy; getting what she needed required one very special leftover from a raid on a house-brownie data farm.

Small gates emptied one wall cubby into her palm. At first glance, it was a plain black rubber thimble like the sort available at any office supply store. She gently raked her fingernail around the latticed nibs. Tiny legs uncrossed, and a pincer dug into the meat of her finger's pad.

"Aww, good morning, little fella," she cooed to the technology bug. "I'm so glad you haven't expired yet."

Its rubbery skin wriggled as the worm rolled over her fingertip, its antennae searching for electrical charges. It bent toward her smartwatch.

"Go ahead, take a look-see at what I need from you," she cooed.

The bug stretched out like a caterpillar at dawn and made its way along the back of her hand to the latest tech. It crept along the band, completing the circle three times before compacting itself through the fine seam around the projection lens. Within moments, the watch's screen lit up.

Hello, Bix.

"Hello, my friend. Operate in secure mode."

We are alone now. What secrets shall I find today?

"Review data from last open transmission. Identify unanswered questions. Prepare to crawl extensive databases for solutions."

Sage. Spy. One Thirty-Two. MWA.

"Everything you can find. Four degrees of separation."

Storage capacity may limit degrees. Proceed anyway?

"Prioritize by overlap, then degree."

Ready.

A memory of the server room in the heart of CWIG HQ formed in her mind's eye. With a last glance around her frozen sanctuary, she set out to discover which CWIG mission Loncalaz had blown.

Six layers of gates made a tight ring around eight Merkaba stars of white-blue streams of data wrapped in energy. Each star stood as tall as a man and floated at the center of a cold, dark, windowless subbasement. Staggering the gates shielded Bix from the cameras, the heat sensors, the motion detectors, and, most importantly, the gelatinous blue coating on the floor that looked like a massive cooling mat but would conduct a down-to-the-DNA scan and eradication of whatever disrupted its surface. Stone tiles in the ceiling had been etched with potent spells and wards to prevent magical observation and infiltration.

The CWIG was a security agency. They really hated it when someone breached their headquarters. Especially burned spies.

Bix's heart sped, and her skin tingled. A smile crept its way into being. The thrill of breaking into the brains of the CWIG never got old.

Her very first Dark Ops team leader, the one who'd recruited her out of the CWIG academy, had instilled in her a resistance to the intelligence concept of "need to know basis." Dark Ops teams always needed to know more than what management deemed necessary. Her team leader had developed a hazing ritual in which new team members would have to hack the brains of the CWIG and extract the complete files of the latest mission.

The catch, of course, was that no agent, no matter how well trained, could do the hack alone. It normally required five people, not coincidentally the bulk of the team: gatekeeper, hacker, muscle, distraction, and overwatch. Today, she didn't have five people. Her original Dark Ops team had been disbanded and scattered in the wake of high-level scandals that had rocked the entire guild. Her last team had been murdered by angels. There was one survivor, but he'd gone MIA. So, she had to do the best she could with what she had.

A bug.

Bix removed her watch with the bug waiting inside and tossed it into the nearest Merkaba star. It vanished into the data streams amid an array of sparks.

An earsplitting siren wailed. The flooring brightened. Strobe lights flashed in a seizure-inducing pattern. Blocks in the walls pivoted, forming arrow slits for snipers. Red dots cut through the strobe lights to be swallowed by the gates.

Shit.

Apparently, the CWIG had improved their security during her absence.

Bix covered her ears as the sirens rattled through her skull, making her teeth ache and her eyes bulge. The darkness beneath her skin rippled along her spine and pushed its way through her flesh. Tentacles of shadows and midnight crossed through the gates and slithered along the floor of the server room, shorting out the sensors. They swept up walls and crumbled stone, filling the arrow slits. They continued farther into seams and seals. Strobe lights shattered. Sirens ended on pitiful bleats. The living darkness gouged and marred the ceilings, rendering wards and spells useless.

Bix cursed silently as the server room filled with predatory night. The sensory assault had provoked the magic of a Shadow Caster to rise in her defense. She had no idea how to wield this completely new magic. It was why Phobos had given her Devana's card, but now wasn't the time to study.

As long as her tentacles stayed away from the Merkaba stars...

The double doors to the server room flung wide. A large masculine form overfilled the frame. The brick-house build and curled horns were enough to tell her who was about to bust her heist.

The Director of the CWIG.

He hadn't liked her when she worked for him. He liked her even less for getting her team killed. Not that she blamed him for that last part. She'd hate herself too if she'd been in his clodhoppers.

"Someone get me a fairy orb," the director barked. "Bring up the wind jets. Let's see if we can clear the air."

"Snipers are moving to secondary positions," said a voice over the director's earpiece, set too loudly to compensate for the now defunct siren.

She should bail. Take the threat of the darkness with her. She and the director would never be friends, but she didn't want to kill the guy any more than she wanted to destroy the servers. Information was all she was after.

Yet, the moment the director stepped fully into the room, he'd be dead or she'd be busted. The gates provided sufficient visual distortion, but he and she had tangoed often enough during her tenure that he'd recognize the slight displacement of native magic her presence caused. Being arrested wasn't a concern, and detaining her was something even gods couldn't do. No, the director would go the vindictive route. He'd take her watch, break the bug, find the intel she was after, then bury her in a mountain of misinformation. By the time she sorted truth from fiction, she'd have lost any chance of keeping Cian and Tobek from turning into rocks.

That said, Loncalaz had invoked a one thirty-two instead of returning to the CWIG. She had to learn why. To get that answer, she needed everything the CWIG had on Loncalaz and anything mentioning bioagents. Thanks to Loncalaz's callous disregard for humanity, she also needed the CWIG files on Cian to help the MWA at Grimtebel counter whatever effects were about to come from the injection. Cian had been adopted by one of their agents. Damn skippy, the CWIG had all of the kid's medical files plus those of his birth parents, grandparents, and all the great-grands. CWIG investigators did not mess around with the friends and family background checks. So, if her bug could grab the intel…

"Snipers, stand down. Whoever is in here, show yourself. We might have a job for someone with your skills," the director coaxed, setting one big wingtip loafer into the room.

The darkness enveloped his shoe. He yanked his foot back with a hiss. Only an argyle sock covered it.

Three of the Merkaba stars sparked.

The darkness shied away.

"What if it's the gatekeeper in there, sir?" Again with the paranoid guy on the too-loud earpiece.

"Blacking out a room isn't the gatekeeper's MO. She'd take this whole floor—including the walls—and let the building collapse around our ears. This is something new." The director held up a ball of rose-gold light. Her darkness swallowed the glow but made no attempt to cross the threshold in pursuit of the director.

She was grateful for its restraint.

The star farthest from her flared. Her watch shot across the room, straight at the director. The darkness caught it midflight and enfolded it. With the faintest tickle, the darkness affixed the watch to her arm. Slowly, shadows retracted from the ceiling and walls.

Swallowing a madman's cackle, she opened departure gates and checked the watch.

She froze.

An avatar of a golden Bi Xie galloped across the screen. Someone had bugged her bug. A very specific someone.

Son of a bitch.

CHAPTER 4

A cold pre-dawn breeze stirred the linen sheers framing the open balcony doors. The city lights of Rosslyn, Virginia, scraped up the walls of the high-rise to bathe the demigod leaning on a cane and watching the cloudy sky. Damp, dark curls streaked with gold caused his ivory shirt to cling to his rigid shoulders. Bandages added texture beneath the cotton.

Ashtad Ba'al, Bix's erstwhile Dark Ops team leader, the same team leader who'd made hacking the servers at the CWIG a hazing ritual. He was the only person at the spy guild who hadn't believed the smear campaign against her.

Ashtad alone used a Bi Xie like the one on her watch to signal her. The Chinese protector totem of a lion's body, an antelope's horns, and a raptor's wings was a favorite of hers.

"Bring the brandy out with you, Bix," Ashtad said without turning.

Lights within the penthouse flickered on. Manipulating electricity was Ashtad's specialty, and he did it with impunity. Sometimes, his emotions got the better of him; thus, he lived in a nonflammable glass house. The walls were covered in pastel mosaic tiles. White marble floors, counters, and tables were balanced by plush pale aqua seating on rubber-coated legs. Only on close inspection could grids of highly conductive metals be seen in the grout, in corner joints, painted knobs, and switches. He had enough enemies that his personal security had to incapacitate the intruders without alerting human authorities.

"You look like roadkill." Bix grabbed a snifter and the decanter off the tray by the door. She poured two fingers of brandy into the glass and handed it to him.

"And here I was so proud to finally have been able to bathe myself without assistance." He took the snifter and swirled the pungent liquid, forming amber legs on the sides of the glass.

"Until the alarm interrupted that?"

"You've always had a knack for horrible timing." He grinned and took a sip. "I set an alert in case anyone accessed your files at the CWIG. Color me intrigued when I saw what it was and who had unleashed it."

"Did you break my bug?" Bix put the stopper in the decanter. She wasn't surprised the bug had tried to fetch the file the CWIG kept on her. She was a point of overlap for Cian and Loncalaz.

"I trapped it in a tangle of encryption." He shrugged. "You can't hack the server room alone, Bix, you know that."

"I would have called on Drew, but he's still lost in the ether. So I'm down the lone surviving member of my spy squad." She offered a half-hearted smile. Drew was a draugr, a body thief in common parlance. Like Bix and Ashtad, he was an Other World being. He was also the only other survivor of the angel attack on her Dark Ops team. That he was her best friend was a bonus. "Turns out, when you're convicted of leading your team to be slaughtered by a superpower, recruiting a new team is sort of hard."

"Drew would have relished the chance to screw the CWIG." Ashtad snorted. "Why didn't you come to me first?"

"Because you work for the guild? Because you have integrity? Because the last time you helped me, you ended up like this?" She wagged the butt of the decanter at his banged-up body.

"It's my job to locate the leak and its network inside the guild."

Ashtad gave her a chiding look. "Your hack tonight will merit a chat with the director, particularly since your bug also grabbed the files on your final op for the guild. It's not the first to go looking for those records, by the way. Since your conviction, we've had multiple attempts on the main and backup servers that store the records for all Dark Ops units. Those have yielded interesting leads. Regrettably, most of those leads wind up dead shortly after we gain any kind of traction."

"So much for you being on sick leave." She braced a hip against the balcony's railing. "Do those leads have anything to do with why the director was manning the graveyard shift tonight?"

"Six people on that shift have gone missing in the last few months. The director has taken a personal interest in the investigation." Ashtad stared into his drink. "It is four in the morning. Why are you hacking into the CWIG at this hour?"

"If I told you, I'd have to kill you," she teased.

"If you want your bug cured, you'll tell me." He sipped his drink. "And you'll focus on what Loncalaz has to do with your hunt for who burned you and your team. Don't forget you worked for me at the time you tried to get the elf canned."

"Really wish I'd been successful." She wrinkled her nose. "But I didn't hack the CWIG for my own case. Loncalaz enacted a one thirty-two, and I just happened to be standing there when he did it."

Ashtad blanched. "Who did he infect?"

"Vidya's kid."

"Special Agent Asariri? He went after a family member of a fellow agent?" He closed his eyes and swore in twelve languages.

"It gets better. He got Tobek too."

"Chief? He infected Chief? Good. Very good." He nodded as his gaze darted about. "Smart move on Loncalaz's part, then."

Bix scowled. "I don't think the Berserkers agree. Plus, he went full battle mode down the street from HQ. Why didn't he come in instead?"

He snorted. "Why didn't you try to come in when your final op went south?"

"I knew we'd been compromised from the inside." Bix sighed. "You're saying Loncalaz didn't screw up his mission. He was sold out."

"The Mid World Army is the only third party equipped to handle chemical and biological warfare incidents. They're also the only ones who could be trusted in the event the CWIG was compromised, which we apparently have been. They'll be meticulous in their documentation. That will give us the evidence we need to call out the conspirators." He thrust his empty glass into her hand, unhooked the watch from her wrist, and hobbled inside the condo. "That means the informant was right. The Consortium killed the original investigation."

"What original investigation?" Bix stood dumbfounded as her brain whirled. "How…when…what…the Consortium is involved in this?"

The four ruling magical races—angels, dragons, gods, and Fates—comprised the infamous Consortium who oversaw the population, prosperity, and protection of the hundreds of Worlds comprising the Mids. Bix had complicated and hostile relationships with the majority of its members.

"Oh, they're more than involved," Ashtad called back. "There is a faction inside the Consortium terminating lives way ahead of schedule, and they're using their top-secret research labs to do it."

From human to spriggan, all indigenous life-forms of the Mid Worlds were created through a series of contracts struck among the four superpowers who comprised the Consortium. It started with souls—the basic building material of all Worlds—which were supplied by the gods. The dragons and the angels made the fleshy bodies that housed the souls, using the native magic of the Mids. Fates then bound the soul to the body with threads of Fate, weaving a destiny as minimal or robust as the contract dictated. Death was the scheduled termination of the contract. This was commonly known as the Cycle of Souls.

Any breach of those carefully negotiated contracts caused

frictions, frictions caused skirmishes, and skirmishes escalated to a war that would engulf all the Mid Worlds.

"Are you kidding me?" She chased Ashtad inside the penthouse, replacing the decanter on the table and desperately wishing alcohol had any effect on her. "Some idiot is mucking with the Cycle of Souls? And the CWIG put Loncalaz on it? Why choose him?"

"Thanks to you, he never rose high in the ranks." Ashtad leaned against his uncluttered marble desk and opened his laptop, smoothing the watch along the top of his keyboard. "He stayed below all radars. His posting in the boonies left him with minimal interaction and a lot of free time, which he used to educate himself in the alphabet soup that is research sciences. Now, you may not know this about Consortium scientists, but they are a pompous, pretentious, bigoted group of know-it-alls. When the informant dropped this bomb in the director's lap, the dark elf fit the need—in knowledge and personality."

"Rewarding an asshat is how they breed, you know," she muttered.

"He's done a damn fine job under pretty wretched circumstances." Ashtad's fingers flew over keys, and his screen flashed like disco lights. The face of Bix's smartwatch mimicked the patterns. "Trescop ab Liath is his cover identity. He's part of an all-star group of renowned experts in their assorted fields at the Consortium's research facilities."

"You're telling me he was undercover inside a place that designs custom cooties to infect the lesser races purely so those lesser races—the bulk of lives in the Mids—are tastier to the superpowers who feed off them." Bix pinched the bridge of her nose at the absurdity of facts. "He used one of those cooties on the child of a fellow agent and a commander in the Mid World Army. How is this not a disaster of epic proportions?"

"Because you're involved now." Ashtad turned too quickly and sent his cane flying. "I used to think guild politics were cutthroat. They're nothing compared to research politics. We thought he was holding his own. Apparently not if he invoked a one thirty-two."

"Let's back up to before my head exploded." She retrieved his cane from where it had skidded across the floor. "There are two Consortium research labs. One run by the dragons and one run by the angels. Which lab does the CWIG think is behind the premature terminations via cooties?"

"Both labs. Has to be to hide what the faction is doing from the Consortium's oversight committee." Ashtad winced as he sank into his chair. "We knew that going in."

"From your informant." She guessed. "Who is...?"

This time, his wince wasn't due to his lingering injuries. "Mirri."

Bix's girlfriend. Ex-girlfriend. The Norse goddess she'd left behind to run the infamous op that had resulted in eight dead agents and ten years of exile for Bix. The goddess who'd spent those ten years fighting for Bix's freedom until very recently, when Mirri had been the victim of a heinous assault.

Bix closed her eyes and struggled to control the riot of emotions hearing Mirri's name triggered. There was a lot of guilt, so much guilt, and a fair heaping of wrath aimed at the people responsible for the attack on Mirri, even though they'd been caught and made to pay.

More to the point, however, while Bix had been in exile, Mirri and her partner had quietly investigated security breaches involving high-ranking members of the Consortium. Mirri and her partner's investigations had come to an abrupt halt when both had had their bodies maimed and their brains turned to pudding. Mirri was currently in a healing stasis in the Under Worlds. Her partner was in a similar situation with the dragons.

All the evidence they'd collected was in a Norse pantheon diplomatic pouch. That pouch was the package Cian had been on track to retrieve tonight, until Loncalaz had intervened.

Chicken meet egg.

"It has to involve some seriously high-ranking Consortium members for Mirri to try to hide the investigation by burying it within the CWIG." Bix puffed out her cheeks. "When you can't go high, you've got to go low."

"Or you tag in the Chimera," Ashtad whispered. Tiny electrical sparks danced around his fingertips, betraying his heritage as the son of a storm god. "Now that you've been freed, you *are* the best person for this case. You are the bogeyman of the superpowers. The High Executioner for All Worlds. Hunting the corrupt and misanthropic, then punishing them is exactly what you do. What you've done since time immemorial."

And there it was, the elephant that had recently butted its way into the middle of their friendship. When seven gods had taken her memories, they'd taken her knowledge of the monster within her along with it. A very old enemy had delighted in telling her the truth, and a handful of frenemies had confirmed it. Her actual friends and the people she'd trusted? Well, that was a sore subject.

"We haven't talked since the wretched revelation." She swallowed the lump of fear building in her throat. Ashtad was a constant and a confidant whom she completely trusted. "Please believe me when I tell you I found out who I was at the same time you did. I didn't lie to you, betray you, or deceive you. I choose to believe you didn't do the same to me, even though you are a demigod who is coming up on your four hundredth birthday."

"A quarter of a century to go, thanks." He massaged his temple. "I was a kid when the mighty Chimera vanished, the center of my own reality. The Mids were hemorrhaging from your last stand during the Great War. I have to admit, you're nothing like the stories my father would tell to keep me in line."

According to the long-lived and immortals who'd known the original Chimera, she'd disappeared for three centuries. Bix's memories kicked in thirty years ago, and she'd spent the last ten of those years in exile.

"I like to think I'm nothing like the unholy terror from the stories I've heard too." Bix toyed with the two pendants she wore. "So how does my being the Chimera change our relationship? Does this mean we can't be friends?"

Ashtad dropped his hand and stared at her as if she was daft. She stared back. Long moments later, he broke into laughter.

"I'm a demigod questing for full godhood. To achieve divinity, I have to embroil myself in increasingly dangerous and impactful feats that surpass the wildest imaginations. Only at the apex of the next Great War will my worth be judged by my pantheon. Something tells me that aligning myself with the Chimera as she rediscovers her powers and purpose—"

"And history," she interjected. "I want my memories from the gods holding them hostage."

"And past," he completed with a mild reproach, "is the best place for me to be."

Bix picked at her sleeve. "You sure? If you want to cut ties with me, I'll understand. I'll be sad, not going to lie, but I'll understand. This is a limited-time offer, though. Breaking up with me later will not go over well. Consider yourself warned."

"If only the women I dated were so forthcoming." He placed his hands over his heart and pouted. The pout slowly retracted to an earnest thin line. "I told you before, Bix. We've been in the line of fire together far too many times for anyone or anything to ever break the bonds between us. You don't always have to like me, and I'm certain there will be times I don't like you. However, you will always hold a place in my heart, much like an annoying little sister of whom I cannot be rid."

She gave him a coy smile. "Kind of like wet toilet paper?"

"Never an image I want." He gestured to his computer screen. "Something you should know, Loncalaz's original handler went missing a month ago. Agents investigated but hit a wall. The case is technically still open."

"You claiming it as part of your investigation into the CWIG leak?"

"Unofficially, I am now." He extended her smartwatch to her. "I just checked on his latest handler. There's been no word from her in forty-eight hours. I've alerted the director and flagged the mission as compromised."

"What are the odds you can run a welfare check on all deployed agents and their handlers? All cases, all Worlds?" She handed him his cane and took her watch. The Bi Xie was gone and *Query Complete* shone in its place.

"Above my pay grade, but I can suggest it to the director. Do you have a reason you think will convince him?"

"First the guys on nightshift at HQ, then Loncalaz's handlers, now Loncalaz?" She drummed her fingertips against each other. "The director should want to know if the issue is contained to this mission, or if all of the CWIG's covert operations have been compromised. It's too easy to be myopic with intel coming in from only one source."

"Are you questioning Loncalaz's integrity?"

"No. Not this time." She waved off the accusation. "I do question his motivation, though. It bugs me that he went after Vidya's son. That's not done among agents on the same side. If word got out, he'd be higher on the shit list than I am. So why do it?"

"To bait Chief?"

"No. Loncalaz could have detained the kid instead. Injecting him wasn't necessary to draw out Tobek." Bix puckered her lips and scrunched her nose. "He knows the kid is a Sage who—like the kid's mother—is a Fate-in-training. Tobek is a Berserker. Berserkers are the Fates' contributions to the Mid World Army, their tax payment to the Consortium so they can reap benefits from playing in the Mids. That says to me the Fates are putting this in my path and Loncalaz was their tool. The last time the Fates pulled this stunt, a bad-enough issue turned out to be a colossally horrible issue."

Ashtad exhaled loudly. "Be careful answering the Fates' calls. The Angelic Host burned your Dark Ops team to ashes and forced you into exile, but it took the actions of more than one Fate to put you all in the angels' line of fire."

Bix chewed her cheek. The rage of that betrayal remained raw and festering even after ten years. "There are moments I wonder if Tobek is in my life now to atone for that—not that his actions can replace my team's lives—but I do wonder if the Houses are trying to apologize."

"Don't be so certain Chief's assistance is altruistic in its motivations," Ashtad cautioned. "Excessive bed rest has given me ample time to look into the history of the MWA and the Chimera. The legends paint a very bleak story. Be smart. Stay on your guard with Chief and his Berserkers. Long-lived means planning for the long game, and he's a renowned strategist."

"Yeah, well, you're not so shabby as a strategist either." She quashed the malignant thoughts lurking at the edges of her mind. "Right now, you're my hero who is all wrecked up and stuck in your ivory tower. Is there anything I can do for you? Bring you breakfast? Dinner? One of those grabby sticks?"

"I'll call if I need anything. I expect you to do the same." He wagged his cane at her. "I've unencrypted most of the data you took from the CWIG. Those files will help you and the MWA with this case."

"Only most of the files?" she asked with a hint of indignation.

"I wiped the others." He thumped his cane on the floor. "Certain intel in the hands of the MWA will do *you* harm. Whether or not you were aware, many of the missions you undertook during your time with the CWIG were to thwart or subvert one or more branches of the army."

"A few ops, sure, bound to happen," she dismissed. "Right hand and left hand competing for the same resource or intel, that's totally expected. The Berserkers shouldn't get their panties too bunched over that."

The look he gave said he pitied her delusion.

"You sure there's nothing in those files *you* don't want *me* to see?" The moment the words were out of her mouth, she regretted them. It was a dick thing to say to a demigod who risked his chance at immortality for her time and again.

"Come on, I trained you to not stop at a barrier to information. I'm not dumb enough to *be* that barrier. The files in question are here." He knocked a knuckle against his laptop. "Whenever you want to take time to learn the contents, you and I will do it together. I've got your six, trust me at least that much."

Chagrined, she nodded. "Of course. You're right. I'm sorry."

"Go home and get some sleep," he urged. "Rest will be a rarity once the subversive faction within the Consortium learns the MWA is responding to their unsanctioned bioagent. Whatever their endgame is, their timetable has moved up due to Loncalaz's actions."

"How high up do we think the faction reaches?"

"That's part of what Loncalaz was trying to find out." He crossed his hands on the top of his cane. "Bix, even if the Chair of the Consortium herself is involved, you have to neutralize the bioagent and the brains behind it before these idiots unleash a plague."

That was no small task. Anything concerning the Consortium was risky for everyone associated with Bix. The Consortium had done the worst they could to her—mentally and physically—and she'd survived. Their only recourse against her now was to punish those people about whom she cared. However, she couldn't do this mission alone. That way lay failure for certain. Success would be had or lost based on her relationships, on the trust she could extend to others and that others afforded her. Trust the bogeyman of ages. Trust the Chimera.

Oy.

CHAPTER 5

Half of Bix's face was warm. Half of it was freezing. Both sides pounded against her brain like a Varèse percussion section. She untangled her hands from the nest she'd made in her comforter and groaned. Her fingers touched damp plastic.

What the…?

She lurched. The mattress abruptly ended. She tipped over the edge. A big arm caught her and dragged her atop a nice toasty half-naked body.

"Easy. You're safe, you're safe, you're safe," a deep voice rumbled into her hair. "It was an ice pack."

Tobek.

She opened one eye. The broad expanse of tattooed images and symbols confirmed her pillow. She opened her other eye. The clash of his blond beard and her teal mop obscured a view of the room.

"You still in quarantine?" she whispered.

"Hence the tiny bed." He tucked a lock of hair behind her ear. "You traveled again while you slept and came for a visit. Looks like you got in a fight before you got here."

Traveling to random places and Worlds while she slept happened all the time. She'd start off in her bed like any normal

39

person and wake up who knew where. Once her conscious mind checked out for the night, her subconscious took whatever problems bothered it and dictated her journey. Where her mind went, so too did her body. Part of the gatekeeper package.

Fortunately, Tobek was a good sport about her crashing his bed as long as she didn't steal the covers…which she'd apparently done.

"At least I brought the comforter *to* you, right?"

"It'll have to be incinerated now, but yes, at least you shared my blanket with me this time," he drawled. "How'd you know which isolation pod was mine?"

"Your toe. It was in the pic you sent me." She scratched her chest and noticed something missing. "Did the docs take my shirt?"

"No." He snugged the comforter tightly around her with his lone arm. "Did you borrow one of my T-shirts when you went to bed last night?"

She nodded. "The Mopar or No Car one."

His chest vibrated with his chuckle. "Then you probably lost it when you left the Mids in your sleep. Cotton grown in the Mids can't survive beyond the reach of native magic. That's why you have a closet overfilled with clothes made of Other World fibers. That includes pajamas."

"I know." She batted at the tickle of their tangled hair. "But your shirts are so, so, so very soft. I didn't plan on losing it. Sorry."

"It's all right. I have others." He caught her chin on his finger and lifted her head so she looked him in the eye. "Do you remember who you fought or maybe where?"

"No. I must have gone to the ether to look for Drew and happened across a husked god or some other entity. For a place where things aren't meant to exist, there are some real nasties loitering out there." Bix gingerly examined her chilled cheek. It felt like her face had gotten between the corner pocket and the eight ball. Her skin was hard to pierce, but it didn't mean she couldn't sustain injuries. Damage didn't last long, assuming she was well fed and well rested.

Thanks to Phobos and apparently Tobek, she was both. However, hurting this much now, meant she'd either just gotten back from the ether or she'd taken a doozy of a beating. Her unconscious mind had a fast flight reflex that kept her alive. That she'd stuck around long enough to incur this level of injury worried her.

What the hell was going on in her head?

"Anudrengr—Drew—will find you long before you can find him," Tobek chided lightly. "But he'd look for you at home, not here."

"True, but I'm a horrible friend if I don't look for him. I'm the reason he's MIA." She snuggled against Tobek's chest and savored the unthreatening warmth of human contact. After ten years of being exiled from all Worlds and forced to survive among the things in the ether, a kind touch meant a lot.

"As much fun as it could be to hang out in bed with you all day—"

"Ugh, get a room with opaque walls, you two," an insolent youthful voice cried, interrupting Tobek. "Besides, I thought you were into girls, Bix."

Bix pushed up on Tobek's chest and looked past the blue-green glow of sensors and scanners embedded in the walls of the isolation pod. Cian, in his own isolation pod, hunched over a computer, typing madly.

"Hey, I picked up something for you and the docs here at Grimtebel." She covered her bosom with Tobek's beard and scowled at said dirty old Berserker, who grinned unrepentantly. She rolled her eyes as she opened tiny gates connecting her to her nightstand at home.

Tobek caught her wrist. "Drop not grab. Quarantine, remember?"

"All right," she said slowly but did as he asked, shifting the gates so two flash drives tumbled into her hand instead of reaching through the gates to pick them up. As her fingers closed over the portable tech, she finally saw what had him concerned.

Crystals formed a fine mesh over his skin from shoulder to amputation. The jagged border of crystals curved around where her head had lain.

Her gut sank. She choked out his name on a trembling whisper.

"Please don't look at me like that," he rasped. "At least we know Loncalaz infected me with the same thing with which he'd been infected. That's good news. We're dealing with only one toxin."

Nodding, she looked away while she tamped down helpless panic. Yes, Ashtad had cautioned her against Tobek, but he didn't get the "thing," the "it," that made her so comfortable around the Berserker. She didn't understand it either, but until it bit her in the ass, she was going to enjoy it.

"Being happy about a cootie is a weird silver lining," she muttered. "Are you banking on your contract with the Fates saving you from a future as a geode?"

At some point in his mortal life, Tobek had made a deal with the Fates. Whether it was the same deal that had bestowed his commission as a Berserker, she didn't know. All she knew for certain was that the Fates couldn't let Tobek die. They had to maintain his body in the same condition it'd been on the day he'd signed his life over to them. Now, because Fates were dicks, they didn't reset him instantly. They liked to let him suffer for a bit first.

"Humbled and hampered, right? Still, there are some advantages to being their lackey." He grunted, then frowned. "I wish the same truth held for the boy."

"That makes two of us," Cian called. "Don't suppose you can get me the same deal you have?"

"Different paths, Cian, different paths," Tobek answered.

She held up one of the drives. "Is it safe for me to give this to Cian?"

"I don't know, truthfully," Tobek said softly. "We need to establish if contact transfer is possible. Especially if your dreams are going to keep bringing you to me."

"There's a load of ego riding that last statement," she taunted, trying to rally to a place of positivity.

"Guilty." His easy grin appeared. "I know you don't want to undergo testing, but can we find a compromise? If the doctors give you a swab kit, will you do your own tests?"

"If there's a chance I could spread this," she gestured to the crystals on his arm, "then yes, that's fair. No docs in suits near me, though. No strangers watching while I'm nude. I can't…I…"

Shuddering racked her as memories she desperately wished she could forget smeared their taint over her equanimity. There'd been things she'd endured in the ether and the fight for survival thereafter. There'd been interrogations she'd withstood after her arrest by the Consortium. Then there'd been situations she'd brought on herself with the last god who'd provided for her, acts she should have been strong enough to stop…

The darkness beneath her skin writhed.

"Easy," Tobek soothed. "Easy. You're in control here. There is no threat. No exploitation. Look at me and breathe. Slowly. Breathe. Good. Slowly. Good."

Shame burned her cheeks as she screwed her head on straight. "Sorry."

His eyes glowed faintly as his hand squeezed hers. "Never a need to apologize for that. Ever."

She furiously wiped the tears threatening to fall. "I'll do the swabs. You probably want a set before and after I bathe, right?"

"We'll have you use one of the decontamination chambers." He tipped his head at the wall now displaying an image of a stainless-steel box with water jets. A spark plug of a dude in a white coat held up a plastic box to the camera and set it on a shelf. "Three sets. As you are now. After a soap-and-water shower. After full decon, if soap and water don't remove it. Chamber is voice activated. We'll turn off the cameras now."

The view of the steel room went dark, then the projection faded from the translucent wall.

"Can't take tech into water, so where do I put these?"

"Might as well give me mine now." Cian rapped on the clear wall of his cube. "I've already been injected and have the blotch

43

to prove it. Not rocking crystals, though, so score one for the resilience of youth."

"Cheeky, boy, cheeky," Tobek bantered. "The toxin leaves a distinct mark at the injection site. Mine's a bit obscured by my ink. Go ahead and give him the files. Probably can't do more damage than has been done."

"Such an optimist." She used gates to deliver the flash drive to the kid's cot. "Cian, I assume you've already hacked into Grimtebel's system?"

Cian gave her the uh-duh look as he picked up the drive.

"Good, then you can send me a pic of the blotch." She mimicked the kid's expression. "As for the drive, it might have more information than you want, but I'm all about oversharing."

"I'm a Sage." He held up his arm and pointed to the green leaf inked in the bend of his elbow. "I'm destined to absorb all kinds of TMI on my quest for Fate-worthiness. I am addicted to the drug of knowledge."

Sages, like their feminine counterparts the Oracles, were humans in training to become immortal Fates. Proof of their trials appeared as small tattoos on their bodies. For Sages, how they fared on each test was reflected in the health of the resulting leaf. From the looks of it, Cian had done well on whatever his first test had been.

"Then consider me a cuter drug dealer than your last one," Bix quipped.

"I don't know, the last one was pretty sexy what with his braided back hair and all," the kid teased as he plugged in the drive. His mien changed from typical teenage know-it-all to wounded puppy. "Th-this is my medical… This is my *whole* life. Holy shit. My birth parents?"

"I don't know who mine are. If someone could tell me, I'd want to know." Bix shrugged. "Took the chance you would too."

"Rather sudden and impersonal way of finding out," Tobek murmured.

"What? Did you want me to take him to a candlelit dinner first?" Bix poked Tobek's chest. "Cian, the explanation for why Tobek is showing crystals and you're not might be in that file. Maybe you can figure it out while the docs focus on the cootie itself."

"I'm a math genius, not a physiology one," Cian countered, not missing a beat as he hunkered protectively around his laptop. "Besides, Chief already called in the Consortium's scientists."

A chill snaked down Bix's spine. "The Consortium is coming?"

"Standard protocol for a bioagent event is to clone as much as we can and send it forward to the Consortium's research facilities. They respond with the requisite vaccinations or cures for our soldiers. If there is an antidote for what we've been injected with, this is how we get our hands on it." Tobek's brows furrowed over his crooked nose. "What is it that you know that I need to know?"

Bix leaned down and pressed her lips to his ear as she placed the second flash drive into his hand. "The toxin was created in a Consortium research facility. Unsanctioned. Finding who and why was Loncalaz's mission. The mission is compromised. That's why he didn't go to HQ. That's why he came to you. Details on this."

"If I view it here, it'll get fed up the food chain whether we want it to or not." Tobek curled his fist around the drive nestled between their bodies.

A pulse of native magic punched Bix's chest like a balloon bursting. Tobek opened his hand and put the shattered bits of the drive into hers.

"Keep it off the grid," he murmured, nuzzling her temple. "Tell Gurp and Xipil. They'll get you the resources you need to complete that mission. Let me manage the science and the politics that come with it from here."

"*You* are going to play nice with politics?" she sniggered against his neck.

"Old army guys are forgiven their lack of tact." He bent his good arm behind his head. When he spoke again, it was louder, for the sake of their observers. "Probably want that shower before the Consortium's reps show up, eh?"

CHAPTER 6

Grimtebel's staff was efficient. The first round of swabs had tested negative for cootie transference but positive for Tobek's tainted sweat. His sweat was still being analyzed for all its hazardous potential. Swabs after her shower had been negative all around, nullifying the need for full decontamination.

Directed to a locker room off the main lobby, Bix had cleaned up, dressed in her own clothes that she'd pulled through gates, and reattached her earpiece and smartwatch. Sure, she could have gone home. The idea of being within five hundred feet of anyone from the Consortium goaded her darkness. However, the Consortium was sending scientists to deal with the unsanctioned cootie. Since Tobek—an upper-ranking officer in the MWA—was infected, the odds were high that the Consortium would also send a rep of commensurate status. No agent of any repute would miss out on a chance to gather intel on people like that.

The bug in her watch greeted her.

Hello, Bix. Connect to new network?

"Yes, undetected."

Security vulnerability identified. Exploitation by third parties in process. Piggybacking.

Bix didn't have to think too hard about which hacker was

mucking around in the MWA's system, probably verifying the contents of his CWIG file. Hopefully, Cian wouldn't be too traumatized by the information. His reaction had seemed genuine enough, but the thing about Fates and Fates-in-training was they were all a bunch of sneaky little shits who would lie like a stack of rugs at a poetry slam. The closer to full Fatehood an Oracle or Sage got, the worse their deceptions became until the behavior was second nature.

Cian's mother was a prime example.

"Alert me when Consortium representatives arrive," Bix said to her bug.

Representatives on premises. Arrival in lobby in 10...9...8...

Bix headed into the unwelcoming lobby of stainless-steel walls, hidden doors, and the seal of the MWA etched into the ceiling. She put her back to a corner and took the moment to check her mail for the image of the injection-site stain. The kid had delivered the pic. Definitely looked like a symbol, a brand maybe. Too consistent in coloring to be a bruise, but decidedly subcutaneous. That was one funky drug. Cootie. Drootie?

She forwarded the image to Ashtad with a request to be alerted should the CWIG encounter it. She included a biohazard warning out of courtesy to the men and women of the intelligence guild. The everyday schlubs she respected, even if most of them wanted her dead.

Three sharp bleats brought her head up. One wall slid apart, opening to a brightly lit corridor. Judging from the barrel-like structure, lack of windows, and dampened footfalls, the facility was underground.

Good to know in case she ever had to rip this place from its footings.

Four well-armed Berserkers led the way into the lobby. A squad of equally armed Consortium guards in their matte-black uniforms with embroidered Consortium logo bracketed two women and an older man. Four more Berserkers brought up the rear.

Holy dick-slinging contest.

Why, oh why, would the Consortium send armed men to a remote and hidden MWA sick ward? And why had Tobek dispatched armed men to greet them? For two groups who supposedly collaborated a lot, this display was...odd.

"What is *that* doing here?" demanded one of the three Consortium reps, flicking a long pale finger in Bix's direction. Honey-brown waves of perfectly highlighted locks escaped the braids wrapped around the woman's perfectly shaped head. Perfectly symmetrical features were augmented by perfectly thick lashes and perfectly plump lips. A perfectly lithe body in perfectly tailored clothes swayed beneath a perfectly pristine white lab coat as one of the two female Consortium reps made her way toward Bix.

All that surface perfection couldn't hide the inner rot of an angel. The whole race was so damn foul, it'd turned their eyes black.

Bix let the slight pass. An operative had to be smart enough to withstand insults without rising to their bait. Every member of the Angelic Host hated her. She hated them with equal fervor. Carping at each other in front of an audience wouldn't establish anything new.

"Kashdejan, what does it matter if the Chimera is here? That she is not in isolation means she's not infected. Therefore, her presence is irrelevant to our purpose, yes?" The thick Danish accent of the second woman didn't hide the annoyance in her tone any more than her questions were intended to elicit answers. Petite yet muscular in body, her dark loamy skin, plum eyes, and a matching shade of close-cropped curls identified the second Consortium rep as a dragon.

The Consortium mandated the use of humanoid forms and commensurate size in all collaborative environs. Most of the dragons Bix had met opted for the glamazon appearance. This one had not only foregone the stature, she hadn't even bothered to change out of her ratty sweatpants and tank top.

Bix liked her on the spot.

"Yashanee," the angel Kashdejan sighed and looked down her nose at her dragon counterpart. "Her presence is relevant because any criminal with a record like hers involved in an attack on a decorated soldier and a young Sage begs a lot of questions."

"Even for us, toxins and diseases take time to develop. The Chimera has only recently been paroled. Again, her presence is irrelevant to our purpose." Yashanee turned to the nearest Berserker. "I would like to see the infected people now and claim the solid remains of the dark elf."

"No one said *you'd* get the remains," Kashdejan admonished.

Bix bit her lip to keep from snickering. Natural enemies forged by the very magic they wielded, dragons and angels existed at opposite ends of the creationist spectrum. These two clearly existed at opposite ends of every spectrum.

Let the battle of the winged superpowers begin.

"Trescop was a member of my team," Yashanee countered indignantly. "Therefore, his remains are mine to examine. The cause of his death is mine to solve. You shouldn't even be here, Kashdejan. There is no press pen or photo opportunity, so you probably feel out of place."

It took a heartbeat for Bix to recall Loncalaz's cover identity had been Trescop, which made Yashanee his boss. As an agent, his goal would have been to get as close to the suspects as possible. Piffle. Maybe the dragon wasn't so awesome.

Still. Angels. They totally deserved the benefit of the blame.

"It is because the elf was a member of your team that my team is better situated to take on the necessary discovery," Kashdejan countered with sickeningly sweet pity. "We can be objective and analytical without worrying about our emotional attachments to a man we didn't know."

"That you did not know Trescop is a flaw. You lack insight into his lifestyle that may indicate an environmental influencer." Yashanee dismissed the angel with a sniff.

Bix jabbed a fingernail into her arm, desperately trying not to laugh out loud. Or snort. Or give anything but a poker face.

"Enough," interjected the only unarmed man in the lobby. "As the Chairman of the Oversight Committee, I decide who gets the remains. The science is what matters here, and the angels' facility has the larger staff of immunologists and virologists."

"Sunan, we should not assume what we're dealing with is a virus instead of a toxin," the dragon argued. "Kashdejan's lab is rife with magics that will affect the outcome of any tests, and her lab is in a densely populated World, compounding the risk to civilians. My lab is in a minimally populated World, the native magic is well-grounded, and my team is personally invested in finding the right answers."

"But not quickly," Kashdejan quibbled. "Nothing comes out of your lab in a timely manner. Speed is of the essence here."

"So is accuracy," Yashanee argued, raising her voice.

"Ladies," Sunan barked again, thumping a heavy ornate bronze cane. Sage leaves peeked from under the right cuff of his tweed jacket and again on the right side of his neck above his bow tie. The leaves on his neck, however, ran the color spectrum, which marked Sunan as an ascended Sage, aka a Fate. Like all Fates, he'd started off as a human. By the time he'd finished his trials and achieved immortality, he'd been in his late fifties. He had a wealth of deep lines in leathery skin and wore his thick silver hair long enough to call attention to its unruly waves. He could easily pass as handsome for a gentleman of a certain age.

Sadly, the sneer and the overt contempt with which he regarded Bix ruined the supermodel effect. She'd seen that sort of look on Consortium members before, when they'd exiled her from the Mids. The darkness beneath her skin wriggled. She bid her temper to calm.

"Suit up, ladies. I'd like to get this visit over with as quickly as possible." Sunan cast his disdain at the Berserkers lining the lobby.

The door to the locker room hissed as it opened. The angel swept ahead of the dragon. Yashanee rolled her eyes and lumbered after Kashdejan. Sunan lingered. The thump-thump-thump of his cane echoed in the lobby as he closed the distance to Bix. The weight he placed on the cane said it was a necessary aid, not a fashion accessory.

"I know of your affiliation with the Berserker commander and the boy," Sunan said softly. "Do not, for one moment, misconstrue events into convincing yourself the Houses of Fate wish for your interference in this. My investigators are already at the labs, going through every file, every data point, and every sample."

"The Consortium's investigators, you mean. Not the Houses of Fates', because that'd be awkward, right? Your peers looking into your area of responsibility? If they were, it'd seem like you're either incompetent or complicit in an attack against your own kind." Bix batted her lashes and donned her best bemused bimbo expression.

Sunan's fingers whitened on the ball grip of his cane as he leaned forward, spittle flying when he spoke. "You are a convicted felon. You have no credibility. Any evidence you procure is by default tainted and will not be considered by the Consortium. At best, it will be seen as aiding and abetting your fellow criminals and dealt with accordingly."

"What I am is the Chimera, a secret the superpowers can no longer hide from me."

"You *were* the Chimera. Centuries ago. Now you're a shadow of who you once had been. Nothing more than some World-hopping tramp begging for scraps of kindness. You will never regain any type of vaunted status. That is one issue on which the Consortium is firmly united." He slammed his cane on the ground for emphasis. "Keep away from my investigation, felon, or I'll make sure those you hold dear have destinies rife with anguish."

Bix bit her tongue as Sunan hobbled into the locker room. The crotchety Fate's spiteful words shouldn't have cut into her. They shouldn't have raked along nerves still raw and still angry.

Shouldn't have. Totally did.

Yes, she craved kindness, loyalty, and friendship. She wanted the earnest exchange of trust and respect. Those were the things she valued. Having lost them, having had them used against her to the extreme detriment of others... Exile had crystalized why those things mattered to her. Every day since her return, she fought to build relationships with the right people who could provide what she needed most.

That was why she wouldn't back off finding a cure for Tobek and Cian. That was why she wouldn't give up on locating Drew out in the ether. That was why she wouldn't let Mirri's years of risk and research contained in the diplomatic pouch go to waste.

To hell with Sunan and his righteousness. She didn't need his permission. She just needed to treat all this as a covert op. In that, she had plenty of experience. First step, put together the right team.

Her smartwatch vibrated. A golden Bi Xie pawed at her screen. Ashtad. Already? Was her old boss in her head? Oh gods, that'd be creepy, for both of them.

Saluting the Berserkers and Consortium guards eying her with varying degrees of caution, she left quarantine.

CHAPTER 7

Bix landed on the aqua couch in Ashtad's penthouse. The demigod glanced up from his computer, then resumed typing, seemingly unfazed by her sudden appearance.

"You rang?" she prompted.

"You have a problem," he said, still typing.

She stretched out across the cushions and flipped her damp hair over the armrest. "I have the problem, not we?"

"I'm happy to make it *our* problem, but I don't think you'd like my method of resolution." He turned his laptop to face her. "This is the Red Web."

She lifted her head and frowned. "Looks like bloodstained TV fuzz from the days before digital transmissions."

"The black pixels are worms that will hijack and corrupt all tech on your network. The red pixels are spiders ready to lead you to your electronic destination." He drummed his fingers on the monitor's rubber frame.

"Um." She closed one eye, wondering where this was headed. "Don't sneeze while you're clicking?"

"No keyboard controls, no tapping, no clicking." He turned his laptop to face him once again. "It's all about having the right authentication keys. They're most commonly purchased at the

Crimson Market. A select few Chweds can make their own keys. Less than a handful can use magic to reach the spiders directly."

"Okay," she said slowly. "What does this have to do with the injection-site marks I sent you?"

"Nothing." He shook his head and leaned back. "That query program is still scraping government and guild files from across the Mids for any matches. It'll take a few hours yet."

"Oh." She sat up as the reason he'd summoned her suddenly occurred. "You need me to go the Crimson Market and pick up a key for you? Sure. Show me the destination and a picture of your contact."

"What? No." He scowled. "I'm one of the…This is about your Sage."

Caution pricked at her nape. "What did Cian do?"

"He's recently acquired his own keys."

"He's in quarantine off World." She wrinkled her nose. "You sure you have the right kid?"

Ashtad toyed with the fine china cup beside his laptop, sloshing the tea to the lip but not over the edge. "Once you told me who Loncalaz had infected, I dug into the kid's records. I couldn't get past the oddity of a special agent choosing another agent's kid as a target. It made me think there was more to his reasons than just tagging in the MWA."

"Yeah, I give you that," she concurred. "What'd you find?"

"You know the kid's an addict, right?" He took a sip and glared at his drink.

"Information and drug." She snorted. "Pill popping is what humans do to their young to make them compliant and conform. Kids learn that pills are an easy answer. That's not a lesson even Vidya could unteach."

"He's probably taking the pills to compensate for the physical changes that go beyond puberty. As Sages mature, their human bodies evolve to take in increasingly vast amounts of information. Eventually, the boy will be able to absorb and process more data than all the servers of the CWIG combined." Ashtad wrapped both hands around the cup. A small electrical charge danced along his fingers and over the surface of the tea until steam wafted through the current.

"What the hell do the Houses of Fate need with that kind of ability?" she shrieked quietly.

"Humans functioning as self-repairing servers." He tossed her a commiserating look. "Not all destinies are woven on a whim. There is actual research and planning involved. The Grove of Sages is integral to that. It's the Fates' much older yet much more robust and accurate version of the Internet. All the history of the superpowers and the Mids themselves are contained within the Grove, within those living servers."

"You're saying Cian could be destined to be a supercomputer instead of a Fate?"

"Not everyone who fails their trials ends up with a merciful death. True for demigods, true for Sages and Oracles."

"Immortal races have deeply disturbing means of punishment for their would-be heirs." Bix grimaced.

"Ensures we're well motivated," he noted drolly.

"Well, right now Cian is hooked into the MWA's network." Bix tried not to imagine all the ways Cian unleashed on the Red Web—which was rife with infinitely more predators than the humans' Dark Web—could go wrong. "But Grimtebel is connected through ley lines, right? Not the fiber cables of the regular human-created network. The kid should have a learning curve with data traveling over magic."

"When did you send him to Grimtebel?"

"Right before I came to you last night."

"That was eight hours ago. He's been tinkering on the Red Web for the last six." Ashtad set his cup in the saucer.

"And he made his own keys in two?"

Ashtad snorted. "That's impossible. Not even superpowers or the architects of the Red Web can pull off that feat. It's a security measure. No, his keys were created a week ago. He hasn't used them until today."

Bix had a suspicion as to why Cian wanted access to the Red Web, and it had everything to do with the kid's mom. "Cian can't get to the Crimson Market in person. The toll keepers at the public portals would flag him as a Sage and re-direct him into the waiting arms of a trafficking ring."

"So how did a human teenage boy acquire keys most Chweds don't even know exist?"

Bix closed her eyes and swore. "The leather bar at which he works. Caters to a mix of Chweds and humans. He must have made the arrangements there."

"Keys aren't cheap. What does a kid like him have that he can sell or barter?" Ashtad challenged. "I've checked his finances and his mother's. They've never been flush. The folks who create keys don't need a hacker's skills. What's left?"

Someone must have figured out Cian had the evidence pouch. There weren't many who knew about the pouch's existence, much less what it contained. Ashtad knew, but he didn't know Cian's mom had stolen the pouch, then given it to her kid with instructions to hide the damn thing. Ashtad would never, ever let Cian near the secrets that pouch contained. He'd kill the kid to safeguard the balance of power, no question.

She had to tread carefully.

"You're clearly tracking where Cian's going on the Red Web." She crossed her arms on the back of the couch, peering over the laptop as she diverted the conversation away from payments. "Any guesses as to what he's looking for?"

"He's trawling for weather purchased events from ten years ago."

"Then he's searching for information on a cabal that's threatening him and his mother," she explained. "Ten years ago, a tornado ripped through a few communities in Maryland, killing school-aged Sages and Oracles. He's pretty sure a cabal is responsible for it."

Ashtad narrowed his eyes. "Ten years ago? Before or after his mother adopted him?"

"Before," she mumbled, seeing the trap she'd inadvertently laid for herself. Ashtad knew her too well to let her dodge it.

"Hunh," he grunted, puckering his lips as he typed. "Ten years ago, prior to his adoption, Cian's mother was one of the analysts assigned to your Dark Ops team for what ended up as your final mission. The Internet says a tornado matching that description hit right before you deployed. The timing is coincidence, though, surely?"

Bix forced a cheesy smile, then dropped it. "I can't verify his story. His mother is in a coma. He was barely seven. Memories of kids—"

"Drew read his mother's soul, which means Drew knows everything she does, and you've been looking for Drew instead of looking at the guilds who could have unleashed a tornado on a suburban neighborhood in the Primary Mid World without getting into trouble with the Consortium," he interjected on one long breath, glowering. "Bix, I know you want the heads of the people who made the call to have you and your team burned. It's likely they are the same people who've embedded a mole inside the CWIG. Our goals are not in opposition. You know I have to talk to the kid."

Trusting someone completely didn't obligate them to do whatever you told them to, no matter how you tried to convince them. Friends weren't drones, and sometimes free will sucked for everyone involved.

Like now.

"A meet with the kid is not going to go the way you hope," she cautioned. "If you try to talk to him about his mother—of whom he is fiercely protective—and so much as hint that she was compromised, he will shut down, lie, or both. The Berserkers aren't going to let you properly interrogate him. Plus, he's in quarantine under the watchful eyes of the MWA."

"Which also happens to be out of the way of anyone else's watchful eyes, even yours." Ashtad sighed. "Isn't it oddly convenient that once he has the protection of the MWA and is removed from direct contact with outsiders, the Sage suddenly has access to the Red Web?"

"I can't shake the feeling that Cian and Loncalaz knew each other before supposedly meeting at the bar. Loncalaz may have been the one to get Cian the keys, but I can't see why they would've planned this whole thing to get inside Grimtebel. Loncalaz is a rock now, I mean an actual rock, and Cian's probably headed for the same outcome. What could they possibly need or want from Grimtebel that would make either of them so foolish?" Bix toyed with her two pendants.

"Loncalaz may have given him the idea, but to get the kid keys means Loncalaz would have broken his cover at the lab. Years of undercover work risked. I don't think the elf went that far," Ashtad posited. "It's more likely the Sage got his hands on confidential info while living with Chief's battalion and sold that to get his keys. He might have needed inside Grimtebel to get more intel stolen from the MWA to feed his habit."

On the one hand, that'd be a horrible betrayal of the Berserkers who had taken Cian in. On the other hand, it was a mess made by the Fates and their minions. It'd serve the Houses right.

"Tell you what, let's see if Cian is street-smart enough to use the Red Web for its true purpose. Whatever he's using for payment on the site will be in the vein of whatever he used to pay for the keys." Bix sincerely hoped it wouldn't be the diplomatic pouch full of evidence. She didn't blame the kid for wanting answers. She was intimately familiar with a knowledge quest. Hell, she'd use every tool at her disposal if she were in his shoes. *She'd* even be tempted to put the pouch on the Red Web if she didn't know the repercussions. But would the kid? He knew it was important, but did he know how important? Would he try to sell it without knowing what was in it? Would he try to open it and barter off the contents piecemeal? It was bespelled to open only for someone from the Norse pantheon. Cian was neither a god nor a Norseman. However, if the kid could negotiate keys to the Red Web, he could probably hook up with a Norse flunky. The moment the superpowers got word that he had the pouch, he'd be dead. Once the contents of the pouch escaped into the wild, they'd shift the balance of power.

A disastrophy in the making.

"Bix, if he sells any of the information you gave the MWA about this case, a lot of people are going to die. Some of them agents."

Her gut said Cian *wanted* to make choices rooted in a place of kindness, loyalty, and compassion. Thing was, making good decisions wasn't innate. It was learned. Mostly it was learned by making bad decisions, but sometimes it was learned by surrounding yourself with the right kind of people. The Fates who wove his threads seemed determined to throw him steaming piles of awful time and again, which made for dismal odds on his surviving his trials, much less coming out with any hint of compassion left in him. There were too many heartless superpowers as it was, so, as silly as it might have been, she wanted to be one of those "right kind of people" for Cian. Maybe then, Cian would become the kind of Fate who actually cared for the people whose destinies he wove.

"It's possible I've misread his integrity," she admitted. "If so, I'll take care of him."

"Hey." Ashtad covered her hand with his and lightly squeezed. "I know you and his mother have an intimate history, but it doesn't obligate you to fill in for her. It's better if you think of the kid as an asset to be managed. As long as we keep on top of him, his risky behavior and new connections could net us the masterminds we're both after. Assuming he lives long enough."

She wasn't keen to mommy the kid. She didn't really lean maternal, but she didn't want to hand him the paint and brush for the bull's-eye either. For now, Cian hadn't done anything to merit a forced redirect. Didn't mean he wouldn't; just meant he hadn't done it yet.

"Thanks for the heads-up." She patted Ashtad's hand and

slid to her feet. "Ping me if you get anything new on missing CWIG agents or that injection-site stain. I'm off to the rabbit hole Loncalaz dug for me."

"Will do." He nodded. "Careful with the cooties."

CHAPTER 8

Bix closed the gate to the kitchen of the modern-industrial-meets-overstuffed-museum basement condo of the renovated coal plant the Berserkers used as their base in the Primary Mid World. To the uninformed, the upper floors were million-dollar river-view lofts with commercial spaces on the main floor. In truth, the only business in the building was Dysmorphic, the tattoo and body-mod shop manned by Berserkers with amazing artistic talent.

There were no windows, no exterior exits, no visible indicators of the massive basement that stretched farther than a pro sports stadium. Tobek being, well, Tobek, had offered her a place to live in this bastion of testosterone. It was heavily warded, constantly guarded, and filled with people who weren't trying to kill her. Two of those people spoiled her rotten.

How could a girl say no to that?

Tobek had told her to loop in their third roommate and his second in command with the data she'd taken from the CWIG. She would, as soon as said roommate finished his animated conversation with the range hood.

Gurp the goblin sat on the top rung of an aluminum ladder erected between the long kitchen island and the range. His mottled greenish-brown arms gesticulated wildly as he chittered in a language she didn't begin to understand. He paused long enough to gnaw on a length of rebar as though it were a licorice twist before continuing.

Goblins were despised by most Chwedlonol for being repugnant living dumpsters. However, in this household, Gurp was the designer, contractor, procurer, cleaner, and portable CSI lab. His senses could identify the microscopic composition of dirt, DNA, and whatever gunk flowed down the drains.

He was a freaking marvel...who seemed to be awaiting a response from the hood.

In all fairness, a Bi Xie had been bespelled into the range hood as a rather effective layer of security. Metal eyes tracked away from the nattering goblin and focused on Bix. She grinned and curtsied. The Bi Xie huffed.

Gurp stopped mid word. His grip on the rebar adjusted, holding the treat like a spear as he turned and faced her. Pond-scum eyes lit with relief when he spotted her.

"Pretty lady home safe," he cheered, scrambling down from his perch. His squat little body disappeared behind the counter before reemerging as he rounded the far end.

"Hi, Gurp." Bix beamed. "I didn't want to interrupt your chat there."

He harrumphed. "Not talk much."

"No, he's proven to be the stoic sort," she said with all solemnity. "But a good listener, nonetheless."

"How Chief?" Gurp set his snack on the mortician's table at the center of the armory adjacent to the kitchen. The basement had been constructed as modular open concept in which bookshelves, display cases, and ancient tapestries functioned as walls. Privacy was relative beneath the soaring industrial ceiling. The aesthetic was wholly masculine except for the small über-feminine oasis Gurp had built for her.

"Not doing well, I'm afraid." She sighed. "The crystals have started forming on him. I don't know how long he has before he completely succumbs."

"He come home? Not alone?" Gurp's bottom lip quivered.

"He has to stay in quarantine," she said, commiserating. "I could really use your help trying to solve who made whatever it is he's suffering from."

"Yes." He clapped. "Yes, I help. I help."

"Excellent." She removed her watch and gave it to him. "Tobek said to tell you and Xipil to keep this off grid. I assume that means something special to you."

Pure mischief lifted his melancholy features. "Come. Come. We sneak. You sneak. I sneak. Come."

Grinning, she followed him through the maze of their home. She had yet to fully explore the basement. She could locate Tobek's altar room, his bedroom, and the TV room without issue. She still got lost getting to her own room, however, and the stairway that led up to the main floor.

Good thing she was a gatekeeper.

Since Gurp had designed the place, he knew all the shortcuts. Before long, they were ascending the dimly lit stairs built into an old water pipe. She listened as he counted the steps. There were thirty-one; both he and Tobek had made a point of telling her that when she'd moved in.

He stopped at nineteen and patted the wall, each touch deliberate and accompanied by a small grunt.

The wall vanished. Warm air gusted into the stairwell.

Bix traced a finger over the smooth opening. "Living with a high warlock who is also a paranoid old Berserker means the surprises never end, do they?"

"Sneak. Sneak." Gurp chortled.

"Indeed." Bix's eyes adjusted to the darker shade of dim. Pale green lines illuminated the edges of the steps rising higher and at a steeper pitch than the stairs running up to the main floor. A light scent of cedar tickled the air as they ascended. Concrete and steel walls gave way to brick and iron. Again, she listened to the goblin count the steps. Since she didn't know where they were headed, she couldn't pop open a gate. By the time she'd climbed thirty-four more stairs in high heels, her glutes screamed objections.

Gurp stopped again and placed his hands on the wall. This time, she heard the locks releasing, chased by the hum of fans and a cool blast. Gray light cut through the darkness. Bix shielded her eyes and turned away. A pudgy, calloused hand took hold of hers and gently tugged.

"Come. Come," Gurp urged.

Blinking rapidly, she allowed Gurp to lead her into a long room lit by dozens of computer monitors showing all kinds of security feeds, data streams, and a few wallpapers of the MWA logo. A cedar conference table with eight leather club chairs anchored the center of the room.

A dozen Berserkers manned monitoring stations. Most gave Gurp a chin-up greeting and Bix a curious double take before returning their attentions to their duties.

"An operation center," Bix said ruefully. "Of course you guys have one. And of course it's not on the main level where anyone could stumble upon it."

"Welcome, Bix." A deeply tanned Berserker stood from his bank of monitors and bowed from the shoulders. The rolled sleeves of his white button-down shirt exposed the thick burn scars on his right forearm. The brown herringbone vest offered a classy balance to his dark jeans.

"Xipil, nice secret lair." She gestured to the room. "Tobek said I should talk to you and Gurp."

"Ah, yes." Xipil rapped on the conference table. "Give us the room, men."

Without hesitation, the guys filed out a conspicuous door that led to a normal hallway. The door clicked shut, leaving her alone with Tobek's most trusted.

"May I assume this is about the drive that vanished this morning?" Xipil indicated the monitors he'd been watching. "You held up two and left with none. The Sage had one."

"You're watching Grimtebel from here?" She sidled toward

the monitors Xipil had been viewing. Sure enough, snapshots from around the quarantine facility filled the screens. They surveilled the doctors, the hallways, the isolation pods, and the rocky terrain above the facility. "You don't trust your own doctors?"

"The Consortium often overreaches during these times." Xipil's smile was fleeting. "How may I be of assistance?"

"Off grid," Gurp grunted and handed Xipil her watch.

"If you'll unlock the encryption for me, Bix, I'll begin the transfer." Xipil powered on one of the laptops docked on the conference table and draped her watch over the trackpad. "Airgapped for precisely these reasons."

"Contents of partitions one and two to copy. Reconfigure encryption to allow Xipil and Gurp read and write rights. Maintain access logs." Bix spoke to her bug.

Transferring. Voice encryption created.

Xipil looked to her in confusion.

"It learned your speech patterns in the conversation we just had." She pointed to the files opening on the laptop without prompts. "This is everything the CWIG had on Loncalaz's mission at the Consortium labs. It includes personnel files of the dragons, the angels, and the handful of upper-caste Chweds they deign to admit into their program. I noticed audit sheets of resources in there too, but there are abbreviations and notations I didn't understand."

Xipil grabbed his phone and hit two buttons. "Meet me in ops."

While Xipil reviewed the data she'd dumped in his lap, Bix watched Tobek pacing his isolation pod like a tiger caged. As she'd suspected this morning, Tobek wore nothing more than his long briefs. Each pivot gave her a lovely high-res view of his battle-honed body. He still had acute bed head, which added to his predatory mien. The inked spells, wards, and stories that covered his chest and arms wrapped around his back. In stark contrast, nothing more than a heavy layer of blond hairs and a smattering of scars covered his sculpted legs.

Then there were the crystals. They'd spread to his pec and shoulder blade, looking like some sort of fantasy armor. Curiously, when Loncalaz had morphed into crystals, he'd shriveled up first, gone gaunt moments before the crystals had spread. There was no part of Tobek that seemed any thinner.

Did the drootie progress differently through different races? Or was the variable the threads of Fate? Tobek's contract with the Fates had undoubtedly altered his threads. Loncalaz had more in common with Cian in that sense.

She checked the monitor observing Cian. Like Tobek, he'd been relegated to wearing his boxers. Unlike Tobek, the kid was still a long and lean teenager: no crystals, no signs of desiccation. No sign of him looking up from his laptop either. She couldn't make out what was on the kid's screen.

"Do you guys have access to the Red Web from here?" she asked Xipil.

"No, Chief has blocked all means of connecting to it from the coal plant and the surrounding three miles. A security measure," Xipil answered without pause.

Bix gnawed her lip. "What about Grimtebel?"

"They run a different protocol. I couldn't say."

"Right. Sorry." She switched subjects to the one of greatest import. "Did the Consortium reps examine both our guys?"

"Blood, skin, spit, you name it." The voice that answered did not belong to Xipil. Xipil was soft-spoken, endlessly patient in tone and delivery. This voice belonged to the only Berserker she knew who shat diamonds. He also happened to be the lead medic for the battalion.

"Runjit," Bix greeted as the Grumpy Gus sauntered into the room. Like all Berserkers, he had a build meant to intimidate and nary an extra ounce of body fat. However, Grumpy was one of the few practicing Sikhs she'd met in the battalion. All the soldiers had unique ways of interpreting faith and religion since they knew the ugly truths of gods and the afterlife. Runjit had made his peace with the differences, at least, he seemed to have.

At Runjit's heels strode his polar opposite battle buddy, all smiles and gregariousness.

"Shwmae," hailed the Welshman as he slid into the chair next to Bix. The raven-haired Berserker sported awesome mutton chops and a large splatter-shaped scar—bright pink with newness—that touched both pale yet hairy pectorals. His unbuttoned chambray shirt did an impressive job framing it. He stretched his legs and crossed his ankles, adding more scuffs to his well-worn jump boots.

"Hywl, you darling angel hunter," Bix grinned. "I'm glad you're up and about."

"He would have been up sooner had he not continually torn his stitches." Runjit took a seat across the table from Xipil. "Reporting as requested."

"Take a look at these audit sheets, tell me what you see." Xipil undocked the laptop and pushed it to Runjit.

"You guys should start with the employee records."

The monitor over Hywl's shoulder went black, then flicked to a video of the Sage in his miserable translucent cell.

"Cian, h-how did you—?" Runjit sputtered.

"You watch me, I watch you. It's always two ways, minimum," the kid dismissed with a shrug. "Same thing happens when Bix hacks my hack. For the record, that old Fate who threatened you while you were in the lobby is a dick."

The four dudes in the room with Bix raised their brows.

"Most Fates are," she reminded. "Try not to become one when you ascend, yeah?"

Cian snorted. "Hey, did you bounce out of the Mids after you left here? I lost your phone's signal."

"A safe house I'd rather keep off the radar," she evaded. Ashtad's place was a dead zone for a whole lot of reasons. "I see you're using your laptop to run riot in the MWA networks. You manage to eavesdrop on the scientists who came for Loncalaz?"

"Pfft, natch." Cian smirked and sobered a bit. "I haven't been able to get into the Consortium labs, though. Don't suppose you want to swing by there with my version of a virus?"

So he could sell the labs' secrets on the Red Web in hopes of finding the cabal who'd coerced his mom into turning traitor? Oh hell no. The cause and cure for every kind of cancer was in those labs, along with a thousand other incurable cooties. Anarchy was not her goal.

"The Consortium has investigators at the labs right now, combing through everything physical, digital, and other. If I add a bug to the systems, they'll find it. Not a battle we should pick, particularly with your life on the line."

"You sure the angels and dragons care if a lowly human dies?" Cian challenged. "Sure didn't seem like it while they were here doing their invasion of my person."

"They'll care because the MWA cares," Xipil assured him. "You're not in this alone."

"Xipil's right." Bix watched Tobek watching the kid, suspicion aging his expression. To distract her roomie, she delivered one of his many sketch pads and cluster of pencils to his pillow. Tobek jerked around. His shoulders shook, and his grin broke through. "Let's do what we can to help the MWA keep the pressure on them. If you hacked my smartwatch, then you have the CWIG files on this case."

"Yeah, I got 'em here. Don't worry, here doesn't mean on the network here. Safely partitioned on my system, here." Cian wrapped himself further around his laptop, whispering into the mic on his machine. "A month ago, Loncalaz pulled a bunch of records from the labs and handed those over to the CWIG. Looks like the CWIG ran backgrounds on all the lab employees. Nothing flagged, so I went wider, scraping social media for first and secondhand presences."

"Secondhand?" Gurp climbed up into the chair beside Runjit and scrunched his face at the screen.

"Your friend has the account, but you're in the photo," Cian explained. "Family members have accounts, so your name comes up in posts. You ride public transportation on your way to work, which puts you in the frame on thousands of video clips. Legacy sites where platforms, services, and tech rose up as the latest trend, then became obsolete—but no one took down their old profiles—are gold mines for finding stuff people thought they'd scrubbed."

"Assuming you know where to look," Bix said more than asked. The kid had hacked the Red Web in less than a day; she didn't doubt his skills.

"The files you stole from the CWIG gave me all the leads I needed to dig into the parts of the net favored by Chweds," Cian boasted. "And while we're talking about things you don't want your coworkers to find, try the thirty-five percent of the labs' employees who subscribe to some sort of booty-call service."

Bix leaned back and blinked rapidly. Lonely-hearts profiles were an agent's wet dream for getting intel on a potential asset, setting up the potential asset to encounter a compromising situation, then using that situation to blackmail the newly acquired asset into compliance. Anyone with any kind of security clearance should've been banned from using those sites.

"What percent of the lab employees are not superpowers?" Xipil leaned on an elbow and cocked his head.

"Eight," Cian answered. "You should see the dating profiles for the dragons and the angels."

"Those are usually predatory," Hywl interjected, lacing his fingers behind his head. "They're targeting the upper castes who want the cachet of hobnobbing with the ruling races at the bargain price of being their meal."

Dragons and angels fed off emotions. Specifically, they fed off the songs played by a soul rubbing against its threads of Fate as it acted and reacted to living. Dragons drank the good emotions. Party with them, and a great time was guaranteed. Angels drank the bad; hence, the reason most mainstream religions pushed fear, shame, guilt, and oppression.

"Consortium investigators are going to be hammering on lab management and interviewing employees." Bix drummed her nails on the arm of her chair. "They aren't going to look too deeply into the Chweds, viewing them as inferior races incapable of pulling one over on the dragons or the angels. The investigators' innate bias leaves one evidence trail wide open."

"Ain't no rumor mill like a minion rumor mill," Cian snarked while typing. "Modifying search parameters to exclude non-Chweds."

"Overlap that with milestones and key dates in Loncalaz's reports. Also, check their social media for patterns in posting." Bix grinned as Tobek held up a drawing of her wearing his now-missing Mopar T-shirt. She did not look the least bit repentant in his sketch. Bedraggled, but not repentant.

"I've got two guys worthy of scrutiny here," Runjit said, plugging in a cable to the laptop. A bank of monitors behind him swapped out surveillance images for employee photos. "Grossly overqualified janitors possessing five PhDs between them."

"Guy on your left, Timai, is a forensic psychiatrist mopping floors at the angels' lab," Cian said. "Chemical engineer who's posing as a sanitation worker at the dragons' lab on your right. Name of Hu Jian."

She studied the faces, not recognizing either of them from her days with the spy guild. "Are we guessing CWIG agents?"

"Most likely," Runjit confirmed. "They were put into play within the past year. Twelve months and eight months, respectively. Both within a week of Loncalaz filing reports of Chwed employees going missing."

"Employees going missing," Xlpll echoed. "Not sick? Not reassigned?"

"Missing," Runjit insisted. "There's a note here to locate them, but nothing in the files that says they were."

"Got it," Cian cheered loudly, then cleared his throat and more quietly explained, "Four researchers with patterned postings to social media."

"I've got four with patterned purchases on their financials." Runjit pushed a new set of photos to the monitors.

"Hey, those are my four," Cian groused.

"Nerd wars," Hywl whispered behind his hand, tossing Bix a wink.

"It's a good thing," Xipil assured. "Verification allows us to focus our search. Explain what makes them notable."

"While scientists are known to be creatures of habit, these four developed a pattern of making public appearances." Runjit clicked more keys, and financial records appeared next to the photos. "For example, it is a habit to get dinner on the way home from work. However, it is a pattern when that dinner is picked up every Wednesday at half-past seven. Not a minute before or after."

"Thirteen minutes later they post a photo on their social media of their meal," Cian added. "Thirteen minutes precisely. Each time."

"This repeats in multiple nonwork aspects of their lives," Runjit noted. "It is as though they are making a concerted effort to appear to be maintaining a schedule."

"Alibis," Bix and Hywl said at the same time.

Bix flashed the angel hunter a smile. "Did the CWIG catch this?"

"Pfft," Cian scoffed. "No. These guys passed the guild's review, no flags."

"I bow down in awe." Bix bent over her clasped hands as she stood. "Thank you, all, for your help. I'm off to do an in-person welfare check for the suspicious six, starting with the janitors."

"May I suggest beginning with Elmira, a sylph employed at the dragons' facility?" Xipil motioned to the picture of a waifish albino. "According to the files Loncalaz pulled from the labs, she hasn't reported to work in three days."

"Yeah, that is weird." Bix retrieved her watch from the corner of Runjit's laptop. "Okay, I'll start with Elmira."

Front-loading location images in order of repeat visits. Residences first.

"Lobbies, courtyards, or exterior hallways preferred," Bix requested of her bug. "If any of these folks are home, I don't want to scare them. Best to start with a nice-girl approach and save the monster Chimera for later."

Re-sorting images.

"I'd like to go with you." Runjit stood and smoothed the shawl collar of his camel sweater that complemented his darker brown turban.

Bix snorted. He stiffened and scowled, a scowl that could not be hidden by his meticulously groomed beard.

"Of course, you are more than welcome, Runjit," she hastened to say. "But just so you know, the less you trust me, the more your soul will fight the transport through the gateways I create. I'm told it's a nauseating trip for the doubters, and we're going to be bouncing a lot in order to quickly clear these locations."

"Understood." Runjit cleared his throat. "If we find these people, I'd like to check them for the unusual staining at the point of injection."

"Oh, if they got poked in the ass, you're going to need someone to talk them out of their clothes." Hywl gained his feet, wincing.

"Which I am sure the Chimera is more than capable of doing," Runjit argued. "You are not yet healthy enough to expose yourself to an infection of any kind."

"I didn't think exposing myself would be necessary, but I'm not opposed." Hywl waggled his brows and twirled his shirt tails. "And if I have to stay inside this fortress any longer, I'm going to peel paint off the walls with a dull razor."

They looked to Xipil expectantly.

"The Chimera is running this mission. We are tasked to provide support."

Runjit and Hywl looked at her, one with wariness, one with puppy-dog eyes.

She held up her hands. "I have a grown-ass man policy. If you say you're up for an adventure, I'm going to believe you know you better than anyone and that you're aware of the burdens you're placing on the other members of the team."

"You've no idea the burden he loves to be." Runjit glowered at his battle buddy.

Hywl blew him a sloppy kiss.

Runjit rolled his eyes, then looked at Bix. "Grimtebel sent over lab results of Chief's and Cian's sweat. They share a common element. I'd like to test the homes of these scientists and the places they frequent for evidence of contamination."

"Swabbing." Hywl thumped his chest. "I'm absolutely healthy enough to wield some cotton swabs."

Runjit shook his head. "I've a testing kit ready to go in the clinic. Give me one moment to grab it."

CHAPTER 9

The dragons' lab existed on a Mid World in an area resembling a quaint resort town. The massive coral-colored laboratory hugged one side of a large clear lake. Cottage villages peppered the remaining beachfronts. The air held the scent of tropical seas with a hint of flowers. The temperature was on the cooler side of warm.

Bix opted to arrive in a small park of orange grass, fuchsia trees, and winding blue paths. Surrounding the park was a quaint preplanned community of colorful bungalows with porches, rocking chairs, and picket fences. Upper-caste Chweds chitchatted in clusters while children played games of magic at playgrounds built for such challenges. Cloudless rosy skies and gentle breezes stretched for miles without obstructions of high-rises, cell towers, or mountains. The lake lapped against the beach three blocks from the park.

The native magic here wasn't Bix's biggest fan. It shoved at her Other World body, savagely attempting to expel her foreign presence. All Mid Worlds exerted some level of rejection. Countering it came as easily to her as breathing, but sometimes on some Worlds, she had to try a little harder to stay on World.

"Well, isn't this a fairy-tale town." Hywl stepped through the gate with the casual ease of traveling with a gatekeeper he trusted.

"Rather public point of arrival," Runjit said through a long exhale as the gate closed behind him. His white-knuckled grip on his kit and the greenish tinge around his hairline gave away his discomfort.

"In closed communities like this, word will spread no matter how inconspicuous we try to be. You guys are built to stand out, so we use that to our advantage to make the weak links nervous or overconfident. Either way, they slip up and we slip in." Bix allowed the medic his dignity, smiling as the park's occupants took notice of their presence. She followed the path out of the park and headed for the aqua-and-lime home across the street.

Yes, an undercover op would have been preferable, especially in light of Sunan's threats; however, she needed a body thief or time to make that work. She had neither. Plan C was to distract from her presence by keeping the company of big beautiful Berserkers. Hywl, with all his charm and thick accent, made a perfect surface decoy. Scientists would be drawn to Runjit's simmering competitiveness and skepticism, if only to satisfy their subconscious need to prove themselves.

She had to hand it to Xipil, he knew how to pick the right guys for a job.

A little white fence framed a well-tended front garden of the cozy bungalow. Hywl reached for the gate latch, but the gate swung wide without assistance. White flower buds bloomed along the hedges leading up to the arched white door.

Hywl placed a halting hand in front of Bix and offered an apologetic smile. "If you'll forgive an old soldier's paranoia, I'd like to go first."

"Who am I to deny a gentleman's desire to take a blade for me?" Bix fluttered her lashes.

Chuckling, Hywl strode to the front door and raised his fist to knock. The door vanished. He paused with his fist in the air.

"Well, hello there, Berserker," cooed a lithe ganconer appearing in the doorway. His sea-foam eyes raked Hywl with lecherous appreciation. Cousin to the light elves of the Upper Worlds, the ganconer had the beauty one expected of the upper castes set in pastel hues all the way down to the slightly blue tint of his skin. The ganconer shared the height of the Welsh warrior but only a fraction of the bulk.

"Please pardon my interruption." Hywl lowered his hand. "I'm looking for Elmira of the sylphs."

The ganconer leaned to the side, peering around Hywl. "Now what would a Berserker in the company of the Chimera want with Ellie?"

It still flustered Bix to be recognized as the Chimera. The superpowers had kept the secret for so long. Once they decided to let it be known, though, it'd spread faster than chicken pox. She wasn't too sure what they'd hoped to achieve with the sudden outing. That part worried her.

"We need to ask Elmira a few questions," Hywl answered smoothly with a slight shrug.

The ganconer eyed Hywl again. "This is about those fifty test subjects who died, isn't it? Figures the Consortium would bring in the Chimera for the official inquiry into Yashanee. Can't be too careful when investigating the cousin of a dragon queen. Come in. Come in."

"It's a dragon-run lab, yet you don't find it odd Yashanee's cousin didn't hush up the scandal?" Hywl turned to the side and motioned for Bix to enter the house before him, mouthing, *Queen? Shit.*

The dragons were ruled by seven queens who alternated eras of reign. While the race was long-lived, the rotation of rule prevented the matriarchy from becoming stagnant and the race from being stuck in the past. They were nearing the end of one queen's era and preparing for the ascension of the next. Naturally, there were those within the race and outside who'd rather end royal rule altogether. The political clusterfuck around the unsanctioned cooties would be infinitely more fraught if Yashanee was cousin to either the reigning queen or the queen ascendant.

"I found it odd Yashanee put a dark elf in charge of the section of which she is most protective. Fitting that he stabbed her in the back. I mean, really, what did she expect from his ilk?" The ganconer shuddered dramatically.

Bix maintained her smile and made note of the eagerness with which the ganconer threw Yashanee and Loncalaz under the bus. Ballsy at best, suspiciously stupid otherwise.

"Drink?" the ganconer offered, leading them into a beach-themed great room opened to a very white and bright kitchen. "I'm Ozmar, by the way. Ellie was my housemate, but she took a job at another lab after the kerfuffle with the test subjects. Management hasn't assigned me a new bachelor or bachelorette bunkmate yet."

"It's a lovely home. I'm surprised Ellie was keen to leave." Bix perched on the edge of a rattan barstool as Ozmar poured some sort of icy blue libation. "Have you heard from her lately?"

"Oh naturally. We're besties." Ozmar presented the drink to Hywl with a coquettish smile. "She sends me emails now and then, seeing how everyone's doing, if there's any scoop or scandal. You know how it goes. It's one thing to leave the people. It's something else to leave the gossip."

Hywl declined the drink but didn't shy away from the attention of their host. "My friend's unaccustomed to traveling with the Chimera. Would you mind if he used your facilities?"

"Sure, sure. Everybody has to be a rookie sometime, right?" Ozmar gestured to the only corridor in the home, never taking his eyes from Hywl.

Runjit headed down the hall, utterly silent with kit in hand.

"I can't believe there's a better offer out there that would take anyone from this patch of utopia." Hywl planted one large hand on the counter and hooked the thumb of his other in his jeans pocket. Somehow, oh somehow, his unbuttoned shirt managed to expose all of his very muscular chest. "What sort of gig lured Ellie away from friends like you?"

"Fieldwork." Ozmar rolled his eyes and skimmed his glass over his bare chest, leaving condensation along his skin. "Can you believe? Took a cut in grade and prestige to conduct field observations of atmospheric anomalies in the protective layers of various Mid Worlds."

Bix's heart skipped a beat. The Angelic Host was in charge of monitoring rips in the layers. The angels and the dragons were not friends. If an angel poached one of the dragons' scientists, there'd be a spat for sure.

"So no forwarding address, then?" Hywl pouted.

"I can give you her email address, if that'll help." Ozmar pivoted, giving a rear view and a little wiggle as he plucked a flower from a vase beside the sink. A bit of origami mixed with magic made a card that he presented to Hywl with flourish. "My address is on there too."

"Thank you," Hywl purred. "Now, what can you tell us about the death of those fifty guinea pigs?"

"Only rumors, I'm afraid. I'm not cleared to be anywhere near that part of the lab." Ozmar put his drink beside the pitcher and set his forearms on the counter. His fingers danced around Hywl's planted palm. "Trescop, the dark elf who actually runs that section, doesn't even allow the janitors on the floor. Techs have to do all their own cleaning, including waste bins. But when you work for a dragon with a penchant for foregoing process and procedure... Well, really, I'm sort of grateful for the ban."

"Science over safety, is it?" Hywl tsked. "And those test subjects? Unauthorized dev trial?"

"Yashanee totally skipped the rats-and-monkeys phase, went straight to testing on people. Chweds, specifically. Mid and lower caste. Rumor says there might have been a few uppers in there too. Employees that..." Ozmar blushed and fanned himself. "Silly me, talking out of school about things I can't say are fact. Scientists, we like facts. Big. Hard. Facts."

"What about outside the lab?" Bix almost hated to interrupt their game, but Runjit had returned to the great room. He gave a slight shake of his head. The house was clean of contaminated sweat, so part of the ganconer's story held. "Does Yashanee fraternize with anyone?"

Condescension filled Ozmar's guffaw until Hywl's congeniality vanished. The ganconer cleared his throat. "Yashanee *lives* in the lab. Same level as her prized research section. She never leaves the lab. Ever."

But Yashanee had left. She'd gone to Grimtebel to fight for Loncalaz's remains. The ganconer's alibi might have meant something if dragons needed doorways, walkways, or gateways to travel. Like the angels, dragons could go anywhere in the Mid Worlds unless the destination had been warded against them. However, what a dragon or an angel could take with them when they traveled was limited. A case of syringes was totally portable. An entire research section? Not so much.

"Thank you for your time, Ozmar, and your help." Bix slid off the stool and smoothed her skirt. "Do let Ellie know to expect to hear from us."

"It'll be my privilege. Always glad to be of service to the Consortium and the Chimera," Ozmar trilled, escorting them back to the door.

Bix and Runjit paused at the picket fence as Hywl lingered with the ganconer.

"Thank you." Hywl wagged the address card and winked. His sensual grin adopted a hard edge as he walked away from the house, pulling his phone from his pocket.

They ambled to the park as Hywl took pictures of both sides of the card, then handed the enchanted slip of paper to her. A pair of tiny gates deposited it in the destructive ether.

"Gods damned upper castes," Hywl seethed under his breath the moment the gates closed. "They all think we Berserkers earned our commissions by being able to follow orders and kill real good. Like I didn't feel the crawl of his magic the moment I touched the card. Like I'm too dumb to know they use those things as eyes and ears to track our locations and conversations."

A Welshman affecting an Appalachian accent… Bix couldn't keep it together. She broke up laughing.

"At least you didn't have to convince him to take off his clothes," Runjit quipped deadpan.

Hywl scratched his mutton chop with his middle finger. "You notice where he said Elmira went? Fieldwork for atmospheric anomalies in the protective layers?"

"Also known as the rips through which ether is seeping into the Mids. No way is the Angelic Host letting anyone outside a very specific choir of angels near those," Runjit murmured. His Berserker's blue eyes constantly scanned their surrounds. "So either the sylph lied or the ganconer is."

"I sent the email addresses to the Sage." Hywl rubbed his palms on his thighs. "With his skills, the kid should be able to pinpoint Elmira's location, especially if Ozmar lets her know Bix is looking for her."

"Assuming it's really Elmira at the other end of that mailbox." Bix swiped through the images on her smartwatch.

"Interesting tidbit that Loncalaz had reported his boss to someone in the food chain, yet all three Consortium visitors acted like they had no idea what is growing on Chief," Runjit pointed out.

"They make a lot of cooties in those labs. We shouldn't jump to conclusions." Bix homed in on their next location. "You guys ready for another house call?"

"Please get us out of here," Hywl whimpered. "I can feel Ozmar staring at my ass."

Snickering, Bix opened gates.

The second scientist with a curious case of the alibis lived in a community adjacent to Elmira and Ozmar's. Set farther away from the beach, these craftsman-style homes sat on larger lots. Picket fences had been eschewed for flat lawns and slate walkways. The occasional cyclist pedaled by with a basket full of oddities strapped to the handlebars. The community lacked playgrounds and parks.

Music flowed from open windows, the kind performed by actual practitioners, not playlists.

"We're heading to the home of Udara of the iron dwarves. Her specialties are in engineering and nanorobotics. On the off chance she has a habit of bringing her work home, I suggest gloves for those of you with porous skin." Bix held up her hands and waggled her fingers.

Both Berserkers tugged wads of black latex from their front pockets.

"A habit from working in the shop. Always keep spare gloves on you." Hywl snapped on his gloves as he led their little band up the path to a home of olive green and dark wood trim. Every window was closed and the curtains drawn.

His knock echoed.

No one answered.

Again he knocked. Again it echoed. Again no one answered.

"Might be at the lab," Runjit suggested, shouldering his way to the front door. He thrust his case at Hywl. "Hold this. I want to test the doorknob before you pick the lock."

"Pretty sure a gatekeeper doesn't need my lock-picking skills." Hywl dutifully held the case, grinning at Bix. "He'll learn the advantages yet, my lady."

"Good to know you're my Plan B, Hywl." Bix peered through a window's sheers. The home was barely furnished save for a few stools and a very, very elaborate Rube Goldberg contraption spanning all the rooms she could see. "Let's head around back. It looks like the front of the house is booby-trapped."

"This will just take a moment." Runjit pulled a cotton swab tethered to a vial. After thoroughly rubbing down the door latch, he squirted a bit of clear liquid into the vial—bathing the swab— and shook the combination. The swab turned black, the water a pale brown.

"Is that a positive result?" Hywl croaked.

"It confirms the presence of the contaminated sweat." Runjit grabbed a handful of clean swabs, then shut the case. He handed half the swabs to Hywl. "Use these. We need to get a sense of path and pattern."

"I'll go left. Meet you two in the backyard." Hywl gave Runjit the case, then leapt over the porch onto the manicured lawn.

Bix followed Runjit around the right side of the home as he swabbed windowsills and siding. A small round face watched them from the upper floor of the neighboring house. The ears of a teddy bear held apart the slats of the blinds. Bix smiled and waved. The child's bear waved back.

A noxious notion slithered across Bix's mind. She checked her phone and Udara's file for any mention of a child or a dependent. One child. Deceased. Three years ago. Cause of death, drowning. In the lake mere blocks away. Bix winced, unable to imagine that hell.

She often wondered if, somewhere in her lost memories, lay the beauty and wonder of having had a child. Those musings were quickly chased by the horror at the idea that she'd abandoned that child.

"Over here, quickly," Hywl bellowed.

Bix was five steps behind Runjit as they rounded the corner to the rear of the house. The bottom half of a Dutch door clacked against the frame; the top half dangled by one hinge. Runjit used his case to hold the bottom wide. Hywl slinked behind him and into a large kitchen. Drawers and their contents littered the floor. Appliances stood warped and contorted from the obvious use of magic. The Welshman kicked aside a broken pantry door and crouched over a shriveling body. Crystals expanded over a tawny torso and limbs, hardening auburn hair and creeping into the edges of a square, gaunt face.

Gray eyes fixed on the Berserker, then slid up to Bix as she loomed over Hywl's shoulder.

"Udara," Bix gasped. "Someone got here before us."

"I've a full geode in the front room," Runjit called. "She was meeting someone. Maybe Elmira? Maybe one of the other two alibied scientists from the angels' lab?"

Confusion lit a tiny spark within the dwarf's dulling gaze.

"Udara, we know there's a conspiracy," Bix said. "We're trying to unravel it. We don't want to damn you, but we don't know how to help you."

The dwarf slid her gaze to the floor. Scattered silverware vibrated. Forks twisted. Spoons contorted. Knives curled. Words took shape.

Too late for me. Too late for Hu Jian.

Crackling from Udara's body turned audible. The spread of crystals completely enveloped the dwarf, constricting at a rapid pace until she was nothing more than a lump of glowing rock.

"By the unholy gods," Runjit swore from the archway separating the kitchen from the rest of the main floor. "Seeing it on the camera feeds was bad enough, but hearing it…"

"That's a sound that'll haunt my sleep." Hywl stood and tipped his head at Udara's final message. "Hu Jian, that was the janitor you'd flagged, right, Runjit?"

"As a probable CWIG agent." Runjit held up a handful of blackened swabs. "This whole house is contaminated and a crime scene. We need to invoke quarantine and alert the lab along with the Consortium investigators."

"I'm leaning toward one of those investigators being behind this. A minion of the faction. The timing of the attack is a little too coincidental what with their arrival at the labs just hours ago. Either they found something worth knowing at the lab, or they've known all along about Udara's involvement." Bix studied the destruction in the kitchen, then headed for the front of the house. Every piece of metal, from window latches to doorknobs to the newel posts on the stairs had suffered damage. "Udara fought back, that's why all the metal in this house is contorted. I'm going to check upstairs."

"Been up there. There's no evidence the fight made it that far, but it is covered in contaminated sweat." Runjit paused beside a small Ferris wheel in the elaborate Goldberg contraption. In one of the bucket seats, a fist-sized lump of rock pulsed in the hues of threads of Fate.

"Guys, we've got company coming up the front walk," Hywl cautioned. "Kids with boxes full of scrap metal and wood. What are the odds this thing was a community project?"

"Probably some sort of therapy to help her cope with the loss of her daughter." Bix peeked out the window opposite Hywl and counted seven kids, two of them human. A human population amid the Chweds must have been what Yashanee had meant by grounding the native magic here. The dragons had invited humans to inhabit this World. Unusual.

"Bix, we can't let these kids near this place," Runjit urged.

Bix poked her earpiece. "Call Tobek."

The ringing at the other end didn't finish before her housemate picked up. "Sweetheart?"

"I've got a midsized craftsman house coming in hot with two victims in geode mode. I need confirmation of identity and the house processed for evidence."

A plink on her phone and the small screen projected a stretch of barren landscape.

"Use this uninhabited land on the southwestern planes of Grimtebel," Tobek said sharply. "I'll dispatch teams to start processing immediately."

"Tobek, my gut says the bad guys knew we were coming."

"Then watch your back. At some point, they'll stop running from you and start trying to intercept you."

"I'd rather the latter. House incoming now." She eyed her Berserker escorts. "Staying with me or staying with the house?"

"With you, my lady," Hywl answered.

Runjit nodded.

Bix planted a hand on the wall of the home to move the house and only the house, leaving behind whatever sewage and electrical systems ran underground. A second thought moved her and the Berserkers independent of the structure.

The third community supporting the dragons' lab hosted commune-style single-story apartments fitted together around garden spaces. No children played here. No music filled the air. Instead, the bark of orders bounced off watercolor stucco walls as Consortium guards swarmed the space like ants on cake. Residents filled the courtyard, clustering and whispering.

"This is Hu Jian's place," Bix murmured under her breath, closing the gate a few feet behind a crowd of onlookers.

"Odd that they're looking for a presumed janitor," Runjit mused quietly.

"Unless his cover was blown." Bix checked her vibrating watch. The familiar logo of a CWIG alert spun in 2D animation. A tap on the screen projected the image. "We've got a report of someone with an injection-site stain. I say we let the Consortium have this win. Agree?"

"One sec." Hywl pulled his phone from his pocket and recorded the Consortium investigators at work. "We need to build a file on the Consortium team. Best to start with faces, especially if one of them turns out to be the mad needle wielder."

"Or takes to following us," Runjit added.

"Okay. I'm good." Hywl tapped his phone's screen. "File sent to Chief."

"What are we in for next?" Runjit nodded to one of the onlookers who finally noticed the big Berserkers.

Bix held out her arm so the men could see the image of a fire-damaged room with long shadows and a scaly lizard-like man staring into the camera.

Runjit leaned over her wrist, then stiffened. "That's the janitor from the angels' lab."

"Who is also an undercover CWIG agent like Hu Jian." Bix ran a fingernail along her bangs. "He's not alone, so expect some political pissery and inexplicable feelings of worthlessness."

CHAPTER 10

Whispers rolled like tidal waves crashing upon the helpless and increasingly demoralized Berserkers. Runjit pressed his forehead to a soot-stained wall, muttering to himself. Hywl vibrated from the strength with which he clenched his muscles. His blue eyes blazed with the rage of a Berserker, casting the small room in an eerie glow.

The object of Hywl's ire? The massive horse-faced, crimson-skinned, black-horned leader of the Cross-World Intelligence Guild. If Beelzebub ever needed a stunt double, the director could easily step in. Hell, the director had probably schooled Beelzebub in misanthropic douchebaggery.

"Knock it off, Director," Bix snapped, closing the gate behind her. Her knees bent a little too far, causing her to stumble into the tattered satin wingback chair occupying the center of the room where sat the distressed agent from the alert. She'd expended more energy than she'd realized resisting the push of native magic while on the World of the dragons' lab. This World didn't fight to expel her anywhere near as violently.

"What are *you* doing here?" the director snarled at her.

"If you insist on torturing high-ranking officers in the Mid World Army, you're going to have your ass flayed by the

Consortium." Bix rested her forearms on the top of the chair. "And I will happily, happily I say, deliver you to their chambers forthwith. I did spend some lovely days there on trial. The destination details are very clear in my mind."

The whispers stopped. The director faced her. "You didn't answer my question. How did you know where to find us?"

"Really?" She stared at him through her bangs. "You could introduce me to Timai here, and set your agent at ease. That is if you want to know what the very strange mark he's shown you is, why he can't go back to the angels' lab, and why you need to check on his handler immediately."

"I think you owe me a shoe, don't you?" The director glowered at her. Most people receiving that look would've melted into an acquiescent puddle, but Bix had gone stiletto-to-loafer with this man many, many times. Half of those many times had been before his big promotion to the head of the spy guild. Once he'd become head honcho, he'd hung her out to dry in front of the Consortium, blackballed her within the Intelligence Community, and propelled her out of the shadows into the spotlight of public infamy. They would never like each other; however, there had been one time they'd managed to work together—eh, more like work *adjacent*—for the greater good.

This needed to be one of the adjacent times. Joy.

"You're no Cinderfella, and I'm not auditioning to be your Princess Charming." Bix batted her lashes, unable to resist needling him. "How're your kids? Take any interesting trips lately?"

He growled like the beast befitting another fairy tale.

"Wh-what does this mark mean?" Timai, the lizard man, pulled his hand away from his upper arm and jerked up his sleeve.

"You've been infected with an unsanctioned bioagent." Runjit rolled his shoulders, tugged his sweater, and picked up his kit as the effects of the director's magic subsided. "You have anywhere from a few minutes to a day before your internal organs dissolve and the husk of your skin crystalizes, trapping your magic and possibly your mind in something the size of a duck egg. At least that's what happened to two of your fellow spies."

Timai closed his eyes and swallowed audibly.

"How far along are the MWA and the Consortium on a cure?" The director spun his gold signet ring around his middle finger.

"Nascent stages," Runjit said. "We need to know how, where, and when you were infected, Timai."

Timai looked to the director. With a grunt, his boss nodded.

"I've been under for a year in the angels' lab. Once you get past the mission of the lab—creating diseases for the lower races—and its use of people as lab animals, it's all fairly routine. The facility is massive, a hundred and fifty floors above ground and an estimated twenty below ground."

"Estimated?" Bix prompted.

"The subterranean levels are strictly off-limits to even the janitorial staff," he explained. "Yesterday, there was a surge in activity on the lifts to the undergrounds. A bunch of security was added. Only angels allowed. I inquired about the flurry and got told to keep my mouth shut and my eyes down if I wanted to keep living."

"Who told you that?" Hywl asked, the glow from his eyes still bright.

"Consortium goons. Yesterday, it was a handful of them. Today, there are dozens crawling all over the lab." Timai winced and rubbed his waist.

"Wait, *yesterday* Consortium investigators showed up at your lab?" Bix looked to Hywl. "That's around the time Loncalaz was infected, and before the MWA sounded the alarm."

"Might have nothing to do with this case." Hywl sighed, pulling his phone from his pocket. "Angels are a twisted lot."

"He's right about that." Timai wiped his cheek on his shoulder. "Once security tightened on the subs, I could finally get close to the virology lab. Today, I passed a woman in the hallway, on her cell phone. Which was interesting, because phones aren't allowed beyond the lobby."

"Standard security measure." Bix nodded.

"Gets weirder." Timai wiped his brow. "The woman is crying, begging to please not make her…make her do what, I didn't get close enough to hear."

"What time today?" Runjit pulled out his flashlight and shone it at Timai's face.

"A few hours ago. Start of my shift." Timai held up his hand against the light. "You mind?"

"When did you realize you'd been infected?" Runjit swung his light at the injection stain.

"I'm walking home from work, two bus stops from the lab. Crowded street. More crowded sidewalk. People bump into each other all the time. Except by the time my brain processed that I felt a prick, I'm a block farther than I was with a thousand people between."

"Yesterday you're cautioned to stay away from the subterranean levels. Today you catch a private phone call. Today you're infected on the street. It's got to be the call that incited them." The director crossed his arms. "Who was the woman?"

"Sarina, a sylph." Timai tugged on his collar and exhaled loudly. "She's one of the 'Chwed Success Stories' that the angel Kashdejan touts in her recruiting spiel."

Sarina the sylph. One of the alibi researchers.

"We'll check on her next," Bix assured. "In the meantime—"

"Timai, how long have you suffered hot flashes?" Runjit interjected.

Bix took one long step away from the chair.

"Since I got here." Timai fanned himself with his shirt.

"You've become progressively gaunt in the short time we've been here." Runjit motioned to Timai's chest with his flashlight. "Your shirt is notably looser on you. We need to get him to Grimtebel immediately."

"Like hell," the director growled. "This is a CWIG agent. Our scientists will take care of him."

"Absolutely not." Runjit returned his flashlight to his kit. "This is a quarantine protocol. Your scientists don't have the slightest clue—"

"Neither do yours," the director snarled.

"I thought I had more time," Timai panicked.

"So did we." Runjit stroked his beard. "Something has escalated the spread."

"Something that Loncalaz had but Cian doesn't. Something that Loncalaz had in common with Udara and the other CWIG agent. Something that isn't tied to the dragons' lab because you're suffering it too."

"*What* other agent?" the director demanded.

"Hu Jian," Runjit said, while Hywl muttered into his phone.

"Magic," Bix blurted. "That's why Tobek is already showing signs. Cian's still human. Humans ground magic; they don't possess it. Sages don't trade their humanity until the final trial for Fatehood."

The director eyed his man. "Timai, have you wielded your magic since you were injected?"

"If you count shapeshifting." Timai pivoted slightly in the chair. "I had to shift forms to get to this abandoned building undetected."

"That's what turns it on, speeds it up, whatever the scientific word is." Bix steepled her fingers in front of her lips. "Loncalaz used a lot of magic in the fight with Tobek."

"Within a few moments, he was a rock." Hywl looked at her, phone to his ear. "Udara used her magic to fight off her attacker."

"Presumably Hu Jian had done the same," Runjit added. "Bix, we need to send Tim—"

He didn't have to finish his statement. Bix sent Timai and the chair to a vacant isolation pod. Sirens blared through Hywl's phone.

"Yes, she just delivered him," Hywl said to whoever was on the other end of the line. Probably Tobek.

"Bix, you're hanging yourself with the very short rope of our truce," the director seethed. "That is my agent you've abducted."

"So was Loncalaz, and he enacted a one thirty-two. He waited until I got there to do it. One could even say he waited until I got there to tag me in." She stepped to the behemoth, close enough that the toes of her colorful pumps touched his spit-shined black wingtips. "My friends and I retrieved the remains of the second agent you had embedded in the dragons' lab. He should have been pulled the moment you were notified the mission had been compromised."

"Hu Jian was there with a scientist, you said," the director challenged. "That's two scientists infected, if you account for Loncalaz's cover. The mission is about exposing the faction inside the Consortium. The development and manufacture of the drug are the means. Don't lose sight of the mission."

That right there was the issue she had with guild management. Agents should never have been considered disposable resources. An agent in the field had to be able to trust the guild to keep them in the loop and up-to-date on all threats in order to do their job effectively. The director had known of the danger to his agents and had chosen not to pull them.

That made him guilty of the same kind of crimes for which she'd been convicted and exiled.

"Three agents are *confirmed* victims," she snarled. "There's a chance the scientist Udara was collateral damage. You need to put every undercover operative and their handlers on alert for that damn stain and tell them not to wield their magic if infected."

His finely arched brows furrowed.

"You don't see it. Why are you here instead of Timai's handler? Hmm? Was his handler not available? What about the handlers for the other infected agents? Are they accounted for? Are they well? Are they noticing tails and trails?" Bix tried for a sympathetic smile as the darkness scrabbled under her skin. "Director, until we have corroboration, you need to assume your in-house problem has compromised *all* your assets in the field. Those you can't pull, you need to warn. Whoever created the bioagent might have chosen to run unsanctioned in order to target your guild."

"That's a leap," he scoffed.

"Not if your guild is standing between them and what they're really after." Bix held his yellow-eyed glare. "You're a security agency. Occasionally, you do your job well. That's bound to be a problem for some very powerful people."

"Both Timai and Hu Jian were infected after the Consortium was notified by the MWA, and after Consortium agents arrived at the labs to begin their investigations. That means whoever is behind this isn't afraid of the superpowers. They're determined, and they're not backing down," Runjit noted, coming to stand by Bix's left flank.

"If anything, the exposure is pushing up their timeline. Three agents in less than forty-eight hours will become how many more in seventy-two hours?" Hywl asked from her right flank.

"And you think my agents were removed because we have or know something that the faction within the Consortium doesn't want us to." The director frowned but nodded. "I'll task some analysts to find what that could possibly be, but we're looking for a needle on a World of haystacks."

"You know how to reach me." Bix stepped aside.

"Gentlemen," the director said to the Berserkers as he headed for the char-trimmed door.

"Director," Bix called after him. "May I suggest they focus on the Dark Ops missions with retrievables?"

The director ducked under the doorway and paused. "You think this is about something we have in storage?"

"This sickness is not killing the victims outright," she admitted. "It's putting them in stasis. Small, hard-shelled packages. Convenient size. Theoretically protected."

The director straightened his suit jacket. "Bargaining chips?"

"It's an idea." Bix shrugged. "What other organization would have something so valuable that the enemy would spend years developing this kind of plan to get their hands on it? They clearly ruled out brute force, covert reclamation, and political pressure."

"They couldn't break us with external forces, so they're hitting us on the inside with fear as their primary weapon." The director grunted.

"Death isn't scary. It's the dying," she said, quoting the popular human cliché.

"It's the uncertainty of whether you're really dying or being prepped for a more hellish life. That's what our agents fear most." The director left the tiny room and clomped down an internal staircase.

Bix waited for his heavy footfalls to fade before she faced the Berserkers. Hywl's rage had finally ebbed, leaving his eyes vibrant but not glowing. He slid his phone in his shirt pocket and regarded her thoughtfully.

She gave the angel hunter the side-eye. "What?"

"It's a tactic of warmongers everywhere to take the heads of their enemies and publicly display them to induce fear. The head is a universally recognizable feature. However, this stuff turns the victims into rocks. Passersby have no idea who the rock is. They wouldn't even know the rock had once been a person. The average passerby, that is."

"You don't think they're bargaining chips?" she asked.

"Oh, I think you're on to something with that idea." Hywl smiled. "But the bargaining works better if it's between races who can recognize a rock as a person."

"The superpowers," she said and inhaled deeply. "All the more reason to stick to our original plan and visit the scientists who carefully crafted alibies. We have two left. Might as well start with Sarina the other sylph, Kashdejan's crying pet scientist."

Sarina's home was straight out of a modern living magazine. Minimalist. Clean lines. Lots of white and glass. If not for the bold orange area rug in the foyer, the two-story condo on the upper floors of a high-rise could have been mistaken for a lab.

Speaking of mistakes, someone had left the front door ajar.

Hywl nudged the frosted glass door wider with his boot. Not so much as a creak of a rusty hinge or the chirp of an alarm system gave them away. The main floor was open concept with sight lines out the balcony to the neighboring high-rise. Dusk bathed the densely packed city of more glass and white concrete in roses and plums.

Hywl checked the corners and the balcony while Bix silently made her way up the floating stairs with Runjit at her heels. To the left of the landing, two small bedrooms with doors wide, beds made, and no personal effects. An unremarkable and unoccupied bathroom sat across from the landing. To the right, another frosted glass door left ajar.

A gentle breeze slithered through the gap.

Runjit laid his hand on her shoulder and sidled around her. He tapped his ear twice and headed for the third bedroom. Bix waited in the hall. Hywl quietly ascended the stairs and gave a slight shake of his head.

"We have a body," Runjit called.

Bix entered with Hywl right behind her. A small thin man lay in repose, eyes wide, partially dehydrated with a kitchen knife through his heart. Runjit set his kit on the foot of the bed and retrieved from it two pairs of latex gloves. He handed one pair to Hywl.

"Check him for the injection stain. I'll verify the room's contaminated."

"Well, that's one hell of a way to stop the change." Hywl rolled the body to its side, mindful of the blade in the chest. "Confirmed. Right hip. This guy weighs less than a ream of paper."

Bix studied the room. Except for the bed, it was like the others. Nothing was out of place. No signs of personalization save for one pair of reading glasses on the bedside table.

"This whole room is contaminated. From the nightstands to the adjoining bathroom." Runjit announced from said bathroom. "There's moisture in the shower. Someone was here recently. I doubt it was the guy in the bed. There isn't enough of an angle to the blade rammed in his chest for it to be self-inflicted."

"There's barely any blood." Hywl pointed to a small interrupted spray pattern on the white sheets. "A body that'd been dead and then stabbed would still have released way more than a little piddle. Clearly this poor guy was in the throes of the desiccation stage of the illness when someone ended it for him."

Bix crouched and peered under the furniture. A white ceramic case the size of her hand caught her eye. She kicked it out into the center of the room. Runjit retrieved and opened it.

"One syringe missing. The other four are here and loaded."

Bix surveyed the room again. She turned toward the breeze and the open window.

Movement on the balcony of the adjacent building caught her attention. A child with a teddy bear stared back. A familiar child. Slowly, the child turned to the east. Bix followed her distraction.

Gossamer wings fluttered between buildings. Long white hair danced in the rising wind, engulfing a petite woman in a blood-spattered blouse.

Sarina the sylph raised a fist, thumb high. Hate hardened her delicate features.

The sylph's thumb pressed against her curled fingers.

"Bomb!" Bix shouted.

CHAPTER 11

Gates opened. How many and where, hell if Bix knew. A thousand tentacles of darkness snapped and writhed around her, undirected and uncontrolled. Her head lolled heavy upon her neck. Her limbs trembled. Native magic shoved at her, attempting to expel her Other World body into the vast ether. The second pendant she wore burned with the magic trapped within it, magic that cast out invisible grappling hooks tethering her to…

Where *had* her mind chosen to send her?

She looked around but saw only the brilliance of the explosion seared into her retinas. In her ears roared the din of detonation. Her lips tasted of heat and ash.

"Hywl? Runjit?" she shouted. Maybe she only thought she did; she couldn't tell anymore. Every one of her five senses was shot. She stayed still, mostly because she didn't have a choice. She focused instead on her breathing, slowing her erratic panting to controlled counts. Inhale, two, three, four. Exhale, two, three. In, two, three, four.

The thrashing of the darkness slowed to match her breathing until the tendrils danced like shadowy partners to a simple waltz. Through their sways, she glimpsed a dark sky around the auras holding dominance in her gaze. Red lights twinkled at the periphery.

Either she was surrounded by emergency response vehicles or she'd set off a full-scale alarm.

Well, shit.

This promised to be unfortunate. If she opened a gate to leave, she was too exhausted and hungry to control the size of it. She'd probably cause this World to collapse in on itself. That might be bad, depending on the World.

On the other hand, she'd visited a dozen or so Mid Worlds that could benefit from a cosmic flush.

A large cool palm cupped her cheek. She jerked back. Fingers tightened in her hair and pulled her face forward.

Raw energy. Potent and divine prickled over her skin. She inhaled sharply, drinking the sustenance her body craved. With each long draught, her senses were restored, her strength rebuilt, and the aspects of gatekeeper and Shadow Caster rebalanced. Her vision cleared, leaving her staring into the red pupils and amber irises of Phobos, the Greek god of fear.

Praise be. Dinner that delivered itself.

Phobos released her head and assessed her with narrowed eyes and pursed lips. Behind him, red and blue strobe lights cut through the night sky. The deafening *aoogah* of an air-raid siren blared at mind-numbing intervals. Phobos snapped his fingers, and the siren went silent. He jabbed a pinky in his ear and wiggled it, wincing.

"If you are collaborating with the Mid World Army, why are they raising the alarm at your arrival? This is like the old days. Though, I much prefer their screams over the siren." Phobos rebuttoned his silk shirt and smoothed the fronts of his three-piece charcoal suit.

Bix scanned the ground and breathed a sigh of relief at the boulders vibrating around them. "Grimtebel. I defaulted to Grimtebel. Good. Good. Good move, brain."

Red lights flashed on the horizon, which she could only assume came from the terrain above the quarantine facility. The blue strobe lights advancing on her position had to be Berserkers coming to subdue the invaders or rescue their own.

"Hywl? Runjit?" she called again.

"You dumped your bodyguards and a sylph inside the MWA building. The smoldering condos you dumped on these poor creatures." Phobos retrieved a rock sliding closer to his foot. He held the carnivorous stone like a pet, stroking its rugged surface and cooing to it. Damn if the thing didn't snuggle closer to him. "You were supposed to meet Devana and arrange for lessons in mastering your Shadow Caster aspect. She informs me you have yet to make contact. Then you were supposed to find a new food source. Instead, you summon me to this delightful oasis of deepening terror. Is this how you apologize for your blatant offenses?"

A god's sense of humor wasn't normal, so she took his query as being earnest.

"I intend to meet up with Devana as soon as this crisis is put to bed. Since I'm still not entirely sure how I summon you, I..." Bix grimaced. Showing any contrition would shift the power dynamic between them and not in her favor. "Thank you for the top-up. You're invigorating as always."

"Oh no, Chimera." Phobos clucked with a wealth of sinister condescension. "You're not getting rid of me now. In fact, you need me to enter that disease-riddled quarantine with you."

Bix recoiled. "I'm infected?"

"Of course not." He scowled at her. "But your involvement in this political skullduggery has drawn the interest of multiple pantheons."

"Speaking of the pantheons, why do the gods even allow the Consortium's research labs to exist? Cooties used to be your bailiwick."

"The naïveté of your question disappoints me," he derided. "Yes, there was a time when plagues were wholly the purview of the gods. Then the angels, the dragons, and the Fates decided we were too adept and too...fond of our little hobby."

"Things were said, feelings got hurt, and pantheons refused to play along anymore?" She didn't have to guess too hard on that. A god's ego was easily wounded, and they had no impetus to grow up.

"Something like that." He dismissed any further explanation with a flick of his fingers. "So, you and I can go into that facility together as collaborators, or the pantheons will send other representatives while you're not around to protect your enemies."

"Enemies?" Bix shivered as the wind blasted over her exposed spine and rippled through her tattered dress courtesy of the darkness she couldn't control. "The Berserkers aren't my enemies."

"It fascinates me, how giving up your memories ripped away eons of emotions and relentless conditioning. You're proof that instinct can be learned and unlearned. For that, I pity you." He set the rock on the ground, then held out a hand to her.

Bix stared at him as a lump grew in her throat. There was no way the Berserkers were her enemies. They'd welcomed her into their home. Their fortress. They backed her up without question. They protected her and helped her. They were nothing less than completely supportive.

But Ashtad had warned her about the Berserkers too. He'd warned her about Tobek, about his true intentions and purposes. He'd warned her that Tobek was a master strategist.

This whole thing could be a long con by the MWA.

It was conceivable that they were training her to trust them as they learned her methods and weaknesses. Then when the command came down from on high, they'd use it all against her.

Their chief *had* confessed to a shared past with her, and he patently refused to discuss it. According to Tobek, his silence was so he didn't taint her personal rediscovery with his bias. Was that why? Was it because they'd been enemies before? How weird did it make him that he'd bring her so closely into his fold if they'd been enemies?

Nah. Gods were the furthest things from trustworthy. She'd put her faith in the Berserkers' actions over Phobos's words. On the off chance Phobos turned out to be right, well, her weaknesses weren't the only ones being studied.

For the record, though, not having her full memories really, really sucked donkey balls.

"Phobos, you have an unfortunate way with women." Bix placed her hand in the god of fear's. "Anyone ever tell you that?"

"Every passing second." Phobos patted the fob tucked into his vest pocket. The fob contained the heart of the woman he'd loved, the woman who'd screwed him over.

The heart still beat.

CHAPTER 12

B ix stepped into the lobby of the Grimtebel quarantine facility with Phobos at her side. A dozen automatic weapons locked on them.

"You all having fun working with a gatekeeper yet?" Bix smiled at the room as one by one the weapons' aims shifted from her to Phobos. "How are my guys doing? They okay? Medium rare? Pink in the middle?"

One of the guards pressed a finger to his ear. "Chief, we have unauthorized access. How to proceed?"

"Shoot me, please," Phobos purred, straightening his pocket square.

"Don't you dare," Bix hissed to the god more so than the guards.

"Let them through," Tobek's surprisingly weary rasp came over a central intercom. "Sweetheart, you'll have to go through decontamination."

Bix pouted and whined but headed for the locker room.

"Oh, for…" Phobos snapped his fingers.

A whirlwind of navy and mulberry spun around her. Whisper-light touches caressed her from hair to toe and all the intimate spots in between. Before she could cry out her indignation, the cloud dissipated. She stood there clean, coifed, and redressed. Even her nails had been buffed and her tech polished.

"Exceptionally thorough, aren't you?" She glowered at the god beside her.

"When it suits." He motioned for her to move along, unfazed.

She plodded through the assorted stations, following Tobek's navigation coming through her earpiece. He guided her to the field house where she'd deposited all the injured and infected. More machines of all sizes and interfaces had been added to the space, lining the exterior walls. People in hazmat suits worked deftly in front of a few of the machines. At the center, five modular isolation pods faced each other in pentagonal alignment. Gaps between each pod allowed quarantine personnel access to the center.

How quaint, Phobos chirped in her head, not her earpiece, but inside her mind.

Gods.

He stepped aside as a person in a hazmat suit pushing a stainless-steel tray of bandages, unguents, and implements left the center of the cell configuration. Again, Phobos motioned Bix to move along.

Bix's insides clenched, and she braced for the worst. She'd tried to get everyone clear of the explosion, but she couldn't control in what condition they'd made it. She didn't know if they'd live or if they'd end up like her Dark Ops team. Worse, what if they'd incurred damage their contracts didn't cover? Not all Berserkers had a full-reset clause like Tobek. They were long-lived, not immortal. They could die, or they could be like Loncalaz, trapped in a rock, praying death was an option.

I know it's not fear making you hesitate, the god of said emotion drawled in her head. *Is it guilt?*

"Concern," she corrected aloud. Sucking down a deep breath, she walked to the center of the pods.

She spotted Cian first. The kid raised a hand in greeting. He was still in good health from what she could tell. No crystals. No weight loss. The same could not be said for the guy in the pod next to him. Tobek was flat on his back on the floor in corpse pose, his only hand over his heart. Crystalline netting had grown down his shoulder to cover his lower body and abs. Only his face, arm, and one pec remained free.

"Shit," she sighed under her breath.

That is unexpected, Phobos harrumphed in her head.

"Not if it's magic the drootie is feeding on." She turned to the three new pods.

Hywl stretched out on his cot, dressed only in his smiley-face boxers, hands laced behind his head. He had a few new pink blotches to complement the old. A white bandage wrapped around his right calf in stark contrast to the dark hair covering his pasty legs. He lifted his oxygen mask from his face and beamed.

"Many, many thanks, our Lady of Darkness."

"Hywl, are you okay?" She went to the door of his pod and bit her lip, searching for obvious signs of damage. "Did you tear your old injuries again? Did you get infected?"

"It's a precaution. Contaminated room. Contaminated projectiles. Our open wounds. The doctors are running tests now," Runjit answered from the pod next to his battle buddy. He looked far worse for wear. Hazmat people tended to his injuries, carefully separating his charred clothing from the burns covering the left side of his body. The blistering reached his face. Scorched bits of his turban tumbled into his lap. His once-glorious long hair looked like it'd been attacked by a toddler with blunt scissors.

"Oh, Runjit, I'm so sorry." Bix struggled with a wave of grief seeing this very proud warrior clinging to his dignity with the fraying rigid fibers of his battered body. Some people, all they could claim as their own was the pride they mined within themselves. It wasn't arrogance; it was the only root they had left to keep themselves anchored to sanity.

It made sense why Tobek had paired Hywl with Runjit. One needed to be steadied on the path, and the other needed to learn to veer.

"The apologies are all mine," whispered a feminine voice through the comms.

Bix spun around on her heel to face the occupant of the fifth pod. A waifish albino woman huddled behind her long white hair as more doctors in hazmat suits worked her over with all kinds of gizmos.

"You must be Sarina the sylph," Bix said with contempt. "The angel Kashdejan's pet. You were clearly expecting someone to show up at your condo tonight. Was it us?"

"No," the sylph blurted. "Oh gods, no. I had no idea anyone else knew. I thought I was alone in trying to stop them. I recognized your face after my thumb hit the button on the detonator, far too late to stop the explosion. Never in my wildest fantasies did I imagine that *you* would come to my aid. I am so, so sorry."

"Blowing up your home and your spouse is a drastic move. He was your husband, right?" Bix planted her hands on her hips. "I have no idea how many of your neighbors are injured or dead because of what you and I did tonight."

"My real neighbors moved out years ago. Those units are vacant except for when they're used to spy on my family or to provide access to my home." The sylph held out her arm as doctors inserted some sort of PICC line.

"Who is 'they'?" Bix demanded.

"I don't know. In the beginning, I tried to find out. While I'm very good at research, they seem to be even better at hiding." Sarina ran a trembling hand through her hair. "All I know for sure is that there is a third laboratory in which they're using scientists like me to cook up bioweapons they don't want anyone to know about."

"A third lab?" Hywl sat up. "Where?"

"No idea." Sarina gave a sad smile. "I know you don't believe me. No one else does. My husband didn't until he was dying. My boss didn't, still doesn't. His boss sent me for a psych eval, and my doctor sent me home with drugs. Some for anxiety. Some for paranoia. Too much stress, don't you know, born from the need to overachieve in order to keep up with the angels working at the lab. Upper-caste Chweds don't really belong in a Consortium lab unless we're there as test subjects."

She has a point. Why retain Chweds to construct their own demise? Everyone in those labs thinks they're gods, entitled to all the same powers and privileges, Phobos derided.

"That's a…not unexpected perspective of the superpowers." Bix refrained from snapping at the god behind her. "We'll come back to the where in a moment. Why did you and three of your peers from other labs need alibis?"

"Ellie, Qiang, and Udara." Sarina's lids fluttered closed. "We met in a support group. Qiang was the last to join, yet one of the first to share his story. I was too afraid to tell mine, lest therapy prove that I really had imagined it all. Ellie and Udara had been going longer than I. I'd assumed they'd already shared. But as Qiang spoke, I wept, because his story was my story, and as it turned out, Udara's story."

Oh please, not a story. Please spare me the story.

"Tell me your story, Sarina."

You did that out of spite.

"It started as a dream. Yet another dream about the office, about the work. You know those dreams where you pick apart your day, your process, or the problem you can't unravel? That's what I thought it was." Sarina let the doctors position her. Her hair afforded modesty. "After about a week, I realized it was the same problem every night. The deviations were how I went about it. The place was the same, but it wasn't my lab. There were never other people, not even those who weighed on my mind while I was awake. And my clothes changed, reflecting what I'd worn to bed. If I'd cut my hand during the day, the cut was still there in the dream."

"It wasn't a dream," Bix prompted.

"I'm a scientist. A hypothesis has to be tested before it can become a theory." Sarina glanced over her shoulder at Bix. "So I set up the tests. I learned 'they' fill my condo with gas at night after my husband and I go to bed. When I wake, I'm in a Spartan lab. My research progressed slightly, as though someone else has been working on it."

"That's got to be aggravating," Bix noted.

"Pales in comparison to the greater picture," Sarina dismissed lightly. "I pick up where things have been left off. Log my details. Then I'm gassed again. I wake up in my bed exhausted. Injuries incurred in the dream are still with me in the day. I tried sleeping in any bed but my own for months. They still found me. Still gassed me. Still put me to work."

"Months," Bix echoed. "How long have you endured this?"

"Five years. Do you have any idea how hard it is to fight for your sanity for five years while being abducted every night?"

"No, I can't begin to imagine," Bix answered truthfully. "You said you told your husband, your boss, and your boss's boss about this. Did you tell them about the abductions as well? Surely it would have been easy enough for them to verify you weren't home."

Sarina spun the plain silver band on her finger. "My husband accused me of concocting an elaborate story to cover up an affair. There comes a point when you realize those you trust the most don't trust you. It's humbling and humiliating."

Bix glanced at Tobek's pod but stopped her brain before it took any detours. "What about corroborating your story with anyone you came in contact with during this ordeal?"

"R&D is pretty solitary until field trials. Most communications happen through terminals and tech. I know there are others at the lab. I know because the place is riddled with cameras and sensors. There is new research, progress and failures, most of which I cannot claim to have done." Sarina hung her head. "But do I know who they are? No. Not until I met Ellie, Qiang, and Udara."

"Each of you is a specialist in a different field, so how likely is it you were working on the same project?" Runjit piped in, the distraction of the interrogation seeming to help him relax as the doctors bandaged what they could.

"We didn't connect the dots until I hit a breakthrough and the nature of my assignments changed. That's when we realized what they wanted me to do and that's when I started sabotaging tests."

Make her continue. I love a good sabotage.

Bix looked at the god behind her. Phobos stared back, his expression inscrutable.

"So for five years, you knew you were working on a contagion, yet something changed recently that triggered your dormant morals?" Runjit again. If he could rise to pique, then the pain meds must've kicked in.

"You saw my husband in our bed," Sarina snapped. "They infected him to punish me."

"We found the case of loaded syringes in your room," Runjit argued.

Sarina spun around, facing the quad. She slid her hair over her shoulder, exposing a painfully bony torso and the blue injection stain above her navel. "They need me, or they would have killed me when I reported them to my superiors. No, they need me now more than ever, so I took myself out of their arsenal."

Cian surged up from his cot and planted a hand against the glass door. "If you gave yourself a suicide injection, then you know for certain there's no cure."

"A cure?" Sarina's shoulders slumped. "Oh, you poor boy. No. There is no cure. You can't develop one when you can't identify the base organism. We know it's organic. We know it easily transmutes to crystalline structures once it bonds to its host. But what it is, at its very core? We have no idea. It is nothing we have ever seen before. That's what makes it so hard to work with. That's why it's taken us five years to find suspension fluids that can serve as carriers that allow the base organism to survive long enough to make it from creation to delivery."

That made all the doctors in the pods pause.

"If they don't know what it is, where the hell did they get the base organism?" Hywl cried.

"Is it contagious?" Runjit inquired over his friend.

"They'd like it to be, contagious that is." Sarina let her hair cascade over her chest again. "That's been the ultimate goal. It's not particularly useful if you have to inject it directly into your target."

"Assassins would love that stuff," Bix muttered. "Have loved that stuff, apparently."

"If it can't work large-scale and across races, we're not interested," Sarina quipped, then quickly blushed. "We being Consortium labs, that is."

"Oh, your bogeymen are definitely using Consortium lab resources, so I'm comfortable believing they want broad spectrum infections too." Bix motioned for Sarina to continue.

"The catch is that the base organism likes to stay with its host once it bonds. I suspect there's someone else in a position similar to mine with the task of making it a communicable disease. I sincerely hope they don't succeed."

Bix scratched her forearm. "So what did they want you to do that finally pushed you over the edge?"

"Aerosolize it."

That earned a full chorus of curses from all the men.

"That's why they need a sylph. Sylphs are members of the air elementals. Their magics are uniquely geared toward manipulating climate and atmosphere, including everything carried on the wind." Bix wagged a finger at Hywl and Runjit. "Sarina, could Ellie complete your work? Once you die, could she step in?"

"Doubtful. She's Queen of the Terrariums." Sarina chuckled, then waved it aside. "Sorry, inside joke. She's an environmental engineer. Biomes are her thing. We suspected she was testing the effects of the bioagents I made on other life-forms. If aerosolized deployment was achieved, what effects would it have on the ecology and how would the varying ecosystems affect the bioagent? Similarly, can we use the environment to spread the bioagent through contact with water sources, native flora, and so on."

"That's a standard part of cootie R&D?" Bix confirmed.

"Oh yes." Sarina bobbed her head. "We have to provide the

Consortium with a full product life cycle before we're authorized to release anything."

"Ellie's place had a nice garden, but we didn't see any terrariums there," Hywl noted. "Seems to me one or two would make the perfect parting gift to your supposed best friend and roomie, right?"

"Ellie didn't much care for her roommate. He had boundary issues, as in a total disregard for them." Sarina winced as crystals crept over her emaciated hip.

"How did these unseen taskmasters want you to deliver the aerosolized bioweapon?" Tobek asked, finally joining the conversation.

"Through the nanites Udara was being coerced into making. The nanites would score soft tissue and deposit the suspension solution along with the base organism into the bloodstream." Sarina swayed, and one of her doctors guided her to her cot. "Eyes, nose, mouth, etc. That's when I realized I was building a weapon of mass destruction instead of an evolution catalyst."

"Evolution catalyst?" Runjit mocked. "That is how you guys justify designer diseases? Evolution?"

"Of course," Sarina said, tilting her head. "That which does not kill you alters your cellular structure. Cells are derived from native magic. The change in your cells forces native magic to be altered. To evolve. To grow. Evolution. Even humans understand the concept."

"A day doesn't pass that I don't dislike the Consortium more and more." Hywl flopped back on his cot.

"They killed Udara's daughter to force her compliance three years ago, then probably threatened to kill those kids we saw coming up her walk to keep her in line," Bix mused aloud. "Yet today, they decided they no longer needed her. Either they have another nanite specialist, or her part of the research is done."

"She had a functioning prototype, but she couldn't go any further until I delivered the final stable solution." Sarina sighed. "The last time I met with Udara, she was planning to release other nanites into the secret lab to ruin that prison from the inside. I don't know if she ever did, though."

"Cian, if Udara built the naughty nanites at her home and they were still there, could you detect them?" Bix called to the kid.

"If we know what she used as their power source, then yeah, no prob," he answered.

"And if we have no clue?" Hywl asked.

"That'll take longer, natch." Cian rubbed his neck. "Maybe a week? Depends on how fast I can get stuff out here in quarantine."

"You've already delivered her house to us, so we'll take ownership of that ball," Tobek whispered.

Bix couldn't look at him, again. Not yet. She wasn't so sure the darkness within her wouldn't react to whatever was forcibly changing him.

"Okay, then." Bix clapped her hands. "What about Qiang? What's his deal, Sarina?"

"Qiang impaled himself on a piece of lab equipment when the Consortium's investigators showed up this morning," Cian answered instead. "He left behind three kids and a husband. His suicide is all over his husband's social media account."

"Oh gods," Sarina whispered.

Do not blame us, Phobos objected. *Politics keeps us far from the labs.*

Bix ignored Phobos's wounded ego. "I doubt it was a suicide. What role did Qiang play in R&D?"

"He's a gateway specialist," Sarina said softly, staring at the floor. "He had to transport the bioagent across Mid Worlds, then study it for any changes in its structures. His findings would come to me for verification. Like Udara, our research was directly linked. Once we suspected what was going on, we'd encode messages to each other in our findings."

"What sort of messages?" Bix prompted.

"Sanity saving." Sarina's voice cracked. "Harmless. Confirmations that what we were experiencing was real. That we were not alone. That we were not mad."

Not to quibble, but she is well on her way to full Medea-level madness.

"Sarina, you may be the last lead we have to stop the people behind this." Bix shook her head. "Do you remember the third lab? The place to which you were abducted?"

"You think my trauma made me block it out?" The sylph tapped her temple. "I committed the most inconsequential details to memory. Chipped tiles, cracked stones, stained bits of molding. All of it."

"Oh, aye, that's my cue." Hywl rubbed his hands together. "Paper and pens, my lady, and I can have a photo-quality sketch ready for you."

"Take a clean pad from my bedside," Tobek murmured.

Gates dropped a pad and colored pencils on Hywl's lap. The Welshman cackled. "If only a beer could be delivered so quickly."

A second set of gates deposited a cold six-pack from Tobek's fridge. Hywl whooped with glee, causing his fellow poddites to chortle.

Bix flashed him a grin, then turned back to the sylph. "Sarina, once you and Hywl finish with the sketches, use whatever time you have left to tell these lovely men in cootie suits everything you know about what you made and any hypotheses for how we can defeat it."

"Happily." Sarina pointed to her face. "If I was still capable, I'd cry with relief that the Chimera herself is intervening in my nightmare. Thank you. Thank you so very much."

"One more thing." Bix stepped aside as another dude in a hazmat suit rolled a tray up to Sarina's pod. "Did you ever tell Kashdejan about any of this? She was your mentor."

Sarina pressed her fingers to her lips. "She's the one who sent me for a psych eval."

"Typical angel," Bix grunted and faced Phobos. "You get what you need for the pantheons?"

Possibly. It is curious that the creationist powers of the Mids cannot or will not identify the base organism.

"Yeah, I noticed that too," Bix drawled. "Yet you say the gods aren't involved."

We are now.

A cloud of mulberry and navy formed around his feet. In a breath, Phobos vanished.

Bix shuffled to Hywl and Runjit. "If Sarina's telling the truth, then you guys aren't infected. Hopefully that means you can come home soon to complete your recoveries. Is there anything I can bring you in the meantime?"

Hywl gestured to the beer. "I got all I need."

"Runjit, anything for you?"

"No." Runjit groaned as a doctor helped him lie down on his unburned side. "Thank you for pulling us out of there. In all my years of service, I've never been so close to an explosion that I tasted colors."

"We're a team, Runjit. No one left behind, right?" Bix forced a smile as his lids drifted shut. Sensory screwups were signs of brain damage. With any luck, it was only temporary or at least covered by his contract. Leaving him to his rest, she stepped to Cian's pod.

"Cian, I—"

"You're working the links, the relations, and the motives," the kid interrupted, knocking gently on the glass. "That's your lane. That's where spies do their best work. That's what Mom taught me. She encouraged me to find my own lane, said that I'll know it once I get rolling. Thanks to you and this mess, I think I've finally found it."

"Make sure the lane is one you consciously choose, not the one someone steered you into, okay?" She glanced at his screen, noting a red glow off its monitor.

"You don't have to baby me, honest." He shoved a hand through his dark ginger mop and grinned. "That was a god, wasn't it? That guy you brought with you? A real god."

"Don't get starry-eyed, kid. They're all assholes," Runjit groused, his eyes still closed.

"I haven't been thinking broadly enough." Cian leapt on his cot, grabbing his laptop. "You're brilliant, Bix. Mom said it made you unpredictable and that's what made you..."

Bix waited for him to finish his spiel, but Cian fell silent as his fingers flew over his keyboard.

"You've lost him," rasped a weary bass.

Bix summoned her courage and went to Tobek's pod. Sheaves of paper covered his cot and littered the floor. There was a pencil crushed under his crystalized hip, as if he'd fallen on it in the throes of succumbing. If not for his voice, she'd doubt he could breathe at all. As it was, crystals prevented his chest from expanding. He couldn't take full breaths. Short gasps, barely audible, twisted her heart and taunted her darkness.

"How soon before I lose you?"

CHAPTER 13

Bix relocated Tobek's pod to a dim, unoccupied corner of the larger room. The cube was transparent, so actual privacy was off the table. This shadowy spot was the best she could do. Within the pod, gentle illumination came from the glowing frames of the cameras and the scanners embedded in the corners and floor.

Tobek's eyes tracked her movements as she entered his isolation pod and slid down the leg of his cot to sit beside him. Not so close as to touch, but close enough to feel his aura. Normally, he exuded a simultaneous clutch and push. The latter was due to the wealth of Mids' magic imbued in him that naturally rejected her Other World presence. The former, well, she didn't know its source, but it was no less palpable. Tonight, however, there was a third element in his mix, one that recoiled from her. If she focused, she could sense the ripples of its retreat.

Those had to be caused by the organism spawning the crystals.

"Turn my comm off," Tobek said to the speakers embedded in the walls.

"Comm off," answered a voice over the speaker. A chirp followed.

Tobek held her gaze for long moments of silence. After a

while, his easy smile crept into place. "Quarantine means you're supposed to stay on the outside of the protective barrier."

"I didn't drag your comforter with me this time. Baby steps." She wagged a finger at his supine status. "Why are you on the floor? The bed too soft?"

"In case your dreams brought you to me once more, I didn't want you land on what I've become."

"I have a lot of dirty comments, but I'll spare you." She gathered the pictures he'd scattered over the floor as heat seared her cheeks. "Got some talent here, young man. Ever think about going pro?"

He laughed, then groaned. "Maybe they'll get me a job at a tattoo shop."

"I know a guy who might be able to help. He's a bit of a stiff, though." She flipped through the pics, noting their common thread. She didn't recognize a single setting, just the subject. "Where are we in this one?"

"Ga—ah, nice try," he groaned, digging his hand into the pectoral unaffected by crystals. "I've told you, I'm not going to talk about our past."

"But has your subconscious used your boredom to make you draw it, I wonder?" She studied the landscape and attempted to open a gate to the destination depicted. Her gatekeeper magic reached out. Denial ricocheted back, skittering over her nerves with an echo of sadness. "It's not a real place. At least not anymore. Was it ever?"

"Shouldn't you be more interested in the picture Hywl is working on?"

"Oh, I'm sure he'll flag me down when he's ready." She collected pictures from the cot and scanned through them. Her frown deepened with each flipping page. "In these, I'm engulfed in darkness, like I'm hiding…and I'm sad. Why am I sad?"

"We lost our—" His word drew out into a pained gasp.

She peered over the stack of papers.

He stared at the ceiling. His jaw worked side to side. His

fingers dug into the ink along his pec. Green glowed around his fingertips as he invoked his magic.

"No, no, no." She tried to pull his arm away. "Using your magic makes the crystals spread faster."

He resisted her easily, continuing to wield. Tiny silver spikes rose from the green glow and pierced his skin. Blood welled, then ran into a lattice pattern of a variation on the Eternal Knot. Dark blue-green edges framed his blood's path, caging it within the pattern, a pattern barely perceptible beneath the layered ink of his many tattoos.

"What is that?" She jerked her hand back. "Is that a spell? Should I get you help?"

He looked at her with soul-deep agony, then looked away. He exhaled loudly and winced as he withdrew his magic from the bloodied pattern. Red blood turned dark green and was absorbed into his skin, into a tattoo that left no hint of the Eternal Knot beneath.

"What was that mark? Is that like the scarring the angels have done to you? I will space the whole damn Angelic Host if they're coming for you in this condition."

The Angelic Host got their kicks carving trackers into their prey. At various points in Tobek's long life, he'd been hunted by the angels. Those trackers went hella deep into the skin.

"Not the Host," he said through clenched teeth as the lattice of crystals crept up his neck. "I need you to do something for me."

"Of course."

"Once my mutation into a geode is complete..." He struggled to swallow. "Take me out of the Mids."

She huffed, half in humor and half horror. "Kill you, you mean?"

"Force the Fates' hands," he corrected between gasps. "Accelerate my reconstruction and ensure I'm cured of whatever this thing is."

"Do you want me to fetch you back to the Mids too or leave

you in the ether?" she asked with heavy sarcasm. "I want to be clear on how dead you want to be before you're satisfied."

He closed his eyes. "A day should do it."

"A d-a *day*?" She stammered. "Five seconds will more than suffice."

"A day," he insisted. "A full twenty-four hours. The organism is bonding to the threads of Fate, as you suspected. Fates and what they weave are not as vulnerable to the ether as a body made by Mid World magic. If my calculations are correct, it will take twenty-four hours for the corrosiveness of the ether to wear down the solidified threads that make up the geode. At twenty-five hours, it'll have access to the soul and husked body of Mids' magic."

She rolled her eyes, then kept looking at the ceiling. "If this kills you, I will hunt down your soul, rip it away from whichever god thinks they're entitled to consume it, and then I will torture you until I'm no longer persecuted by your compatriots here in the Mids. Are you willing to pay that price?"

The crystals hampered his smile as they overtook his beard, forcing him to speak out of one side of his mouth and slurring his words. "I do solemnly swear."

"You're a dick for requesting this of me." She sighed loudly. "Also a grown-ass man with a reset button, so fine. But don't be surprised if I keep you company for those twenty-four hours, just in case using the ether as cosmic sandpaper doesn't go as planned."

The skin around his eyes crinkled. "Bring your own blanket."

Static crackled in her ear.

"*Noswaith dda*, my lady, and pardon the interruption," Hywl purred through her earpiece. "We have a few pictures of the third lab ready for your review."

"Be right there," she said, sending Tobek's sketches through gates to a bolt-hole. His sweat may have been funky, but the cootie wasn't contagious. She wasn't worried about spreading the sick anymore. However, there was information in those drawings, whether Tobek had meant to reveal it or not. She wasn't going to let them be incinerated. "All right, bed buddy, I'm off to see a secret lab about secret cootie."

"Don't go alone," he gasped. "Wait for me. Not too long left."

"I suspect you'll be fully pocket-sized by the time I return." She struggled to produce a smile. "Make sure you don't go anywhere in the meantime, okay?"

CHAPTER 14

B leach. Industrial cleaners and bleach. The acrid smells burned Bix's eyes and nose as she stepped through the gate into a concrete bunker. The air tasted metallic. Ultraviolet light flickered through the shards of what had been frosted interior walls. Her stacked heel crunched through thick layers of shattered glass. Remnants of normal incandescent bulbs mixed with upended beakers, vials, and tubes that had been deliberately knocked out of stands and shelves. Stools had been ripped from their wheels. Counters slashed by large claws.

Destroyed. All of it.

The third lab, the best lead she had to the people behind the cootie, ruined. Someone had beaten her to the big clue. Again.

Which was odd all on its own.

Sure, Sarina blowing up her condo would have alerted the minds behind this, but knowing that the sylph had survived, such as it was, to tell a gatekeeper where their hidey-hole was? Doubtful. No, this was either a misdirect by the sylph or a scorched-earth cleanup by the faction. If it was a cleanup, then the method of destruction could tell her who had been contracted to do it. If she learned who the cleaners were, she could track their bosses. Naturally, she needed proof that this had been the infamous third lab. Without it, she couldn't know for certain that Sarina had been telling the truth about being a cog.

First things first, where was this lab, how populated was the World, and how easy was it for a non-gatekeeper to travel here?

It wasn't on the Primary Mid World. The push of native magic against her Other World presence was feeble at best. Probably one of the newer Worlds added to the collective Mids where native magic hadn't had the time to saturate everything yet.

When weaponizing an organism that fed on native magic, it was probably best to mitigate the odds of overfeeding it. However, there was enough native magic present that all these trappings and this very structure could exist.

About the structure…

The concrete outer walls were not concrete at all, rather a less porous replica. A fair number of Chwed cultures on various Mid Worlds had spun fashion movements centered around twentieth-century human warfare. Doomsday bunkers and nuclear silos led the architectural trends.

So this was a newer World added in the last hundred years. Something about it had made it special enough that the Consortium had taken it under its protection. That required the full body of the Consortium to agree. It was way bigger than a committee decision, but a committee would be responsible for monitoring its integration. Not the same committee in charge of keeping tabs on the official Consortium laboratories. That'd be way too convenient, but the lab's location confirmed the treacherous faction had plants in multiple committees. Always good to know where allies would not be found.

Which brought her back to the destruction surrounding her.

It had a pattern. Overhead, the mangled aluminum tracks of the drop ceiling and clusters of exposed wires dangled from twisted support rails. Some of the wiring probably belonged to the lighting, others to the surveillance system. A refrigerator tilted against a fume hood; its stainless doors gaped, held open by a mound of cracked tube racks spilling out to the hallway. Something fat and tubular had imprinted in the stainless-steel casing of the fridge.

Bix put her hands on her knees and swung her tush from side to side. The denting wasn't aligned with other battered and busted machines. She stretched to her tippy toes and pawed at the air. Some of the ceiling support rails should have been severed or at least sheared, not just dinged. The wires should have been sparking. Ultraviolet light said there was still power in the facility. Full power hadn't been cut, only specific lines.

Suspicion niggled at her.

She headed out to the long hallway. Narrow. Barely wide enough to fit that fallen fridge. Hip-high scuff marks should have been deeper with less transference of whatever black gizmo had scraped against it. Evenly spaced gouges marred the hall floor. Walking heel-to-toe, she counted off the distances between. Eight feet.

She took it all in one more time...and laughed.

Chweds had tried to make the damage look like a dragon's tantrum.

During her time in the CWIG, she and her team had staged a lot of break-ins and break-outs. There was an art to creating ruin for a frame job. There was also a two-week workshop at the academy on it. Whatever team had done this deserved a failing grade.

Firstly, when framing a superpower, one never, ever used chemicals. Dragons and angels wielded incredibly potent native magic, nullifying any need of chemicals. Even the lowest of lesser gods could wreak havoc without stooping to bleach. Secondly, if the building was to be left standing, then the damage had to reflect a temporary loss of control by said superpower not a total loss of control. A total loss of control by a god or a dragon would destroy the building, therefore, the damage had to be contained in one section.

Whoever had done this job had run riot as far as the eye could see.

Pfft. Rookies.

Bix's toe punted something small yet unforgiving. She yelped and hopped on one foot as she tracked the sound of tumbling over broken glass to a pile of halved tables. She crouched to peer into the shadows under the unstable mound.

Rainbow hues pulsed in the darkness.

Her guts sank as she retrieved a fist-sized geode.

Someone had picked off the scientists outside this lab, and now she had proof at least one had died inside the lab in the same manner. One wasn't irrefutable proof. It could've been a plant, but it was enough to make her keep looking. She could've been holding Ellie, for all she knew. Yet in a place this big with this much equipment...

Testing a theory, she focused on the interplay of native magic, her presence, and the geode. As faint as a fly on her arm, it was there, the displacement of retreat. It didn't like her. She didn't take it personally. The scientist inside that geode wasn't aware enough to discern one person from the next. No, no, it was the infectious organism that shied from her, just as it had done in Tobek's isolation cell.

Interesting.

Tossing the geode from hand to hand, she ambled toward the center of the large lab, searching for more scientists as she dispatched UV lights into the ether. Once she removed the last light, she groaned.

Dozens upon dozens of tiny rainbows illuminated the darkness like stars in a tragic sky.

Sarina had suspected other scientists had been working on the project. How many of the geodes glowing before her had been trapped in this black site and for how long? Years like Sarina?

There were far too many geodes to carry, so she made her way back to the huge fridge. A few well-placed gates righted it and allowed her to close the doors. A few more gates popped holes in the sides to allow air to circulate. One by one, she retrieved the geodes and loaded them into her makeshift travel cooler. The fridge didn't need to keep anything cold, just contained. It should serve well enough as an isolation pod until she figured out who these poor people were. Scientists for sure, but who and from where? No way could these all be Consortium lab employees. This many missing Chweds would be hard to explain to the communities supporting those labs.

Radio static peppered the silence, bringing Bix up short. It wasn't coming from her earpiece. The chirps of beginning and ending transmissions echoed, though muted. Bix eschewed walking along crunchy shards for the silent movement through gates. As she approached the radio noise, others could be heard. Clattering. Boots squeaking. Metal scraping.

Coming from the other side of a faux cement wall.

More radio noises. Military call signs. An exfil countdown.

Shit.

If she could get her hands on even one member of that team…

Without an image of what was on the other side of the wall, she had no choice but to remove a chunk of the wall and with it any element of surprise. Hopefully, it wasn't the side of a furnace or the supply shelf for all the bleach they hadn't used.

She planted a gate in the wall and let it grow.

The bunker trembled.

She snapped shut the gate. That shouldn't have happened. The gate wasn't that big.

A sonic boom shook the bunker. Dust drifted down from the ceiling. Not her doing. The boom had been a programmable gateway opening, displacing atmospheric pressure. Every type of gateway beckoned to her gatekeeper magic. A playful batting, like a puppy wanting attention.

Son of a bitch.

Any doubt she'd had about a military being behind this cleanup was gone with the use of a programmable gateway. They were rare, heavily monitored, and heavily guarded. Tobek had one at the coal plant. The CWIG had one in HQ. It took a whole lot of a special kind of native magic to change the destination. It wasn't set by a bunch of privates trying to sneak off base.

At least she now knew how Sarina and the other abducted scientists had gotten to this place. And now, she had a means of tracking who had brought them. Be all that as it may, it was the cleaners' means of exit. Time was ticking.

She blew the gate wide without care for the destruction and stepped through to a long room with an open door swinging at the far end.

Twelve rows of twelve columns of bunk beds filled the chamber. Every bed had a set of shackles and an empty clipboard.

Every bed held a pulsing geode.

Test subjects, had to be. Two hundred and eighty-eight test subjects. A shudder racked Bix as she imagined the stark terror they must have felt watching their peers succumb. Those poor people. How had they ended up here? Focus group gone horribly awry, or had the faction opted for straight-up abductions?

Her shoulders slumped further and further with each geode she sent to the fridge. Over three hundred lives trapped in a stasis of terror. A thought sent the fridge to her bolt-hole in Jotunheim. Hopefully, all the spells that had hidden Ogun's pet would serve to hide the geodes from the Consortium. It was the only option for the time being. Delivering the fridge to Grimtebel with the possibility of the Consortium reps showing up? Um, no. Best to keep all these victims hidden for now.

She slowed as she neared the door. The interplay of native magic and her presence changed the closer she got. There was a dead spot. Not as in end-of-life dead, more like a neutral zone, one she normally felt when in the company of humans. Since humans grounded magic, they caused a small pocket of stillness amid magic's normal tumult. The Berserkers didn't give off that pocket because of their modified Cycle of Soul contracts; they weren't technically human anymore. As for Tobek, he was his own special case of exceptions to all the rules.

That said, there was definitely a human on the other side of the door.

How and why would a human be out here? Why hadn't she felt

their presence earlier? Curious yet cautious, she stepped through the doorway into the UV light bathing a long tunnel.

A young girl clutching a teddy bear waited at the far end.

Bix's pulse sped as recognition dawned and rage awakened. Tentacles of shadows and midnight slithered from Bix's back into the dark passageway. She'd seen this girl before. Udara's neighbor. Then again at Sarina's before the explosion.

Logic checked her wrath and stilled her darkness.

Her first instinct was to blame the faction and its cleaners. She'd narrowly missed them at Udara's, and they may well be racing toward their exfil at this very moment. However, they hadn't been at Sarina's, not anytime close to when Bix and the Berserkers had been there.

The girl had.

Now the girl was here. Watching her.

That couldn't be good.

"Hi there." Bix cautiously approached the child, pressing out again with her senses to confirm the neutral space of a grounding human presence. Definitely a ground…but there was something else, an anomaly barely perceptible that Bix couldn't identify. She sent her darkness to search for the source. Whatever it was had to be the girl's means of transport. Was it a danger to the girl? Was the girl's presence some sort of odd plea for help? Bix had to proceed carefully lest she upset whatever was using the girl. "I can take you to safety. Would you like that? Would you like to get out of here?"

The girl hugged the bear to her chest and stared at the shadows moving with Bix. Were the bear's eyes moving too?

"My name is Bix." Bix smiled in what she hoped was a reassuring manner. "What's yours?"

The tunnel shook. The floor cracked. A fissure started as a hairline and rapidly grew, spidering out to the walls and up to the ceiling. Rubble rained.

Different threat. Different source. Ground source. Below the tunnel. Not whatever was pulling the cleaners out above them.

Shit.

Bix lunged for the girl. Tentacles reached farther than her arms and closed around nothing.

The girl and the bear vanished.

The floor split open. Tunnel, chamber, and lab tumbled into a yawning wet maw.

Bix threw open gates as fetid saliva washed over her.

CHAPTER 15

Bix shivered in the concrete hallway outside the bathroom she shared with Tobek and Gurp. It was never a good idea to pop straight into the bathroom without knowing precisely where both her roommates were.

"Gurp," she called. "Gurp, are you home?"

Metal scraping against concrete answered from somewhere near Tobek's altar room.

She lifted her sodden hair away from her unbugged ear. A long thick string of saliva twirled from her hair like a corkscrew wind spinner. "Gurp? Is that you?"

"I here."

Bix flinched as the goblin appeared at her elbow wearing striped pajamas and a matching long-tailed cap. "Hi, stealthy guy. I'm sorry to awaken you."

He rubbed the wart on his nose. "No sleep. Too worry."

"We'll get our third Musketeer home soon, promise." She smiled and jiggled the slobber string. "What are the odds you can tell me from what creature this came?"

Gurp grabbed the dangling wad and rubbed it into his hands like lotion. He sniffed his hands, then sniffed her. He reached for her arm and paused. "Okay?"

"Take as much as you need to know the answer. I can give you my clothes if that'll help." She bent down so he could reach her hair and closed her eyes.

His taste buds were his best research tool, but she didn't want to see any part of that. She respected the skill—had mad respect for it—and watching him eat live ordinance was mildly entertaining. Witnessing a secondhand spit exam? No thanks.

Gurp's touch was awkwardly gentle as he scraped saliva from her. He muttered and grunted. Took more samples. More muttering.

A long fart chased a squeal of epiphany.

She held her breath and opened one eye.

He pointed to the bathroom. "You clean. I get book. I get book."

"You know what the creature is?" she wheezed, heading into the bathroom.

"Yes, yes. I know. I know." He bobbed his head, then shook it. "Not dirt. No tell source dirt."

"We'll start with the creature, then see what the boys upstairs can tell us about the World. Sound like a plan?" She cranked the knobs in the huge shower and looked over her shoulder. No sign of the gaseous goblin. Amazing how quietly that guy could move, but if he ever went on a covert op with her, she'd need to get him some charcoal-lined undies.

She stepped under the harsh blast of cool water, still clothed, and groaned with sweet relief while her mind wandered to those troubling final moments at the lab.

The human girl. The anomaly in the neutral space. The attack of the slobber monster. Were the three related? Why did the girl keep appearing at key sites related to the researchers? What was causing the girl to intersect with Bix? Some weird spell, or were the Fates up to something? The girl *had* warned her about Sarina detonating the bomb, and maybe the girl had tried to warn her about the slobber monster. But how was the girl getting around without a gateway? Dragons, angels, and gods, any of them could move through the Mids without a gateway. Depending on their rank, they could move a human with them, but their use of magic should've tripped Bix's senses.

Unless there had been no final exit for the girl.

Perhaps the girl had been abandoned at the lab. Served her purpose and was discarded? Or was the girl like the Little Mermaid, challenged to deliver a message yet had failed and was doomed to die? When it came to spells involving Mids' magic, Bix didn't know enough about how they worked to be certain that the girl had escaped. With the lab destroyed, she couldn't get back there to verify. She could only open a gate to a destination where her mental image of an existing place was accurate. Hungry subterranean monsters tended to change the landscape.

If she could find the World, she might find the girl who might be there and might be trying to give Bix a message that might be important to the mission. That was a lot of "mights" and not a lot of time. She still had a picnic in the ether with Tobek to force his reset, which needed to happen sooner than later because she was running low on uninjured teammates. She had a strong suspicion which military group had destroyed the lab, but she also had a strong bias that could blind her to other options. Tobek had fought enough wars with, for, and against every armed group existing in the Mids. He'd know for sure who the cleaners had been, and he'd know how to deal with them. Cross-referencing to whose military the cleaners belonged with the committee responsible for monitoring the World that had hosted the lab and she'd have a lead on two more members of the faction within the Consortium.

It was the ass crack of dawn. As much as she wanted to go from shower to bed, she got dressed and went in search of Gurp. He was in the modern library, the one with books allowed to be read rather than the thousands Tobek kept under ward and spell throughout their home. The goblin motioned for her to join him at the small table set between two sleek leather chairs. He pulled on the pair of white chain mail gloves resting beside a tome made of…not paper. Skin maybe? The pages were thick and irregularly cut, the binding laced with gut string.

The magic rolling from the book was palpable, and it wasn't Mid World magic. Neither were the gloves. She wouldn't be surprised if the cover had a big eyeball staring at the burled wood of the table. Maybe some teeth instead.

"You guys ever worry that the god to whom this book belongs is going to come looking for it one day?" Bix perched on the edge of the seat as Gurp turned the book toward her and pointed to a crude drawing of a rather familiar maw and some fancy swirls around it. "Yes. That's the mouth. What's the book say it is?"

Gurp stared at her bemused for two heartbeats.

"I can't read whatever language that is. Missing the knowledge I once had," she said, chagrined. According to third parties, the Chimera of old had known all kinds of things, including fluency in every language since the dawn of time.

"Nabaziix," Gurp said slowly and pointed a cautious finger at her pendants. "God hunter."

"That thing was chasing a god?" she echoed. Was it a god moving the girl around? Phobos had said the pantheons—plural— had taken an interest in the cootie.

"Maybe…" He stared at the floor and whimpered.

"Maybe, what?" she prompted gently.

"Maybe hunt you," he mumbled.

"I'm not a god, though I do feed off them, so maybe it tracked that to me? Or maybe it was drawn to the Other World energies I exude. Either way, extremely helpful. Thank you, Gurp. That is…" She paused and tipped her head as a stray thought intruded. "They're not native to the Mids, right? Not a long history here? Kind of like that book?"

He made a middling mewl and a seesaw motion with his hand.

"More of a 'sort of.' Okay, not as clear a lead as I'd hoped, but a very useful one nonetheless. Thank you, again." She stood and smoothed her skirt. "I need to check in with Xipil. What time do you think he'll be up?"

Gurp chortled and closed the book. Four skeletal hands shot from the covers, grabbing for him and recoiling when they touched his gloves. Juddering, the hands laced and sealed the pages within their boney clasp.

Less monstery than she'd expected, yet still not suitable for the public library.

"He up." Gurp held the book at arms' length. "In ops. Take Chief shift."

Bix made the point of appearing at the secret door in the ops room, lest a sleep-deprived Berserker try to relieve her of her head. She'd expected to interrupt a handful of bleary-eyed men mainlining cans of caffeine.

She was grossly mistaken.

All the chairs in the ops room were occupied, all the monitors lit, all the landlines and cellular lines in use. Runners darted in and out of the main door. Chatter held the undercurrent of coordinated purpose instead of casual banter.

"Sir," one of them called. "Company."

From a ring of bent heads at the far end of the conference table, Xipil's familiar face emerged. His smile was polite as he caught her eye and completed whatever he was saying to the men around him. Those men pushed away from the table, rolling to assorted monitoring stations to confer with their peers. Xipil met her at the door and bowed from the shoulders.

"Good morning. How may I be of assistance?"

"I'm sorry to interrupt." She glanced around the room. "Is everything okay?"

Crow's feet appeared at the corners of Xipil's Berserker-blue eyes. "This is normal. While it is early dawn for us, with time zone variances, this window is most convenient for other battalions to report on missions currently underway across this World and many others. For example, information from central

Africa directly impacts troops on maneuvers with the light elves four Worlds away."

"CHWINT." Bix mentally slapped herself for not realizing it sooner. "Chwed Intelligence. You guys are a collection and analysis unit. You're the military version of the CHWINT in the CWIG."

"There may be *minor* similarities," he demurred. "May I assume you successfully located your last target?"

She smirked at the familiar rise of hackles. Certain CWIG sections despised being compared to their counterparts in the MWA. "I did and it was destroyed by a Nabaziix."

Xipil flinched. "A Nabaziix? You're sure?"

"It tried to eat me, so yeah." She didn't blame him for his reaction. At some point he'd clearly encountered the slobberer too. "I need your help identifying the World on which the lab had been built. The MWA is kept apprised of new additions to the Mids, right?"

"Protecting all the Mid Worlds is part of our larger mission, so yes." He tapped the shoulder of the man at the nearest station. "Need to borrow your seat."

The Berserker stood without quibble—speaking some fascinatingly fluid language to his phone—and joined a cluster at the conference table. Xipil offered the vacated seat to Bix. She politely declined his chivalry. Xipil settled in and pulled the keyboard to the edge of the table.

"What can you tell me about it?"

"It's newer, within a hundred years. Probably closer to seventy-five. The old magic has gone, but Mids' magic has yet to fully saturate it." She stood at his shoulder while he entered the information. "There should be a trace of atmospheric displacement caused by a programmable gateway. Military grade."

His hands hovered above the board. "Did you see what kind?"

"No, the lab was underground. The cleaners were finishing when I arrived. I only heard bits of the radio communications.

Never laid eyes on the squad or their means of escape. Saw the damage they'd wrought. Heard the gate opening above ground."

"Male or female voices?"

"Can't say for certain." She tugged at her sleeve. "I know it's a long shot, but I'm hoping seismic-activity monitoring is part of your SOP along with monitoring programmable gate usage. The intersection of those two should give us the exact World. There is a small chance a child survived the Nabaziix and the cleaners."

Xipil wasn't the only Berserker to pause. None of them looked away from their stations, but it was a notable count of ten before activity resumed.

"What of the child's family?"

"Just the child," she murmured.

"Understood." He struck a few keys and sighed loudly. "I'm afraid Chief is the only one with the clearance for the programmable gates logs. However, I can narrow down our search to five Worlds that have entered the collective within the set timeframe and whose terrain can support a Nabaziix."

"Five Worlds is still a lot of ground to cover, but way better than five hundred." She sighed but hastened to add, "Thank you. We need that third data point. I guess I should abduct—"

Bright green light surged from the walls, stopping Bix midsentence. All work around her ceased. Three men sailed their chairs across the room, commandeering a spate of workstations. A dozen monitors displayed the perimeter of the coal plant, from roof to river.

Again, green light surged from the walls. This time, in a shorter burst.

"Sir, it's a customer at Dysmorphic."

The shop wasn't open yet. Wouldn't be for a few more hours. The local Chwed community knew that, but they also knew they could come to the shop in cases of extreme distress.

Bix followed Xipil to the security monitors. A glaistig pounded against the door to the body-modification shop on the main level. The glaistig's eyes rolled, wild in her gray face.

Her mouth moved somewhere between words and full-lunged screams. River algae and blood stained her golden hair as she clawed at her body. Her goatlike legs pawed the pavement and kicked the door.

The poor woman exuded abject terror.

"She shouldn't trigger the wards," Xipil said. "Turn on the mic so we can hear what she's saying."

"The sheep! The sheep are eating me alive! Gods help me. The sheep," the poor woman wailed. Her caterwaul pitched higher, causing every man in the room to cover his ears. The glaistig beat her head against the door hard enough to break skin as her panicked fervor ratcheted higher.

"Her hands are clear. Subdue the glaistig," Xipil shouted into a phone Bix hadn't seen him pick up. "Tranquilize. Use only necessary force. Healers will meet you outside."

Three Berserkers burst out the door of Dysmorphic and tackled the glaistig to the ground. Still her terror would not abate.

Movement on another monitor caught Bix's eye. A moon-faced young woman with a trident of hooks on the back of one hand waited patiently beneath the parking lot's light.

A psychopomp. An escort of souls.

Bix's guts dropped as she watched the glaistig work herself into a fatal frenzy within the hold of two of the Berserkers while a third readied an injection. It wouldn't be necessary.

Gods. Fear. Sheep.

Such a jackass.

The moment the glaistig collapsed, Bix opened gates.

Bix didn't pause to appreciate the entertainment of the Woolly Barrel. No, she made a beeline for the god at the farthest bend of the bench lining the balcony.

"Most people use a phone."

Phobos raised a brow and gave her a long once-over. "I am a

god, Chimera. Be grateful I sent a messenger instead of plaguing every Berserker in that fortress."

"Death by dreams of sheep, really?" She planted her hands on her hips. "How bored are you?"

"I don't choose an individual's fear, though I enjoy encouraging it." He stretched his arms along the couch and rested his foot on his opposite knee. "You need to visit Nergal of the Mesopotamian pantheon."

"He's a god of war. Why would I go see him?"

Not all gods were her friends. Most were not. Many, many had reveled in her bleakest moments. Now that she knew why—once upon a time being the entity who'd held them accountable for bad behavior—she looked forward to the day she could hold them accountable again.

"Nergal specializes in the science of war, and he is an expert in plagues. Whatever the unknown organism infecting your warlock and your Sage, he is most capable of discerning its source."

She stared at him dumbfounded.

"I warned you the pantheons were interested." He shrugged.

"Interested enough for another pantheon to use a human child to send me a message?"

It was his turn to look perplexed. "Gods use humans all the time for all kinds of reasons, though not usually to contact the Chimera. What did the child say?"

"Nothing. I'm not even sure it was a god puppeteering." She shrugged. "Back to the cooties, if the pantheons are involved now, why not bring it up to the greater Consortium? Why am I going to wherever Nergal is?"

"You know politics, and we all know you." His sneer sent a shiver down her spine. "Nergal resides in the Under World of Irkalla with his queen, Ereshkigal. They are consort and queen, not husband and wife. It may seem like a semantic difference, but the difference is key to understanding their power dynamic. They are from a time long before the cowardice of patriarchy stripped the proof of women's might from the public consciousness."

"Is her ego so fragile that she needs others to remember who truly reigns?"

"The power of a god is rooted in the beliefs of others," he chided. "There are some who believe she's a titan biding her time. Others believe she is a creation goddess who surrounds herself with the dead as inspiration for the new. Either way, she is banned from the Mids and most other Worlds."

"Banned for a reason?"

"Fear, mostly." He smiled with actual delight, which was wholly disturbing. "She's not particularly well known among the lesser races, so she can't expand the quantity of souls that come to her like Hel or Hades have. It doesn't seem to affect her power, though. She remains unquestionably formidable."

"This just gets better and better," Bix drawled. "I seem to recall there's a locked gate at the entrance to Irkalla."

"You'll have to pass through seven gates to get to the actual temple there. Each gate is a trial. You will be judged by Ereshkigal, Nergal, and the lesser gods who rule the cities of the Irkalla."

"Lesser gods as in demons or as in disappointments?"

"Demons, definitely demons."

"Okay, as soon as I——"

"Now," Phobos commanded with menace. "Do not treat this as you did my referral to Devana. My patience with your ignorance is limited. Be grateful I choose to see your egregious insults as a folly of your muddled mind."

Oh hell no. She'd let this sort of shit pass once with a male god. It'd escalated into an abusive relationship very quickly. Being free of that last douche had been the only good thing about her exile.

She placed her hands high on Phobos's thighs and leaned forward until she tasted his raw energy. "Do not confuse my appreciation for your assistance for any kind of weakness. Be grateful I have a modicum of control over my temper, lest you learn how quickly I can take more than you are willing to give."

For long moments, they stared at each other, breaths mingling, neither willing to move.

The corner of his mouth twitched.

"As for Nergal, never lose sight of the fact he is a scientist above all other things," Phobos cautioned. "Scientists are interested in discovery and accumulation of knowledge more than the greater good. Do not appeal to him on the grounds of right and wrong, or even on the welfare of the souls from which he and his queen feed. The only person for whom he cares is Ereshkigal."

"Who can smite me if I threaten her or her husband." Bix wrinkled her nose and straightened.

"Consort," he corrected. "You are on your own for the introductions. The Mesopotamians and the Greeks don't like to get along. Beware his queen. If you are the lady of darkness, Ereshkigal is the empress."

CHAPTER 16

If Nergal could cure Tobek and Cian, Bix could skip the whole risky business of taking Tobek into the ether. Her faith in the cosmic-sandpaper plan was not strong, which was why she stood before the great earthen gate to Irkalla instead of an isolation pod in Grimtebel.

Tobek could wait a little bit longer. Beauty of being a rock.

The first gate to Irkalla had been designed to look like compacted loam. In truth, everything in the Under Worlds was made from drained souls crafted to resemble whatever the deities desired. Ereshkigal apparently desired dirt. Perhaps this appearance of soil was to ease the transition for the souls returning from the Mids.

It'd been thirty years since Bix had last roamed the labyrinthine passages connecting the hundreds of Under Worlds. Back then, she'd had one of Hades's hounds to help her find her way. Back then, she'd been feral, stripped of all her memories and ignorant of all things but the dangers in the ether. Hades had taken her in and taught her how to feed, speak, and defend herself. While he'd gone about the business of being a god, she'd explored the wonders beyond his domain.

Most Under Worlds did not have a locked front door.

Intricate reliefs in the massive circular gate framed a smooth mound at the center. The odds of those reliefs being warnings were high. Alas, they could also say *Ring Bell for Service* and she wouldn't know.

"Hello?" she called.

No answer.

Not an auspicious start. Yet, without a mental image of her destination, she had to go through the seven trials. She had to make the trek on foot in slightly impractical and thematically appropriate pumps. She was particularly pleased with the ghost-shaped heel and glow-in-the-dark ghoul pattern.

In moments of crisis, a little bit of joy never hurt.

"Hellooo?" She raised a fist and knocked on the first gate to Irkalla.

She cracked a smile, imagining Hywl doing it. If anyone could sweet-talk their way through seven trials, it'd be the Welshman.

The dome in the center rotated. Carved eyes opened. A wide mouth yawned.

"Hi." Bix smiled. "I'm here to see Ereshkigal and Nergal."

Tones flowed slowly from the wide mouth. Really, really slowly. So slowly that it took her ten counts of thirty to recognize the tones as words. It gave her attention plenty of time to wander until it caught on the head's silver and gold lip piercings. They weren't the usual labret ball piercing. No, these were thick heavy talons of engraved gold and silver that wrapped under the chin. The guardian of the gate had worn these for so long, they'd rubbed notches in the earthen ring holding his head snugly in place. More interesting was that the metals hadn't been worn down, aged, or tarnished.

Drained souls were as sturdy as the magic forming them into shapes was strong, but those piercings... If Bix were a betting girl—and she was—those piercings weren't native to the Under World.

Anyone's Under World.

With a thought, tiny gates separated the piercings from the

guard and deposited the shiny baubles in her palm. They made her skin tingle with the wealth of magic imbued in them. Upper World magic.

The head howled, projecting its agony in slow motion.

Bix focused on the gaps left between the divots and the howling head. She opened a small gate in each divot and let them grow.

Howls of indignation took on the tones of terror.

Bix paused and smiled again. "I'm here to see Ereshkigal and Nergal. Open the gate now and swiftly, or I will destroy it and you."

Consternation took no time to form on the guardian's expression. The passageway quaked. The head tucked until its bald pate showed once again. The ring framing it spun clockwise. The circular earthen gate spun counterclockwise. Like a mighty sawblade, it cut into the ground. The gate and the guardian vanished below the surface, but the sound of the gate in motion did not cease.

On the other side, a bright desert sun shone upon a rocky path between two arid hillsides. Tufts of grass dotted the hills. Artfully formed souls twisted and moaned in pitiful welcome. In the distance, the blue shimmer of a sea beckoned.

Not being the sort of girl who enjoyed vivisection by whirling sawblade or long walks along unpaved terrain, Bix took a shortcut through gates she controlled to cross from one trial to the next. She held fast to the piercings.

One should never trust anything or anyone in the Under Worlds.

The second gate to Irkalla lapped against shorelines, stretching as far as the eye could see. Lakes, rivers, creeks, every Under World had an abundance of what passed as water. Probably some sort of building code. Water that no one could drink, filled with souls eager to drown the newest denizens. Misery loved company, as the saying went.

Ereshkigal's sea-bound souls leveled up the requisite torment by morphing into images. The one directly in front of Bix assumed her appearance and laughed with a hand out, as if waiting for her to grab it. Yeah, not going to happen. To the left and the right of that pseudo-reflection bobbed scads of people and creatures she didn't know. The eyes connected them, though. Deep-set, upturned, and the colors of distant nebulas.

Kind of cool, but not what she needed.

There was no boat to break the flat horizon of endless water, which meant the guardian wasn't a ferryman. That'd be too easy. No, whoever the guardian was, he was in the water. She had to figure out which of the strangers bobbing with the currents was the one who could open the gate.

She strolled along the shoreline, rubbing the piercings from the first guardian between her palms. Each image she passed assumed her identity, but each bore different attire, a different state of well-being, and a different emotion. Some displayed her scars, some didn't.

She almost missed it. The flaw.

Backtracking three people, she spotted it again. It was small, ever so small. Her reflection portrayed her most shameful moment. Before Phobos, there was another god from whom she'd derived her sustenance, who had ensnared her with glimpses into the past she no longer remembered. She'd become an addict hooked on that god's information, and he'd become the asshole who'd abused her. The reflection before her now showed her naked, his fluids seeping from her as she huddled in a shadowy corner, bereft. The truth of her situation had finally sunk in, a situation she had put herself in time and again. The realization that she *couldn't* stay away from him had destroyed her spirit, so strong was her addiction. The shame of that night. The humiliation of every time thereafter.

Her skin turned clammy thinking about it.

But that wasn't what had caught her attention this time. Her bedraggled reflection clutched a sprig of purple bellflowers. Flowers had never been in that god's home whenever she was there, and she certainly didn't make it a habit of toting them around. No, the flowers belonged to the guardian. A guardian who stared up at her with watery eyes, their pained disgrace a fabrication.

"Open the gate, guardian."

"Open the gate, guardian," her reflection echoed.

With a thought, she seized the bellflowers from her reflection. They were brighter in person than they had been in the water. Their fragrance was gentle yet potent. The Upper World magic holding them in stasis rippled over her skin.

"Give them back," shrieked the water. Her reflection distorted as a funnel spun up. "Give them back to me now."

"Open the gate, guardian," she repeated.

"Never, you thief," it shrieked, and the sound skittered over the sea.

While she was willing to play the gods' games, she felt no compulsion to play it by their rules. So on the horizon where sky met sea, she opened her own gate and let it grow. Her gate displaced the water, pushing it farther and farther ashore. Angry tides rose with the furious screams of the guardian, but the waves could not crest over her creation.

"Open the gate, guardian, and I will stop the destruction of your home."

"My flowers, please." The guardian took the shape of a woman of pure liquid. "They were a gift, and I cherish them dearly."

"The gate," Bix repeated coldly. The sprig of flowers remained in her hand.

With a mournful wail, the guardian formed a second funnel pushing far into the sea. The front of the funnel parted, revealing a stairway of black glass illuminated by a red-orange glow.

Even if the heat hadn't reached up to slap her, Bix guessed what the third gate had to be. She closed the gate displacing the sea and opened another on a step amid the fire.

The sea slammed shut above her with a deafening boom. She blinked a few times to adjust to the brightness of flames leaping from the walls of a circular chamber. A ring of fire she'd anticipated, albeit on the floor. The whole yawning pit of blazing damnation, hey, she'd read the comic books, they'd created a certain expectation. Walls of fire surrounding a pit of vast nothingness? Nope. Nope, hadn't seen that coming.

Where the steps ended, she couldn't discern. She dipped her heel off the side of the step. Flames shot up from the pit.

"Pay the toll, and you may pass," the fires mocked.

"Ah yeah, there you are." She set both feet firmly on the step. The awakened fires of the pit danced around her. "Open the gate, guardian."

"Pay first," the flames insisted. "I will take what you have stolen from the first two guardians and then I will take your… shoes."

"Will you let me walk across burning embers and broken glass afterwards?" she derided, scanning the flames for the form of the guardian. Either the glow prevented her from detecting him or he simply *was* the flames.

"Possibly, but what care have I for the journey you make after this?" The flames leapt as he cackled. "I care only about the now, the moment, the instants you and I are sharing in the present."

The fiery walls churned scorching heat of which she was not remotely a fan. She did not do hot. Ever. The sweat. The slime. The ick. The no. Just. No.

"You're right," she sighed dramatically. "What care should I have for you beyond this moment?"

The darkness beneath her skin rippled and ripped its way free. Tentacles rushed into the flames, beating them down.

"Stop, stop," the guardian bellowed.

She didn't. Couldn't. Both. The darkness extinguished every ember on the walls, then dove for the sources within the pit.

The guardian screamed.

The flames died, all but one tiny flicker, revealing a mountain of hoarded treasures. All the things with which the dead had been buried. Tolls and tokens meant to give the soul a favorable and swift passage. Jewelry. Coins. Casks and urns, probably filled with oils and wines.

But only at first glance.

Those treasures were echoes of items created from Mid World magic. Items that souls couldn't carry with them beyond the boundaries of the Mids. Yet within the illusion and the echoes, there was an actual item. A small box with a crank.

Even from the step, she felt the Upper World magic imbuing it. When it was in her palm, alongside the piercings and the flowers, it appeared so plain and yet equally powerful. The thin metal crank turned, gears clicked, then music played.

The darkness retreated beneath her skin.

"Give it, give it to me," whined the lone flame tethered to a wick embedded in the glass floor.

"Open the gate, guardian."

"You are cruel, heartless. Unloved and unlovable," the guardian mewled as segments of the floor separated, leading down to a massive feather, docked and waiting for her on a sea of turbulent air.

And so she progressed through the gates and the trials. Fourth, fifth, and sixth. Howling winds, honed blades, and hungry flora. Upper World trophies filled her arms as she stood before the seventh and final trial.

A wall of writhing nude bodies woven together, the warp and weft of limbs and torsos, stretched to the high and the low and the sides and the everywhere.

She rolled her eyes.

"Will you have me take the last of his gifts, Ereshkigal?" Bix called. "Nergal brought these with him when he descended from the Upper World for the final time. They are tributes to your guardians whom he mercilessly quashed after your first assignation. Each gift tells a segment of his story. Each gift also binds him to Irkalla. If I take the last piece, he is free to leave you."

Eyes of the bodies within the wall opened. Whispers of gibberish flowed from their mouths. A random cry rose here and there.

"I know the feel of your magic, Nergal," Bix coaxed. "I know you are scanning me through these tokens I hold, just as I am using them to locate the fragments of the final tribute embedded in this gate. By now, you know who I am and that it will take only a thought to destroy the protections the final tribute affords you."

The volume of noise from the wall cranked up to eleven.

Bix didn't raise her voice. She spoke to gods. They heard her no matter the interference.

"If I unlock this last gate, Nergal, they will come for you. They who sent you here to steal your queen's secrets eons ago will come for you. Your pantheon will do nothing. In their eyes, you have been corrupted by your tenure down here. You will be husked. The secrets you hold stolen from you. You will fight them as a mighty god of war should, but you will fall beneath their greater forces. They will use those secrets against your queen. She will unleash the dead to avenge you, and in so doing make herself vulnerable. They will strike at her weakest moment and render the lesser gods useless. Irkalla will crumble. Its cities will be ruined. Scavengers will come from the passages above to steal the souls and sell them to other pantheons. And all for what? To test my worth? My allegiance? My deceitfulness? My hate?"

Bix didn't fight the ripples of Upper World magic rolling over her as they increased their intensity. Thank the powers that be for Internet searches and a whole lot of articles on the myths of Nergal and Ereshkigal. She'd done her homework before leaving the Mids. While the human records had created a framework of possibilities, the trials and the guardians had narrowed the stories down far enough that her experiences with pantheons and treachery made it easy to extrapolate the most likely concerns a pair of gods in love could have.

Of course, she could be way off base and about to be attacked by a god of war. But for the lives of those in the Mids, she was willing to take big risks.

Sudden silence gripped the wall. Laced limbs bent, breaking the weave down a jagged line. The gate swung wide, opening onto a short promontory jutting over a landscape of ten cities surrounding a grand temple that must have been the capital. Shades of greens and teals illuminated the Under World.

At the edge of the promontory stood a man in a white button-down shirt that was mostly unbuttoned. Seven gold chains of various lengths dusted his lightly furred muscular chest. His hands rested in the pockets of loose dark slacks that billowed around his legs as crossing breezes lifted the sounds of the undead population going about their business. His dark hair, closely cropped on the sides yet longer on the top, swooped over his brow to frame pale golden eyes and crimson pupils. His smile was slow and brilliant.

The trophies in her arms vanished, yet the surging power of Upper World magic remained. It flowed from the man himself.

Nergal.

"Welcome back to Irkalla, Chimera. You have been missed."

CHAPTER 17

Bix ambled in silence alongside the Mesopotamian god of war and plagues through the streets of Irkalla. Each city had a theme of means of death: sickness, old age, starvation, war, and so on. Nergal had chosen to lead her through the City of Executions. Souls here held the shapes of their last lives, still glowing and full of experiences. They'd yet to be drained for food. With ten lesser gods and two wholly powerful ones, the surplus spoke well of the queen and her rule.

"Did you put them back," Bix asked, "the trophies?"

Nergal nodded.

"The piercings were nice."

He paused on the steps of the capital and faced her. "You favored the piercings?"

"Well sure, I've a predilection for shiny metals, and those were definitely shiny." Bix squinted to spot the top of the steep stairway leading up five square tiers to a crenelated topper. On the third tier, the stairs passed under a sleek archway floating out from the main building. The very precise angles, the perfect linear construction, and bold geometric accents reminded her of American Art Deco architecture. She never would have guessed the movement's roots were millennia old.

Nergal resumed walking. "It used to be the music box you favored. You'd borrow it whenever you'd visit."

"And I did that often?"

"In the timelines of immortals, yes, often would be accurate."

For a god, he wasn't very chatty. They ascended the rest of the interminable stairway in silence. The worst thing she could do was keep talking and risk annoying him. Then again, she was on a schedule with a great big Berserker shoved into a little tiny rock waiting for a picnic she didn't want to happen.

"I assume you know why I'm here."

"I know why your conscious mind brought you here, and I know for what your subconscious mind is desperate." He motioned her into the temple at the top of the capital. "More importantly, she knows."

Darkness blanketed everything. Not a single dot of luminescence no matter how feeble penetrated the temple. The presence within the darkness was potent, its awareness palpable.

Ereshkigal.

Summoning her courage, Bix strode into the pitch. She kept to her normal stride, not too long, too short, too hesitant, or too bold. Darkness scrabbled over her body, light as feathers, sharp as pinpricks. Bix didn't balk or fight. She allowed the supreme goddess of Irkalla the inspection.

Ereshkigal yanked on Bix's two pendants. Hard. Darkness twisted the corded necklace until it bit into Bix's skin and threatened to garrote her.

Darkness exploded from Bix's spine. Like assailed like. Grappling. Jabbing. Tearing and thrashing. Bix held her ground, but deep within her, a seedling of sinister desires grew, feeding on the hostility.

Ereshkigal withdrew—her attack and her presence. Delighted laughter filled the temple. Torches of glowing aquamarine souls flared to light. Thousands of tendrils of darkness contracted into the feminine form of the goddess. Ethereal darkness became black skin, blue-black hair, and crimson eyes. Black robes shot with golden fibers draped her curves.

The goddess clutched her fists to her chest and beamed. The words she spoke flowed like a beautiful song.

Bix was clueless to the lyrics.

Ereshkigal's joy crumbled. Her questioning gaze cut behind Bix.

"She does not recognize her old name or the languages of the ancients," Nergal explained. "It is ignorance, not malice, that causes her to greet you so."

Pity, the depths of which Bix hadn't seen before, contorted the goddess's features.

"My dear girl," Ereshkigal soothed in a language Bix could understand. "Your darkness is as wild as it was when you were an infant."

That snagged Bix's full attention. "You knew me as a baby?"

"Oh," Ereshkigal tittered. "Yes. Yes, I was there when you came into this existence swaddled in your mist and midnight. Nebulas burst in colorful arrays from the joy you brought to us all. Your mother captured them and placed them in your eyes."

Her. Mother. This was the first confirmation Bix had of her family. She wasn't a creature created from cow sweat or some such silliness.

"You-you know my family. Are they nice? Are they worried about me? Are they looking for me?" Bix's brain said to stop with the twenty questions, but her mouth was incapable. "Do they even like me? Do I have siblings? A spouse? Children?"

Again, Ereshkigal looked to her consort. Nergal went to his queen's side, took her hand between his, and kissed her fingertips. "My love, you were there when she made the sacrifice. You mourned her. Rejoice in this moment. She has returned, curious and eager. Unburdened by all she does not know, frightened by what little she does."

Ereshkigal frowned but nodded. Her gaze shifted to Bix. "She is so vulnerable now. I do not want to let her go back to them."

"A prisoner cannot feel love for their jailor." Nergal tucked a lock of hair behind his queen's ear. "Let her choose your company because her heart brings her to you, not her desperation. Love her enough to give her the choice."

Ereshkigal drew both of Nergal's hands to her cheek and gazed up at him with such affection, it made Bix's chest hurt. "Will you stay, child?"

"I am incapable of staying anywhere for too long." Bix winced, bracing for the goddess's wrath. "Plus, right now, I have a plague problem affecting my friends in the Mids. I'm sorry."

"Had you told me anything else, I would know you were lying." Ereshkigal wagged a finger at her. "The aspect of the gatekeeper fosters your restlessness. It is your dominant aspect right now. As you reconnect with the other aspects you are unconsciously suppressing, you will regain balance. You will be able to spend the night in the arms of the man you love."

"Or woman," Bix noted.

"You executed the only woman you've truly loved," Ereshkigal said sadly. "It was the last act of fealty you performed for your family, and it is what drove you from them."

Bix rocked to her heels. "Wait, what?"

Ereshkigal stepped closer to Bix, curiosity plain on her elegant face. "That pain is gone? It does not linger even without the understanding of why?"

"I've been cautioned that I could not handle the pain of my past, so I gave up my memories." Bix shrugged. "Seems to have worked."

"You could not...?" Ereshkigal sang out in peals of bright laughter. "What fiend told you that lie? Child, you gave your memories to seven gods so that your secrets could not be stolen from you while you were too weak to defend yourself. It was a precautionary measure. You anticipated extensive injuries and a long recovery."

"I spent three hundred years as a husk in the ether. If that's recovery, I have a bone to pick with my doctor."

"Of course you were in the ether." Ereshkigal stared at her, utterly bemused. "You are one of the creators of the ether. You gave every ounce of your power and every bit of your essence to strengthening that protective barrier against an incursion by old foes."

Bix's head imploded. Her knees turned to rubber. Ereshkigal caught her with the darkness before she hit the floor.

"It is perhaps too much information for her all at once, love," Nergal cautioned.

"She is only as fragile as we permit her to be," Ereshkigal scoffed, slowly setting Bix on her feet before releasing her.

Monster. Bix now knew for certain she was a monster. Tales, legends, myths, they only scratched the surface of her depravity. What other description could there possibly be for someone who'd created something as destructive as the ether? It was the place the pantheons discarded their unwanted, weak, and husked gods. It was seeping into the Mids through tiny fissures and dissolving everything it touched. It was a danger to everyone.

What, if not a monster, created a thing like that?

"It's not your fault my peers turned it into a trash can," Nergal noted dryly. "In the beginning, the ether served a secondary purpose as a haven for husked gods to reincarnate. However, appreciation depreciates over time. Great sacrifice becomes expectation, then fades out of issue entirely. A tragedy, but a truth nonetheless."

"If my plan was to keep the bogeymen out, I failed," Bix confessed. "They've set up camps in the ether. They prowl the perimeters of the Mids looking for ways in. We think scouts might have succeeded."

Nergal scowled. "This is recently?"

"The scouts? Within the last five years."

"And you come to me looking for a cure for a *new* sickness that baffles the Consortium's finest?"

"Y-yes," Bix stammered, bouncing her attention between the gods.

"And how long has the Consortium been working on or against this sickness?" he asked.

"At least five years." Bix's guts clenched as she connected the dots. "That has to be coincidence. Why would entities powerful enough to thrive in the ether bother with a sickness in the Mids? Can't they smite at will?"

"Plagues work best as a means to weaken the enemy but not destroy them." Ereshkigal turned contemplative. "Most often, sicknesses allow an immune people to claim rule."

"Assuming the invading forces are looking for new or expanded territory," Nergal added.

"Similarly, plagues allow looters to ransack nations with little threat to themselves. Again, some immunity is required," Ereshkigal mused, tapping a finger on her lip. "Plagues are particularly useful when an opposing force is searching for something specific yet sacred to the natives. Something fragile, perhaps, that would shatter in the face of violence. Or something elusive that will slip their grasp if they show a strong presence via war."

"These entities in the ether could be looking for something hidden in the Mids? Something the greater Consortium isn't willing to give?" Bix asked. She'd warned the CWIG director that the faction was after something the guild had in storage. If they were after it at the behest of an Other World third party despite the greater Consortium's refusal, it explained why the faction hadn't been able to simply demand the item from the CWIG.

Still, plague as a means of coercion? That was pretty drastic and not at all efficient. Just how long had this third party and the faction been after the item?

"Much depends on the nature of the plague being used in terms of who would succumb and how quickly," Nergal ruminated. His gaze sharpened on Bix. "Bring me your warlock, and we shall see if this is coincidence or causality."

Bix opened her mouth to object, then shut it.

She shouldn't be surprised the gods knew about Tobek or his condition. Plus, the grown-ass man had made her promise to take him out of the Mids to induce a reset. Ether. Under World. Both were detrimental to anything created with Mid World magic.

Either way, the Fates were going to have to kick in his restoration clause toot sweet.

That was the goal, right?

Right.

CHAPTER 18

The pod from Grimtebel disintegrated the moment it cleared the gate dropping it out of the cocoon of Mid World magic. All the tech… Poof. Less than dust. Cot. Toilet. Gone. All that remained was a man. The lattice of crystals fully encased his body, leaving tiny gaps no larger than the nib of a pen. Skin tattooed and plain pressed against the hardened threads of Fate as though it were pulp trying to escape a sieve. The radiant blue light of a Berserker's rage added brilliance to the glowing crystals masking his face.

There remained one bare spot, one decidedly untouched, unmarred, perfectly delineated bare spot on his pec in the shape of the Eternal Knot. The same spot that had bled in his isolation chamber. The same spot into which he'd pumped his magic.

Skin that should have been desiccated still held enough tone to resist compression. Bones that should have turned to dust still provided the structure. Lungs that should have vanished still struggled for breath within a suit of stone.

Bix's heart stopped. She stood frozen to the spot, waiting for Tobek's body to deteriorate if not from the toxin, then from his mortal presence in Irkalla. She waited for his contract with the Fates to shed the rocky casing and cure him.

She waited…

Waited…

Nothing changed.

"I don't know how much longer those threads of Fate are going to protect him from being down here." She skimmed her fingers over Tobek's Eternal Knot, expecting it to feel anything but normal. Yet his skin was warm and goose bumps spread under her touch as his heart hammered beneath her fingertips.

"This crystallization is worrisome," Nergal said. "You were right to come to me, Chimera, but now I must get to work."

In a blink, Nergal and Tobek vanished.

"Oh, child," Ereshkigal sighed. "Of all the allies available to you in the Mids, you chose *him*?"

Bix faced Ereshkigal. The goddess was the third to question her relationship with Tobek. "Why wouldn't I? He and his men have been nothing but supportive."

"May that illusion hold for you this time," Ereshkigal whispered.

"This time?" Bix crossed her arms. "You know my history with him? Sure you do. You knew me as a baby, why wouldn't you know all my past including the parts involving him. Why do people affiliated with the pantheons warn me away from him?"

"I could speak of it endlessly, but my words will not give you the answers you truly desire or answers you would believe," the goddess countered sadly. "Even those you loved most were unable to win that level of trust from you."

"Too trusting is a flaw of which I've been accused," Bix scoffed. "Not trusting at all? That's how someone ends up the lone prisoner in an isolation of their own making."

Ereshkigal's darkness gently brushed against Bix. "When you were young, you trusted implicitly as all children do. Your family used it to break you, repeatedly. Out of self-preservation, you turned to your darkness to seek out proofs, evidences, and verifications. It quickly became the aspect on which you most relied."

"Wow, my family, a real bushel of peaches there," Bix muttered as Tobek's drawing of her engulfed in sadness and darkness drifted through her mind.

"Would you like to learn how to make your darkness your strength once again?"

"You-you would teach me to be a Shadow Caster?" Bix narrowed her eyes. Everything gods did came with strings. "What would it cost me?"

Ereshkigal drummed a finger against her cheek. "Time. It will cost you time with me, while Nergal sees to your warlock."

"I would love that," Bix rushed to say, "but I've got leads about the cooties in the Mids I need to track before the idiots behind this release it as a bioweapon."

"What if I told you your darkness can be used to locate your lost friend, the draugr?"

That grabbed her attention. "Drew?"

"Drew," Ereshkigal confirmed. "The draugr would be useful to you in this inquiry, yes? The ability to read souls, to wear bodies that may still be in use, to infiltrate the Consortium's laboratories despite their investigators? All that would be helpful, no?"

"Well, yes, of course," Bix admitted. Really, she wanted Drew back because she missed him and didn't want him to hurt or be scared anymore. That's what friendship was about, that and loyalty.

Loyalty meant a lot.

"Results wouldn't be instantaneous, not without a lot of practice," the goddess cautioned. "You'll have to concentrate on using your aspect to search instead of destroy. But it would be more effective than prowling the ether in your sleep."

"How did you...?" Bix pointed to Ereshkigal's darkness. "It told you that?"

"I withdrew it from you." The goddess gestured to the black tendrils braiding around Bix's thicker tentacles. "Your darkness is churning, confused, directionless. It is very easy to tap to gain… What is it you call it? Oh yes, *intel*."

"And if I learned to control my darkness, I could pull secrets from others?"

"Other Shadow Casters, yes. It is the strength and the weakness of the ability." Ereshkigal tilted her head from side to side. "It is better to think of the darkness as a limitless army of spies. You could even find that god-hunting Nabaziix and the girl who weighs so heavy on your conscience."

The girl with the teddy bear. Drew. Plus, she'd be near Tobek in case he needed her. Friends. They were the reasons she was involved in this mess in the first place.

"Okay, I'm game…for as long as my mind allows me to remain," Bix quickly qualified.

"I am pleased." Ereshkigal clasped her hands together and smiled. "The first thing to know is that light is the great excluder. Darkness welcomes everything. Wherever there is darkness, wherever there are shadows, wherever light cannot reach, you can and you need not open a gate to get there."

Bix blinked rapidly. "How is that possible?"

"Think of darkness as one big pool. You're tapping into it. Each shadow you unleash is a set of eyes and ears."

"I don't know how to release just one shadow."

"The quantity of shadows you unleash is not the challenge," Ereshkigal dismissed. "How to bring in information while pushing out directions is your first test. Otherwise, other Shadow Casters will pull information from you once you tap the pool."

Bix held up her hands. "That we don't want."

"No," Ereshkigal chuckled. "That *you* definitely do not. Expect to be overwhelmed by the information as it comes in. The longer you can stay in the pool, the easier it will become for your mind to adjust and compensate."

"So, I should expect it to suck for a while, eh?"

"Ah, the figurative use of 'suck.'" The goddess bobbed her head. "Yes. Should it be the literal, focus on pushing out an image of Drew with the command to find him."

K. A. Krantz

"He's a body thief, I have no idea what he looks like right now," Bix opined.

"Then focus on whatever details or senses define him. How would you identify him if you were doing this in person? That is what you push out." Ereshkigal let go of Bix's darkness. "Now, find a shadow, a dark place within this temple, and tap the pool."

It took quite a few tries to get the tentacles to go where Bix consciously desired. All to Ereshkigal's amusement. The goddess provided instruction while Bix grappled with the basics. From there, tapping the pool was easy. But holy gods, being in the pool was like being trampled in a mosh pit at a speed metal festival during a monsoon.

"Push. Drew," the goddess spoke in Bix's ear. "Push. Drew. Find. Drew. Push."

Bix pushed the directive. The darkness pulled answers from thousands of places. A crippling headache gave way to nausea, forcing Bix to sit with her head between her knees as her mind acclimated to the influx. In time, she learned to focus on one sound, one scent. But when she focused on one image, the aspect of the gatekeeper physically took her there.

Fortunately, now that she knew what the temple at Irkalla looked like, getting back to Ereshkigal was a simple matter. The goddess welcomed her each time, her patience seemingly limitless as Bix reengaged with the pool under her guidance.

The nth time Bix returned to the temple, Nergal awaited her.

His grim expression caused her heart to clench.

"Is he…" Bix forced her mouth to articulate words. "Did the Fates fail him? Is Tobek, is he dead?"

Nergal cocked his head. "Would it bother you if he were?"

"Yes," she cried. "What is it with people thinking I'm heartless?"

"Would it bother you even if he's not the man you believe him to be?" Nergal challenged.

Bix looked to Ereshkigal. The goddess regarded her with pity. Anger rippled down Bix's spine and her darkness answered, slithering around the temple aimlessly. Bix jabbed her fingers into her hair and harshly kneaded her skull as despair wound with rage and exhaustion.

She was an idiot. She'd rolled up to these gods all casual like, interacting with them as if they were normal people even though she knew better. Damn she did know better. She'd been burned by being this stupid before. One rule when dealing with gods. One cardinal rule:

Contracts first.

Never do anything for a god and never request anything from a god without locking down a very detailed contract first. Gods were dicks looking for someone to screw. Always. And here she'd blithely handed over the one man who'd tirelessly supported her without hesitation. The one man who had to be so strong for everyone else had asked her to help him while at his most vulnerable. What had she done? She'd handed him over to a god of war, a god of plagues, a scientist who cared more for the science than the lives. Here, take him, take Tobek... Not one assurance. Not one promise extracted for his safe return. What had she done? What had she done?

"Oh, child," Ereshkigal whispered, reaching for her.

"No," Bix seethed, wrath edging out sorrow as she turned on Nergal. "I understand a god's regard for human life is lacking at best. However, I delivered my *friend* to you so you could find a cure for a bioweapon that threatens the whole of the Mids. I did not bring him as a sacrifice to your ego."

Nergal's eyes narrowed and his body angled away from her. "Fascinating. Completely husked, all memories wiped, all training stripped away, all instincts reset to the fetal condition, yet the wrath that shaped so much of who you were is still there. It is desperate to grow."

"Where is he?" Bix yelled.

"Find him yourself," Nergal bellowed with the full breadth and volume of a god. The temple shook and torches flared.

The god's voice echoed in her bones, but Bix refused to cower.

Tentacles spawned tentacles, casting eyes and ears across Irkalla. She pushed the image of Tobek as crystals, as a geode, as a man, and as a soul long accustomed to the shape of his mortal body. Answers didn't come, so she drove her darkness into every nook, cranny, bowl, urn, shoe, passage…and laboratory.

What the darkness saw confounded her. Gates brought the vision to her.

Tobek. In flesh. In the flesh that had been created by Mid World magic, flesh that should have been melting away from its exposure to the Under Worlds. Yet there he stood. Beautiful as any painting. A big blond bear covered in ink and eyes bright with rage. His amputated arm did nothing to detract from his allure. In fact, it was a bold reminder of what he would sacrifice to win. For better or worse. That determination and the intelligence to back it up were more attractive than any six-pack.

Yea though and alas, unlike the defiantly nude models of old, he wore loose pants.

She shambled toward Tobek, unsure if what she was seeing was real. The closer she got, the more his aura pushed and pulled at her. Familiar yet unbalanced in its conflict. This far from the Mids, its magic's rejection of her was barely perceptible. It showcased the ferocity of the pull whose source she still couldn't discern. Gone was the hint of retreat that the cooties had caused. Her hand trembled as she laid her palm against his chest. It was as warm and firm as it ought to be. Its welcome was tenfold.

"Say these tears aren't for me," Tobek rasped, brushing his thumb against her cheek.

"How are you…?" She drew her hand along his shoulder and down his amputated arm, tracing the scars. It really was him, perfection to the finest detail. "How are you surviving this? No matter how often your contract resets you, Mid World magic cannot exist here. *You* cannot exist here."

"The answer you don't want to accept is the answer nonetheless," Ereshkigal said softly.

"I want to hear the truth from you," she said looking directly into Tobek's raging glow. "No evasions, quibbles, or nonanswers. Can you do that?"

"No," he whispered.

"'No' you cannot answer that, or 'no' you will not answer that?" She withdrew her hand from him and laced her fingers in front of her. His deliberate silence released the wrecking ball of a lie she hadn't suspected and shattered her.

Tobek wasn't human. He wasn't a Chwed either. He'd gone out of his way to make her believe he was. Not being human or Chwed wouldn't have been a big deal if he'd just told her, but he hadn't; he'd *chosen* to lie to her in words and actions. What sort of friend lied about a basic thing like what they were? Why was the lie even necessary? What was he hiding from her that required him to ruin her complete trust in him over something so inconsequential?

She bit her lip and drew a steadying breath. When life crashed and burned around her, the only thing to do was soldier through. She wasn't a fan of airing dirty laundry in front of an audience. All the things she had to say to Tobek could wait. Bigger issues and whatnot. She schooled her features, steadied the trembling of her hands, and turned her back on pain.

"Nergal, my apologies." Bix mentally shifted gears to the actual issue that had brought her to Irkalla. She couldn't look at Ereshkigal. The goddess had warned her, and like a real deet-da-de, Bix had ignored it. "Did you have enough time to develop a universal cure?"

"I'm afraid a cure is off the table for anyone without the ability to regenerate from a pure state." Nergal scowled. "I did, however, discover the source of the base organism."

"It must be some oogie stuff if it infected Mister Not Human and Not of the Mids." Bix tipped her head toward Tobek.

"Indeed." Nergal inclined his head. "It is sourced from the worst possible thing in all existence."

"No," Ereshkigal gasped, eyes wide with a hand to her bosom.

"What? What is the source?" Bix prompted.

"The blood of our old foes." Nergal thrust both hands in his pockets. "The blood of a Devourer."

CHAPTER 19

"What exactly is a 'Devourer'?" Bix asked, swaying as the physical price of continuously tapping the pool of darkness weighed on her. A warm palm on her side pulled her against a bare, muscular chest.

"If you faint from exhaustion, your mind isn't going to let you stick around to get your answers." The damn not-a-man murmured into her hair. "Lean on me. The rest we'll hash out later."

It wasn't as if Tobek was going snap her neck in front of two Mesopotamian gods, and he was sturdier than a wall. Might as well use him like one.

Ereshkigal watched their interaction with open curiosity. "The Devourers come from Worlds far beyond ours. They consume all types of magic—world-native, god-native, Fate-woven, all of it. The magic they dispel is corrosive and poisonous. They lack the ability and the desire to create sustainable environs. They do not believe in partnerships, only enslavement."

"Once they've killed everyone and everything, they move on to the next beacon of thriving magic." Nergal sneered. "They are an incurable plague, militaristic in their culture. Their occupation of a territory is devastating to the effect that the World will eventually collapse in on itself and implode."

"While death normally provides the fertile bed for new growth, what Devourers leave behind in the fumes of a destroyed World are so toxic that creation gods dare not try to build a new World there." Ereshkigal looped her arm around her consort's.

"Well, shit," Bix groaned. "How long does it take for them to drain a World?"

Nergal rubbed two fingers over his lips. "Depends on the wealth of native magic available to them, on the size of the invading force, and how deeply they have to burrow to poison the roots of the native magic."

"Your best guess as to a large force taking over the Mids?" Bix coaxed.

"One hundred years if the army is under the command of a general with something to prove." Nergal looked up and to the left, as if recalling a memory. "Three hundred if it's an experienced campaigner."

"From their perspective, they're foraging for food," Ereshkigal added. "Gluttony is a careless use of resources, yet commanders with aborted vision and tenuous leadership use it as a reward for their troops."

Bix eyed the souls still formed and sort of living in the cities of Irkalla. Ereshkigal had clearly mastered resource management.

"In less than two hundred years, the native magic of the Mids will reach its cyclical apex," Tobek growled. "The Phoenix will burn and reset the balance. I am loath to believe the timing of their incursion is coincidental."

"Agreed." Nergal gestured to Bix. "The Devourers tried before at the apex proper, but the Chimera did her duty to the Phoenix, then gave the last of what she had to the ether. It is clear she is unable to repeat the feat at this time. The pantheons must rally to oust them now, before they gain a foothold in the Mids."

Bix pinched the bridge of her nose and tried to ignore the loadstone dropping in her gut. The Phoenix burned every five hundred years, and she was the foe that forced him to it. According to the long-lived and the immortals, it was an appointment for an execution she never missed. These days, she didn't know enough about that rendezvous to know if she *could* skip it and take on the Devourers instead. The years leading up to and immediately after the burning of the Phoenix were years of internecine warfare among the superpowers while everyone who was anyone jockeyed for more power. While the superpowers were in the throes of coups and regime changes, the humans and the Chweds died by the hundreds of thousands across all the Mids. Killing the Phoenix out of cycle simply extended that period of brutal war until the next cycle reset everything and reestablished the Consortium. No history of any race portrayed those war-torn years as a pretty time.

It was, however, the perfect time for a third party to infiltrate the Mids, destroy the Consortium permanently, and seize whatever they wanted. What the Devourers didn't raze would perish anyway. Without the Consortium, there would be no more Cycle of Souls contracts, no more repopulation of the Mids. Nothing to encourage native magic to grow. Angels and dragons would die off while Fates and gods starved.

It would be the end of all life in the Mids; indeed, the death of the Worlds themselves.

Fuck.

"The cogs of the political machine that is the multitude of pantheons are reluctant to move." Ereshkigal steepled her fingers. "We'll need lobbyists to impress upon pantheon leadership that this is an immediate priority. I will speak to my sister Ishtar so that she may gather supporters to the cause. She lost a favored consort to the Devourers. Her hatred of them is deep and inexhaustible."

"What happens to the immortals who go up against the Devourers and fail?" Tobek asked. "What is their fate?"

"Those who fall are husked and imprisoned. We've managed to free a dozen or so over the eons that we have fought the Devourers." Nergal looked to Bix and grimaced. "Their captives are trapped in the savage state of reawakening. Once the captives' magic is no longer dormant, the captives are drained again. It is a cycle of torture that forced us to send those we recovered into special rehabilitation."

Bix closed her eyes and shuddered. She'd been there, in that feral state of starvation and complete ignorance. Cognizant but less capable than an embryo. Fear and the will to live were the only things that registered. How many times could a god endure that before it imprinted permanently? What if husking couldn't erase it from their minds or their bodies? What if it twisted the very essence of their divinity?

Broken gods were probably how true evil came to be.

"My love, I must leave Irkalla." Nergal cupped Ereshkigal's face and stared into her eyes. "It is war for which we are preparing. I must meet with my peers and convince them of the threat and the urgency."

"Yes, the gods of war must succeed where the lobbyists fail." Ereshkigal's eyes watered, and she pressed her hands over her consort's. "Do not be gone too long, love. Please."

"I will work in darkness so I am never far from you." Nergal kissed his queen with a passion that made Bix blush and stare at her feet. "Until I am in your arms, I cannot be whole."

"I'm going to focus on the cootie," Bix said, breaking the moment. "Whoever is making it is getting that source material directly from a Devourer. Whether that Devourer is a scout who snuck into the Mids through one of the holes in the protective barriers or whether the scientist-idiot is working with a third party to traverse the ether to get it, I'll find out."

"I'll alert the MWA who will pressure the Consortium into action." Tobek sighed. "Two questions, though: what does a Devourer look like, and how do we kill it?"

"They can look like anyone, any race, any gender." Nergal indicated the four of them. "You will know them by the way their toxic magic displaces Mid World magic, leaving behind a taint perceptible to the upper castes. I'm afraid the lesser castes are, on the whole, defenseless."

"And how do we kill them? Take their heads? Spear their hearts?" Tobek prompted.

"Weapons of the gods or the wrath of the Chimera at her full potency." Nergal shook his head. "Beyond that, I know of nothing within the Mids that can help you."

Bix winced at the reminder of her subpar status. "What about a counter-cootie? If we have their blood in the toxin infecting the Mids, can't we use those samples to concoct something to infect them?"

"I have wasted millennia working toward that very end, yet to no avail," Nergal bit out.

"But it could be possible if you had other highly competent minds to challenge you, to push you to innovate?" Bix asked.

"She means no offense, love," Ereshkigal interjected, casting a chiding glance at Bix.

"I don't, really, I don't," Bix hastened to assure. "You are the expert without question."

"I doubt there is such a mind out there that can provide any beneficial challenge, but if there were…" Nergal lifted one shoulder. "It is possible in as much as anything is possible. The trick would be infecting only the Devourers without laying waste to all other life-forms. I would not pin the future of the Mids on the hopes of biological warfare against a race that is poisonous by their very nature. Our attempts could backfire completely and strengthen our enemy. There are so many unknowns."

"Go rattle the sabers of the other gods of war," Ereshkigal urged her consort. "I will consult with the governors of Irkalla's cities. By the time you come home to me, we will have begun work laying the foundations for a counter-biological weapon. If the Chimera can find someone competent enough to stymie our governors, then we will present that candidate to you for potential collaborations. Worry first about the reception your peers will give you after so many lifetimes in the Under World."

"Their bigotry is of little consequence, for we gods of war are very well acquainted." Nergal looked over Bix's head to the not-man behind her. "One could even say there's a modicum of respect exchanged, begrudging or not. It comes from warring against and amongst each other for eons. I have not forgotten which of their weaknesses are best to exploit for our cause."

In a blink, Nergal was gone.

Ereshkigal grabbed Bix's arm. "Child, you must reawaken all your aspects if there is to be any hope for the Mids against the Devourers."

"I need my memories to do that." Bix sighed. "I don't even know where to look for them. Seven gods, that's the only clue I have, and most gods aren't my biggest fans."

"That's why you chose to implant your memories in those gods whose magic is rooted in the Mids." Ereshkigal frowned. "Every pantheon has to contribute a Mid World guardian if they want to reap the benefits of the Mids. Some pantheons designate more than one. The guardians didn't have to like you, but they knew consequences to themselves, their food source, and their pantheons' power if they failed you."

"Man, I was ruthless, eh?" Bix groaned. "That's over a hundred gods to pick through. I don't suppose you know which of the guardians I chose?"

Ereshkigal crossed her arms and huffed. "No. You denied me that knowledge. You did not trust me to leave it with them, as if I was a lowly thief of dreams or fears."

Bix bit her tongue as the hairs on her nape stood on end. It was easy to forget that there were no such beings as benevolent gods. They were happy to help if it got them something in return. For Nergal, he got the chance to leave Irkalla, trumpet the horns of war, and tackle a plague that could take him off the blackballed-gods list. His wins were pretty clear.

What did Ereshkigal get from this? Gods of the Under Worlds planned for the extra-long game. It came with the territory. What was Ereshkigal's long-term goal? More importantly, did Bix really want to know right now? Probably not. Might prove to be one too many cans of worms she'd feel obligated to juggle. Better if she focused on the current mission and remained grateful for the goddess's favors thus far.

"I am blessed to have been so loved," Bix said instead.

"Indeed." The goddess relaxed and smiled. "I will monitor the darkness for *intel* regarding the Devourers. Should you choose to do the same, be aware they too have Shadow Casters among their ranks. Once they discern your presence in the pool, they will attempt to extract information from *you*."

"I'll practice a bit more before I chase the white whale." Bix laced her fingers and held them to her chest. "Thank you for everything."

"Visit often, child. I do miss your company."

CHAPTER 20

Bix returned with Tobek at her side to the Mid Worlds, just not the Primary Mid World. Rain pelted the tangerine shores of an uninhabited island once used by her Dark Ops team as an interrogation site. Young and hungry sea serpents slithered through piles of bones and headed into inky waters, escaping from her intrusion on their hunting grounds. Larger predators' haunting songs beckoned from the acidic waves, luring the ignorant to their doom.

"What are you?" Bix stepped out of Tobek's comfortable hold and faced him.

Tobek dropped his chin to his chest and sighed. "Must we do this now?"

"We're partners. We're roommates. We rely on each other. It is not unreasonable for me to want to know what sort of entity purports to have my back. Conversely, I also need to know the best way to help you when I'm covering your back—a responsibility that is hampered by not knowing *what* you are." She curled her hair around her finger, taking advantage of the rain for a reset. "Grimtebel treated your affliction in a mortal manner. You would never have had to endure complete crystallization if I'd known I could safely take you into the ether."

"I needed to go through that to fully understand how the toxin assailed the body. I've been a doctor many times, I know how to discern normal bodily function from atypical."

"So you can tell me that you were a doctor, but not what you are," she countered, not willing to indulge his attempt at diverting the conversation. "I've seen you bleed. I've seen you suffer. I've seen you interact with people and magics in a wholly human way. Why did you need me to believe you were human?"

"You assumed I was, and I saw no purpose in embarrassing you with a correction." He wiggled his toes in the sand. "In actions and words, have I not proven to be your friend, ally, and even protector? Why this need to find a flaw in the trust we've already established?"

It would have been one thing if he didn't want to talk about his own history. For the long-lived and the immortals, that was a pretty common stance. But he knew she was memory impaired. He knew she was desperate to relearn who she'd been, to eradicate the vulnerability of not knowing her old enemies, and to shore up her defenses against threats that still had her in their sights.

These were all issues a plain old chat could resolve. That he steadfastly refused to engage on those topics merited scrutiny.

"Since you are determined to treat this as a game, I'll play." She forced her lips to form a smile but made no effort to hide the weariness accompanying it. "Tell me what you are. Lie or choose not to answer, and I will cause the Worlds on which each Consortium lab is located to collapse in on themselves, including Grimtebel."

"Bullshit," he mocked. "It goes against everything for which this version of you stands."

"This version of me is trained to destroy the things that threaten to destroy the whole of the Mids." She shrugged. "To that end, the most expedient path is to obliterate all potential stores of Devourer blood, execute anyone with even tangential knowledge of the toxin, and foment hostile environs to prevent any sort of collaboration that might lead to the re-creation of the toxin."

He eyed her warily. "That is the anarchist crap the CWIG teaches their operatives."

"Remember, I don't have to be on a World to open a gate large enough to destabilize it. Something, I suspect, you've witnessed me do more than once in our shared past." She inspected her fingernails, internally gauging the strength with which his presence increased his rejection of her Other World proximity as he reconnected with the Mids' magic. The clutching tempered as his push and pull balanced, returning to the familiar dichotomy.

"Only whe——" He bit down on an agonized cry and gripped his chest, curling forward. Blood welled between his fingers.

"Tobek?" She reached for him, but he retreated from her. The green of his magic glowed around his hand.

"Get away," he gasped.

"No. Let me help you." Darkness responded to her frustrations and ripped from her spine. Her tentacles yanked his hand away from his pectoral. The Eternal Knot pushed up through the layers of ink on his skin, blistering and blackening. "What is that? Tell me. *Tell me.*"

"C-can't," he groaned.

Had she been a decent person, a kind and merciful sort, she would've recalled the darkness. She would've backed down and let the man heal himself. Sadly for him, what had once been a tiny seed of malice had grown frilly tangles of roots, a shoot, and probably a thorn or two.

Nergal had been mostly right about what had remained within her after her husking. It wasn't wrath, though. It was whatever malice grew up to become.

"If you really know me, you know the monster within me," she whispered. "Your damned prevarications are feeding it."

A part of her expected his pacifism or even patronization. Instead, his eyes took on the faint glow of an angry Berserker. He looked everywhere but at her.

His evasion was the wrong response. Her tentacles knocked bones into the sea and repeatedly speared the sands, lashing out at everything and nothing. Yet, only one tentacle assailed Tobek.

She wasn't sure if that was her doing or his.

"Your suffering will not end this line of interrogation," she cautioned. "I will have your answer."

He glared at her from behind the veil of his sodden hair. A sneer framed his pained stammer. "C-cursed. You. C-cursed me to n-never s-speak of our p-past."

She straightened, and the darkness stilled. "Liar."

His eyes rolled until the whites showed. He sank to his knees. She bid the darkness to return to her. The instant the tentacle released Tobek, he slammed his hand to his chest and caged the charring scarification of the Endless Knot. The native magic he wielded flowed in greens and silvers until his breathing normalized and the bleeding stopped.

"I haven't lied to you, sweetheart," he whispered. "Not from the moment you crashed into my home. However, your assumptions are beyond my control."

"Funny, for a man who gets off on pain, you don't seem to be overly fond of this kind," she quipped, feeling like a piece of shit, but how was she to have known? Chimera version 1.0 had not messed around with protecting herself. That meant Tobek knew something significant about her. Version 1.0 hadn't killed him; she'd opted for a curse instead. What sort of intel did he have on her that would have prevented her from removing the threat he posed?

More importantly, what did that mean for her now? For the Chimera version 2.0? Should she trust him? Should she get as far from him as possible before he turned on her? Knowing she'd cursed him didn't really make her feel all warm and cozy about shacking up with him. How he'd refrained from going all "Here's Johnny" on her was disconcerting.

"The physical pain I can endure. It's the rest that..." Tobek stood and dabbed at his chest. The scorched Eternal Knot faded beneath the images inked over it. "If you're done establishing our boundaries, can we go home and deal with the significant issues at hand?"

She massaged her temple. "I'm not sure."

He shoved his wet hair out of his face and raised his brows. "Answering more of your questions is going to render me catatonic for a rather lengthy period. This isn't the best time for me to go AWOL, and who knows how long we've already been gone. Time flows differently in the Under Worlds."

"Three days. We've been gone three days in the time of the Mids," she answered offhand. She bounced a lot between the two settings. Her mind instinctively tracked the variations in time.

"Three?" He shut his eyes. "The part about being a member of an army is that your troops notice when you're missing. Certain protocols are enacted the longer I'm gone. I need to report in."

"Relax. You're not my prisoner. Nor are you the only source of information about the original Chimera or even your own history. That buys you a short reprieve before we go toe-to-toe again on those topics. And there will be a return to those topics, I assure you." She perched on a massive skull at the edge of the beach and watched the play of water along the horizon. Peaceful on the surface, vicious and deadly from shallows to the deeps.

"Warning acknowledged." Tobek widened his stance and slid his lone hand in his pocket, waiting. A mantle of patience and concern settled over him, softening his mien.

She drew a long breath and mustered up some strength from somewhere. There were pressing issues, timely issues, things that could no longer wait. She needed her teammate on the same page so they could finally make some progress. It didn't require complete trust, just mission level. She was intimately familiar with the difference. Carrying her ass out of a burning building? Mission level. Knowing the locations of all her bolt-holes? Yeah, not even Ashtad knew that.

Maybe Ereshkigal had been a little bit right.

"While you were out of pocket, I found the third lab. However, a militarized team of cleaners beat me there. They neutralized over three hundred scientists and test subjects by turning them into geodes."

Tobek swore. "Sarina succumbed as well. Add the three CWIG agents and yours truly, and that makes a successful field trial. Cian, so far, is their only anomaly."

"Because *he* is human. No magic for the Devourer blood to feed on. If it can't feed, it can't bond to the host." She shook the sand out of her shoes. "The lab was destroyed, but I need Cian to continue working on tracing Udara's nanites."

His eyes cut left and right. "You're hoping they've attached themselves to the cleaning team?"

"You don't spend five years working on a bioagent that proves successful and then quit. You clean house because you don't need the researchers anymore."

"You take the successful formula and move it into mass production." He nodded. "Meaning they took Udara's prototypes and made them functional."

"Even microscopic robots run some sort of code. If we can't stop the bioagent from being deployed, maybe Cian can find a way to counterinfect the nanites. If he can tell me what sort of expert assistance he needs, I'll get the people. Spies are pretty good at collecting assets."

"As soon as we get to the coal plant, I'll make sure the Sage is paying more attention to the nanites than his computer. I'll see to gathering the willing experts too. Anyone we have problems with, I'll send you a dossier."

"Thank you." She stared at a water droplet dangling from her soggy bangs. "I need *you* to pull the origin and destination logs of every programmable gateway and cross-reference it with the new Worlds Xipil identified."

"That's highly classified." He scratched his jaw. "Not that I'm unwilling, but my request will draw attention. It's a political grudge match with a lot of weight thrown around to get those lists."

"Legit reasons for it. The cleaners used one of those gateways. It should tell you who the cleaning team is, who they work for, and why they tried to frame the dragons for hosting the third lab."

"Frame? The dragons?" He groaned. "I had forgotten how you—"

She winced with him as he covered the Eternal Knot, once more countering the pain he incurred when he mentioned their history. "One last task for you before I send you home and allow you a break from stumbling over our past."

"Only one?" He grinned. Sort of.

"Hold off on alerting the MWA to the presence of the Devourers and the role they play with the toxin." She stared at the rain pooling in her lap, mesmerized by the way it escaped over the creases in her dress. "Wherever the faction inside the Consortium has planted their loyalists, I don't want to tip our hand. Not yet."

"You need to come home and rest." He reached to tuck her hair behind her ear, but she leaned away. "I'll have some answers for you by the time you wake. Then we can make a plan to go after the Devourers, together."

"That's not something we can do on our own. Taking on the Devourers is in the pantheons' hands. We asked for Nergal's help. We need to give him time to come up with a strategy. Right now, you and I need to focus on the immediate problem of the toxin; then we figure out how to dismantle the faction."

"I'll come up with something to placate the MWA in the short-term, but only the short-term. For the safety of the troops, I cannot sit on a critical detail like a god-level threat for too long."

"Fair enough." She nodded. "While you manage the MWA, I'm going to apply what I learned from my studies with Ereshkigal to what I found at the third lab."

"That sounds dangerous." He grinned.

"Always a possibility." She matched his smile. "Someone felt it was important to make the dragons look guilty of a crime, which tells me the dragons are the only ones who are not, in fact, in on this."

"Okay, I can see how you got there." He sobered. "The questions then become who did the cleaners think was going to find the third lab, and who did they think would be so readily biased that they wouldn't look too closely at the staged scene?"

"My gut says the cleaners are from the Angelic Host." She held up her hands to stop the reproof forming on his lips. "I know I've got baggage when it comes to them. But, angels would do a crap job on a frame because learning how to do it right is beneath them. It's a job they'd normally hire out to a group of Chwed mercs, but they couldn't this time because they're dealing with Devourer blood."

"Why would angels need a programmable portal? They can move through the Mids at will," he challenged.

"What they can carry with them is limited though," she countered. "Perhaps they needed to transport certain equipment from the lab to the production facility."

"That leaves the Consortium's investigators or my guys as the ones who find the third lab." Tobek harrumphed. "A supposedly unbiased third party discovering the evidence lends more value than rival races pointing fingers at each other."

"By now, the Angelic Host has probably heard that the third lab was destroyed, so they're scrambling, which means a mistake is bound to be made."

"The Consortium investigators have another two weeks at both legitimate labs before they wrap up their reviews." He sucked in air through his bottom teeth. "That gives the angels plenty of time to plant the right kind of incriminating evidence at the dragons' lab."

"They'll do it sooner than later so their cohorts in the faction can get back to their mass-production schedule while everyone else is focused on the dumpster fire of the dragons colluding with enemies of the gods." She pointed her finger at him and fired her imaginary gun. "If I time this right, I can them in the act of the set-up."

"Even if you're right and it is the angels—which I'm not totally sold on; it could as easily be mercs hired by the Consortium faction—your very recent history with them is very contentious.

Sunan is an ass, but he has a point about any evidence you find being dismissed by the superpowers. Are you sure you want to take lead on finding the planted evidence?"

"That's why you're going to check those programmable portal logs, and that's why all eyes are going to be on you and your progress."

He arched a brow. "While you play in the shadows?"

"Oh, I've been spying on top-secret locations for ages. Shadows aren't necessary for that." She stood. "Anyway, thanks to you and Nergal, I know what I'm looking for now. I'll be in touch."

"Wait." He danced away from the gate opening behind him. "At least grab your comm, in case you need me. We're partners, right?"

Bix glanced at her naked wrist and grinned. "A comm isn't going to work where I'm going."

CHAPTER 21

Bix took a detour on her way to Devourer Detection Duty. Not knowing what sort of entity Tobek was bothered her in much the same way Loncalaz choosing Cian as his target did. There was something going on at a macro level that she needed to know. It was like being tasked with an op but not getting the full intel packet.

There was only one person she could go to for help.

She caught Ashtad exiting his bedroom...without his cane.

"Do you need help getting to a chair or to bed or something?" She yelped as high voltage electricity raced up her legs to her wet hair, releasing a plume of steam.

"Damn it, Bix." Ashtad closed his fist, and the charge stopped. "I'm sorry. Wasn't expecting company."

"I probably should have used the front door." She wrapped the ends of her hair around her fingers to stop the random sparking. "But seriously, do you need me to get your cane for you?"

"It's been a few days since your last check-in. I'm somewhat ambulatory now. Not for long stretches or with more speed than a septuagenarian's shuffle, but I'm getting there." He swept her with a disapproving look. "Drowned Pomeranian is not a good style for you."

"I need your help."

"Obviously. Get yourself some towels from the bathroom." He hobbled toward the pristine kitchen and gestured to the spacious master bath. "I took the liberty of laying in a few supplies for you after your return from exile. Check my closet. I'll be in the living room, whenever you're ready."

Bix watched him shamble around his kitchen just long enough to make sure he really was steady on his feet before she snagged a fluffy towel from the bathroom and darted into the adjoining closet. It was larger than his living room and lined with built-ins. Two center islands. Floor-to-ceiling angled mirrors with a tailor's pedestal at the far end. Ashtad had always been a clotheshorse, but, whoa, the demigod did not mess around.

She took two laps around the room before she dared open one of the garment bags. His undercover clothes. Mechanic's acrylic work shirt with the name "Ahmed" stitched on the chest. Pilot's uniform. Desert BDUs. Leather fringed jacket.

Latex chaps.

Nope. Nope. Nope. Didn't want to know.

She zipped that bag and opened three others before she touched the telltale fabric made to survive beyond the Mids. It was a beautiful backless number done in black with a damask Bi Xie pattern. Three other dresses of similar exquisite tailoring and progressively bolder patterns rounded out the selection.

Who was he kidding? The Bi Xie won every time.

The sleek underpinnings were in a smaller bag attached to the hanger. He'd given her the choice of two pairs of delightfully impractical shoes. She chose the pale pink T-straps, polka-dotted with glitter emojis and a clear spiral heel filled with more glitter suspended in solution. She dumped her wet, dirty clothes through a pair of gates, then dressed.

Presentable once again, she located Ashtad in the living room tapping madly on his rubber-coated keyboard.

"How much do I owe you for the wardrobe?"

He lifted his hands from the keys as if she'd interrupted a

maestro in the midst of his grand composition. The question on his lips converted into a smirk as she perched on the edge of his desk.

"I knew you'd pick the Bi Xie. I'll have the other dresses redone to suit."

"No, no, please don't go to more trouble for me."

"It's clothes," he said dryly. "Feel free to think of them as undercover attire, which I often provide for my operatives."

She raised her brows. "Your operatives? And am I speaking to the CWIG's mole catcher or to the seneschal of the demis?"

"Don't give me multiple personalities. I am but one demigod who is extremely adept at multitasking." He sat back in his chair and openly assessed her appearance. "I'll make a note for them to lengthen the sleeves as well. I seem to recall you normally wear a smartwatch to keep in touch with Chief and his merry band of Berserkers. You need the matte surface for the screen's projection."

"Speaking of Tobek…" She grimaced, "Once upon a time, you told me he'd taken you in when you first came to the Mids."

Ashtad nodded. "Yes. I'd angered a few nymphs when I was fresh from the Upper Worlds. They were kind enough to introduce me to the monotheistic god-fearing human race during the Spanish Inquisition. Imagine my significant dose of humility having been captured and tortured by nonmagical lesser beings."

"I took Tobek out of the Mids," she blurted.

He looked at her, bemused.

"I took him to Nergal. He survived." She traced the pattern in her dress. "Did you know he could do that? Did you know he's not human or even a Chwed?"

"Wh-what?" Ashtad sputtered. "He went to the Under Worlds with you? All the way in the Under Worlds, not lingering in a gateway connecting the Mids to the Unders? Fully Under?"

"For three days, in Mids time." She glanced at her erstwhile spymaster. "Do you know what he is?"

"Based on that intel bomb, a god is the first thing comes to mind." He spun his teacup on its saucer, his composure regained, but his mind clearly working furiously, examining all the angles. "But I'd like to think I would have noticed that at some point during the century I lived and trained with his battalion."

"It never came up, even among his men?"

"Every Berserker is there because the head of a House of Fate plucked them out of the great unwashed masses, modified their Cycle of Souls contract to include some kind of longevity and restoration clause, and sent them to the MWA. As far as I know, the Berserkers are all mortals who've shown exceptional skill on the battlefield. It's an unspoken assumption that everyone there was human before gaining their commission."

"How long did it take them to know you're a demi?"

He laughed. "Not long. I was supremely and tragically cocky."

"He can't be a god. I feed off gods' raw energy. I would have noticed if I was living with my dinner," she argued. "Not a dragon or an angel because they can't exist beyond the Mids either."

Ashtad sipped his tea. "Okay, then, what do you think he is?"

"A Fate? He *says* it's a contract that resets him, yet Nergal mentions Tobek's ability to 'regenerate from a pure source' as the only cure for Loncalaz's bioagent."

Ashtad snorted. "If Fates could regenerate from a pure source, they wouldn't be old, they wouldn't still have the markings of their trials, and they wouldn't be missing a body part."

"Tobek's missing a body part." She poked Ashtad's arm. "And all his ink could be covering up his Sage's leaves. Plus, plus, he is old for his time."

"It's not uncommon for the Fates to live among the lesser races," he conceded.

"But I've seen him bleed, red blood, copious amounts." Bix wrinkled her nose. "You and I have seen Fates bleed. Their blood comes out red but quickly changes to rainbow rivulets."

"I too have seen him bleed copious amounts and you're right, it is not the same as a Fate's blood." He tapped the frame of his computer with his fingers. "We can't ignore the way he uses native magic. You and I have seen him wield it repeatedly and to significant effect. That's no scam. Fates can't do that. Their magic is all about designing interactions to create situations and affect outcomes."

She squeezed her eyes shut before blurting, "A demi is the only thing left. You guys eat, sleep, bleed, and wield magic like mortals. To the casual observers, you're like enhanced Chweds but with an endgame of divinity instead of death."

Ashtad laughed again, but this time it tapered into a sound of contemplative horror. "A demi who has been in the Mids for as long as he has, continually absorbing magic and emotion for eons... No. No, there's no way his pantheon would allow him to stay here and become something more powerful than a titan."

"What if they couldn't remove him? What if the Houses of Fate did something to block his extraction?" She poked the scars in her arm. "Can they do that? Can Fates block a demi from ascending to full godhood?"

He whistled low. "They can certainly weave paths to impossible challenges around the demi, but our failure would mean death, not a delay in ascension. Remember, demis don't have threads. Fates can't directly stunt our development."

"He definitely has threads of Fate," she insisted. "I've seen them meshed over him like the trussing of a turducken. What would a demi be doing with threads of Fate?"

"Over him, you say?" Ashtad sat forward and braced his elbows on the table. He laced his fingers and pressed his thumbs against his lips. "It would depend on the weave and on who wove it."

"What would depend?"

"I guess it's possible, however remotely..." He bounced his fists on his lips. "There's a story my grandmother used to whisper to her pets. No one believed it contained a mote of truth."

Bix rolled her eyes. "Crazy grandma stories. Awesome. What'd she say?"

"Restraints." He looked at her with sadness. "What you saw could be restraints rather than threads that sew a soul to a body.

Like a net tangled around a fish, they're there to trap and restrict the divinity of the god or demi."

"Pfft, of course no one believes that," Bix dismissed. "A god can break threads with a thought."

"Back when the Houses of Fate fought the pantheons for their independence, they reached out to the enemies of the gods for assistance. It's wholly possible that those Fates learned how to bind a god. If they can bind a god, they can bind a demi." He shot her a glance. "They might even be able to bind an Other World entity like you."

She waved aside his warning. If the Fates could have bound her, they would have done it long before now.

"Tobek can't be Other World. The meals I've seen him pack away? Dude can eat food. Mortal food. He doesn't go hunting for souls or primordial essence. He prefers his steaks rare and his vegetables steamed. He has a love affair with coffee."

"All in line with the behaviors of a demi." He glowered at his keyboard. "Let me look into the netting. Weaknesses, side effects, the whole shebang."

"Thank you, but no. I don't want you running afoul of Tobek or incurring the wrath of whichever Fates know how to trap a demi and bind a god."

"I can be discreet," Ashtad pointed out. "It *is* the essence of my job. Plus, if the Fates really are capable of something like this, I need to know for purely selfish reasons."

She couldn't argue with that. "Keep in mind, he has a contract with the Fates. That's beyond dispute. It'd be worth knowing if the netting happened as part of it. If it did, it means he *let* the Fates bind him. What could have been worth the price of his divinity?"

"Love and ego are the universal weaknesses of gods and demis alike." Ashtad mulled the question some more. "Whatever it was isn't common knowledge."

"If it was love, his tale should be as popular as Hades and Persephone or Isis and Osiris." She hopped off Ashtad's desk.

"Ego would put him up there with Prometheus and Loki. He'd be known."

"Those are stories of gods acting out against other gods and titans." He shook his head. "I bet the pantheons buried his story because they don't want anyone to know about the Fates having that kind of weapon against them. They want history to forget it."

She tapped her temple. "I must have known, the old me, pre-memory wipe."

Of greater interest, why hadn't she—the original Chimera—freed Tobek from his bonds? They'd known each other. Multiple sources had confirmed that. By all accounts, he was and continued to be a guardian of the Mids. Regardless of what type of entity he was, Tobek most definitely held a high rank in the MWA. If she'd been so worried about the Devourers back then that she'd sacrificed everything, why hadn't she helped Tobek ascend to his full power so he could've helped defend the Mids?

Had she been that heartless, or was there a dark side to Tobek that she'd wanted to keep contained by Fate's bonds? Was his dark side the real reason she'd cursed him to silence about their past?

"Bix, if we're right, it explains why Chief doesn't talk about it." Ashtad pinned her with a knowing look. "If his reticence on the topic—or any closely related to it—is why you showed up here peeved, maybe you should cut him a little slack."

"Maybe he doesn't talk about it because he physically can't. For example, he can't talk about the history he and I share because of a curse I put on him." She rocked her head from side to side. "Maybe I'm the one who had the Fates bind him."

"Whoa," Ashtad wheezed. "I hate to say it, but that sort of cruelty would fit with the stories of the old Chimera."

"Right? Sort of hard to verify without my memories, though." She chuckled miserably. "Hey, while I'm here, anything on Cian's malfeasance with the Red Web I should know about?"

"Lots of unwise moves and trades of midlevel info he's siphoning off the MWA, but nothing too dangerous yet." He arched a brow. "Bix, if the Chimera cursed Chief to silence instead of executing him, she needed him alive for a reason."

"He must know something she couldn't drag out of him." Bix shrugged.

"It might not be information that makes him valuable. It might be the man himself."

"Like a jealous stalker ex sort of thing?" She thought of the pictures Tobek had drawn of her, and of the obvious emotional connection between subject and artist. Didn't exactly clarify which one of them was the stalker.

"More like a very special ingredient in a very special spell." Ashtad splayed his fingers above his keyboard, a new composition ready to flow. "I'm going to do more digging into the history of the Chimera and the MWA. I'll pull some favors, see what the scuttlebutt among pantheons is."

"I'm going to go be the spy you trained me to be and do remote recon on the labs." She gave him two thumbs up. "Might want to warn the director that I'm going to ruffle wings, feathered and scaled. If he's found any of the needles in the World of haystacks, now would be a good time to share."

"I'll check in and let you know." He set to typing. "Stay away from the Consortium's goons, Bix. If the faction figures out you're on to them, they'll use any excuse to negate your parole and exile you once again."

CHAPTER 22

It'd been three days since the Nabaziix had destroyed the third lab. By now, the angels and the Consortium faction probably knew their frame job of the dragons had a hiccup. To nail a dragon, they'd need to level up their evidence and to stage a bogus research section somewhere within the dragons' lab. Equipment for the fake lab could be easily pilfered from legit uses within the dragons' facility. The only unassailable proof would be a cache of pure Devourer blood. Bix had to get her hands on that proof before the Consortium's investigators did.

Nergal had said Devourer blood would displace Mids' magic with a hint of toxicity. Bix had just the tool to locate it: ether.

Mid Worlds abutted each other like flowers in an overstuffed bouquet. Ether not only surrounded the bouquet, it slithered through the gaps to fill every crevice. If one stood within the ether, the gaps appeared limitless. However, if one knew where to stand in the adjacent World, the ether became a useful spy tool. It adjusted scale and stripped the viewed World of color and sound. Native magic existed as a sepia tone. Only extremely powerful magic could emit color that defied the ether.

Any part of a Devourer ought to register like a map tack.

Bix set up her viewing station in the middle of an odiferous quagmire on a World of sophomoric bog beasts. Churning gates kept her from touching down in the pervasive muck while she inspected the dragons' lab from the adjacent World. She had an unobstructed view of the lake in which Udara's daughter had drowned. A bit of ambling allowed a review of the surrounding quaint communities. The lot was still vacant where Udara's house had sat; though, now there was a crime scene barrier around it. Nothing registered from Hu Jian's apartment complex or Ozmar's bungalow neighborhood.

That left the laboratory proper, looking more like a coastal resort than the birthplace of myriad diseases.

A few hundred dragons staffed the lab in addition to the hundred or so Chweds. Flares of purple dotted the ether like merry fireworks amid the drab. The flashes denoted the magic of creation wielded by the dragons. The absence of any echoing displacement suggested the scientists were concocting sanctioned cooties rather than mass-producing Devourer-based toxins. However, a spy wasn't worth the title if they didn't delve beyond initial impressions.

Into the sterile belly of the beast she went.

As a skilled gatekeeper, Bix could press the barriers of one World into a neighboring World, enabling her to walk in World A while existing in World B. She kept the layer of ether between the Worlds. It was a little trick she'd learned while reassembling her marbles in the days of her Under World residency. She'd taken one of Hades's hounds whenever she went exploring for the times she'd gotten in over her head or completely lost her head. The latter had happened a lot in the beginning. The vibrancy of life in the Mids had easily overwhelmed her. That was when she'd stumbled upon the solution of the ether buffer.

Bix smirked as she strolled through the front door of the dragons' lab, past oblivious security guards and complex sensors. She paused at the directory posted on the wall long enough to get her bearings. Yashanee, the petite dragon she'd met at Grimtebel, was the lead scientist at the lab. Ozmar the ganconer had said

Yashanee lived here. The best place to plant evidence would be in Yashanee's private domain. Top floor. West wing. Beneath a glass-domed roof. The best place for the bogus lab would be in the least trafficked areas, like down by the utility rooms which were always in the basement.

Better to focus her efforts locating Devourer blood.

The facility bustled with activity. Research assistants, researchers, administrators, and—her personal favorite—robots. Everybody was a rat in their own maze. Even the security teams. Everyone wore a coded armband that translated to area access.

Then there were the Consortium goons in their distinct uniforms, standing guard at every door and elevator. Windows had been bolted shut. Glassed-in lab areas looked as if hurricanes had torn through them. Papers were strewn everywhere, computers tossed, and machines dismantled. Beakers, test tubes, and everything fragile lay in shards across the floors. Despondent Chweds cleaned up.

It wasn't fun to be in the crosshairs of the Consortium. Bix knew that from experience.

She continued her way through the facility, winding back and forth from wing to wing. The higher the floor, the more obvious the progress—or lack thereof—of the Consortium's investigators. She caught up with the actual investigators on the third floor, east wing. Chweds lined the outer wall like the condemned facing a firing squad. Three dragons stared down a goon holding a tablet computer and trying his best to not appear intimidated. The guy totally failed, but hey, he tried. She peered over his shoulder, reading his tablet. He had a cluster of questions and a list of keywords that should occur in the answers. Typical for nonexperts interviewing experts. None of it related to toxins, so she continued her search.

She veered away from the corridors thick with curious people and plowed through walls that didn't exist in her World. The attire of the researchers said more about the work they were doing than the actual research. Lab coats versus goggles and respirators versus full hazmat suits. Up on the fourth and fifth floors, magic was happening. The intensity of purple flares made her wish for sunglasses as spots echoed while she wandered.

Up on the top floor, those spotted echoes weren't echoes at all.

Half a hundred pewter dots peppered the ether, causing the sepia tone of native magic to ripple until its concentric circles collided with another dot's circles and cast wavelengths that whited out her view of the World.

The planted evidence. Had to be.

Bix went wide and low to see around the squiggles of displaced magic. Definitely a personal abode. Bed, small bathroom, and a computer screen that occupied an entire curved wall displaying assorted molecular structures. Beneath the domed glass ceiling paced the petite dragon from Grimtebel.

Bix's heart stopped and darkness writhed under her skin as she took in the glass shelves across from the huge computer screen.

Geodes. Fifty geodes had been carefully displayed and tagged with a name, race, location, and date. So much for her idea that the dragon had been framed.

The image on the monitor wall changed. Molecular modeling disappeared. Large text came in its place.

Come all the way in, Chimera.

Bix fully entered the dragon's private chambers and braced herself for an attack of pure native magic. The only action came from the collection of geodes on the wall, where the taint of the Devourer blood within them recoiled from her.

"Your presence angers native magic. Those of us with royal blood can feel it." Yashanee tapped her tablet, and models reappeared on the screen. "You've been in the building for a while now. Did you find what you were looking for?"

"About fifty examples of you being the ringleader in the unsanctioned development of a toxin that targets the threads of Fate." Bix pointed to the wall of geodes.

"Ringleader?" Yashanee's dark plum brows furrowed, yet her focus never shifted from the tablet. "I'm the one who reported the beginnings of that research to the Consortium years ago, for all the good it did."

Bix crossed her arms under her bosom. "I'm going to need more than your word on that. I was there when you feigned cluelessness at Grimtebel, remember?"

"On the contrary, I told Sunan and Kashdejan we were dealing with a toxin, not a virus. Your friends were the first confirmed subjects who had yet to morph; hence, my urgency to reach them before they changed. If my haste offended you, that's your problem."

Bix snorted. Ah, royalty. "Proof, Yashanee, I need proof that you're the whistle-blower."

"The proof you want is no longer available. What remains is corrupted, courtesy of one of the Consortium agents. I'm having difficulty pinning down which one breached the facility's security and installed a worm." Yashanee continued to tap on her tablet.

A chill danced down Bix's spine. The evidence planting, it *was* underway, but why when these geodes were damning enough? Unless the faction didn't know the geodes were here? Or Yashanee was lying about the worm. Not enough info to know if the answer was a, b, or e—none of the above.

"Yashanee, I will either help you get to the bottom of this or deliver you to the Chair of the Consortium right now. Choose your next words wisely."

Yashanee exhaled loudly and lowered her tablet, finally looking Bix in the eye. "Mirri."

"Excuse me?"

"Mirri," the dragon repeated, returning to her tablet. "The former Norse Ambassador. She came to me after the oversight committee buried my report. We talked, I told her about the anomalies I'd discovered through my routine audits of this facility, she promised to look into it."

And Mirri had found something that had sent her to the CWIG instead of the Chair of the Consortium or even the Norse pantheon. The answer to why had to be in the evidence pouch Cian had hidden. Oh, what she wouldn't give to have her hands on that pouch right now.

"Not long after, Trescop arrived." Yashanee smiled at a geode dead center in the shelves of other geodes. "By now you probably know that was a false name. His real name is Loncalaz, and he is a spy for the CWIG. Most of the trapped souls on those shelves are CWIG agents. The rest are from assorted branches of the Mid World Army."

Bix's jaw dropped. Half a hundred agents and soldiers.

The director of the CWIG had questioned why she'd insisted on welfare check-ins. That many missing agents merited a broader investigation. They couldn't all be affiliated with the Consortium labs case. As for the MWA soldiers, they couldn't all be Berserkers. Otherwise, Tobek would have led the hunt for his men instead of wasting time being infected.

"Misfortune befell Mirri, Loncalaz is a rock, and the digital evidence files are thoroughly trashed, so as I said, the proof you want is no longer available." Yashanee huffed. "I had hoped upon seeing you at Grimtebel that Loncalaz had successfully relayed our problem to you. He had a strange confidence that he could get you to help. I couldn't fathom how. That he infected your friends...I am sorry. That is not the means I would have chosen."

"Well, it worked," Bix admitted, tipping her head at the wall of geodes. "How did a routine audit lead to discovering all these fallen agents and soldiers?"

"This first one connected the dots." Yashanee gestured to the placard one shelf above the center. "She was Loncalaz's original handler. He found this in his bed. He brought it in, thinking it was a prank played by one of the staffers here. The bio alarms went off when he entered the building. The microscope wasn't necessary to know what it was. A touch was enough."

"A dragon's magic creates flesh and body, so you didn't need science to show you the broad strokes of the geode." Bix puffed out her cheeks. "You had to tell him it used to be a person."

Yashanee nodded. "He'd pieced together who it was within a few hours. I asked my cousin to verify the Cycle of Souls contract associated with the geode. Loncalaz was right."

"Your cousin is a queen, right?" Bix knew the answer but played dumb. "She must be in order to verify a contract."

"My cousin is the reigning queen," Yashanee corrected.

Bix choked on a wheeze. "The *reigning* queen of the Dreigiau is aware of all this? And she's done nothing?"

"What can she do? I already have an entire laboratory staffed with the best minds available. Until I can give her something actionable, the best she can offer is the confirmed identities of the afflicted. When one is a queen, conjecture is suicide and a cause for war."

"She still could have alerted the CWIG or the MWA, through back channels, of course." Bix read the card on the center shelf and swore. "Did you take Loncalaz's geode from Kashdejan's lab?"

"I swapped it with one of the others before we left Grimtebel." The dragon returned to her obsession with the tablet. "I couldn't leave him with the angels. They would have cut him open, killing him in the process. They would not have respected the man or his remains. You understand, don't you?"

Yashanee didn't see it, how in trying to save a friend, she'd incriminated herself. That was two strikes against her of her own making. That didn't include the angels' or the faction's efforts. The dragon might have been science smart, but a mastermind of complex subterfuge? No. Not in the ball game. Not even at the same ballpark.

Bix's mind raced as she tried to figure out how to help clean this up without making it worse.

"What about the other people here?" Bix drummed her fingers against her hips. "How did you know about them?"

"Loncalaz brought them to me. He said he was following a hunch." Yashanee motioned to the bottom shelf. "When he brought in the soldiers, he voiced the idea of involving the MWA. He believed it had become too big an issue for the two of us. The field trials were expanding, and no one was taking responsibility for it. No one was acting on our escalations of it. We were being ignored, and someone out there was using it to assassinate his peers and MWA soldiers."

"Why didn't you call in the MWA yourself?"

"You heard about the fifty test subjects for which I was reprimanded? The ones who'd died and Loncalaz had reported their deaths? I did kill them. It was the successful completion of a new kind of gene-modifying disease that my lab had been officially tasked to work. The issue wasn't that the subjects had died, but that I'd bypassed certain unnecessary protocols that oversight committee had recently inflicted upon me. Members of the committee picked those details from Loncalaz's final report and made them an issue."

"A political assassination of your reputation, and they waited until now to do it," Bix mused aloud. "They waited until their toxin was in field trials, and somehow Loncalaz got his hands on it. Do you know how or when he did?"

"I didn't know he had until the MWA notification came in." Yashanee hung her head. "I am ashamed to say we never made it much further than what you see before you. I'd figured out the base element was an Other World biologic. But, since each thread of Fate is technically an Other World biologic and is unique to an individual, I can't separate the unknown foreign biologic from the thread without destroying both."

"You couldn't derive a pure sample of either. Without those, you can't make a cure." Bix nodded. "I'm getting the gist of the science issue."

"I invited Sunan to assist since he is a Fate. I even gave him a geode. I've heard nothing from him since."

"He already had a geode when you all went to Grimtebel to fight over Loncalaz's remains?"

"Yes. He'd had it for a few days by then."

"Did you tell Sunan about Loncalaz? That he was assisting you in this?"

"I didn't need to. He was already aware, and he was aware of the elf being an agent."

Son of a bitch. The CWIG leak. She needed to tell Ashtad it was linked to the Consortium.

"What about Kashdejan? Did she have any clue about this before Grimtebel?"

"I did not include the angel in the distribution of reports, nor did I invite her speculations." Yashanee stared at the floor. "I did not want her participation."

"A dragon and an angel not wanting to collaborate? Go figure." Bix rolled her eyes. "Would you be willing to share with me the list of victims? These fifty plus the two you gave to your peers?"

Yashanee flipped her wrist twice. Violet magic sparked, then ebbed, leaving behind a sheet of paper. She thrust the page at Bix. "Here. Fifty-five victims' names, the dates they were found, and the places they were found. It includes the three I destroyed in my initial attempts to understand what they were."

"Loncalaz and the queen verified they were all agents or soldiers?" Bix took the page and scanned the list. She recognized a few from her days with the CWIG.

"Yes." Yashanee stared at her without blinking. And kept staring.

Bix gave her the side-eye. "What?"

"You need to leave. Now." Yashanee turned toward the door. "My cousin is coming. She's not alone, and she is livid."

Bix didn't question the bond between a dragon and her queen, much less blood-related dragons. She did question why now, why right now. She looked again at the geodes. "Yashanee, they're coming to arrest you. Let me take you somewhere safe."

"Arrest me? For what?"

"That worm you found in your system, the removal of Loncalaz, your ruined reputation… You've been framed as the mastermind behind this toxin. I think I know by whom. But if they catch you with these geodes, nothing you say will save you."

Yashanee's skin rippled. Her petite humanoid form wavered. "This isn't about science, is it? Something big is going on."

"A faction inside the Consortium is behind this. They're tying up loose ends. You pose the biggest threat to their getting away with their grand scheme."

"But I'm not, not anymore, am I?" Yashanee's voice dropped octaves and grew in breadth as skin gave way to scales and mass multiplied. "You know. The Chimera reborn. You can stop them."

"Almost. I'm close, but I'm not there yet. I could use your help."

The dragon cranked her neck as her spine extended and her face elongated. "Dragons need joy to exist, and there is no joy coming from those geodes. Take them. Cure them if you can, if not set their souls free."

"Yashanee—"

"Go. Now," the dragon roared as the door to her quarters flew off its hinges.

Bix caught a glimpse of the dragon queen in the company of Sunan and a phalanx of armed guards as gates snapped open and shut.

CHAPTER 23

With the geodes of the CWIG agents and MWA soldiers keeping the company of those from the third lab, Bix turned her attention to the angels most likely to have prompted Yashanee's arrest. Something had changed. Something had spooked them. Something had happened within the last few hours to have caused the arrest to happen now.

The concrete-and-glass high-rises on the World hosting Kashdejan's lab jutted up like a trap of spikes keen to impale the unsuspecting visitor. An oppressive blanket of cerulean blue showed through the ether's filter, covering the city and the suburbs. Above the skyscraper of the angels' lab, pulses of bolder blues turned the blanket opaque.

That required a whole lot of magic from angels at a constant burn.

Bix's first impulse was to turn the World in on itself and watch it implode. Nothing she found as she examined the area argued for its continued existence. Too many people jammed into a cloned experience functioned like drones on conveyor belts. Sameness abounded from the architecture to the fashion. Why bother populating this place with soul-tethered life-forms when homogeny seemed the desired outcome?

The entire point of putting a soul into the Mids was for it to lead a rich life so it would play the songs that fed the dragons and angels, so it would expel the refined magic that fed the Fates, so that it would absorb experiences that would feed the gods.

If she'd been a superpower, she'd have asked for a refund for the soul that'd been stuck here. Of course, this was the lab led by angels, and those fuckers drank depression like cheap wine.

Quick, grab the mason jars.

Bix's examination of the angels' research facility began at the tip of the building's spire. It took time to sort the bursts of collaborative magic wielded by the scientists versus the hub maintaining the blanket over the city. Once she trained her gaze to discern the constant from the variables, she headed inside.

The internal structures of the skyscraper were clear. Walls. Tables. Floors. Elevators. Chairs. The optical illusion from the very top brought to mind Dante's pit of the damned, an endless spiral of increasing misery. Except she knew there was a bottom, and finding out what the hell they needed an army of angels to guard…well, her money was on a cache of Devourer blood.

The dark silver wisps seeping from the basement sort of gave that away.

Bix pressed down from the upper levels of the facility, scanning for the paler hints of pewter that would denote the not-Loncalaz geode and any samples of the toxin Sarina or Qiang might have smuggled from the third lab, but all the gray seemed restricted to the basement.

Whoa.

On the sixty-first floor, armed angels formed a barricade. Wings out and overlapping, they blocked a contingent of Consortium investigators. Researchers clustered on surrounding floors, trying to sneak peeks. Whatever work they were supposed to get done today wasn't going to happen.

A wee bit of a detour couldn't hurt, especially if the angels were flipping the Consortium the middle finger.

Just because she could, Bix passed through the walls of

investigators and angels. More than one feather-brain jerked their chin up, but none broke the line. At least they were alert enough to note the reaction from native magic her presence caused.

Farther into the maze of clear walls and sliding glass doors, angels dismantled furniture, equipment, and cameras. Refrigerators of samples were wheeled down the hall under heavy angel guard.

None of it gave off the wisp of gray, so Bix paid it little heed. She passed a pair of Chwed researchers weeping in the corridor under the black-eyed watch of another angel. Three angels in lab coats formed a semicircle around an angel in combat boots and cargo pants holding a tablet. Judging by the head bobs and shakes, it was an incident interview, but what incident?

It'd been four days since Sarina had blown up her condo and Qiang had impaled himself on lab equipment, so whatever this bit of housekeeping was about had to be new.

Bix passed through two more clusters of angels cataloguing every binder and hard drive. A faint hint of gray, barely more than a speckle of dust in the sepia tone, drew her farther into the lab.

She drew up sharply.

Biker boots. Dark denim. Round butt. Snug Henley. Ridiculously broad shoulders. Blond man bun. Even with clothes on, that backside was recognizable.

Anger spiked.

Tobek. Cured and in public. *He* was the catalyst. Gah. Guess he couldn't resist answering the summons of the honey-haired angel at his side. They bent over whatever gave off the smudge of gray, heads touching.

Kashdejan placed a hand on Tobek's shoulder, lightly stroking him. He made no effort to shrug her off. Bix made a heroic effort not to dump the angel into the ether. Instead, she moved closer to see what had been so urgent Tobek couldn't have kept a low profile. A glass ball. An empty glass ball. An empty glass ball that gave off a tinge of Devourer essence. The ball must have contained what remained of the geode Yashanee had swapped out. It'd taken the angels nearly a week to kill whoever that had been. Surprising.

Tobek's head snapped up. His eyes narrowed. He held up his hand, his natural hand.

Kashdejan stepped away and signaled her guards. All activity around them stopped. All eyes trained on Tobek's raised hand.

Pressure pushed against the layers separating the Worlds, firm, precise, and aimed squarely at Bix's chest. A pinprick of vivid green pierced the ether straight from Tobek's hand.

Son of a bitch.

She'd known he was powerful, even when she'd believed him a high warlock. His ability to pierce the ether with magic that bright confirmed Ashtad's suspicions—Tobek had to be a tethered demi on his way to surpassing a titan. Once this toxin issue was put to bed, she would figure out Tobek's pantheon and the House of Fate who'd woven that net.

In the meantime, he had to learn not to push against things that would absolutely push back. Peevishness unleashed her darkness. Tentacles speared through the gates and knocked Tobek across the room.

Kashdejan's face contorted, releasing what might have been a scream. Whirling shadows told of an alarm going off. Wings unfurled from angels' spines as chaos overtook the lab. Chweds hit the deck. Angel guards collided with angel scientists. Consortium investigators crouched with arms covering their heads.

The seed of malice inside Bix shook out another root.

Laughing with a hint of mania, Bix trailed the angels who took wing over the balcony of the sixty-first floor and plummeted down the atrium, into the thick of the telltale pewter wisps. Wide freight elevator doors opened to an empty shaft and in the angels went.

So did she.

The deeper underground they flew, the thicker the silvery gray. Thicker. Thicker.

Totally opaque.

She couldn't see a thing beyond the presence of powerful magic. Not exactly the best time to go blind. Still, needs must, so she opened a gate into the elevator shaft and crossed Worlds.

Bix counted five blips of the alarm's red lights before the angels flying down the empty shaft realized they weren't alone. Gates intercepted their hasty dive and moved them out of this World into random other Mid Worlds like pellets from a shotgun's blast.

Unlike the Chwedlonol races, angels—along with dragons—could travel between Mid Worlds with ease. They didn't even have to be an archangel or a royal dragon to do it. So, wherever she dropped them, it had to be someplace cloying, claustrophobic, and utterly disorienting in order to buy herself enough time to wrap up the recon.

Frankly, she'd prefer to toss them into the ether knowing they'd poof out of existence entirely, but these angels were just guards doing their jobs. They didn't deserve to die for it.

Yet.

A lot depended on how much Devourer blood Kashdejan was hiding down here in the bowels of her evil lair.

The elevator car parked at the bottom of the shaft zoomed closer. Bix loved a good free fall as much as the next adrenaline junky, but not so much the splattering on landing. She layered gates to slow her descent until her impractical pumps touched down gently atop the car. She tossed open the emergency hatch on the roof and jumped inside. A press on the Door Open button, and voilà.

The doors opened to a wide hallway. Not bright and shiny like the lab above. No, it was all dark, hammered, aged iron. The whirling red lights glowed like bloodstains along the dimly lit splintering corridors.

Might have been bloodstains for all she could discern. The howls, yowls, and keens riding under the din of the alarm's sirens certainly lent themselves to the horror-movie setting. All that was missing were a few dozen meat hooks and a whirring chain saw.

Without the ether acting as a filter to identify potent magic, she had to rely on the common five senses and a thorough boots-on-the-ground sweep. There had been a time when she'd had a team of fellow agents to scan and clear top-secret sites with her. Then angels had burned her teammates to ashes.

Still bitter. Very bitter.

A pair of hazmat suits scampered across a perpendicular hallway. Three angel guards turned down her corridor. Their startled expressions changed to indignation as they tumbled into gates. Time and again, she picked off roving patrols as she searched for the Devourers' blood cache.

The dueling wails of sirens and Chweds dulled to a drone in the back of her mind. The dark walls swallowed all shadows of movement. Strong antiseptics wafted on the forced air, overpowering any identifying smells. That left taste and touch as her guides. She wasn't keen to touch anything down here, and she sure as shit wasn't going to lick the walls.

Tracking her target meant tuning in to the sensation of native magic being displaced; therefore, wherever native magic offered the least resistance to her presence, she went.

Lessening pressures led Bix deeper into the dark labyrinth, passing by caverns lined with cages filled with upper-caste Chweds. The well-being of captive Chweds worsened by sector as she headed farther into the maze. White-coated researchers worked around their subjects, misery feeding off despair.

Now and again, she caught the eye of a scientist. They quickly looked away, heads low. They were as much prisoners of this World as the Chweds in the cages.

She hated angels. All of them. Feckless fearmongers.

Two more turns brought her before a squad of guards unwilling to abandon their position before a blackened double door. Angel fire leapt to their hands. They got off a few blasts before the gates closed over their heads, nipping the tips of their wings.

Sorry. Not sorry.

Guards holding their ground was the kind of behavior that said something interesting waited behind closed doors. The lack of native magic thrust gave her a good idea what it was.

The cache of Devourer blood. The evidence they'd intended to plant on Yashanee until Tobek had resurfaced and pushed up their timeline.

Dusting the singe off her sleeves, Bix planted a gate in the middle of the sealed doors and let it grow. Steel buckled and bent, twisting the doors off their hinges. Blasting it open would have been more satisfying, but shards tended to be tricky in populated areas.

This area was definitely populated.

A platoon of armed angels stood between her and a whirlwind. Not a cell. Not a cage. Not a wall. Not even a box. The angels were using a *tornado* to keep the cache secured.

One guard or a thousand, it didn't really matter to her. They were all relocated with the same ease. In a heartbeat, she stood alone with a screaming siren and a tornado separating her from the proof she needed to nail Kashdejan and her entire staff of angels.

The darkness inside her rippled.

"Stop!" demanded a melodious voice that made Bix's stomach heave.

"You're way too late, Kashdejan." Bix placed a gate in the wall of the wind.

"Please, Chimera, stop before you do irreparable harm," the angel pleaded.

"Kash, what are you hiding down here?" Tobek demanded over the din.

Kash? *Kash?* Oh, lookie what Berserker had an intimate history with an angel. Bix hadn't anticipated that one at all. And the angel hadn't told her lover what was down here? That made Bix even more eager to find out. She grew the gate until it made a pretty archway. Glaring white lights beat down upon a half-naked man prostrate upon the floor. Long black hair fell in tangled waves around a crown of silver horns, unruffled by the wind surrounding him. His skin was gunmetal gray and taut across well-formed muscles. Down his right side, tar-black scrollwork gleamed under the lights.

She didn't need an introduction to know exactly at what she was looking.

A Devourer.

It wasn't a cache of blood the angels had been hiding. It was the godsdamned source.

"Kashdejan, the evidence against you just keeps mounting, doesn't it?" Bix called out triumphantly.

The Devourer struggled to lift his head. Pale silver eyes, bright as polished titanium, fixed on her. Exhausted resignation faded, and loving relief transformed his vulpine features.

"Bixie, babe, I knew you'd find me."

CHAPTER 24

Bix stared at the Devourer. Her feet rooted to the spot. Only one person called her Bixie.

It might have been a Devourer's body, but there was a draugr inside it. A body thief and a soul reader. A minor minion in the arsenal of the Norse Pantheon. A consummate spy lost to the ether where Devourers had set up camps. Above and beyond all that, inside the body of the enemy was her best friend.

"Drew?" she whispered.

He smiled. Giggled. "I tried to take a god for a spin and ended up in one of these. Hella handsome, though, aren't I? You should see my package."

It wasn't the voice; that always varied by body. It was his choice of words, the dramatic inflections, and the blessed giggle.

"Drew," she whispered again, this time with confidence. She laced her fists and pressed them to her trembling lips. Tears welled, turning her vision hazy.

"Yeah, Bixie, it's me." He sniffled and held out a hand to her.

Bix took one step forward. A firm grip on her shoulder stopped her.

"I cannot allow you near it," Kashdejan asserted. "It has worn many disguises and spoken in many tongues. It has taken the shapes of fallen friends and innocent babes. It is not what it claims to be."

"Look at me, Bixie, look at what I can do." Drew bared long pointed teeth and released a gray plume of mist. When the cloud cleared, he appeared as a middle-aged white man with a potbelly and a mustard-stained shirt. He did it again and took the shape of an older Asian woman in hospital scrubs. He did it again and took on Kashdejan's shape. Five more times he did it. Five more times he assumed the looks of people Bix recognized from their history together.

"You see what I mean?" Kashdejan hissed. "It is toying with you, with all of us."

Drew reverted to the body of gunmetal and horns, panting. Base shape. Original form. By the looks, shifting was difficult, but he'd done it to deliver a coded message. They'd worked some heinous ops together, ops that could have gone south quickly if either of them had misread the other's body language. The fact Drew changed bodies all the time spoke to just how well she could read him. His current attire of Devourer didn't change that.

She'd gotten his message. Loudly. Clearly. And wholly disappointingly when it came to Kashdejan. The angel had no idea what was really going on. She didn't even know Drew's relevance to the cootie case. His appearance here was the very setup Bix had feared the angels were endeavoring to apply to Yashanee. For whatever reason, the faction had felt it necessary to frame Kashdejan too.

That begged the question: what did the angel know that threatened the faction?

Bix slowly turned her head and met the black eyes of said angel. Her peripheral vision tracked Tobek standing to the side, stance wide, arms crossed. His blue eyes glowed, but not at a full raging blaze. His attention shifted from the angel to the Devourer. He said nothing. Did nothing.

Mission-level trust. Bix had to remind herself that whatever his reason for being here, he'd earned mission-level trust. But if he pulled another stunt like he'd done upstairs, he'd find himself dumped in the Under Worlds without a taxi home.

Bix dropped her gaze to Kashdejan's hand upon her shoulder, then up to the angel's small sneer, flared nostrils, and unblinking regard. "The only reason you are not vivisected and scattered across the ether is because I know precisely how long the draugr inside that Devourer has been missing from the Mids. It is far short of the five years that scientists from the two Consortium labs have been laboring—under duress—on weaponizing Devourer blood."

Kashdejan gasped and stiffened. "You lie. Every word from your accursed lips is a lie."

"One of your scientists came to you years ago and asked for your help, for your intervention, and for your protection. You dismissed her as weak, delusional, and inferior." Bix faced Kashdejan fully and smiled without warmth. "Instead of looking into her claims, you sent her for a psych eval."

"Sarina lost her mind due to the pressures of her job. Yes, I should have terminated her instead of sending her for her treatment. My mistake," the angel hissed. "But how dare you hold that up as definitive proof of my participation in some elaborate conspiracy?"

"How dare you be so stupid as to believe your whirlwind is effectively containing the *peer of a god*?" Bix maintained her smile and her quiet tone even as the darkness slithered from her spine and headed for the shadows. "The only reason anyone in this building is still alive is because the draugr inside that Devourer is forcing it to heel."

"Sing it, girlfriend," Drew trilled, obviously equipped with the hearing of a godlike entity. "This asshole does not like having me onboard. Keeps trying to evict me. More insistent than that slumlord at my last condo in Adams Morgan."

Kashdejan jerked away from Bix and turned to Tobek. "Back me up here. You know the Angelic Host wouldn't jeopardize the whole of the Mids to collude with an unknown entity."

"The Angelic Host isn't under suspicion. However, the

evidence against you—personally—is staggering, Kash." Tobek flexed his prosthetic hand against his bicep. "Your employees. Your tainted lab equipment. Your possession of the unique source of the toxin. She's trying to give you the benefit of the doubt. Anything less than immediate and complete cooperation compounds your guilt."

"My g-guilt?" Kashdejan sputtered. "I asked you here to tell you the geode in my lab was actually an MWA soldier, not Yashanee's elven flunky, and this is how you show your gratitude? There was a time you at least *tried* to balance your responsibilities to the Mids against your obsession with the Chimera. Now you've become its lapdog? I'm sure your peers in MWA will find this change of fealty incredibly enlightening."

Bix made a mental note for the painful tête-à-tête she and Tobek were going to revisit. she and Tobek were going to revisit. Especially if he was hooking up with angels, who, as a race, loved to torture him. However, it was a teeny bit reassuring that his reason for being here was in his capacity as a Berserker commander duty bound to follow up on the welfare of one of his men. He wouldn't have sent Xipil in his stead, not if he feared his second in command could've been infected by whatever was afoot here. Bix could forgive him for putting his men's best interests before his own. He might stab her in the chest, but he wouldn't do it to his men.

"Jealously and pride are blinding you to the larger picture." Tobek uncrossed his arms and straightened. "I am uncertain what you thought you'd gain by keeping your prisoner a secret. I'm also uncertain of how you came into possession of him. Regardless, she is going to move the Devourer to a secure location. You and I are going to have a nice long chat about who is intent on framing you."

"Framing me?" Kashdejan pivoted repeatedly between Bix and Tobek. "You said I was guilty of the conspiracy."

"He said the *evidence* makes you look guilty," Bix corrected, massaging her throbbing temple as she pushed and pulled intel from the pool of darkness. "Someone placed you squarely in my path. It's no secret that I despise your entire race. My bet is that they hoped I would annihilate every life-form on this World for the transgressions committed against my very dear friend here; thus, allowing you—postdeath—to absorb all the blame while the true culprits continued their work."

"Benefit of the doubt, Kash," Tobek repeated. "You didn't stop to question why she didn't kill your guards today or even harm them. She merely distracted them. You let your bias corrupt your conclusions."

"But-but that Devourer is a threat to our very existence," Kashdejan argued, gasping as she continued to bounce her attention between Bix and Tobek.

"So why is he here?" Bix recalled her darkness from the shadows and rolled her shoulders as it resettled beneath her skin. "If he's such a danger, why did someone bring him to you instead of the archangels, the royal dragons, or—better still—the gods? Why, when you've yet to link the organic source in the syringes the MWA handed over to you to the blood of your basement prisoner, did someone want you to have him?"

"That's the organic base? That thing?" Kashdejan groaned. "That rodent. He played to my ego, and I embraced all of it without a second thought. I am a fool who helped frame myself for the sake of vanity. I wanted to be known for discovering a new Other World race."

"The Fate Sunan," Bix said more than asked. "He convinced you to take the Devourer, thus making sure you appeared guilty to investigators when they inevitably came knocking."

"First contact research, he said." Kashdejan nodded. "I have the better facility. I have the better teams. I have the better resources. All the respect…Sunan went to small yet great lengths to set me against Yashanee. And he succeeded."

The hairs on Bix's nape tingled. "*You're* the reason they've arrested her?"

"Yes. Right after I contacted Tobek, I reported her to the

oversight committee for leading the unsanctioned development of organic bioweapons." Kashdejan laid her fingers against her cheek. "She swapped the geodes, proving she had foreknowledge and multiple samples. What else was I to think?"

Bix couldn't blame the angel for Yashanee's mistakes. No, this was all on Sunan and his cronies. They'd gone after second-tier influencers within the Dragon Horde and the Angelic Host. They didn't target the dragon queens or the archangels directly; they were using family and lieutenants to weaken the highest ranks. Similarly, they weren't going after the leadership of the MWA or the CWIG; they'd targeted the rank and file. Loncalaz had nailed Tobek to intentionally expose their research.

All right. This part was a game she knew, a game of puppeteering, of working behind the scenes to effect desired outcomes. This was the game of spies and mercs, of intelligence and counterintelligence. Shadow ops, strangely enough. Who better than a Shadow Caster to change the rules of the game?

That she could do with a little help from a new asset—the one angel with a vested interest in protecting her own ass from being hauled before the greater Consortium.

"There is a faction within the Consortium protecting the key players behind this toxin's development. Sunan is a member. They've framed Yashanee because she figured out what they were doing," Bix explained.

"And I just gave them exactly what they need to ensure she's executed at the end of her trial." Kashdejan threw her head back and glared at the ceiling. "I'll go to the Consortium chambers now and wait for them. Then Yashanee and I will formally accuse Sunan."

"If you do that, you make yourself look guiltier," Tobek cautioned. "There's a wealth of evidence against you, and now there is evidence against Yashanee. We have nothing concrete against Sunan."

"Of course you don't." Kashdejan sighed as her lids drifted shut. "Publicly, he's deferred everything about the toxin and this

Devourer to me. Privately, he never did anything more damning than have conversations—unrecorded conversations. The delivery of the Devourer was done with such secrecy that it can't be linked directly to him. I can't believe I was blind to the trap."

"Hubris isn't only for humans," Tobek drawled.

"Why did they come for you now?" Bix asked the angel. "What did you do that was unusual shortly before Sunan approached you about the Devourer?"

Kashdejan chuckled sadly. "I was at a recruitment fair when I was accosted by a collective of concerned family members. It seems I'd hired some of their loved ones, and one by one, they'd fallen out of contact. The families gave me a list of names and pictures."

"You didn't recognize any of them," Bix guessed, knowing now how Sunan had staffed the third lab.

"No." Kashdejan shook her head. "I personally interview every employee of this lab. I'd never heard of any of them, so I made a few inquiries. Within a week, Sunan brought me this new specimen they'd captured coming through one of the rips in the protective layers surrounding the Primary Mid World."

"Could at least have given me a couch and a book, you know," Drew groused from his idle sprawl.

Bix smirked at his pique. "What are the chances those missing Chwed scientists made up the second-best R&D team for a new toxin?"

"There were enough people to make many teams many times over." Kashdejan placed both hands against her cheeks and closed her eyes. "I don't know how to undo this. I think I need your help, Chimera."

The resignation and reluctance imbuing those last words would thrill any asset handler. Bix let the request hang there unanswered for a few heartbeats. Antici…pation.

"Okay," Bix said at length. "We'll figure it out, but it isn't going to be a one-and-done. You get that, right? This is the Consortium we're dealing with."

Kashdejan winced but nodded. "I understand."

"You'll be expected to testify at Yashanee's trial," Bix began.

"I can't lie. They'll know," the angel interjected.

"I don't want you to lie. It'll only make you look complicit. All I want you to do is tell me when they read her sentence."

Kashdejan opened her eyes. "It'll be too late by then. There is no delay between sentencing and it being carried out. Yashanee's chances of being found innocent are slim."

"For now, that notification is all I need from you," Bix insisted calmly.

"A trial of this importance will take a few days for the prosecution and the defense to present their cases before judgment is issued." The angel stepped away and rolled her shoulders. Golden wings unfolded from her spine. She plucked a feather and handed it to Bix. "We'll keep it simple. If this turns green, Yashanee is innocent and will be freed. If this turns red, she's guilty and will be dead within moments."

The power contained in that one feather prickled over Bix's skin and raised the hairs on her nape. "Thank you. Now, I'm going to take your prisoner and leave you and Tobek to do whatever you two do."

Tobek raised his brows. "Kash, I need to debrief you on the details of the Devourer acquisition and those missing scientists. We can do it at Grimtebel."

The angel's shoulders slumped, yet she nodded as she tucked her wings once more beneath her flesh. "Thank you, Chimera, for not believing the worst of me. It must have been difficult for you."

"An archangel once told me that when the times to defend the Mids arise, we all have to set aside the crap that's built up in the off years and do our duty. He might have been right. We'll see." Bix sent the feather to her bolt-hole on Jotunheim and Yashanee's list of fifty-five CWIG and MWA agents to the keyboard of Ashtad's computer. Hopefully, her old spymaster would get the message.

Where she and Drew were headed, neither the list nor the feather would survive.

CHAPTER 25

Around table and four armchairs awaited Bix and Drew in the temple of Irkalla. Drew clutched Bix's hand, then convulsed and gasped, snatching his hand back.

"Damn, Bixie," her bestie whimpered. "We more than don't like you. I think we're allergic to you."

Bix held her hand a hair's breadth from Drew's shoulder, learning the way the Devourer's innate magic reacted to her. Where the small sample of blood in the geodes had recoiled like a twitch, Drew physically moved. As in full body retreat.

"It's like you're shoving me away," Drew cried with mock indignation, slapping his hand over his shoulder. "It's not a nausea thing. It's a GTFO thing."

"Due to one of the aspects you are subconsciously repressing, child," Ereshkigal said by way of greeting as she glided under an archway. "I regret the discomfort it causes your friend, but keeping you two close together is necessary to keep the Devourer weakened."

"Aw, Drew, you didn't tell me I make you weak in the knees," Bix teased, laughing as Drew batted his lashes at her as he sat. "Ereshkigal, did you tell Nergal what I was bringing?"

"He regrets that he cannot be here in person. However, he

is making progress in his efforts among his peers." The goddess took the seat across from Drew. "I am pleased you tapped the pool to reach me, child. Very pleased indeed."

Bix frowned. "If Nergal's not coming, who gets the fourth seat?"

A blast of frigid air and the clicking of a hound's nails across the floor answered her question. The hound brushed past Bix, yet a second and far more potent presence lingered behind Bix. She turned and came nose to sternum with studded leather stretched tight across a small bosom. Looking up the plank-straight white hair, Bix met frosty pale irises and blood-red pupils. The goddess had gotten her impressive height from her mother, a giantess. Dad was a chaos god, which meant this particular goddess knew every trick in the book and did not find that shit funny.

Hel.

Goddess of the Norse Under World and current ruler of the entire Norse pantheon. Also the woman who'd arranged for Bix's early parole after enforcing her exile. They had a complicated relationship.

"Hello, creature," Hel purred, tracing her finger over Bix's bottom lip. Sparks of divine energy leapt from her touch, taunting Bix's appetite. "Keeping busy since last I saw you, eh?"

"You said I had to rise to the occasion." Bix eyed Hel, then Ereshkigal. "Can't say I expected you two in any kind of partnership."

"Well, that makes you the fool, then, doesn't it?" Hel flopped down in the fourth chair and kicked her legs over the armrest. "We're queens of our respective Under Worlds. We're into casserole exchanges, block parties, book clubs, you know, all the usual neighborly things."

"I invited Hel because of how the Devourer was captured," Ereshkigal explained. "It was information new to me. Information I did not have in the last war against our old foes."

Hel sat upright and thumped her boots on the floor. She dragged her chair closer to Drew, so close that her breath moved his tangled hair. Drew whimpered through clenched lips and leaned away from the goddess.

"Anudrengr, you sly little minx." Hel crossed her arms on his chair's armrest. "I'd wondered where you'd scurried off to."

"Sort of hoping you'd forgotten me, goddess," he whispered.

"Forgotten you? Forgotten you? You were my very first creation way back when I was a little ankle biter. How could I ever have forgotten you?" Hel propped her chin on her palm.

Bix gawped. Sure, she'd known Drew was old. She knew Anudrengr was a name he despised. She'd always known he was a draugr. Draugrs, as a category of minion, were way, way down the food chain. Half step below soul compacter. Bix didn't care about caste or rank or any of that. She cared about the individual. She cared about Drew himself. But he didn't talk about his ancient past, and she couldn't talk about hers, so they'd agreed to a thirty-year window of reminiscing.

To learn that he was a creation of a child god who'd grown into one of the most powerful goddesses of modern times? Holy shit. Children of gods couldn't make diddly-squat until they embarked on their demigod trials. Hel *shouldn't* have been able to create anything as a child.

But she had. Drew was it.

"You've created countless minions since then, my goddess. Surely they are dearer?" Drew kept his attention on the large dog sitting on his foot.

Hel's hound licked its big maw. Its red gaze never wavered from Drew.

"Some, true." Hel raked her nails down Drew's arm, drawing tarry blood. "I don't like the fashion choice. Have to admit."

"Happy to remove it, if you'll tell me where you'd like me to slough it off." He closed his eyes and screamed from behind sealed lips as Hel scored him again.

"Stop it," Bix snapped.

Hel arched a white brow. "Watch it, creature. Ereshkigal may have infinite patience with your shenanigans. I do not."

"I should like to hear from your creation how it is able to control the Devourer," Ereshkigal said, taking Bix's hand and giving her an indulgent smile.

"Getting in wasn't hard," Drew rushed to say. "He let me. It was a simple negotiation. I told him I could show him where to access the Mids in exchange for a ride inside. He wasn't keen to let me lead, but, much like a boy at a middle school dance, he finally surrendered to my insistent redirections."

Bix snorted. She'd danced with him often. Sometimes he wore the body of a guy and he led; sometimes he wore a girl and Bix led. Once, he'd worn a bear. He'd definitely taken the lead that time.

"And he's left you in charge the whole time?" Ereshkigal asked incredulously.

"Oh no, no no." Drew waved his hands in negation. "The moment we touched our big, clumsy feet on terra firma created by Mids' magic, he lost it. That's given me the upper hand since."

"Lost what?" Ereshkigal prompted.

"He got sick," Hel translated. "Too much Mids' magic all at once, eh? Overdose, did you?"

"That's putting it mildly." Drew placed a hand on his scarred abs. "However, he's still capable of quite a few impressive feats, including shapeshifting. Markings on his side are his name, rank, specialty, and troop insignia. They also serve as a locator beacon for the other members of my squad."

"Not unlike the angels with their choir markings, then," Bix mused aloud, pondering the logistics of moving, housing, feeding a foreign force, even a small one. "As a godlike entity, can you hop Worlds at will?"

He shook his head. "The protective barriers continue to pose a problem. Once I'm in, I'm trapped until I find another hole in the barrier to get to the ether or a gateway between Worlds. I can shapeshift well enough to fool the scans at the public portals."

"That's something I'll put to the Consortium," Hel noted. "Modifying the scans is resource intensive, but we should be able to justify it under health and welfare."

"Why not call it what it is? A security measure." Bix fought a sneer. Nothing was straightforward when dealing with divinity.

"Public paranoia, mass hysteria, and capitalist opportunists." Hel shrugged. "Anything under security encounters more resistance within the Consortium and local governments. Sell it as a health benefit, and only the angels bitch."

"Speaking of angels, Drew, how did Sunan get you to the angels' lab?" Bix hoped the answer contained something about netting that could bind a god's peer.

"Sunan's in deep with the Devourers," he spat. "I mentioned I'm trackable, right? By my troop? They found me pretty quickly once I entered the Mids. Our orders are to establish footholds here. Sunan is our guy inside. We change our appearance to look like Consortium guards, following the old Fate around like dutiful goons, gathering intel and identifying other places for our peers to infiltrate."

"Fucking Fates," Hel muttered. "Never should have given them their independence."

"Consortium guards," Bix blurted. "Timai had said a group of Consortium guards arrived before the MWA raised the alarm."

"That'd be the day Sunan left me at the lab. He screwed up when he injected your old buddy Loncalaz the elf. Loncalaz got away before we could catch him. Sunan was already nervous about Kashdejan asking questions about the Chwed scientists he'd abducted, and Loncalaz's escape made him desperate. He demanded a volunteer from the Devourers to frame her. I made sure I was chosen." Drew smiled at Bix. "I knew if I could get to the angels, you'd find me, Bixie. I knew you'd give me a clean out. Can't exactly let this suit rejoin his troop and blab about me."

"Sorry it took me so long." Bix reached for him but stopped herself as he twitched. "Hel, is this enough for the Consortium to convict Sunan?"

"And save your dragon friend?" Hel shook her head. "Anudrengr's affiliation with you invalidates his testimony. Besides, you could march every Devourer in his troop in front of the Consortium and ninety percent of the members will find a way to affix the blame to you. Or did you forget your last appearance before my esteemed colleagues?"

Bix's darkness rippled. Ereshkigal took Bix's hand in both of hers, calming.

"Anudrengr confirmed your weak link." Hel stared at Ereshkigal's hands. "Keep the pressure on Sunan. He's your key to the others."

Bix rolled her eyes. "The faction inside the Consortium is a poorly kept secret, isn't it? Do you know all the members or just some?"

"Not all. I have my suspicions. No proof." Hel rapped on the table and stood. "You know the game, creature. It's about evidence and presenting it to the powers the culprits truly fear. They don't fear their peers and until you fully regain your aspects, they aren't going to fear you."

Bix grimaced. "I'm working on it."

"Work faster," Hel demanded.

"If I may be bold?" Drew piped up. "The effects of my host consuming too much Mids' magic is wearing off. He's regaining his strength. I cannot survive inside him much longer. If there is someplace you want me to take us, now is the time."

"Hang on, I need one small thing." Hel rammed her hand into the Devourer's body. Drew screamed and writhed. His eyes rolled back in his head. Hel smiled and buried her arm up to her elbow inside the Devourer, fishing for something. All the crackling and popping sounded like rice cereal landing in a bowl of milk. Hel pulled free of the Devourer. Boils and pus blackened her arm. "Just as revolting as I remembered."

Bix fought the urge to grab Drew's hand. It wouldn't reassure him, only cause him more pain. "What did you do to him?"

"Well, I can't exactly make more if I don't know what makes Anudrengr special." Hel shook her arm, and the damage repaired itself.

"*Can* you make more like him?" Ereshkigal inquired.

"Exactly like him? No." Hel smirked. "I'll shoot for close enough, though. Creature, when you find the Devourer's friends, make sure you send me one. Throw it in a conference room in Helheim. I'll take it from there."

"Thank you for coming, Hel." Ereshkigal stood. Fine filaments of darkness flowed from her.

Hel's hound yelped and bolted.

"It's been fun, ladies. Until the next book club."

With that parting salvo, Hel and her hound vanished.

Bix waited until she was sure Hel had left the building before turning to Drew. "Drew, is it safe to assume your troop of Devourers is not bunking down with the other Consortium goons?"

He nodded. "They're hiding on a World with minimal Mids' magic, holed up in some high-tech production facility as masters of their new domain. We're talking at least a city block in size."

"Is that where you got your injuries?" She gestured to his scabbed abs.

"It's like reliving the Spartan agōgē, the original one, minus the singing and man-cuddles. It's all sadistic military drills all the time. They don't stop training when they draw blood, they keep going until they blackout. Their blood runs into drains that are kept remarkably sterile."

"Do they even know they're supplying the base for the toxin?" Bix said with disgust.

"In their opinion, Sunan might as well be collecting their pee. These guys bleed for the fun of it. Total dick wag."

"How many are there?"

"I make lucky thirteen." He held up a quieting hand. "And before you say it, this ain't my first recon rodeo. Leave me with one of the artists from Dysmorphic, and we'll get you an accurate enough picture of the location for a drop-in visit."

Bix opened her arms to hug her bestie. Drew danced away from her and wagged a finger. Chastised, she turned to the goddess watching them with rapt fascination.

"Ereshkigal, I know Nergal is banned from the Mids, but do you think it's too soon to request help from his peers who still have privileges there?" Bix bit her lip, not sure how the goddess would take it. Nergal had said only gods could take on Devourers, and she was inclined to believe him. In order to put an end to the toxin, she had to put an end to the source.

"He would be insulted if you faced Devourers without him, regardless of location. Twice so if you are going to the facility where they make this toxin and think to deprive him of information he might find useful." Ereshkigal reached inside her robes of darkness and retrieved a very familiar music box. "Turn the crank when you arrive at the site, then get out of the way. You are not yet strong enough to survive a clash of deities."

Bix took the music box from the fire gate of Irkalla. "I understand. Thank you."

"Now, I must take your prize before it smothers your friend." Ereshkigal unleashed her darkness.

"Please, don't hurt him," Bix begged.

"Oh child, these bonds you forge. I do not know whether to be happy for your current joy or sad for the pain I know will come." The goddess covered Drew in darkness. He screamed again and again. His tone adopted a bestial howl.

Bix stood there, transfixed, torn between her fear of interfering in something she didn't understand and trying to stop her friend's pain. Drew's howl escalated to braying as Ereshkigal peeled away the body of the Devourer from the draugr. Plumes of gray smoke attempted to elude the goddess's darkness, but she allowed none of it to escape.

Phobos had hinted at the unknown depths of the goddess's power, but there were no accurate words to describe the swiftness and surety with which Ereshkigal dissolved another godlike entity. She was more potent than sulfuric acid on whipped cream.

"Visit me again soon, child," Ereshkigal whispered as she and her prisoner blended into the shadows. The darkness departed the temple, leaving behind the glowing ice-blue crackling energy of a genderless being caught somewhere between wolf and giant. It shielded its face and turned away from Bix.

"Drew?" She'd never seen her BFF without a borrowed body. The Under Worlds were the only places he could be corporeal, and he didn't like coming down here.

"Don't look at me, please. I'm hideous. A figment of a tormented child's imagination brought to life." His voice was low, and his words seemed to struggle up from his throat, like a vinyl record played at the wrong speed.

"Oh, you great big dork, you don't know how much I've missed you." Bix wrapped him in a hug that would've broken bones if he'd had any. His body prickled against hers, his energy alive and raw. It held only a hint of that primordial essence that made a god…edible.

"Bixie, please, I can't take your pity."

"Pity happened when you went undercover as a blobfish on that selkie-versus-kelpie mission." Bix tucked her head under his malformed chin and held him tighter. "Then you had to sing through that mound of gelatinous oog."

"I sprayed sea snot everywhere." He laughed over a sob. "Oh my gods, it was pop-star meat suits for weeks after that before I could bear look in the mirror."

"What say we go find you a dead pop star to take for a spin?"

He snuffled and nodded. "I want to be a petite and delicate flower."

"K-pop singer it is."

CHAPTER 26

Bix ascended the stairs to the second floor of the Woolly Barrel with a petite brunette wearing a blinged-out cat-ears headset, PVC short-shorts, and a triple-wrapped scarf that hid strangulation marks. While Drew could exist in a living body like the Devourer's, the draugr preferred the recently deceased. No fighting with a soul for dominance, no leaving a taint on the soul that the gods could taste. Drew's essence delayed decay long enough to have mostly harmless fun.

"Bixie," Drew giggled. "You are causing some serious whispers. No more undercover work for you."

"Right? The infamous Chimera is famous. Thanks to the Consortium and the CWIG, everyone knows the face that goes with the name now." Bix smiled as a big tie-dyed cousin of the Yeti cleared out a cozy circular booth in a delightfully secluded section. His hairy mitt held open the dark lace drapes. A small tray of shiny metal rings awaited her at her table. Drew picked up a handful as she slid into the booth.

"And they bring you toys unprompted? Me likey." Drew scooched closer to Bix until their thighs touched, whispering, "Not that I will ever object to hanging out in swanky one-percenter clubs with you, but, um, I thought we were headed to Dysmorphic

221

to ask a beefcake to draw us a picture."

Bix turned the flat of her forearm up and spoke to the bug in her smartwatch. "Display last incoming message."

Last message from Herr Schmidt: ____

"It's blank," Drew mumbled.

"It's not the contents, it's the sender. Herr Schmidt means there's trouble on the home front." Bix scanned their surrounds, staring down those who stared too long and relocating those who didn't take the hint. It was weird to do. She'd been trained to use attention as a tool, something she could take in and out of her bag of tricks. These days, though, she needed to learn how to be inconspicuous while being conspicuous. Different tool altogether, probably a different bag even. "While you were trying on new suits, I grabbed my comm and tried to get a sitrep. I've been cut off from Tobek and the coal plant. Same for Cian and Grimtebel."

"Did Chief lock you out of the house?" Drew held her hand and pasted on an adoring expression. "Can he?"

"No." Bix slid one of the rings on Drew's finger, playing to the part. "But just because I *can* burst in doesn't mean I *should*, right?"

"So if they've gone radio silent, who are we meeting?"

"An artist Ashtad knows." Bix didn't like the setup, but keeping a god waiting to run riot was never good and with Sunan on the defensive plus the time lost in Irkalla, she had to roll with the circumstances. Adapt and innovate to complete the mission.

"Good, then we have a minute to discuss an elephant."

Bix gave Drew the side-eye. "If you want to antagonize poachers, I will take you after we wrap this up."

"What? No." Drew bumped her shoulder. "I mean the *figurative* elephant. The literal one we should totally schedule for the spring."

Bix managed a half smile.

"I feel the hesitation you have, that you've never had around me before," Drew murmured. "Out with it before we have a rift that kills me."

"I looked for you every day," Bix confessed. "I hunted the ether as best I could, because I didn't want you to spend one more second out there. I'm so sorry I couldn't find you."

Drew leaned away from her. "You ninny. Of course you looked for me. I never doubted you would, despite me telling you *I* would find *you*. We both know the ether is not conducive to hide-and-seek. I grabbed the closest suit and came in from the cold, just like a good little agent would."

Bix gnawed her lip. "Are you really okay, Drew?'

"No," the draugr squawked. "You're avoiding the elephant because you don't want me to feel bad. Shame on you. We've haven't become a dynamic duo by stowing our baggage. Let the bitch flag fly. I'm not that fragile, and neither are you."

Bix struggled with a surfeit of emotions, unsure of which one to choose or which one should win. Which one did she have the right to feel? The seed of malice within her had many opinions, but those she tamped down. This was Drew. *Drew.*

"Say it, Bixie," Drew cajoled. "Whatever it is can't be worse than what I imagined while I was stuck in the ether."

"All the long-lived and immortals know who I was and who I am. My situation is not that different from a husked god reentering the game, I get that. However, they have family, friends, and a pantheon wanting to fill them in on the details of the lives they left. I don't, and I don't understand the widespread secrecy." Bix paused and bit her lip as tears filled her vision. This was harder than she'd thought it'd be. Drew was her best friend, yet she had to *ask* when Drew should have told her. Why did the people she wanted close to her not tell her the simplest of truths? Spoken truths were the demonstration of integrity and respect, which were the cornerstone of healthy relationships. It shouldn't have been hard. Wasn't the friendship she offered good enough to merit simple truths? "I don't understand why you—my best friend in all the Worlds—didn't tell me I was the Chimera. It was a pretty big secret to keep from me."

"Yes, it was." Drew nodded rapidly. "But I don't regret keeping it."

Bix stared at the ceiling as a tear fell.

"Oh, Bixie, you are trying so hard to figure out how and where you fit with a heart so big and nature so loyal. I am beyond honored to be with you on this leg of your journey." Drew gripped Bix's thigh with both hands and angled to face her. "I didn't tell you because I didn't want you to focus on who you'd been while you're in the throes of becoming so much more. Better, by leaps and bounds."

"You mean you were afraid I'd turn into the monster I once was." Bix looked anywhere but at her bestie as her voice quavered.

"No, honey, no, no, no." Drew violently shook her head. "I knew the last Chimera mostly through other people. She rarely stepped out of her darkness. It was a shield that kept her isolated. I don't want that for you. I never want you to feel ungrounded, homeless, or friendless. I never want you to feel alone or abandoned. People are going to use you, they're going to take advantage of you, and they are going to do their damnedest to make you feel like crap every chance they get. Then they'll have the audacity to demand you do things you hate for the greater good. Neither of us can stop that. We can't control other people..."

Bix puffed through her tears and gave Drew the side-eye.

"Okay, technically I can control the meat suit," Drew amended with a small smile. "But, Bixie, babe, you are never alone. You have me, even when I'm bobbing for gods in the ether. Now and forever. I can't stop the bad things from happening, but I swear I will stand right beside you as the crap blasts us in the face. Knowing me, my mouth will be wide open too."

Bix laughed, the tumult of conflicting emotions dissipating. "Good thing your senses are muted."

"Right?" Drew gasped and flopped a hand over her chest. "Seriously, I don't get those coprophilia fetishists. There's a reason I prefer dead meat suits. The dead shit only once."

"Gah, the images," Bix groaned, wiping away her tears.

"You know you missed me." Drew leaned into Bix's side and looked up at her, fluttering her lashes.

"More than you think." Bix hugged her friend. A frisson made her stiffen.

"What is it?" Drew whispered.

"Our artist is here." Bix felt him before she saw him. The push and pull of his existence colliding with hers; otherwise, she wouldn't have recognized Tobek as he slid into the booth beside her, setting a black leather portfolio on the table and drawing the curtains.

All his glorious hair was under a long black knit cap. His beard had been dyed black and waxed into a sculptural piece. Colored contacts and tinted glasses hid his blue eyes. To top it all off, he wore a suit. Suit. Mind, he'd chosen a turtleneck instead of a tie to cover up all his ink, but... Suit. Tailored too.

A delicate ringed finger under her chin closed her mouth. "Need a bib, Bixie?"

Bix kicked her bestie under the table and marveled that Tobek's sleeves didn't burst at the seams as he reached across the table and took Drew's free hand in his, kissing the air above her knuckles.

"Welcome back, Anudrengr," he purred with a hint of an accent he rarely let slip. "She has missed you terribly."

"Oh, snookums, I know you missed me too." Drew blew him a kiss. "Loving the artsy, fartsy, darksy look."

"Never been one for trends." Tobek pushed the pile of rings and tray to the outer edge of the table and waved his hand over the top. Misty green magic cascaded over the little mound of metals. Seemingly satisfied, he threw one arm along the top of the bench seat. He stared at Bix for a few heartbeats. She met his unblinking regard and waited. Slowly, his wicked smile crept into place. "I've blocked the sound from traveling outside our circle. We can speak freely now."

"When Ashtad said he was sending an artist, I have to say I didn't expect you." Bix raked him over once more, silently cursing that indefinable "it" that existed between them. She was still peeved about his stunt in the angel's lab when he'd cut through the ether to attack her, so, no, she didn't return his smile. "No bolt of magic straight to my heart this time? Am I falling in your esteem?"

He winced. "All I felt was the disturbance. I assumed it was a Devourer. I had no idea it was you until you retaliated."

"Having now been in the room with a Devourer, can you tell the difference between us?" Bix asked. "Can you differentiate their poison from my presence? Or have I always been toxic to you?"

"Oh, dayum," Drew muttered, watching the two of them like a tennis match.

"Sweetheart..." He pressed his fingers into his chest, where the curse of silence was etched beneath his ink.

"You know what? Don't bother with an evasion." She held up a hand and shook her head. "I'll assume that because you are here, you continue to be onboard with our original mission. Are your guys okay?"

"You gave me three tasks last we conferred," he said coolly, still managing to evade a question. "The first was to make sure Cian was working on Udara's nanites. The good news is he found three caches in the house, each of a different style. Two of the power sources have been identified. The third is proving a challenge."

"That's huge," Bix conceded. "Finally, a break."

He reached for her hand, but she pulled it back. His eyes narrowed behind his glasses, but he inclined his head and withdrew his arm from the back of the bench. "The bad news is Sunan has seized Udara's home and all related research on the Grimtebel network in the name of the Consortium."

Bix sighed and massaged her temples. "There goes our chance at counterinfecting the nanites and stopping an aerosolized bioweapon."

"Don't forget, we unleashed a teenage Sage on this." He peered over the rim of his eyeglasses. "The kid has his copies of the research squirreled away. Only now, Sunan has a good chunk of it too."

"Sunan's scientists hit a wall with the nanites. Success rate is eleven percent," Drew piped in. "If Sunan thinks the kid can improve that rate, he'll take the kid."

"He tried," Tobek growled. "Went over my head. The MWA

was happy to give him custody of Cian. A Sage under the guidance of a Fate was deemed more appropriate than under the diverse protection of a battalion of soldiers. I disagreed, so Ba'al and the CWIG have him now."

"A-Ashtad has Cian?" Bix stammered. All the issues of the diplomatic pouch, the Red Web, Cian's mother being a traitor, the CWIG leak… Ashtad had found a way to get his interview. She sincerely hoped he remembered the dangers of pushing the wrong buttons with hormonal youths. Especially hormonal youths who could blow up a square mile of Washington, DC, in a fit of fuck you.

"Sunan is afraid of challenging the CWIG because he doesn't know how much Loncalaz communicated to HQ. The CWIG's big bosses in the Consortium are already demanding to take over Sunan's so-called investigation into the labs." Drew stroked the ears of her headset. "Ashtad pulling the kid under the CWIG's umbrella is not as bad as you're thinking, Bixie."

Drew knew all about the pouch, so if she wasn't worried, Bix would try to chill. Try.

"If anyone can help Cian with the nanites, it's Ashtad." Bix nodded, searching for a silver lining. "He knows the kid was infected and that there's no cure. He'll be on alert for crystallization on the off chance it happens."

"The second thing you requested was a review of the programmable-portal logs to identify the merc team who'd cleaned the third lab to frame the dragons." Tobek unzipped his portfolio. "You didn't mention there was a child left behind on that World."

"A chance, there was a *chance* a child was left behind." Bix hung her head. "She's tied up in some spell to track me, or tied to a superpower I couldn't detect."

"Xipil took a team. They did a twenty-mile sweep around the site of the Nabaziix surfacing. Ran thermal scans and ground-penetrating. No geodes, no girl. No signs of advanced life at all. If anything, it appears to be a breeding farm for Nabaziix."

"Nabaziix?" Drew echoed. "Since when have the Mids become home to god hunters?"

"Since the faction decided the creatures would make an excellent security system for their secret lab to keep the scientists in and the gods out." Bix slid to the edge of her seat. "Praise to Xipil for searching for the girl. That means you found the World, which means you found whose military was using the portals."

"That's why the coal plant is on lockdown and my men are tethered to base." Tobek pulled out his sketch pad and two pencils. "You were right. It was a military group."

There was a bite to his tone that raised her hackles. "Whose military, Tobek?"

He fisted both hands on his pad. "Mine."

Bix's heart stopped. "Berserkers?"

"Not Berserkers, another branch of the MWA." He forced his fingers to uncurl with visible effort. "The programmable portal they used is housed in another MWA facility. That I pulled their logs raised flags. That my queries were too on point has me heading in front of the MWA Tribunal in a few hours."

"Tobek, I am so, so sorry," Bix whispered, her mind reeling from the revelation. Yes, she was miffed at the man, but she'd never intended to set him at odds against his organization. She didn't have faith in any so-called justice system, and Sunan had warned her that he would make those around her pay for her interference. Sunan had succeeded with Yashanee, almost succeeded against Kashdejan, and now he was going after Tobek. Whatever the Fate had arranged, the repercussions of the MWA Tribunal could be staggering to Tobek and his men.

Shit. Shit. Shit.

"Where do they think you are right now?" Drew asked.

"Sequestered in my chambers at the Tribunal's compound. Holograms are inordinately useful." He spun a pencil and worked his jaw. "We can use this to find out what the hell the MWA is doing colluding with Devourers. This is hardly my first time on the receiving end of the inquisition. It'll be ugly and time-consuming, but I'll get what I'm after. Don't you worry."

"If you need to throw me under the bus, do it." Bix crossed her arms under her chest and sat back. "My reputation is already shot. It might even give me a useful boost in the criminal circles. There is nothing the MWA can do to me that the Consortium hasn't tried. I need you around for the bigger battle. You hear me?"

"Sweetheart, considering the trust issues you currently have with me, there is no way I am going to make them worse," he scoffed, looking pointedly at her posture.

"Yeah, but this time you could tell me what you did to screw me over." She slowly uncrossed her arms and put her hands in her lap. "Recent history not covered by the curse, true?"

Tobek pursed his lips and did not answer.

Drew's brows furrowed as her attention bounced between Bix and Tobek again. If Drew had known about the curse and hadn't told Bix… Bix didn't want to go there, not now.

"Chief, make sure the men and women you'll be addressing are, in fact, the persons they seem to be," Drew cautioned. "Devourers are shapeshifters. My last suit and I had a lot of fun being a Consortium guard."

"The list of soldiers," Bix blurted. "Yashanee gave me a list of soldiers whose remains Loncalaz had found. Sunan has been using his toxin to remove specific agents and soldiers. Loncalaz figured out his pattern. That is how the elf was able to collect so many."

"So many?" Tobek echoed, arching a dyed brow.

"You two work on the sketch of the manufacturing plant while I write down the names." She patted his portfolio. "Paper, please? I can't email them to you while your comms are being monitored."

Drew crawled across her lap to sit next to Tobek. Bix gave them space, texting with Ashtad while Drew relayed the location details of Sunan's Devourer squad. By the time she finished transcribing the list, the drawing was done.

"Will this work?" Tobek slid her his sketch, and she handed over the list of fallen soldiers.

The plant was a modern marvel of stainless steel and glass. The view was from a loft overlooking rows of round machines, square machines, tall machines, squat machines, and a network of tubes and gauges. Committing the details of the image to memory, Bix tested a gate at the destination. Five potential destinations vibrated in answer. "It's not unique enough yet. Try adding odd shadows, random stains, cracked panels, or rusting beams. Anything that gives me more detail."

"Best way to stymie a gatekeeper is to clone facilities. Seems they used a lab template from the Primary Mid World," Tobek ruminated. "That said, this is three times bigger than they should need."

"There's a, um, pile, about as tall as I currently am, in the corner, here," Drew murmured, her finger tapping the back corner of the loft.

"Okay, a pile of what?" Tobek held his pencil over the indicated spot.

"Limbs, torsos, partially eaten bodies." Drew looked a Bix and hung her head. "There will be spatter and streaks on the wall there from the Devourers chucking their unfinished meals. Sunan often freaked out about it compromising the sterile environs, but my squad insisted it stayed. It was a cultural thing with the Devourers."

Tobek scratched his cheek with the flat end of his pencil. "The Devourers eat people? I thought they absorbed native magic?"

"It's not osmosis, hunksome." Drew adjusted her scarf. "They live down to their name by actually consuming concentrated sources of native magic in whatever form that magic takes. Artifacts, plants, people."

There were a few races of Chweds who ate people, not many, but enough that Drew shouldn't have been reluctant to mention it. So why the shame?

"Whose bodies, Drew?" Bix gently prodded. "Who did you eat while you were in the Devourer's suit?"

"Remember how I said I brought my suit through a gateway I knew to be guarded by angels?" Drew tried for a half smile, but it read like a pained one.

Tobek swore under his breath.

"It wasn't touching down on terra firma that made your suit sick, was it?" Bix took Drew's hand in hers. "Your justified dislike of angels coupled with your suit's hunger made for an opportunity you couldn't resist. Am I right?"

"Turns out Devourers can only consume native magic commensurate to their own magical ability. My suit had minimal abilities. The angel guarding the rip in the layer was too much for us, it essentially put my Devourer in a diabetic coma. That's when I took full control of the suit. I would force it to overeat to maintain control." Drew slid her hand from Bix's. "Angels are way too potent, plus they regenerate, which created an unacceptable risk to my squad. So we leveled-down to upper-caste Chweds. Those proved too much too. That pile is proof of our failures. We eventually figured out higher-end mid-caste Chweds are on our level. Devourers eat the entire body, skin to bones since all of it is fashioned from native magic."

"And how many of your meals were MWA soldiers or CWIG agents?" Tobek struggled to keep his tone flat and set to updating his sketch.

"Berserkers aren't imbued with enough native magic to be worth the effort. Your guys wouldn't be eaten, but they would be killed for being a minor obstacle." Drew sniffed. "However, you, Chief, would be a prize-winning main course for a Devourer commander."

"And none of us can defend ourselves against these anti-gods," Tobek grumbled. "What about the souls? Do the Devourers eat those too?"

"No, no." Drew shook her head. "The spittle of a Devourer makes the threads of Fate tangible. They rip those free of the body, then weave a container for the soul."

"Sort of like the geodes," Bix noted.

"Just so." Drew nodded. "Devourers keep the souls purely to deprive the gods of that food source. Sunan took the ones from our squad. No idea what he did with them."

"How's this?" Tobek turned the updated facility sketch toward

Bix. Dismembered corpses and spattered walls marred the corner of the loft.

Bix wasn't squeamish. She'd seen a lot of death, but being eaten alive was not kind of thing she wished on anyone. She tested the destination gate again. One vibrated in answer.

"That'll do." Bix used gates to her bolt-hole in Jotunheim to swap her smartwatch for Nergal's music box. She squeezed Tobek's hand. "As always, thank you. Good luck with the Tribunal. If you need me…"

Tobek held fast to her hand and captured her gaze. His intensity caused his colored contacts to glow. "I don't like you doing this alone."

"She's not." Drew slapped Tobek's chest. "Hello. Sitting right here in thread-free disposable armor. Nothing will happen to me if I get pricked by Devourer cooties and this suit doesn't radiate enough native magic to be of interest to them. The same cannot be said for you."

"Be careful, sweetheart," Tobek rasped. "You're dealing with a very old Fate. Who knows what Sunan's anticipated and who he's going to throw into your path."

"I'll be fine." Bix grabbed the music box and Drew's hand. "I'm planting a beacon. The rest is up to the gods."

CHAPTER 27

Planting a beacon wasn't the only thing Bix intended to do at the manufacturing plant. Any idiot knew Devourers were not making the toxin themselves, and with the Chwed scientists having succumbed to their own creation, that left a different contingent of victims staffing the facility. Since the toxin fed on magic, she shouldn't have been surprised to see a hundred humans hard at work on the plant floor.

Paper masks, paper hair nets, paper gowns, and paper booties… At least Sunan had granted his captives the illusion of safety. On the other hand, he'd screwed the pooch by bringing them to a remote Mid World to ground the negligible infusion of Mids' magic. Without sufficient native magic, humans would expire at an accelerated rate. Their bodies simply couldn't withstand the hostile environment. On the third hand, at least they were safe from being eaten by Devourers since they didn't possess any magic to entice the anti-gods.

"We don't have long before my former kith feel your presence," Drew murmured. "If you want to save these people, it's now or never."

"Small problem." Bix pushed against the feeble native magic. The scamper of Devourer toxicity answered. "Your kith must have felt me opening the gates. They're masquerading as humans and are mixed among the folks before us. I can't batch relocate the humans without scooping up the enemy along with them. We're going to have clear the area one by one."

"Okay. I'll check for souls within the suits, you open the—
Move," Drew barked, bodily shoving her behind a huge stainless-steel kettle as a bolt of black zipped through the space where they'd just stood, rupturing a tank of tarry goo. "That's a batch of Devourer blood. Time to crank the box, Bixie."

"Why didn't the humans scream?" Bix listened to the odd silence around the hum of machinery. "What did the Devourers do to them?"

"Things, babe. Does that mean you don't want to save them? Not judging. Beacon and bolt is fine by me too."

Bix glowered at her bestie. "The gods aren't going to care about the humans. Mortals are disposable and acceptable collateral damage."

"Guess what? Devourers don't care about them either." Drew crab-walked to the edge of the vat racks and peered around the corner. "There are only two of us against a dozen anti-gods. Don't delay the reinforcements to play hero. Crank the damn box."

Bix twisted the crank on the music box three times.

Divine energy, a blend of Upper and Other Worlds, flooded the plant. Four gods of war braced the corners. Nergal in the south carried his mace. Athena in the north armed herself with spears. Ogun in the west had brought an iron machine gun from a sci-fi movie. Menhit in the east spun short swords. Gone were the trappings of their respective heydays. Second-skin body armor had replaced togas and headdresses. Flowing manes were slicked and contained. Only their god-forged weapons harkened back to the days of old. If they cared that they were outnumbered three to one, it didn't show.

Bix was less than thrilled to see Athena among their number. The Greek goddess had interrogated Bix in the cruelest ways possible while Hades had been helping Bix put marbles in her mind jar. The goddess of wisdom and war hadn't believed for one moment that Bix's memories had been wiped. Athena had been determined to prove it to Hades. Along the way, the goddess had inadvertently taught Bix a thing or twelve about mental torture.

As for Menhit, Bix didn't know her beyond the bio the CWIG had on her, but the Egyptian pantheon were members of the Bix-Be-Gone club. She'd learned that lesson on a rescue op when the package had refused to leave their captors if it'd meant going with her. After that, Bix had been sidelined on every mission that had remotely dealt with anything and anyone from the Egyptian pantheon.

That both goddesses had shown up with Nergal said he either hadn't told them she would be here, or Bix had to watch her back with those women.

At the moment, all four gods exuded sinister joy as strange words spilled from their lips, rhythmic and hypnotic. Inhuman cries tore from the pool of humans as four of the Devourers gave up their pretense and morphed into horned gray deities. Black balls oozing dark gray steam formed around their hands. The first volley flew at Menhit. The Egyptian goddess leaned aside, dodging the toxic mass. It collided with the tempered glass ceiling, shattering it.

Bix cast the music box into Irkalla and gripped Drew's shoulder. "How do you want to clear this?"

"Let's run this like a square dance with one small gate." Drew stood and pointed to the reflection of huddled humans in the neighboring rack. "I'll hook my partners. If they have a soul, I'll toss them through. If they don't, I'll call switch. Any Devourer will physically move away from you. If a human is dumb enough to do it, leave them here. We don't have time to chase people. Agreed?"

"On your go." Bix squeezed Drew's shoulder twice as she pondered a safe place to deposit humans who now knew about the reality beyond their insulated bubble. They needed medical attention and to be tested for potential infection by the Devourer toxin. Grimtebel was the logical choice, but it'd been compromised by Sunan and the faction. If she sent people there, the MWA might have orders to kill them or to hand them over to the Consortium. Either way, they'd be dead. She also couldn't send them to the authorized Consortium labs for the same reasons. She couldn't burden the guys at the coal plant, because they weren't equipped and already in deep shit.

This kind of stuff was so much easier when she'd had the CWIG's full support.

A second blast of Devourer magic was chased by three more. The World trembled. Humans dropped by twos and threes, victims of uncaring deities. Fractures enveloped the plant. Menhit and Nergal leapt into the fray with battle cries that broke more glass and sent chills down Bix's spine.

Drew darted to the nearest gaggle of humans with Bix at her heels. "Hi, hi. No time to make friends. It gets weirder from here. You're good. You too."

Bix opened a gate in the gap between her back and Drew's. The draugr slung humans from her side of the reel line through the gate. Hand to forearm, Bix gripped the surprisingly calm humans on her side and did the same. The roof continued to rain glass down upon them as gods and anti-gods waged war. Humans continued to fall in the name of collateral damage.

They'd cleared a third of the humans still standing when Drew jerked to a halt. A Devourer sailed overhead, close enough to ruffle hairs. He collided with a huge machine, warping steel, then slammed into the ground, leaving a crater. The deity regained his footing as though the impacts did nothing more than irritate him. He leapt into the air, unleashing a bolt at Athena.

Ogun's bullets caught him midflight. This time, when the Devourer hit the ground, he didn't get up. Tarry blood pooled around him, too thick to run.

Drew skirted the goo and headed toward another group of humans cowering in a circle.

"You noticing something about the people you're touching?" Bix yelled over the chaos.

"They're all women," Drew shouted. "I've spotted more than one prison neck tat."

"Now we know where Sunan went shopping for new employees." Bix reached for the nearest woman.

Magic recoiled. The woman bolted, her form changing as she flung actual humans in her path. Bix didn't hesitate. A special gate delivered the imposter to a conference room in Helheim, paying her debt to the Norse goddess. Bix couldn't save the human bodies deteriorating from the Devourer's deliberately noxious touch. She couldn't let it slow her down either, not if the few remaining humans were to have any chance at a life beyond this.

Locking down her emotions, Bix chased Drew around a large machine that'd supplied a conveyor belt. The belt was mangled and its contents strewn amid corpses. Bix grabbed a mostly undamaged box from the floor and ripped off its cardboard lid. At least a hundred loaded vials. Bix couldn't risk this getting into the wrong hands, and she couldn't assume the gods were going to do the right thing either.

That left her with one choice.

Drew laid her hand on Bix's. "If you destroy this World, the Consortium will come after you with everything they've got."

"If I don't, there's a chance a part of this—no matter how small—could survive the deities' brawl."

Steel beams crashed down around them as if mocking her assertion. The building groaned as its structure failed. The loft that had once housed the Devourers collapsed into the main floor, casting up thick clouds of debris.

"Bixie, I don't want to lose you to exile again," Drew pleaded, ducking behind her.

"That only worked because deep down I believed I deserved it." Bix held a hand up against the dust rushing toward them. Something moved under the platforms on which cooling units teetered. "The Consortium is going to have to decide who is the bigger threat, me or the Devourers."

"Over here," came a shouted whisper. "Please. Help us."

"Across the aisle." Bix pointed Drew to the last cluster of living humans, reassessing the millions of vials boxed and ready to distribute. The vials now tumbled across the floor, trapped under bodies and in cracks. Some were broken, too many others intact. She couldn't leave all this opportunity here. She couldn't, because she had capitalized on exactly this sort of abandoned disaster throughout her career. Get the vulnerable clear, then this place had to go. The gods would survive the blast, but so would the Devourers.

Fuck it.

Drew moved out, steps ahead of Bix. A Devourer seized the draugr by the throat.

"Trash of the Under Worlds," the Devourer seethed. "How dare you rise against—"

The Devourer gagged on its final words as tentacles of darkness pierced his body. A tentacle shot through his wrist, forcing him to release Drew. The Devourer fought against the shadowy spears; yet the more he writhed, the worse the damage he wrought upon himself.

Drew scrambled along the floor, over the corpses and the debris, her throat bubbling with toxic pustules from the Devourer's grip. "I know I look like hell, sweeties, but if you want out, you're going to have to give me your hands."

Three eager hands shot from the humans' hiding place. Drew took each one, then threw a thumbs-up over her shoulder.

Bix cut a gate beneath the four of them and snapped it shut before the tanks could follow. Drew was safe and the humans freed, what few she could. Now, she stood amid the melee of deities, hooked into divinity. Her laughter sounded off to her own ears as her darkness drank the poisonous essence of the Devourer. She expected it to taste like a garbage dump smelled, but there was no flavor to the primordial strength coasting through her. It wrapped her senses in silken batting and muted emotions until all that remained were base needs. Alas, this meager sample was not as robust as her customary meals; the potency compared to dining on a minor god. Yet, where a god's essence invigorated her, the Devourer's numbed. The difference was...curious.

"Chimera, behind you," Ogun boomed as he fired on two Devourers rushing at him.

Time slowed as Bix turned to face the new threat. A two-fisted bolt of toxin flew from the hands of a Devourer. Her darkness surged toward him, digging in for a fresh draught of cosmic Novocain.

Shiny metal shimmered out of the corner of her eye. A golden spear pierced her from the left as a short sword impaled her from the right.

Goddesses. Those bitches had picked the wrong prey.

Bix's body seized, but her mind registered no pain. Instinct reacted without the fetters of thought or fear. Her darkness sank into feminine power. The divinity of the goddesses collided with the divinity of the Devourers within the vessel of Bix's body, pushing her cells apart.

Spontaneous inhuman combustion.

Bix ensured the World exploded along with her.

CHAPTER 28

Sandalwood, black pepper, and musk, with a hint of gardenia. The heady masculine blend of aromas lured Bix into consciousness. Silk caressed her cheek and naked body. Soft furs cocooned her in warmth. The crackling of fire whispered in the distance. Water lapped nearby. Sublime decadence.

She made the mistake of moving. Hunger built with each stretch of her aching muscles. She raised her arms over her head, and her sides shouted in bruised anger. She pushed out with her senses, and native magic welcomed her. Not Mids' native. Other World native.

Confused, she opened one eye.

Burgundy tapestries covered the black lace enclosing an ornate zebrawood canopy bed. Engravings of demonic cherubs watched her with hollowed red eyes. Smoke traveled through a mirrored medallion at the highest point of the canopy; red eyes stared through the haze.

To the coddled, it might seem like a twisted hell; yet to anyone who'd been through a twisted hell, this was being coddled.

"Hiding from me, Phobos?" she purred, her voice husky and rough.

Engraved beasties lashed out forked tongues, drawing apart the curtains. Braziers glowed on the far side of a cobalt moat that lapped against the raised ebony dais on which the sprawling bed sat. Night stretched beyond the army of brass fire bowls.

"You were injured and needed rest," answered the disembodied voice of the god of fear. The shadows chittered and chirred.

"Is that all I've needed?" She slid her spine along the silk sheets as hunger rode her. "I'm clean. Did you eschew magic and dare to touch me yourself for once? Did you lay your big, strong hands upon my broken body, hmm?"

She blushed as the words slipped from her mouth, but deep within her, the sprout of malice had new roots and two new leaves. The roots twitched with the infusion of Devourer essence. Both leaves bore a goddess's name. Her whole body demanded a tribute and a feast for the transgressions of the divine.

She knew how to bait a man, a god.

"Phobos," she moaned, throwing one hand over her head as the other trailed over her body. "Did you cup my breasts as you poured water over them? Did you watch the streams as they trickled down my chest, pooled in my navel, then drenched my hair, my sex? Did you take your time with the lather? Did you stroke me? Caress me?"

The last word barely passed her lips when Phobos appeared beside the bed. His dark hair was mussed around his angular face. His eyes were hooded; his nostrils flared. His undone silk robe hung from his heavily scarred shoulders and dusted his loose lounge pants. He said nothing. Didn't need to. The rapid rise and fall of his chest gave him away.

"You did." She chuckled quietly, triumphantly. "How did I feel, Phobos? Was I soft in all the right places and firm in the others?"

The arteries in his neck bulged, and a muscle twitched in his jaw. "From whom did you feed?"

"You told me to find someone else," she taunted, rolling to her knees and allowing the covers to fall away. She slid her hands under the fall of her hair and lifted it, giving him an unobstructed view of her assets.

She was hungry, so very hungry.

His gaze held hers, but his chin went up and his hands fisted at his sides. Men. It didn't matter the race, they were all happy victims of seduction. It was why she enjoyed women more—they made her work hard for their permission to play.

"Damn you," he hissed as he hauled her up against him to take his kiss.

She took more than his firm lips on hers; her tongue swept into his mouth and drank his energy. He growled and slid one hand to her buttock, holding her firmly against his rigid sex. She pressed her belly against it, undulating as she fed.

He tore his mouth from hers and searched her gaze. The glow of his red pupils bled into his amber irises as his divinity rallied to replenish that which she'd drained from him.

"Where is it?" he demanded, hoarsely. "Where is your fear?"

"I don't fear you, Phobos." Bix nipped her way along his shoulder, consuming more of the fuel she craved. Her nails dug into his thighs, holding him in place. "I need you. Has it been so long you can't tell the difference?"

He tossed her in the center of the bed and snapped his fingers. Clothes materialized over her body, the corset a few cinches too tight and the skirt snug enough to force her knees together.

She let loose an indignant cry. "What the—?"

"Your fear has never been of me, but of your inability to protect yourself when your addictions overrule your logic." He crossed his arms and widened his stance. "In the past, all I had to do was respond with the slightest bit of interest in your touch and your fear would spike. Now, however, your fear is buried so deeply that it is barely perceptible no matter how far I push you. So again I ask, from whom did you feed? Whose essence did you consume that hid your fear from me?"

Bix rolled out of bed as gracefully as the super tight golden dress allowed. The stiletto heels he'd provided tangled in the lace drape. Cursing, she yanked her shoe free, satisfied by the ripping sound of the damn curtain.

"I'm waiting," Phobos prompted.

"And I'm hungry, so what's it matter?" she groused. In the corners of her brain still wiping away the cottony haze that had separated her regulatory ego from her impulsive id, she recognized her peevishness as being ridiculous, only slightly more ridiculous than throwing herself at him. Why *had* she done that? Thank the powers that be he'd rejected her. He was absolutely right about her fear. The very last thing she wanted to do was succumb to a cycle of addiction that had previously shackled her to an abuser. Screwing her food source was precisely how she'd gotten trapped in that wretched situation the first time.

Yet, when she'd awakened in Phobos's bed, she'd awakened with zero fucks to give about anything and anyone except her hunger. She couldn't recall being that singularly focused since she'd crawled out of the ether. She'd done many, many bad things in her quest for nourishment. Many. In no way could she afford a return to those bleak times.

"It matters because I felt your summons," Phobos answered with a hint of seethe. "If your other source of sustenance responds in the same way I do, then I shall have company the next time I am compelled to answer. Call it selfish if you will; however, I need to know whom to expect when I arrive."

"Oh, well, yes, yes, that's a fair question, then." She kept the bed between them, mostly because she didn't trust herself not to do something else spectacularly stupid while she mentally scrambled to understand what had gone wrong with her self-control. "I, um, I was at the plant with the Devourers and the gods of war…which included your buddy Athena, long may she suffer."

"She is," Phobos assured drolly. "While you rested, I paid her a visit to get her side of the story. You are no longer the helpless creature she once enjoyed tormenting. From what I was able to gather, she and Menhit attempted to husk you. You retaliated by stealing their weapons, then trapping them in the blast of the World exploding. Athena is currently recovering in the company of her priestesses, and Menhit with her pantheon."

"What about Nergal and Ogun? Are they okay?" Bix hadn't considered using a World as a cosmic grenade against divine entities. She filed away the notion on the chance things got worse with the Devourers.

As for whether the two gods who hadn't stabbed her in the back or anywhere else had escaped unscathed, she couldn't quite tell if Phobos's flat stare meant they were fine or not. Maybe he didn't know? Probably better to check with Ereshkigal once she escaped Phobos's scrutiny.

"Athena made no mention of you feeding from her," the god of fear said, drawing the conversation back to his original question. "Was it Menhit?"

Bix shook her head. "Devourers. Two of them."

He sucked in a sharp breath.

"It wasn't intentional," she rushed to say. "My darkness defended me. I think I tried to husk them. I have to say they didn't put up much of a fight."

"Did you kill them? The two from whom you fed? Did they die?"

"I-I don't know," she admitted.

"Two scouts, low-level entities whom you should have been able to eviscerate on a whim, even in your naïve state, and you *don't know* if you killed them?" He scratched his brow. "We're not ready for this. We're not ready to stand against their invasion. We had four gods who are experienced campaigners against the Devourers, and their individual egos wouldn't allow a swift and simple defeat of twelve scouts. What will we do when the Devourers bring the full might of their armies to bear against the Mids?"

It was a rhetorical question, she realized, one that drove home the bigger issue. It didn't matter if the Devourers were looking for something specific right now. Once they figured out they could overtake the Mids and feast on the native magic for centuries, there would be no stopping them. Worse, if the faction inside the Consortium kept up their collusion, they'd succeed in exposing the breadth of the Mids' vulnerabilities to the Devourers sooner than later, vulnerabilities the greater Consortium was incapable of patching. The gods were only the first layer of defense. It would take all the superpowers working together to turn back the Devourers permanently.

Things did not look good for the future of the Mids.

"The pantheons have grown complacent because we used you to fight our battles for us. Now, we will rot in the stew of our negligence just as the titans before us." He looked at her with a mix of disappointment and pity. It faded as his eyes narrowed.

In a blink, he was at her side, seizing her by the upper arms. He kissed her again, without warning or passion. Stunned, she jerked her head away.

"What is that about?" she cried.

He speared his hands into her hair and held her still. Again, he kissed her. Again, it lacked any hint of desire or kindness.

Two could play at that. She mimicked his loveless hold and used it to withdraw as much fuel from him as her hunger demanded. He pulled her along with him as he braced his back against the bedpost. When his body trembled, she leaned in to pin him to the carvings. When his hands slid to her shoulders to gently peel her away, she held fast.

Only when she was sated did she release him. He sank to the mattress, wan.

"Each time you turn creepy, I'll turn full Ziggy Piggy," she cautioned as the pangs of hunger finally dissipated. "Now, care to explain why *you* put the moves on *me*?"

"You're clearly regaining your senses, but your fear has yet to resurface," he whispered. His hand shook as he raked it through his hair. "If consuming Devourer essence repressed something deeply rooted in your psyche, we should investigate what other changes it made to you and how long those changes will last."

She huffed, ready to dismiss such an absurd notion, but stopped. She hadn't been herself when she'd awakened. His tangled sheets were testament to that. "As good an idea as that probably is, you don't know me well enough to know what's changed."

"Does anyone?" His question lacked his usual derision. It sounded earnest, which made the answer even more pitiful.

The answer was no. No one knew her that well. Not Drew. Not Ashtad. Not Tobek.

"I'll check with Nergal to see if any of the Devourers survived. I'll let you know if you have anything to worry about the next time you answer my call."

CHAPTER 29

U nable to go home to the coal plant, Bix headed to Jotunheim for her smartwatch and Kashdejan's feather. The latter remained gold. Yashanee's trial was still underway. Good. That gave her time to make arrangements.

The moment she affixed the clasp of her smartwatch, the screen burped to life.

42 messages from: Director, CWIG

Bix laughed. There were two means by which those messages had found their way to her: Ashtad or Cian. "Ignore messages. Reply with an image of the Ferris wheel at National Harbor, Maryland, Primary Mid World. Time stamp thirty minutes from now. Alert me five minutes before the meeting."

Message sent. Timer set.

"Scan restricted networks for any recent news of Tobek, his men, Cian, or Sunan. Search the last forty-eight hours."

Access to restricted networks limited due to present location. Schedule inquiry for later time?

"Yes. Run query when networks are available."

Bix hopped up on her pile of mattresses and held the feather between her hands. She took a deep breath and unleashed her darkness, directing it at the pitch black of the long tunnel leading down to her bolt-hole. When her darkness tapped the pool, she cast out for confirmation of the destroyed Mid World that had once housed the Devourers and their vanity toxin. Answers rolled to her in images and sounds of faceless witnesses to the grand explosion, of subsequent damage to the surrounding Worlds from the shock waves.

Of the retreat of Devourer troops advancing on that World through the ether.

She pushed for more answers, of the gods on-site, of their status. Of the total death count of their enemies.

Ereshkigal answered. Nine Devourers killed. Two captured. One escaped. Nergal sustained minor injuries. Ogun emerged unscathed. Athena and Menhit required assistance from their pantheons. They'd apparently forgotten the Chimera's darkness was limitless and her wrath instant.

Bix reveled in the affection fueling the rage of the goddess of Irkalla. She thanked Ereshkigal profusely and promised to be in touch again very soon.

Her watch vibrated.

Five-minute warning.

She tucked the feather into her bra and frowned as her fingers brushed card stock. Fishing, she pulled the business card Phobos had given her days ago. Devana's card. Odd. She'd left that on her bedside table at the coal plant. Whatever. She had Ereshkigal as a teacher now; she could disregard the referral. A thought spaced the card into one of the fire bowls in Phobos's bedroom.

If he'd wanted to remind her of the referral, he could've handed it to her again. He didn't need to stuff it in her lingerie.

Grabbing a coat from a stash spot, she opened gates to the Primary Mid World.

Bix strode down the concrete boardwalk separating the five-star hotel at National Harbor from the Potomac River in the Primary

Mid World. It was a sneeze away from the District proper and across the river from Tobek's coal plant. Chweds in glamours, Chweds with humanlike appearance, and humans mixed and milled together. Some were carefree, while others bent to labor. The biting late-autumn wind coming off the river kept quite a few folks wrapped in wools and leathers, scarves and gloves. Puffers and furry hoods abounded as she headed down the docks.

She was so pleased with herself for remembering a coat. The cold didn't bother her, but it was important to blend in when having a meet in a highly populated area. Yes, a silly detail in the greater scheme, yet it proved presence of mind. She hadn't left any marbles behind at Phobos's. She'd only left a smidgeon of her dignity. Alas, she was accustomed to that last part.

A large man in dove gray with salt amid his pepper hair turned as she approached the queue for the Ferris wheel. He extended an arm to her, ever the gentleman, at least in public.

"Retired linebacker suits you, Director," she cooed, taking his arm. "I don't think I've seen you use this glamour before."

"Useful when meeting with humans and their congressional committees." He handed their tickets to the attendant and helped her into the large glass gondola. He waited until their car was in the air before handing her a photograph.

A quaint yellow farmhouse with a wraparound porch and rocking chairs sat on an open plain. A few chickens in the foreground and a boney horse with a swayback stood off to the side.

"Cute," Bix said, wondering where and why. She tested a gate at the destination, and one vibrated in confirmation.

"You deposited thirty-two female convicts into HQ's clinic. Of those, eight were healthy enough to be released. After a complete debrief, we put them up at that house in southwestern Ohio."

Eight. Sunan had damned all but eight.

"Thank you," she said, meaning it. She'd taken a huge risk in entrusting those women to the CWIG. It was bittersweet that the guild to whom she'd once sworn allegiance—the guild who'd hung her out to dry—had stepped up. "What's happened to the others?"

"They're in a hospice run by Chweds. A nice little idyll on another Mid World that offers less strain on their degenerating bodies." He stuffed the photo in his inner coat pocket. "It's been ten years since HQ has been afflicted by random deliveries. Particularly those in need of medical assistance. Is this going to become a habit?"

"Your agents going to make it a habit of tagging me into their cases?"

He grunted and stared out over the whitecaps dancing along the river. "Do we have a body we can bury?"

He meant Loncalaz, Timai, and Hu Jian. He had the grace enough to care about that, which surprised her.

"I'm afraid not."

He scowled but nodded. "Our mutual friend sent me a list of names. Only twelve had reported in."

Bix cocked her head. Ashtad had sent him the list, which meant Ashtad had triple-checked the names. "Every name on that list was verified before being communicated. The twelve who reported in are not your people. You have been infiltrated by non-Chwed shapeshifters."

He stilled, then dusted his lapel. "DNA?"

"Not good enough." She knew the make and model of the scanners the CWIG used to identify the known classes of shifters. "You'll need to go shopping in the vault. God detectors. I do not recommend confronting them. If you want me to remove them, I am happy to do so. They'll be remanded to the custody of the pantheons."

He rubbed the corner of his mouth. "Do we know what they're after?"

"No. One or more needles in those haystacks, which is why you can't let up on the search for said needles. The names on that list are the key. Your man had figured out the pattern. That is what ultimately put him in the crosshairs," she said, referring to

Loncalaz. She laid her hand on the director's sleeve. "He did a hell of a job. You should be proud."

"Tell me you got them. The ones actually behind this." He finally looked at her. "We both know what a frame smells like."

She met his regard and tried to hide her surprise. Did he know she'd been set up? Did the man behind the position disbelieve his own guild's official report? Nah. Not him. Not possible. Their history wouldn't permit it.

"We both know politics will not allow the questions to be asked or answered that would ultimately prove the narrative faulty," she prevaricated with a fleeting smile. "The lab, the production facility, the low-hanging fruit, that's all been resolved."

"The immediate threat neutralized. Good. Good." He rocked his head from side to side. "Unfortunately, it's a symptom treated, not the root. That is buried too deeply for an extraction. We're into a long game. We'll stay vigilant. Enemies close and monitored until we know what they're after."

"You sure about keeping them in play? If any of the people they replaced have families, those innocents are in danger, not to mention their work teams." Bix understood the value of allowing the enemy to lead the CWIG to the prize, but risks had to be weighed. The director did that sort of thing daily, and he had the view of the bigger picture of all the political machinations underway across countless areas. He knew better than she when and how to get the Consortium to listen and take action. She'd given him the intel he needed to make an informed decision. She'd respect whatever choice he made. For now.

"Information is what we need the most at this point. If that changes, I'll let you know." He glanced at her bosom. "You, uh, seem to be glowing."

The angel's feather. Red blasted over her skin.

"Thank you for everything, Director. Do be careful, or you'll find yourself the last legit agent in a room of imposters."

With a thought, she left the gondola turning merrily above the bright lives of Washington, DC.

Bix arrived in Jotunheim in the same breath as a roaring dragon in fully natural form. She kept to the tunnel until the deafening noise stopped. She counted to ten, then descended the rest of the way into her chambers. The iridescence of the dark scales hinted at the dragon's ties to the royal bloodline.

"Yashanee," she called.

The dragon had enough room to turn around without dragging her barbed tail through the water bowl. The cavern granted the space for her wings to unfurl but not flap. Blood dripped from deep gouges and intense burns in her face and vulnerable underbelly. A single plum eye blinked; the other was a charred hollow.

Bix's heart broke. The sprout of malice grew under the brutal evidence of injustice.

"Chimera?" Yashanee rasped, confirming the damage to her vocal chords. "What...how...?"

"I am sorry. I had to let the Consortium believe your execution was successful. Please take as much time as you need to—"

"To accept I wasn't just incinerated out of existence?" Yashanee huffed little plumes of violet smoke. "Where are we?"

"Once upon a time, someone stole a beloved pet and built this prison to hide the beast." Bix pointed to the tiles of wards and spells embedded in the cavern. "While I do not intend for this to be your prison, I do hope it will help you hide from those who choose not to be fooled by my little stunt."

"There are sufficient parts of me smoldering on the Dais of the Damned. Your rescue, however inexplicable, should be believable." The dragon winced and cried out as she shifted forms to the familiar petite powerhouse, which served to highlight how gruesome her injuries truly were. "I did not feel your presence in the Consortium's chambers. How did you know where I would be, much less when?"

"It wasn't that long ago that I stood on that same platform to receive my punishment." Bix shrugged. "As for the when, let me say only that allies can be found in the people we least expect."

Yashanee hobbled to the swimming-pool-sized water bowl and slid into it. Violet magic danced through the depths, turning it opaque. Yashanee sighed with relief. "I do not mean to sound ungrateful, but why the reprieve?"

"Why did you protect me when your cousin came to arrest you?"

Yashanee closed her eyes and twisted her blistered lips into something of a grin. "You are the only one who can stop the faction. Being caught with me would have played into their hands. Frankly, the Mids need you."

"The Mids need you too." Bix opened gates. A collection of battered equipment better suited for the dump appeared at the foot of her bed.

Yashanee's head snapped up, and her eye opened. "I feel the taint."

"Three hundred and fifty victims are in that fridge. Two hundred samples of the working toxin are in those boxes, and the kettle contains pure Devourer blood."

"A cure," Yashanee gasped, swimming to the edge of the pool. What skin had been torn and scorched was bright pink with thin scabs. "You salvaged all this, for me?"

"I have no idea what sort of equipment is necessary, so if you make a list, I can acquire whatever it is…but there is a catch."

The dragon narrowed her eye. "I can't leave?"

"Hardly," Bix chuckled. "The souls of the frost giants here are not going to sing the songs that will sustain you. You will have to be very, very careful about where you go and when. You cannot have contact with anyone you once knew, most especially your cousin and contemporaries. And I strongly suggest appearing as a race that's completely different from the one to which you are accustomed."

"Logical, all of it. My own Witness Protection Program." Yashanee crossed her arms on the edge of the pool and tilted her head to stare at the ceiling. "I will need to modify some of the spells. A few feathers from an angel would help to mask the resonance of a dragon's presence."

A series of gates supplied the feathers from assorted stashes Bix had collected over the years.

"Will those do?"

"Yes, quite well." Yashanee pushed up out of the pool. A twist of her hand and a towel appeared. "What's the catch, then?"

"I need you to collaborate with a god."

Yashanee choked, coughing with enough force she had to plant her hands on her thighs. "Which one?"

"Nergal."

"Are you kidding me?" The dragon blotted her eye and mouth. "The god of plagues? You want me, a scientist dedicated to the evolution of Mids' magic, to work with the god of plagues?"

"You have to earn the opportunity to work with him." Bix offered a chagrined grin. "You'll have to pass all the trials his queen and her governors will present to you, so that you can have the exquisite honor of being derided and dismissed by a dude who believes dragons and angels have no business in the art of suffering."

Yashanee stared at her in disbelief. Bix braced for the countering indignation and inevitable negotiation.

Instead, the dragon beamed. "He's a god. Why would I expect anything less?"

This time, it was Bix's turn to gape.

"Truly, Chimera, I've been a fan of his for eons." Yashanee laughed outright, the sound pitiful due to the damage that had yet to heal. "The opportunity to collaborate—or, as he would see it, annoy—is something of a dream for me."

"He will not make it easy," Bix warned. "Neither will his queen. Their expectations are beyond high."

"Why should it be anything less?" Yashanee limped to the refrigerator and pried open the doors. Her breath caught. "So many. Such a waste."

"Nergal will be focused on developing what we have into a weapon against the Devourers that can be deployed anywhere, from any World. In essence, he'll attempt the reverse of Sunan's efforts. I want you to focus on an inoculation."

The dragon cocked her head. "For individuals?"

"For Mids' magic. Accelerated evolution, if you will. Something that will protect the magic at its very core from the poison that is the Devourers."

Yashanee pulled a geode from the pile and skimmed her raw fingers over the top. "It will take time."

"That's the only thing I cannot give you." Bix opened a partial gate that looked into an empty chamber with a dirt floor and turquoise torches. "This is a window into Irkalla. It will not permit passage since that would be dangerous for all involved. I don't know what the tests will be or when they will begin. Assume 'soon.'"

"Thank you for trusting me with this." Yashanee clutched the geode to her ravaged chest and smiled wistfully. "It was noted at my trial that your human friend who was infected has yet to succumb."

"A young Sage," Bix confirmed as her watch vibrated. A Bi Xie galloped across the screen, dragging an image of a coffeehouse behind it. "The lack of magic inherent to humans has prevented the Devourer blood from bonding to his threads, or so it seems."

"That will hold true until his next Fate-driven challenge sends a shock of magic, however brief, through him as it marks his grade." Yashanee sighed. "When that happens, bring him to me. I will need to run tests that compare his health to the last set I drew. The results will be important."

Shit. The trials of Fatehood. Bix hadn't considered how those would impact Cian and his new condition.

"You'll need copies of all your initial research, of course, to include his original scans. I'll do what I can to reclaim as much of it as possible." Bix projected the coffee shop image onto her sleeve and checked the time stamp.

Now. Ashtad needed to meet now.

"I am not giving up on Loncalaz," Yashanee confessed. "I'm not going to give up on any of these poor souls. Your young Sage included."

"Thank you for that. The sheets are clean, the blankets laundered, and there's a tablet on the pillow there. Whenever you come up with the list of necessities, ping me." Bix held up her wrist and shook her smartwatch. "Be sure to mask your identity on the ley lines. This sanctuary only works if you let it."

CHAPTER 30

Bix closed the gates and breathed in the delightful scent of freshly ground and brewed coffee. White lights from the barren trees outside the shop danced over tan brick walls, covering customers and furniture in speckles. The amber glow of the fire in the centuries-old fireplace beat back the chill of deep night. Conversations stayed at a muted din from artfully clustered velvet wingbacks and tufted club chairs set upon boldly patterned rugs. The tongue-oiled wooden door swung open, admitting laughter from tourists scurrying down the historic King Street in Old Town Alexandria, Virginia, Primary Mid World.

Three miles from the coal plant. Not a coincidence.

Her watch vibrated.

At your eleven in fuchsia.

Bix spotted the plush pink balloon chair, the silver cane, and the ever-elegant repose of Ashtad with a tablet in his lap. The occupant of the facing chair brought her up short. Early twenties. Bright white kicks. Dark hoodie. Brand-new baggy jeans with dirt on the knees. Slight bluing around the nail beds and petechia in the eyes.

"Drew? I thought you'd be with the women from the facility."

"Hiya, Bixie." Drew patted the seat next to him. "I told them we had to finish the job. The gals understood, even offered to do our wet work. They've got a bit of a chip on their shoulders, you see. I insisted they rest, binge on bad TV and junk food. We'll rendezvous with them once we put this to bed. You're going to love them."

"O-okay." Bix nodded and took the offered seat, her attention cutting between Drew and Ashtad. The two of them in the same room. By choice. Had to be a BFD if they could stand each other this long. Some of their animosity was due to their shared history at the CWIG, some of it was due to Ashtad's elitism, and some of it was pantheon related. "Ashtad, good to see you're roving again. Thanks for taking in Cian, by the way. I know that was a big ask. Where is he?"

"With his mom." Ashtad handed her his tablet. A camera feed of the hospital room played. Cian sat bedside, clutching a limp hand to his cheek. Bix couldn't look at the woman in the bed, the way the sheet tapered over where legs should have been. She couldn't quite deal with the machines breathing for Cian's mom, circulating blood for her and pumping drugs into her. She focused instead on the men and women standing guard. The replacements for Tobek's men who had kept faithful watch over the Oracle.

"Demis?" Bix wondered how many favors Ashtad had called in to replace the Berserkers.

"CWIG agents," Ashtad corrected. "The director insisted. Apparently, the recent spate of KIAs are weighing on him. He may also be aware that Loncalaz is the reason the kid is infected with an incurable death sentence."

"CWIG agents aren't going to stop Sunan." She handed Ashtad his toy. "But the gesture is noted. Refreshing proof the director has a conscience."

"Too bad the kid is going to end up an orphan because of the director." Drew took Bix's hand. "I'm sorry to say this, sweetie, but Vidya was ruled brain-dead an hour ago. The kid's requested they keep her on life support until morning."

The news hit Bix...not quite like the falling building she'd expected. After everything she and Vidya had been through, the youthful romance, the bitter breakup, the gutting betrayal that had led to the deaths of Bix's Dark Ops team and Bix's exile, and the painful attempt at redemption; Bix cared, sure she did. She gnawed on her upper lip as she waited for the gutting grief to take hold. She expected anger, but it wasn't there anymore. Neither was the bitterness. They'd had their time to blaze brightly, then burn out. There was only a hollow sorrow, a sadness for a life that could have been lived so much better if different choices had been made.

"Vidya's greatest fear was to have her body live while her mind was ravaged by her oracular gift," Drew whispered. "She didn't want to wake up from this. She hung on for Cian's sake."

Drew had read Vidya's soul the chaotic night that had ended with Vidya in a coma. He knew everything Cian's mom did, so if he said Vidya wanted out, she'd wanted out.

"That's the second mom Cian's lost. My concern is for him," Bix admitted. "He shouldn't have to be an adult at this age. He's smart, so smart, but that's just book smart. He fancies himself street smart, but…"

"He was smart enough to place nanites on Sunan and use them as trackers. We know exactly where the corrupt old Fate is." Ashtad flipped his screen at her. A green dot pulsed on a map of ley lines. "I figured you'd want to handle this part."

Bix studied the map with curiosity. Curiosity morphed to amusement as Ashtad changed the map view to a scenic view. A beautiful biodome in the middle of a barren World engulfed in electrical storms.

"Ellie, Queen of the Terrariums," she said with a smile. "He stole Yashanee's sylph for purely personal reasons."

"There is no public gate on this World," Ashtad warned. "There is no tear in the atmosphere protecting it."

"No tear means no Devourer cronies carting him around. That means it's a god playing taxi," Drew added.

"No, no, not a god or a Devourer, or a public gateway." Bix shook her head as pieces fit together. "I know exactly how Sunan is getting around. He overplayed his hand in logistics and got caught by the master of it."

Drew and Ashtad swapped wary looks with raised brows and tilted heads.

"Sunan is the reason the coal plant is on lockdown and Tobek sidelined." Bix crossed her hands in her lap and grinned. "The MWA is the Fates' contribution to the protection of the Mids. Sunan is a very old Fate with a lot of connections. He is using the gate at the other MWA facility as his personal shuttle, the gate Tobek identified as being tied to the third lab. Tobek is before the MWA Tribunal not to beg for forgiveness but to throw Sunan under the army bus."

"Honk-honk, muthafucka," Drew cackled. "And to think of all the times that fogey Fate made us hoof it through public gateways."

"There is a hierarchy within the Consortium, and the leadership of the MWA far outranks any oversight committee chair," Ashtad conceded. "If the MWA leadership has proof, then they'll have the authority to take down a Fate."

"I need to get to Sunan before Tobek does to reclaim all the toxin research the Fate stole." Bix stood and tucked her hair behind her ear. She had a few questions to put to the mean little prick as well. "You guys, thank you, thank you so much."

Ashtad hooked his cane around her ankle. "Hurry back, because the imminent death of Cian's mom has made the boy an imminent problem."

"How's that?" she asked.

"He's going to sell the diplomatic pouch, Bixie, in exchange for new bodies for him and his mom. The meet is in two hours. Lincoln Park, in the District, not Lincoln Memorial, Lincoln Park." Drew tugged the strings of his hoody, his choice of suit finally making sense.

That was the park to which Cian had been headed when Loncalaz had supposedly surprised him. The simple retrieval mission that had gone from pear-shaped to full-on disaster.

"I know the place." She puckered her lips and sniffed. "There's a dry cleaners and a wine bar across Thirteenth Street. The rooftops should give us a decent view. Bring binoculars. Make that night-vision goggles. You can be certain he'll black out all the cameras and the streetlights in the area. He'll shake his CWIG detail about ten minutes before the meet."

"We can stop the sale now," Ashtad suggested…sort of ordered, really.

"He booby-trapped it with a troll bomb," Bix said. "The sale has to happen for a lot of reasons."

"A troll…" Ashtad pressed a finger to his lips. "Not going to ask who gave it to him."

"Gift from Mommy." Drew leaned forward on the arm of his chair. "You know she wasn't a saint, right?"

"We need to grab his buyer anyway." Bix scanned the coffee shop one more time. The sensation of being watched traipsed over her skin. "And we need to see who else shows to take it from the buyer once the initial transaction is completed. We run this like any other sale intercept."

"We can't let it fall into… You know what? Never mind." Ashtad unhooked his cane from Bix's leg. "You clearly knew this was coming, so we'll continue to play it your way. Though, a little heads-up would have been nice."

She hadn't been certain Cian would sell the pouch, but his loyalty was to his mom, not to Bix, not to the Berserkers, and not to the CWIG. In light of that, she wasn't surprised by his decision. The question was how hard would she let his mistake bite him in the ass before she intervened. How long did he need to writhe in the noose he'd fashioned for himself before he learned to respect ropes, trees, and chairs?

"Assets, have to know how to manage them." Bix tossed Ashtad a wink. "See you guys in two hours."

CHAPTER 31

Bix closed gates inside the humid biodome of Sunan's Tarzan fantasy. Life inside the big glass bubble resembled a giant jungle in shades of green with pops of colorful blooms. The pungent scent of plant life and verdant soil hung heavily in the humid air, as if the artificial breezes couldn't break through the dense canopies that obscured the violent storms raging beyond the dome. The internal atmosphere didn't encourage bugs. No buzzing, dive-bombing, slithering, or nibbling indicators anywhere. Mother Nature had taken a backseat to the dictates of native magic.

A massive manor house had been constructed up in the trees. Smaller treehouses fanned out below. Suspension walkways, vine elevators, and broad-leaf boats on clear rivers made the humanoid life-forms appear like diminutive dolls.

Naturally, the Fate couldn't live here alone. He'd starve. He needed the Chweds living here to expel their magics so he could feed off the refined element. Most Fates resided in heavily populated Mid Worlds, so fuel was never in short supply; that, and they liked to see the destinies they'd woven come to fruition. Normal, healthy, fractious Fates did that.

Fates who conspired with Devourers to destroy the Mids? They liked to play lord of the plantation.

Bix used gates to ascend to the teakwood porch wrapping around the manor house. Rattan doors stood wide. Whitewashed floors led into the house of a hundred windows. Ceiling fans made of sprites turned a gentle breeze. Naiads trapped in sculptural fountains fed the waterfalls. Fire fae imprisoned in light fixtures flashed Morse code.

"Chimera, to what do I owe this unexpected visit?" Sunan greeted from a grand staircase carpeted in the hides of weres... animal shifters, who, upon closer look, still lived.

What a purgatory. Phobos would've loved this place. Bix couldn't wait to leave.

"Come now, you fusty old Fate, my arrival here can't be that unexpected." Bix opted to stay on the floor that she sincerely hoped hadn't been made from trees in which the dryads resided.

"On the contrary, you've developed a habit of collaborating with entities who lack threads. It's so much easier for me to keep tabs on you when you're colluding with the Berserkers or the young Sage." Sunan descended the stairs, relying heavily on his cane.

"So why drive a wedge between us?"

"Alas, I am not the only Fate with an interest in what you do and with whom." He paused and checked his watch. "We have a few minutes before your housemate and his reinforcements arrive to arrest me. Shall we sit?"

His cordial welcome raised her hackles.

"You're not worried? About being found out? Detained? Hauled before the Consortium for the crimes for which you framed the Dreigiau queen's cousin?" Bix headed to the veranda and a pair of rocking chairs. She double-checked the chairs to make sure she wasn't sitting on someone.

He laughed as if she were the village idiot. "You wouldn't have come if you'd wanted them to take me. Even in your diminished capacity, you realize one person with a thread is all I need to arrange my freedom. No member of the MWA will be able to contain me, no matter the numbers they apply."

The notion of delivering him to Ereshkigal and Nergal had

occurred. Hell, it had been Plan A. Now, however, he seemed a little too eager and a little too smug about using her as his exit strategy. If the MWA was coming to get him and he suddenly vanished, they'd know she'd done it—with or without the testimony of the witnesses surrounding them. If she skipped out with Sunan, it would ruin the trust Tobek and his men had given her.

Maybe she needed to come up with a different sort of perdition for the Fate.

"Yet you are guilty of so many crimes, even by Consortium standards," she mused aloud.

"I admit to being surprised that you allowed Yashanee to perish for my sins. The old you would never have stood for it." He set his cane between his feet and crossed his wrists over the ball hilt. The garish white rubber foot cap mocked the rest of his cultured style.

How many hundreds of nanites had Cian embedded in that hideous porous surface? Did Sunan even know that he'd been outsmarted by a novice Sage? A mild case of nanny-nanny-boo-boo tickled the back of Bix's mind.

"As you said when we met, any evidence I provided would be ignored or assumed compromised. There was nothing I could do to save her." She settled in the chair and set her arms wide on the rests. "What did you do with the actual research, the records of what Sarina, Udara, Qiang, and the others built for you? Did you destroy that along with the original files you stole from Yashanee and Kashdejan?"

He thumped his cane. "Now, now, I can't tell you that. It's the last intact copy, and I'll need that to sell to whomever you're planning on leaving me with. Thank you, though, for demolishing everything else—the lab, the facility, even those revolting Devourers. It increased the value of the completed research to, well, it's priceless."

"Help me out, then. There's one thing I wasn't able to resolve." Bix kept her façade calm and civilized; inside, she wanted to stuff him in an iron maiden and drop it into a poison ocean. "The timing of the inciting moment. Sarina said she'd been working on the toxin for five years. Yet you would have needed her *after* you'd identified Devourer blood as something detrimental to the threads. And it was only five years ago that the Devourers could even access the Mids. Fates have never been able to traverse the ether without a ferryman, so how did you hatch this grand plan?"

"You do not recall, but the Fates were once part of the pantheons." He pulled a face of disgust. "The Devourers have been foes of the gods since the time of their mutual creation. Each side takes prisoners. Each side does horrible things to those prisoners. The effects of Devourer blood weren't so much a secret as a piece of history long forgotten."

As a Sage who'd ascended to full Fate, Sunan was his own supercomputer. He had access to all that ancient history in the makeup of his body. Perhaps, even after his ascension, he was still an information addict. Perhaps that was why he'd taken the path of science instead of brute force.

"Your motive in all this was to get the attention of the Consortium," she posited. "That's why geodes instead of killing your victims outright. You were hoisting a caution flag."

"Roughly three hundred years ago, *you* stood before the Consortium—what was left of it at that point—and warned us that the Devourers were at the gate. We, all four superpower races, were in the throes of the cyclical power shift that comes with the apex and nadir of Mids' magic."

"The Great Wars," Bix clarified. "The ones that come every five hundred years when the Phoenix burns."

"Yes, yes, good, good, you've relearned that much." He grunted with approval. "We not only ignored you, we made it your problem. You were one of the creators of the ether. You promised us it would protect us; therefore, it was your responsibility to make sure it did. We had other issues to manage."

Bix snorted. "New alliances, new heads of Houses and pantheons, new Cycle of Soul contracts, new committees and chairpersons of said committees, all the rigmarole. Way to look out for the greater Mids."

"We wouldn't even spare scouts to mind the borders. No one believed you, me included." He held up a hand and wagged a finger. "No, that's untrue. We always believed you—that was part of your power over us—we just didn't *care* about a near-future problem when our immediate future was being decided."

"So, I executed the Phoenix, then tried to shore up the ether, alone." Ereshkigal had told her as much. She recalled the drawing Tobek had done of her, wrapped in her darkness, so painfully sad. He'd said she was sad because they'd lost. Perhaps what had been lost was her case in front of the Consortium?

"For centuries after that, the issue of the Devourers never came up. Not until you resurfaced in the bowels of the Under Worlds, for all appearances having been husked. You ranted and raved in words that weren't even words about the horrible things in the ether."

"The Devourers." She shivered at the memories. The things that had frequently hunted and accosted her had been faceless, amorphous entities. Devourers had the ability to become anything, so sure, bogeymen of the vast nothingness weren't out of the question.

"Hades, your nursemaid, brought it up to the Consortium, where he too was ignored. But there were a handful of us who remembered your warning. That handful of us had faced Devourers before. You see, these younger generations, they don't know. Their biggest fears are of being forgotten. No, they had to be reminded. So I did. I reminded them. Or I would have, had you not interfered."

"That's why you wanted it aerosolized. Maximum infections equal inescapable proof when entire cities of Chweds are turned into geodes."

"Yes." He nodded vigorously. "It would have been a beautiful awakening. A return to the bygone days of actual cooperation within the Consortium."

"Why target agents and soldiers for your field trials? What are you after?"

"I'm not the one searching. They are. The faction. They've been searching for years. For what, I don't know." He levered himself upright. "You didn't honestly believe that your Dark Ops group was the first group of CWIG agents to fall, did you? It wasn't about just you. Your whole team had to go. As for the agents and soldiers who found themselves on the wrong end of a needle, they got too close to figuring out what the faction is after."

"All the Fates in the Consortium knew I was an agent yet still exiled me for being a merc?" She surged to her feet. "You heartless bastards."

He leaned forward until his nose was a hair away from hers. "Threads. You worked with people who had threads. Of course we knew."

"Your cronies used a *tornado* to kill children slated to age into Oracles and Sages. You, a Fate, didn't bat an eye at that?" She refrained from the diatribe about that tornado's death toll being used to coerce Cian's mom into turning traitor.

"The faction backed me in my efforts to shed light on the Devourers. What are the lives of some children when we can always write more into existence?" His watch chimed. "Ah. It's time. Your Berserker is here along with a cross-company of guards. MWA's finest from the five branches. They've arrived on the grounds below. I think I'm flattered. Shall we?"

Bix reached out with her senses, searching for Tobek's presence. It was a faint tickle of the push and pull. She had time… and a new plan. She opened gates at the coal plant and inside the cubbies in Jotunheim, quietly moving supplies into the last place Sunan would foresee. Into the very heart of his own home. She didn't need eyes on her prizes to relocate them; she only needed clear mental images of where they were stored and where they were headed.

"Chimera, come now. I've answered your questions, honestly, even," Sunan chided with thinly veiled annoyance. "We need to go. Unless you want me to get free."

"Well, we wouldn't want that." She looped her arm around his and guided him into the manor house, to the large foyer replete with tortured Chweds as part of the furnishings. All the lovely supplies from her assorted stashes awaited them at the foot of the grand staircase. A massive metal pentagram surrounded by a ring with engraved spells spun slowly in the churn of rotating gates, a glorious focal point to a new installation.

"What is that?" he hissed, slowing.

"Did your friends in the faction ever tell you the details of the work I did that led to my early parole?" Bix smiled at the wonderful piece of art Tobek had made long before their reacquaintance. She was going to owe him big-time for its appropriation, but hopefully he'd understand. Moderate theft versus major betrayal, the danger of befriending a spy.

"No. The details have been kept on a need-to-know. I didn't." Sunan jerked against her, but she held fast, propelling him forward.

"Then you are going to love this. Living art, really. You've been such a connoisseur, it'll be an honor to join the gallery, I'd think."

"Wait, what, wh—"

Gates moved him, trapping him in the finite space in front of the pentagram. Gates also allowed her to grab the very necessary second component of the piece. Very special, very rare, very magical, and very dreadful spikes with fat heads.

"While you were making a toxin to kick-start an epidemic, other people were up to other bits of no good and very bad. I happened to have pilfered some of their more valuable torture devices." She held up one spike, closed one eye…and unleashed her darkness. Tentacles grabbed Sunan's appendages and forced them into alignment on the pentagram. They snatched away his cane. The spikes were hot in her grasp and flew true to their mark. Sunan screamed with the beautiful sound of terrified agony as her darkness hammered the spikes into the bespelled frame. The malice within her grew.

The sounds of the MWA soldiers rapidly ascending the tree drifted through the open doors.

"Wh-where do you think you're going to take me, impaled like this?" Sunan gasped, befuddled.

"Oh, you misanthrope, I'm not taking you anywhere. Neither is the MWA. You see, no one with threads can get you down from there. Without a gatekeeper, they can't move the pentagram either." Bix recalled her darkness and picked up his cane. "What will happen is the army is going to burst through those doors at any moment and they are going to find all your victims, all these poor brutalized Chweds who can testify to your comings and goings and to the confession you just gave on the veranda. The MWA will take all the Chweds from here, including Ellie, whom you need to maintain this fantasy of yours."

"You wouldn't." He shook his head, his hair adhering to his sweaty, blood-spattered brow. "I need them to live."

"No, you need them to weave," she snarled. "You're going to learn the difference. We'll see how well you enjoy starving without the hope for the sweet release of death. I got a real kick out of it while I was in the exile arranged by you and your precious faction. Ten years of your guts gnawing on themselves and your muscles desiccating to the point you can't lift your head... Good times. Good times. Sure, it's not quite the same as being turned into a geode, but it's close."

"I will get out of this, and I will ruin you," Sunan shouted.

"A part of me hopes you will try," She laughed with deliberate mania. "You made a gross mistake using diluted Devourer blood on Chweds because a girl like me wonders what would happen if someone mainlined the pure stuff into a Fate. Would it solidify the blood in your veins? Would it harden your muscles? Would it turn your precious brains to stone? Would it, in fact, *kill* a Fate? Are Fates truly immortal, or was that one more lie your kith wove into the universal history? Your ilk might be hard to kill, but I don't think it's impossible, not anymore."

"By uttering those words, you've turned every House of Fate against you," he panted, sneering.

"I am the Chimera, High Executioner for All Worlds. I

already knew your dirty secret. It was only a matter of time before I relearned it." Bix smiled broadly, feeling the push and pull of Tobek arriving on the veranda. "Welcome to the ranks of the convicted felons, Sunan. I hope you loathe your stay."

CHAPTER 32

Bix turned the collar of her coat against the damp wind blowing the season's first snow across Washington, DC. The clouds formed a thick blanket, trapping the city's night lights. Salt trucks lumbered past while pedestrians scurried with heads down toward warmer destinations.

"Anyone else find the change in tonight's forecast mildly interesting?" Ashtad peered through night-vision binoculars at Lincoln Park. Leafless trees provided enough cover without obscuring the view from their rooftop stakeout.

"It's either a minor god or a weather elemental." Drew stuffed his hands in his hoodie's pockets. "Neither of whom can offer new bodies for Cian or his mom."

"Are we thinking the kid is short-sighted or clueless?" Ashtad asked. "Desperate is a given, but does he not know how the Cycle of Souls works? Even if his buyer—some dragon or angel—does provide the bodies, there is nothing to say the Fates are going to unravel the threads from their existing bodies or reweave them into the new ones. He's signed his own death warrant."

"He did that the moment he publicly admitted to having the evidence pouch." Bix spotted the kid entering the far end of the park. "North entrance. Flannel jacket."

"Bystander, playground, southern end. I don't see the parents. Isn't it awfully late for a kid to be out alone?" Drew bumped Bix's elbow with his. "What? Bixie, what? You stopped breathing."

Bix struggled to swallow. Sitting on the swing, a little girl with a teddy bear. *The* little girl. Udara's neighbor. Victim of the Nabaziix. The girl for whom Xipil and his team had searched.

"It's a goddess," Ashtad grunted. "A Mid World guardian. I can feel her drawing power from the ley lines."

"Impossible, the girl is human," Bix argued. "She radiates neutral space of a human. I've been within twenty feet of her multiple times. She's been appearing at key sites during the cootie case. There might be a god using her as a puppet. I couldn't sense the god though, still can't."

"This demi knows when the ley lines are being tapped," Ashtad countered. "There is a goddess on site somewhere."

"Now, now, Mommy and Daddy, no fighting in front of the children." Drew stretched across Bix and snatched the goggles from Ashtad.

"Hey, using those," Ashtad griped.

"Hogging," Drew corrected. "'Hogging' is the word you meant."

"Scan for dead angels or dragons nearby. The goddess hasn't waited for them to complete the sale to make her move. Cian can't tell the difference among the superpowers when they're in humanoid form." Bix spoke through her hands, her heart hammering as Cian lay on the ground and rolled under the lip of a memorial dedicated to Mary McLeod Bethune, an educator passing on her knowledge to the next generation. Oh, the irony.

"We should get down there." Ashtad slung his bag of spy goodies over his shoulder and picked up his cane. "The kid is in way, way over his head."

"If there's a goddess watching, she'll rip apart this entire neighborhood on a whim the moment we move on that pouch." Bix shook her head. "Stand firm."

"This neighborhood backs to the US Capitol. If that bomb

goes off, it will be construed by the humans as a terrorist attack from which the Primary Mid World will devolve into nuclear war," Ashtad argued.

Same argument Bix had had with herself at the beginning of all this. Good to know the trainee didn't fall far from the trainer.

"A goddess's tantrum will have more devastating effects than the bomb. Stand firm. Let Cian make the exchange. He has to deactivate the bomb before we can do anything." Bix bit her lip as Cian pulled a white box with shimmering seams the size of a case of paper from the platform of the memorial. Troll bombs looked innocuous, which was part of their deadly efficacy.

"Hey, when angels bleed, their blood turns into exotic plants, right?" Drew asked, his attention on a familiar neighborhood to the southwest. "We've got a minor jungle growing in the middle of a side street."

"Those must be the original buyers. Figured it'd be angels." Bix stared at the girl hopping off the swing and ambling toward Cian, bear dangling in one hand. "Leave them for now. We'll check their scarifications for choir and rank after we have the pouch."

Potent magic rippled past them, causing all three to grunt in unison. Definitely a deity nearby.

"Whatever she is about to do, she's about to do," Ashtad warned, setting his cane on the roof. He rolled his wrists, drawing all available electricity to him. It built in crackling blue orbs around his hands.

"Hold," Bix said. "Cian hasn't taken the pouch out of the box yet."

"Holding for your go." Ashtad shuffled away from Bix, giving himself enough room to launch an attack without frying her.

"There's the pouch." Bix shivered. A chill raked down her spine as Cian lifted a dark, iridescent soccer ball from the box. Elven script shimmered under the traffic's passing lights. The Norse diplomatic pouch. The unabridged collection of Mirri's years of investigations trying to prove Bix's innocence.

"He's handing it off." Ashtad glanced at Bix. "Bix, we can't—"

"Not yet. He still has a chance." Bix held her breath. "He has to put it in the girl's hands. Intermediary or not, she'll refuse to give him the new body until she's sure the pouch is what he claims. Who has eyes on the goddess? I can't sense her, and I can't spot her."

"The teddy bear is the goddess," Drew snarled, his rage swift and unexpected. "She's using the neutral space of a human child to mask herself from you. The girl is a poppet, likely enhanced by spell work to conceal divine magic. I repeat, the teddy bear is the goddess."

Bix frowned. "You're sure?"

"No…how…?" Ashtad sputtered.

"Trust me, Bixie, as someone created to be a goddess's plaything, I know which is which." Drew gripped the goggles so tightly, they cracked.

That was all the guidance Bix needed. Cian extended his arms, the polyhedron balanced on his palms. The girl reached for it.

"Bix…" Ashtad urged.

The instant the girl touched the pouch, the darkness ripped from Bix. Tentacles of ravenous night wrapped around the girl and speared through the bear. The bear roared into the fighting feminine form of a ginger goddess, writhing against the darkness. Gates moved Cian, the bomb, and the pouch to three vastly separate locations.

"Chimera, don't you hide from me," the goddess shrieked. Her voice caused the ground and buildings to quake. Alarms sounded. Windows shattered. Traffic lights snapped from their cables. Cars skidded off roads.

"Devana," Ashtad swore, grounding his weapons. "Bix, she's the Slavic Goddess of the Hunt. Completely lost her marbles in the last Great War after facing the Chimera. Cian was never her prey. You are."

"She should've learned this lesson the last time, then." Bix yanked the goddess out to the ether, leaving her human poppet at Drew's feet.

Vast nothingness spread around Bix and her captive. Not even a brave Devourer tainted this placeless space. Every twitch Devana made resulted in the goddess screaming in agony upon the impalements of Bix's darkness. Yet in the ether, there was no damage to be wrought by Devana's caterwauling. The goddess changed her forms, woman to bear to wolf to child to woman, over and over. The darkness never lost its hold. Like any reasonable witness to a tantrum, Bix let it play out. Sure, she could have cautioned the Mid World guardian about resistance making the suffering worse, but, meh.

Finally, Devana figured it out. The goddess settled into her form of muscular femininity, red eyes bright, hair unraveling from its twin plaits.

"Clearly, you are not a Shadow Caster," Bix drawled. "Why offer your services to Phobos, then?"

"How dare you *dismiss* me," Devana spat, chest heaving from exertion. "I gave you an invitation. You ignored it, so I tracked you to see what was so urgent that you could not come to me. You were hunting. I respected that, so I waited. When you'd found your prey, I reissued my invitation. What did you do then? You burned it. Where is the respect, Chimera?"

"I don't know you," Bix scoffed. "Why would I respect you?"

"Y-you d-don't know me," Devana stammered, eyes widening and rolling until the whites showed. Foamy spittle formed at the corners of her mouth as she sputtered and fumed. Her nails dug into her scalp, rending deep gouges that bled.

Bix increased the distance between them.

"You don't *know* me," Devana wailed, pounding on her forehead with the heels of her hands. "I can't get you out of my head. Your memories. Your horrors. Your torments. Voices of one word. Songs of one note. Scents so brief they tease. Tastes so fleeting as to create a hunger that cannot be sated. Your tiny pictures of no meaning and no timing and no story and no context and no *relief.*"

Bix stilled.

Devana was a Mid World guardian. Ereshkigal had said Bix had given her memories to that specific group of gods because only they understood the importance of keeping her secrets for the sake of the Mids.

Devana's nails tore her cheeks from lower lid to jaw as she sobbed. "Three hundred and thirty years of no peace within my own skull. All I wanted was for you to take your poison from my mind."

"Devana, I am sorry," Bix said in earnest. "I had no idea. You are absolutely right. I disrespected you. In my surety that all gods wanted to use me, it never occurred to me that the gods who possessed the one thing I desperately want to recover would actually come looking for me. I had anticipated being the hunter, tracking you all down. A civilized rendezvous never crossed my mind."

"Hunting? Us? Hunting us?" The goddess gaped, slack-jawed and mauled by her own hands. Her breathy titter escalated into full-on manic hysteria. "There is no need to hunt us. We are coming for you. Those of us who have not been locked up or locked down by our pantheons are coming for you. Not all of them are as reasonable as I. None as grounded in reality as I. But rest assured, we are coming for you."

Threat. Staring at a raving lunatic goddess, Bix could only construe that as a threat.

"And will all of you see fit to use a child to get me? Or will the other keepers of my secrets reach higher, closer, deeper within my inner circle?"

Devana's smile adopted a sinister curl. "It is the least we can do to repay you for our prolonged insanity."

"Who are they, Devana? The others? Their names."

Devana threw wide her bloodied arms. "Take them from me. You want information. Take it, but not before you reclaim your memories."

"Did Phobos know?" Bix demanded. "Did he know you hold my memories when he agreed to the referral?"

"The Greek spymaster knows more, sees more, says little. So little. Intercepting souls to siphon their memories before the souls reached their rightful owners. Sneaky thief. I like him. He is a hunter too. Hunting, hunting…" Devana's words spiraled upward into hyenic howls.

Spymaster? Bix had briefly met Phobos while she'd been under Hades's tutelage. Never had either god alluded to Phobos's job for the pantheon. Never had she thought to ask because so few gods had responsibilities to the greater pantheon beyond creating and maintaining believers. Fear was a full-time gig, or so she'd thought. What a fool she was. What a willfully blind fool.

"Take them," Devana screeched, interrupting Bix's self-flagellation. "Take your mind from mine, or I will take every life you've ever valued."

Bix bit her lip and tested her darkness. She knew how to withdraw essence from the gods through her darkness, but her memories? The last time she'd tried it…oof. Not good.

"Give them to me, my memories. Give yourself the gift of sanity," Bix cajoled, taking a chance and not wanting to admit her ignorance.

"Give? Give?" The goddess cackled. "You inflicted them on me. Only you can extract them. Now stop torturing me. Take your memories, Chimera. Use these cursed spears of wrath and malice to withdraw the poison they infused within me."

Bix did her best. She started with the familiar, with the divine essence, but it only fueled her. She cast more tentacles into the goddess, causing Devana to keen. Memories still didn't come.

"Look beyond the goddess and her essence," whispered Ereshkigal's voice in Bix's ear as filaments of darkness banded around Bix, giving her support. "Think of her as nothing more than a shell. Allow your darkness to seep into the riot of her primordial construct, displacing it, forcing it to fade into the background. Find the dust of you scattered within her chaos. Call to the infinitesimal parts of you longing to come home, bid them welcome, bid them to return."

Bix closed her eyes and yielded to Ereshkigal's web of comfort. "Come to me, all that is mine. Come. I am broken, my chasms deep. Come. I want to be whole again."

Lighter than feathers, smaller than motes, they came. The fleeting scents. The singular notes of sound. The hint of flavors. The flash of an image. The twitch of a touch. They came. They collided with the fragments already there, searching for mates.

Bix juddered and gasped. Mist and midnight seeped from her eyes and nose as the influx overwhelmed her, robbing her of lucidity.

Devana's rapturous cry mixed with the onslaught. Her joy was short-lived. Her cry morphed to terror as the goddess of Irkalla drained every last bit of everything from the huntress, leaving nothing more than an ephemeral casing. Hollowed. Husked.

Gods couldn't die. This emptiness was as close as they got.

"N-n-no," Bix choked. "Need her. N-need all of them. The gods. To fight. The Devourers."

"Oh, child, after all these years, her mind learned to adapt to the presence of your memories. When you retrieved that which was yours, you destroyed what was left of her ability to think rationally, to control her base instinct. You've made her worse than savage. She had to be husked for the safety of her pantheon and the Mids. This price was once acceptable to you, though it clearly isn't now." Ereshkigal's darkness stroked Bix's hair and brushed her brow. "Should you need someone to talk to, you know where to find me."

Filaments unraveled as Ereshkigal withdrew her support and her presence. Bix fought for control of her own body and mind as her past attempted to reestablish roots in her present.

It took a while.

CHAPTER 33

Bix massaged her temple and willed her legs to put one foot in front of the other as she stepped into the Mid World of orange beaches, hungry sea serpents, and perpetual rain. She blinked rapidly and shook her head, trying to make sure what she saw was truly in front of her eyes and not an echo of a displaced memory.

A hut of bones had been built upon a platform of large skulls.

"You know, this takes being grounded to a whole new level," Cian called from the shelter he had built.

"How long has it been?" Bix stroked her wrist for her watch and grimaced. It hadn't survived her spontaneous trip out to the ether with Devana. Damn it, she'd really liked her bug.

"No idea. Battery died a while ago." He wagged his smartphone, then stuffed it in his hoodie's pocket. "I can tell you I've slept for three long stretches. Learned that the ocean water will eat the skin off my fingers, rain filtered through sand in a skull is potable, and raw sea snakes are not a delicacy."

"Wow. Didn't know you had a survivalist streak." Bix gestured to the hut. "I'm impressed."

"Mom insisted." He gave her a half smile and motioned for her to join him under his shelter. "She said the Fates were cruel and twice as bad to their own. She wanted me to be prepared in case something like this happened."

Ah, Vidya.

"I'm sorry about your mom, and I'm sorry you didn't get a chance to say good-bye." Bix took a seat beside him.

"The gang from the CWIG made sure I was there in her final cogent moments." He picked at his pants. "Her brain stopped working right after I told her about this case and Sunan and infecting that nasty rubber cap on his cane with nanites. I could've sworn she smiled, you know? Like her last real thought was 'you get 'em, son.'"

"That sounds like the woman I knew. When we get back, I'll help you put together her funeral." Bix draped an arm across his shoulders as he struggled with tears.

"Cremation. She didn't want a draugr taking her out for a final spin or some necromancer making her dance like a puppet. 'Course that would've been hard since she didn't have legs anymore." He huffed at his own joke, sighed, then put his head on Bix's shoulder and bawled. She let him. She didn't offer platitudes or words about his mom's death being a final mercy. When she'd hurt this badly, Tobek had held her in understanding silence. That had been the best thing anyone could have done for her, so that's what she did for Cian. There was no rush. Nowhere they had to be. No one to whom they had to report. Grief was rarely convenient, but this was its time and its place.

"I really screwed up, didn't I?" he asked through his sniffles.

"The nanites were brilliant." She put her head atop his. "The whole scheme you cooked up with Loncalaz about selling the diplomatic pouch to buy your mom a new body? *That* was a colossal screwup."

He wiped his eyes, then his nose on his sleeve and looked up at her. "How long have you known about me and Loncalaz?"

"Agents don't involve other agent's family members. It's a code of honor." She shook the sand out of her shoes. "Loncalaz is an ass with no respect for humanity overall, but your mom was one of the two real friends he ever had. My guess is he reached out to you when he heard she'd been hospitalized. You, in your state of panic and shock, told him about the pouch and the Berserkers. The two of you hatched a plan to get you access to the Red Web and from there make a deal with the dragon or the angel who'd contributed to your mom's Cycle of Soul contract. Sadly, things went south for Loncalaz before the mission was completed, and he injected you with an unsanctioned toxin."

"That was not in the plan," Cian blustered.

"No, but by then he knew his time was up. He was desperate and didn't think through all the ramifications. Like someone else I know."

"I'm sorry, Bix. I didn't know what was in that soccer ball. I just knew it was important to powerful people. I'm guessing, based on my time-out, that it was, is, important to you too."

"Look, everyone is allowed one epic cock-up." She tugged on her ear as sensory memories ran riot, mixing sound bites of the past with the present. "Without it, we never really understand the impact we have on the Worlds. It's one thing to imagine the consequences of our actions. It's something else to be battered and banged up in the maelstrom of repercussions. For someone on the path to full Fatehood, it's good that you did this now with people who get what it means to have a lot of power and not a lot of the right experience."

He rucked up his sleeve and showed her the new leaf connected to the first, a wilted leaf. A silver-dollar-sized fractal of crystals surrounded the leaf. "It was a test, and I failed."

"Failing once doesn't exclude you from becoming a Fate," she assured him. "How long ago did the crystal form?"

"I felt it growing as I handed the ball to that creepy little girl. It hasn't spread since then and there are no other spots." He tugged down his sleeve.

"We need to get you tested, check if the cooties are growing where we can't see them."

"Um, I think you might need to get tested too." He looked at her nose and dabbed his lip.

Bix wiped the indicated spot and groaned as mist and midnight brushed her fingers. "It's nothing."

"If that's how you bleed, that's not nothing." He leaned away from her. "What's wrong with you?"

"Nothing is wrong. I…" She hesitated, debating whether to trust him with her truth. He was part of her circle, an asset in many ways. The other gods, the remaining five out of the original seven, would come for her, and one of them might use him as Devana had. It wasn't fair not to warn him of potential dangers. "A lot of years ago, I split up my memories and gave them to certain superpower keepers. The goddess who came after you was one of them. Now that I'm slowly reclaiming my lost wits, my body and my brain…they, they take a while to adjust."

"You should be careful." He rubbed his neck. "In computing, if you try to merge legacy memory modules with new ones, they often lead to a corrupted operating system and a melted CPU."

Bix wiped her cheeks as the mist started dribbling from her eye again. "Yeah. I think I'm discovering that. Come on, let's get you off this island. Pretty sure the clinic at the coal plant can run a basic health check on both of us."

She'd send all his samples to Yashanee for research, but no way could she have the kid meet the dragon who was supposed to be dead.

"So, um, what *is* in that diplomatic pouch?" He grinned hopefully.

"Dude, trust levels." She snickered. "You screwed up royally. You're going to have to earn your way back to top-secret clearance."

CHAPTER 34

Vidya's memorial service was a small affair attended by coworkers from the CWIG, a few nurses from the hospital, and the Berserkers from the coal plant. A handful of others whom Bix didn't recognize were there too. Drew made a point of getting to know them down to their souls. If the faction had sent representatives, however, they made it out undetected.

A battle for another day.

Today, Bix was grateful for the friends she still had. Ashtad had sent ahead his regards; his cover didn't allow him to mingle with active agents. He'd called in a few favors and spread a bit of disinformation to the human media about a rare earthquake causing the damage near the Capitol on Devana's ill-fated night.

Drew flirted with a pair of CWIG analysts who had no idea with whom they were dealing. The CWIG believed Drew had died with the rest of Bix's Dark Ops team, and the draugr was keen to keep it that way.

Tobek, the sometimes-literal rock, had made all the arrangements for services and cremation after Bix and Cian had returned from their time-out. He'd laughed for hours upon finding Sunan staked to his pentagram. As she'd suspected, the MWA had cleared out the biodome and taken Sunan's prisoners for debriefings, then on to havens. The Fate himself, they'd left where she'd put him. A special prison for a special prisoner. Silent alarms had been set to record any visitors Sunan might receive, on the off chance his friends in the faction saw fit to drop by.

The big Berserker caught her eye as he made his way across the funeral parlor's rooms.

"Cian is off with Xipil and Hywl to spread his mother's ashes." Tobek offered her his arm.

She stared at it, wrestling with emotions, wrestling with the "it" that said trust him without reservation versus the seed of malice that demanded she cut him down first before he could do it to her.

"Hey." He dipped to catch her gaze. "Are we okay? You and I? You've been aloof since Irkalla."

"I accept that some of your evasions are due to the curse." She sighed, taking his arm as people started to stare. "However, I am aware that some of them are not. Until you and I can have frank and unrestricted conversations, we're going to have problems."

He laid his hand over hers as they strolled. The tension in his arm belied his outward congeniality. "The sort of problems that build walls between us?"

"A bit," she admitted softly.

"My actions, they're not enough to allay your concerns?" he grumbled.

"I'm not with you all the time, Tobek, and I don't wish to be," she rushed to add, "so I have no idea if I'm your target in a covert op, or if I'm a thankless fool being overly paranoid. Regardless, that is my truth in this moment."

He inhaled deeply but said nothing. They wandered through the rooms of the parlor, nodding to those who made eye contact, but they didn't stop to talk. Eventually, he spoke.

"I have often wondered what it is like to be the only one who can't remember. To be surrounded by people with whom you share a history, yet be the only one who doesn't know it." He shook his head. "It must be terrifying. Every encounter, every interaction, you are automatically at the disadvantage. You can't tell who is a true ally and who is an enemy masquerading as an ally. Your paranoia is understandable. Frustrating at times, yes, but that is my problem, not one you need to assume for me."

"You sure know the right words, when you choose to use them," she drawled.

"I am ever at your side when you want me to be." He paused and turned her to face him. "When the moments arise that your trust in me wavers or is broken, come to me, give me the chance to explain the best I can, the best I am permitted to, before you cut ties. Please. That is a lot to ask, I know, but I ask nonetheless."

She tipped her head. "You're going to dodge the questions, Tobek. We both know it. Why waste the time?"

"Time with you is never wasted." He drew his hands down her arms. "One day you will have all your memories again. One day you will not look to me for answers, because you will know them. One day after that, I hope that these awkward, uncomfortable, and occasionally painful situations are the things we look back upon and laugh."

She snorted. "You make it sound like we're an old married couple."

His easy grin appeared, and he winked as he refolded her arm around his and set to strolling again. "A quarter mile below this room is a heavily warded bunker, one of the most secure in the Primary Mid World. The proprietor is an old friend of mine. She's given us permission to use it for as long as we need."

"What would I do without you?" Bix squeezed his arm and caught Drew's eye. The draugr slid two slips of paper into her bra and bid farewell to the analysts.

"Are we ready for this?" Drew shimmied and clutched Bix's hand.

"Going to find out." Bix let Tobek lead them through hidden passages and down winding stairs carved into the earth. Torches sparked to light their way, then extinguished once they'd passed. A glyph appeared in the stone walls here and there, markers along the path. They rounded two bends and hostile native magic shoved against Bix.

"Oof," she wheezed. "Potent."

"Should protect the surrounding area from any unpleasant surprises Mirri left behind." Tobek raised his natural hand. Green mist spawned silver keys that flew into hidden locks. As one, the keys turned with clicks and hisses. The stone wall receded and slid to the left, revealing three nested chambers: the outer contained supplies, the middle beds, and the center an octagonal table and chairs.

"Wheehehe," Drew gasped and fanned herself. "This place is not my biggest fan. They've warded against my kind."

Bix stopped. "Will you be okay? We can move to another location."

"Oh, Bixie, babe, I'm no common draugr." Drew slid into the chair Tobek held out for her. "I can hold the suit for, mmm, six hours, let's say. Think that'll be enough time?"

Bix took her seat and puffed out her cheeks. "To open it? Gods, let's hope so. To know everything Mirri stashed in it? That's probably going to take years."

"One step at a time." Tobek sat opposite Drew. "A lot of people have died or wished for death because of this thing. We don't want to be among their numbers."

Bix exhaled slowly and opened gates, retrieving the elusive Norse diplomatic pouch. She plunked its hard casing on the center of the table. It exuded no power, no hint of what lay within. The pouch had been designed to mask the contents, and it did so beautifully.

Drew pressed her fingers to her lips. "Oh my. There you are, my pretty. It's been a long time since we've seen each other."

Bix glanced at Tobek and squeezed his hand. He squeezed back, his presence comforting. Drew pulled the pouch in front of her. As Hel's creation, Drew was a member of the Norse pantheon; therefore, she had the requisite credentials to open the pouch.

"Now, remember, Bixie, the size of the pouch does not reflect the contents. It can be as small as a business card in there or as large as an opera house." Drew waited for Bix to nod before pushing her hands through those of the suit she wore. The draugr stretched her fingers beyond any illusion of normal until each finger touched a different surface. Tiny script glowed on each tile. The tiles burst apart, pieces spinning, then stacking in a pile no larger than a deck of playing cards. There they stayed, inert.

Other World magic flooded the bunker, rolling in waves from a whirling cloud of deep blues and glittering grays. Chirrs and chitters tumbled from the cloud.

"Oh, shit." Drew rocked back in her chair, hands fitted in her suit and by her shoulders.

Tobek leapt up from his seat and stood behind Bix. "How in all Worlds...?"

"...did Mirri pull this off?" Bix finished for him. She slid to the edge of her seat as her darkness slithered from her spine and coasted over the table, closing around the cloud of her very own mist and midnight. Her darkness drew her displaced essence into her. She shuddered and twitched. Her essence, there was something off about it. Not tainted, per se. Something, though. Waving the concern aside, she rubbed her hands together as her darkness withdrew from the contents of the pouch, revealing a seven-sided pyramid of mixed metals. Stamped into one side was the familiar variation on the Eternal Knot.

Bix looked over her shoulder to Tobek. "Yours?"

Tobek scratched the spot on his pectoral where the same variant of the Eternal Knot had been tattooed. His lips pursed. He didn't answer. She took that as a "couldn't" answer.

"Your sigil, Bixie," Drew explained. "The Eternal Knot balanced on a heptagonal pyramid, each face a facet of justice."

"Whatever Mirri was hiding belongs to you," Tobek said. "It doesn't seem to be the evidence files against the superpowers you were hoping for."

"Or the proof against the snerts who set us up." Drew sighed and crossed her arms over her chest. "I thought for sure the stuff Mirri had collected would be in there."

Bix shrugged. "Mirri wasn't in any condition to confirm or deny the contents when we started the hunt for it, so we all made guesses. At least we're the ones who ended up with it, right?"

"Yeah. Yeah, that's right, sweetie." Drew patted Bix's thigh. "Definitely don't want whatever that is in anyone else's possession."

"Why don't we give you some time alone with this?" Tobek squeezed Bix's shoulders. "We'll come get you in an hour. Okay?"

Bix nodded, mute, unsure how to feel. Disappointed? Intrigued? Annoyed? Curious? Kid at Christmas? E—All of the above?

Drew kissed the top of Bix's head, then followed Tobek out of the chambers. The door thudded into place; its locks snicked.

Alone with a very pretty pyramid, Bix stared at it, waiting for a tumult of questions to assail her. Nothing. Not even a rogue memory hiccupped into the complete silence in her mind. Hesitantly, she poked the pyramid. Power skittered up her arm and tickled her ear. The panel bearing her sigil swung open. Golden light blasted forth, grabbing hold of her and forcibly remolding her body as it dragged her inside.

She struggled against the warping of space and time as she plummeted. Her darkness shot out around her, searching for context and clues. Through its webbing, she glimpsed towers of shelves stuffed with books and objects. She jerked to a halt, suspended by her tentacles that had tethered to the scrollwork of iron railings framing one of seven gilded stories of shelves. Books of all shapes, colors, and sizes filled two-thirds of the shelves. Items exuding powers from all Worlds filled the other third.

Overhead, backlit frescos told beautiful tales of characters she didn't recognize from races with which she had a passing familiarity.

Recalling her darkness, she dropped the rest of the way to the plush carpeted floor of deep teals and dark cobalt. Sparkles played within the weave, like stars in a night sky. Myrrh and cardamom lightly scented the air.

"Hello?" she called. "Hello, is anyone here?"

Items jingled. A faint tremor animated the library. A small mirrored prism thumped and rattled on a shelf, then launched toward her. She caught it and flipped it over, looking for anything that would make it more than a pretty paperweight. She held it up to her ear and shook it. A strand of hair got caught in the edge and was yanked out. Thrusting out her bottom lip, she rubbed her head. The prism drew her hair inside its seams.

Odd.

The mirrors warmed in her hand. The library went dark. Bix spun around, pushing out with her senses to detect the threat. Filaments of light escaped the seams of the prism and wove together to create a hologram…of her.

Oofa. She did not look good. Weary was a nice way of putting it. Hunted was more apt. Hungry too. Had someone replaced her contour makeup with charcoal? Oh, her hair, oh, oh, that had suffered a run-in with an angry Goth for sure. Jet was not a good shade on her, and close-cropped was not a good length. Was she wearing Tobek's oxblood coat? She was swimming in it, what remained of it, that is. It was sleeveless, though his shoulders were so broad, the seams dusted her elbows. She did not like the discolored cluster of three old bullet holes in the chest panel where his heart would've been.

"Hi, me," the hologram greeted with a quiet chuckle. "I'm your future. The corniest beginning of every sci-fi movie ever, but it's true. You're probably a little freaked out with the whole space-time contortion thing. Sorry. We had to get the library as small as possible to inflict minimal damage to the flow of time. If we did this right, you've just discovered Devourers in the Mids. I know…"

The hologram looked askance and lowered her voice. Bix leaned closer out of habit.

"I know you were hoping to find the evidence against the superpowers that Mirri and her partner had collected. It's in here, along with other things we thought would help you in the upcoming war." The hologram scratched her neck, leaving behind reddish-brown streaks. Someone's blood? Ew. "You weren't wrong. You and Drew, you guys weren't wrong about the pouch. I remembered that I…you…*we* were fixated on getting it, that we weren't going to let Mirri's hard work go to waste. That's why we used Mids' magic to replace the original pouch with this one. Hopefully, we scheduled it right. Time travel is a tricky thing."

"We nailed it," she assured her holographic self…for no apparent reason.

"Hopefully, you found the Phoenix, and he convinced you to spare the Sage. The kid betrayed us to Sunan in hopes of getting a new body for his mom. That bitch never deserved an iota of forgiveness, she didn't even deserve love, but… I know I made a mistake when I killed the kid."

"I *didn't* kill the kid," Bix blurted. She leaned back and scowled. Whoa. Angry much? Killed Cian? Say who what now? That was some sick twist of…Fate. On the other hand, Cian hadn't betrayed her to Sunan either. He'd helped bring down the old fart. Apparently, changes were already afoot in the timeline. Praise be.

"Loncalaz infecting him was the best thing that could have happened for our cause," the hologram continued. "But I ruined that in my fit of rage. Without the kid, Yashanee can't make the vaccine. Something about his blood makes him special, it makes the vaccine possible. You've got to keep him alive."

The kid tended to put himself in dangerous situations, so walking the line between letting the kid learn a lesson and pulling him back from death was going to be a challenge. Without the Berserkers to keep a vigilant eye on him, she'd have to find Cian a suitable roommate who could protect and monitor him without impinging on the kid's development. Tricky but doable.

The hologram bit her lip. "We're losing the war against the Devourers. They've destroyed all but three of the Mid Worlds. Native magic is poisoned beyond any hope of purification. We have fifty years at the most before there is nothing left but a toxic cloud in this quadrant of the greater universe. Things are beyond bleak. There is a chance, a slim chance, that we—that you—can change this path of destiny. That's why we created this resource for you. The locks on the library are keyed to us. We are the only ones allowed in or out. Should you try to transport anyone inside, they will automatically relocate to an undisclosed location. Sorry, security is paramount. You'll understand soon enough."

Well, considering Devourers were shapeshifters and so were most gods, yeah, yeah, security would be important. Tobek, hoarder of all things powerful and old, would probably have an orgasm just seeing this place, but no, no. She now had stuff he couldn't know. So *thhpp*.

"I've got to go. We're rallying for the last stand on this World." The hologram stood up, then sat down again. "Don't give up on regaining our memories. I stopped when I could no longer assimilate them without succumbing to fits of insanity and jeopardizing our friends. Be braver than I am. Trust in those who trust us."

Sounded like Cian had been right about the legacy memory chips after all. Ack.

The hologram vanished, and the lights in the library came up. Bix set the prism on a shelf and rubbed her hands together. She'd done all this with only a fraction of her memories? She'd built this library? Stocked it? *Sent it through time?* Okay that last one, she sort of knew how that might be possible.

Bix slapped her hands against her cheeks and took it all in one more time.

Where to begin?

OTHER BOOKS BY K.A. KRANTZ

<u>Urban Fantasy</u>
The Immortal Spy Series:
THE BURNED SPY
THE PLAGUED SPY

<u>High Fantasy</u>
Fire Born, Blood Blessed Series:
LARCOUT

The Captured Spy
Available Summer 2018

Want to be notified when a new book is released?
Subscribe to K. A. Krantz's email newsletter at
kakrantz.com

**If you enjoyed this book, please spread the word and
leave a review with the retailer of your choice.**

ACKNOWLEDGMENTS

To my family, for the unlimited supply of Ivory soap. To Jenn Stark, mango slushies with rum make everything better. To Linda Ingmanson, my development editor, for reminding me there's always more to little girls than anyone ever suspects. To Toni Lee, my copy editor and fact-checker, for battling my abuse of hyphens, and for tracking down the logic train when it derails. To the team at Gene Mollica Studios, thanks for capturing my crazy and making it into something beautiful.

ABOUT THE AUTHOR

KAK splits her time between Cincinnati and the DC 'burbs with her ever-faithful hairy beast. When not writing, she indulges in a shoe obsession, conducts a love/hate affair with paint, and pretends she has enough upper body strength to wield power tools.

Visit her website at www.kakrantz.com for free flash-fiction, blog posts about her latest fancies, and more. If you're on Twitter, she'd love to hear from you. Tweet @KAKrantz.